THE RESONANCE WAR
BOOK FIVE OF THE CELESTRIAD

D1741565

Marise Morland

THE RESONANCE WAR
BOOK FIVE OF THE CELESTRIAD

DOUBLE DRAGON

Double Dragon Books by Marise Morland

"Omnia mutantur, nihil interit." OVID

Dedication

This book is dedicated to Sydney Jordan,
whose love of science fiction and support for my
work has been invaluable throughout the creation of
this series.

Acknowledgements

A sincere thank you to the following people who shared their scientific expertise:

Duncan Lunan (astronomy, general science)
Nigel Deacon (chemistry, geology, crystals)
Emma Hall (genetics).

Prelude

+Lydion!+

He stirred irritably. +Can't you let a man rest?+

+Not now. You need to wake up+

He shifted again. Something wasn't right. He normally woke effortlessly, bright and refreshed, but this time something was dragging him down. He sensed the delicate but soporific scent of nightflowers, and vaguely recalled going to the Tyvian Gardens to meditate.

+You're not in any garden. You've been given twilight balm. Now focus, you idiot, while you still can+

Annoyance piqued his muddled senses. +Twilight balm? Why in chaos did you give me that, Drusa? I can't think straight!+ But he rallied his perception, as she'd ordered. There they all were - his friends, his Eldorian mistress, his nephew. He knew them, not by sight or sound, but by their patterns. Only Nefyrra knew how frequently he'd used that unlooked-for ability, especially when working on resonance devices.

"I don't summon it," he'd confided sadly. "It just happens."

Now the patterns shone out brilliantly, seemingly masking the input from his other senses. Memory returned.

+Discord's dreams! He stabbed me - that excrescence Pervain stabbed me! I didn't even know he was there - he walked straight up to me and.... By harmony, I've never seen Laura cry like that. Now she'll have to admit she loves me. I'll tease her about it later. Oh, chaos, that's me on the operating table. Is this - what does Laura call it? - an out of body experience? Laura? Laura!+

+She can't hear you+ said his companion.

+This is amazing. I can go anywhere. Wheeee!+

+Settle down. You haven't acclimatised+

+Anything to please you, Dru. I won't stray too far. Can I just pop over to the generator room and see how Tonor's doing?+

+If it will make you happy+

Lydion ignored the sarcasm. Tentatively at first, then more confidently, he focused on the Lyricon basement. +Would you look at that! Tonor in a chair, asleep! I turn my back for one evening and this is how he behaves.+ He drifted closer to the sleeping operator. +Hey, Tonor! Man that weathershield, you idle lump. It's all yours for the moment, but if you want to keep your job - +

Tonor started awake. "Lydion?"

+He knew you. Interesting+ said the ever-present pattern at his side. +Ah, that explains it. He's resonance-sensitive+

+Tonor? Never!+

+I don't make mistakes+

+Chaos, what's happening?+ Lydion flailed about in a panic, assailed by a fierce new energy source.

+He's started the shield. Close off and I'll guide you back. There's something you must see+

Lydion scanned near-emptiness. +Is this the hospital? Where did everyone go?+

14

+Focus carefully+ came the response, quietly impersonal.

And Lydion, with sudden appalling clarity, knew the body on the table - his body - was dead. He didn't flinch away, couldn't, not until he'd read every chill inanimate detail. A trace of life at the cellular level mocked him with its fading futility.

Drusa, alone with the corpse, kept vigil.

+Dru!+ Lydion tried to touch her, but his incorporeal self had less substance than a dust particle. Then, in profound dread, he refocused on the watchful pattern he'd presumed was Drusa in her healing mode. How could he have been so wrong when the entity before him had haunted his nightmares for decades? Even without the power and menace of the Synectic net, there should have been no mistaking the coldly sardonic mindset of Sarune, once the most reviled woman of her species.

+You don't fear me now+ she observed.

+Why should I fear anyone? I'm dead!+

+No, you're not+ she countered angrily, and dragged him to a far corner of the hospital where a dying man peacefully breathed his last. The aura of twilight balm hung opaquely in the air.

Suddenly a dazzling energy spike transformed the darkening consciousness. Lydion drew back, recalling Pervain's knife. Then, just as suddenly, the charge abated. The man's pattern broke free of his body, maintained its integrity for one brief moment, then dissipated and was gone.

+That squandered energy+ Sarune explained candidly, +is what the Synectics sought to harvest.

15

It typifies the death of the individual, whether Celestrian or Narvellan. I must confess you nearly went the same way, as I'd taken my attention elsewhere. I thought you had years of corporeal life ahead. Fortunately your pain summoned me back in time to intercept you+

Lydion tried to muster some anger, but could only manage weary reproach. +What have you done?+

+It was all done long ago+ she replied. +The night you beguiled Eluthia. The night the Synectics cast their net+

+But you rejected me!+

+The others did. I liked your spirit of adventure, so I marked you. And you began to evolve+

+No!+

+You absorbed the potential via Eluthia+ she went on relentlessly. +You've always known. You knew it when you found the wall writings at Ilonna. You knew it every time you worked on resonance theory+

+I don't want this, Sarune. Just let me go+

+If you insist. Personally, I think you want to live. Let's find out+

She let her influence fall away, and Lydion tried to will himself into nonexistence. Nothing changed.

+Convinced?+ inquired Sarune.

+Why did you come back for me?+ Lydion asked, curious in spite of himself. +With the Synectics gone, aren't I surplus to requirements?+

+Not at all+ Sarune answered coolly. +I'd value your company+

Her audacity was boundless. +Perhaps I don't need yours+ Lydion retorted.

+Are you sure? I'd planned and rehearsed my transition for years, decades - and I still wasn't prepared. I hung cravenly around my life-bonded and his love-child because I couldn't face the solitude. Could you? Could you survive, in the knowledge that only a few sensitives could divine your presence - and then but rarely?+

+Mallina - + began Lydion.

+You have no bond with her. She's oblivious to you. Look, she's dried her tears. Your true life-bonded is long dead+

+Yet I sensed her+ Lydion mused, almost to himself. +Even after her death+

+That wasn't Tarlatine. It was me+

For once Sarune hadn't meant to be cruel, but she'd destroyed Lydion's most cherished illusion. Desolation smote his fragile new senses; he tried to retreat from it, lost focus, then lost awareness. Sarune adroitly encircled his faltering pattern with her own, supporting him.

+All this fuss over an elite-wife+ she crooned. +Sleep, then, if you must. Gather your wits. Then I'll teach you all I know: which resonances sustain us and which threaten us+

Unaware, he drifted. Kalyx portrayed him at the Lyricon, Mallina fell victim to a sniper's bullet, war raged at the edge of the Alda system. The Gloriana took her leave and Scapirian divers raised a time capsule. Clemis gave birth to a son. And throughout these events, Sarune - not normally the most patient of beings - kept faith with her task.

Lydion's pattern began to stabilise just as the scolia-tech tried out the Cadence - two notes at a time.

+Your work, I presume+ Sarune remarked, unsure if he could perceive her. +It has your signature all over it. You couldn't have done it without the enhancements I gave you, so be sure to thank me later. I've observed every detail of this grubby little conflict, so I'm ready for your questions. Now stop moping and snap out of it. I'm not letting you be my second failed experiment!+

Lydion made no reply, but his pattern continued to grow stronger.

Presently he began to dream.

Chapter One

Alda Mexa 4.4.6.4030

"What's next on the agenda?" asked Laura.

Administrator Dessin briefly raised a hand. "I have the statistics you requested, First Citizens, concerning the number of scolia-sensitives in the post-Escir generation. To ensure accuracy I've worked closely with Custodian Nefyrra and regional scolia leaders..."

Idenion, as he was apt to do at such times, let his mind wander. Six years ago, Dessin had been in the forefront of the student rebellion against the Eldorians. It was so improbable that he'd choose city management as a career. Yet the young man had a natural flair for coordinating Alda Mexa's many changes. He, Idenion, would have become fixated on details.

"...so we've established that one in five children is scolia-sensitive," Dessin was continuing, "and some of these have highly developed perception as well. Tafret Academy is looking forward to training new relayists."

"This is marvellous news, but please tell your teams to exercise care," Laura said. "Scolia sensitives must be nurtured, not goaded, and the same applies to relayists. Kyrin often spoke of the frightening tests he had to undergo as an infant, and we don't want a repetition of that - even if we have to make a game of it for the very young."

"Understood," replied Dessin soberly.

"Having said that," Laura went on, "the advantages of early learning are well known, and a sensible tuition programme should be introduced across the city states as soon as one can be devised. We'll make it a priority."

Recordist Sheyell looked up from her notes. "Dare we hope that this increased musicality might lead to a return of the singing voice?"

"I doubt it," Laura said regretfully. "We seem to be heading in a different direction entirely."

"In that case, First Citizeness," ventured Dessin, "couldn't you reconsider our proposal for a statue?"

"Not that again!"

"It's our tradition, Laura! The First Singer has always commissioned a likeness in stone to preside over the Lyricon stage. If there are never to be any other contenders, you should allow us to proceed."

"I've given my answer many times. After the Narvellans left, after the Eldorians were kicked out - and just last year when the Masons' guild asked me again."

"Guildmaster Cleve would render an excellent likeness."

"This isn't a vanity issue, Dessin. Where I come from no one puts up statues to anyone until they're dead. I promise before witnesses that when that happens you can commission as many as you want. But not until. Now, is there any other business?"

"There's one more item," said Dessin. "A request for technical assistance, submitted two days ago by Habbon's team on Alda Four."

"Habbon?" inquired Sheyell. "The Eldorian archaeologist? I thought he was on that dustbowl Dral, looking for evidence of a lost race."

"The race we reputedly destroyed," Idenion said quietly. "After five thousand years there was very little to find, and after suffering breathing difficulties Habbon relocated to Alda Four. He said he'd only gone to Dral for selfish reasons, curiosity mainly, and that now his stamina was failing he wanted to give something back to us, his benefactors."

" He didn't want people – Escir, specifically – finding out he was ill and ordering him to stop work," Laura explained. "So we hushed it up."

"It's only a four-man team and they're living on the base last occupied by the Narvellans," continued Dessin. "But it's in need of constant maintenance and the repairs are diverting the men from their research."

"Which is?" Sheyell asked.

"Habbon had been told about the subsidence at the base, the one that killed Chisrin and almost cost Dena her life," Laura answered quietly. "He believed there had to be a reason for the cave-in, some underground remains of *our* lost civilisation perhaps. That's what he's looking for."

"He wants at least two full-time engineers to keep essential systems running," said Dessin reading from the communications transcript.

"He's well aware every technician's working overtime to support our growth programme."

"We can't let him down," Idenion decided. "Alda Four's yielded many artefacts and we shouldn't assume we've found them all. We'll send him the men he needs, subject to frequent review."

"Seconded," said Laura briskly. "Now, if there's nothing else - "

"There is, actually," said Idenion. She looked at him quizzically.

"It's regarding the library upgrade and the transfer of old stock to the basement," Idenion went on.

Dessin tried not to look bored. The library was no-one's priority save Idenion's. "I thought the transfer hadn't begun?"

"It hasn't. Before we can shift any material we have to know there's space for it, and nobody knows exactly what's in the sub-levels. I requested an inventory."

"And?" Laura prompted.

"This morning, the workers found a locked door."

Instantly, he had everyone's attention. Locked doors were synonymous with one person: Tralvar. Had the late tormented genius one last surprise for his people?

"And this was why you delayed the start of the meeting," Laura surmised.

"Correct. There was no key, so I ordered a forced entry and stayed while it was done."

"What was inside? A weapon?" asked Dessin eagerly.

"Recording equipment?" asked Laura.

"Neither. Behind that door we found the entire contents of Alendis' apartment. Mirrors,

22

furnishings, clothes, all dumped in a heap and forgotten."

"Tralvar could never face clearing those effects," Laura recalled. "He must have had everything shifted downstairs until he felt ready to deal with it. And he never did."

"So what's the problem, Idenion?" This was Sheyell. "Tell your workers to dispose of it. We don't want any reminders of that man."

"Not so fast!" Laura objected. "I'd like to inspect the clothes. Alendis had the best designers working for him."

"Get rid of it all," reiterated Sheyell.

"Or start a museum," Dessin said jokingly. They all glared at him.

"May I finish?" Idenion enquired. "The room also contained a cabinet of Alendis' writings – not just speeches, but private diaries and texts dating from his years as a healer."

Sheyell looked outraged. "You surely don't have any use for *those*?"

"On the contrary," replied Idenion calmly. "I intend to study them."

Even Laura looked taken aback.

"I daresay you'd all oppose this decision, given the choice," Idenion continued. "So, much as it offends my democratic principles, I'm denying you the right of veto. You seem to forget that Alendis' dictatorship lasted a mere six years. As a healer, he had a profound knowledge of the Celestrian mind – not just scolia-sensitives, but relayists and empaths like himself. He may even have foreseen the traits we're witnessing in our children. Laura, will you support me in this?"

"There are always lessons to be learnt from the past," she replied, "even from such an unlikely source. I'll support you as always."

"That concludes the day's business," Idenion said thankfully. The sub-committee broke up in near silence. The third administrator, Ansela, had as usual said nothing throughout the proceedings and voted with the Chair. Now, suddenly, she spoke up.

"First Citizen, what's the use of convening these sessions if you overrule the objections we make?"

"If memory serves me correctly, today's the first time I've done so," Idenion said with quiet courtesy. "Merely naming Alendis was bound to prompt emotional reactions and I wanted everyone to have time to think. Also, this is purely an akron matter at the moment. If it becomes a city matter we'll have a further debate."

Ansela thanked him. "Against that time, please be aware that I'd have voted to keep the documents."

She drifted out. Idenion gazed after her in surprise.

"So, we'd have won the vote after all," Laura said. "That's interesting to know. I'd better view this material, hadn't I, before you have it sent to our apartment."

"Not a bad idea. I should warn you, there's a lot."

"Then I'd best help you read it. Otherwise you'll be accused of neglecting your duties."

Idenion ushered her down a back stair, then another. "Duties, yes. That's something else I've been meaning to discuss with you."

"Do you want me to take over some of yours? I think I could manage a few more."

Idenion didn't reply straight away. When he did, it was with another question. "How old are you, Laura?"

She looked puzzled. "Thirty-seven, of course."

"And in Earth years?"

"Sixty-one," she answered reluctantly.

"And since you always have trouble with the conversion, I assume you already knew that."

"Since we're not on Earth," she replied caustically, "I don't see why in chaos it matters. Surely you don't want us to retire?"

"We can't be First Citizens for ever." Idenion steered her along a narrow corridor. "We both have our careers. At least let's start thinking about our successor."

"Who do you have in mind? Trevone?"

"No," Idenion said emphatically. "He's a bright and innovative First Scientist, and to put him behind a desk would be a big mistake."

"Dessin, then."

"He shows promise, but he's more engineer than diplomat. And he's still very young."

"About the same age as you were when you took over," Laura reminded him. "One for the shortlist, then, along with Kalyx."

"Ah. Kalyx."

"We know he wants the job."

"I'm not sure how much that qualifies him. Let's see how well he does in Scapirion. Whilst we're making our minds up, we could maybe curtail our admin work. There's no need for both of us to be at committee meetings, for instance."

"Today being an exception, of course."

"Of course." Idenion paused by an ancient timbered door. Near the latch, one of Tralvar's intricate spring-locks hung uselessly by one nail. The door creaked grudgingly open after a hefty shove, and a damp must odour wafted out. There were no windows.

After a few moments of fumbling, Idenion switched on a temporary light left by the workmen. "Sorry about the mess. I did warn you."

Laura was silent, staring at a tarnished bedstead which stood adjacent to the door. Its red and black coverlet was stained and faded, but the motif was still starkly visible under the bright lamp.

"Was this on the flags too?"

"There's no need to whisper," said Idenion, though his face was sombre. "I guessed you'd recognise it."

"I know what it's trying to be." Laura turned aside, to be confronted by a portrait of the dead dictator. "So that's your urban myth confirmed. I never quite believed he'd been to Earth."

"I didn't try too hard to convince you," Idenion confessed. "I thought it might have sent your younger self on a guilt trip. Well, let's see if we can salvage anything from his ruined life."

At the far end of the room was a polished wooden cabinet with sliding doors. Inside were rows of neatly bound folders, labelled and dated, containing page after page of Alendis' graceful handwriting.

"At least we won't need anyone to decipher it," Laura remarked. "Are you sure we won't be wasting our time?"

"Positive. He was taught by the best healers on Corayn – and healing employs resonance, similar to perception and the lattice."

"How much of this have you read?"

"Very little. But I heard plenty from the man himself, when he took me on tour. I was something of a captive audience, and a willing one." Idenion grinned shamefacedly.

"Until I came along and rescued you."

He kissed her on the nose. "Come on, let's find someone to take these files to the study before Sheyell decides to send them for recycling."

"I wonder..." mused Laura. "Sheyell's about our age, isn't she? Do you think she had some kind of run-in with Alendis?"

"Maybe," Idenion conceded. "But if she did, it's something she doesn't want to share. There's no point in challenging her about it. Do you fancy a trip to Tafret tomorrow?"

Laura blinked. "What?"

"We need Nohal's input on the entrainment programme. It's important, Laura. There's a lot of raw talent out there – I didn't realise how much until today – and if it isn't correctly managed it can atrophy. And that would mean withdrawn, discontented children."

"You're thinking about Dena."

"Absolutely. Because we were shunted from family to family, her abilities were neglected until she couldn't utilise them. Remember how inhibited she was?"

Laura sighed. "All right, point taken. We'll speak to Nohal at once."

"And we'll tell him about Alendis' files," Idenion declared. "I can't think of a better person to advise us."

* * *

Cheveney, England, August 5th 2011

"I think it's a disgrace!" Caitlin Stretton, at 82, was as nimble and ill-tempered as ever. "Wickens Clump's been part of our village for centuries. They can't just fence it off. I was hoping you could've done something about it, Jack Moffat."

Jack sighed. "I did raise it as the last parish council meeting, but no-one had any bright ideas. These old covenants are complicated, and we're not lawyers."

Caitlin glared down the lane at the nine foot high fence now surrounding Wickens Clump. A large notice read: "Acquired by the Trustees of Cheveney Manor. No trespassing." The only remaining entrance to the Clump was on Manor land. "Well, who are they, these trustees? Haven't you even been able to find that out?"

"Not yet," said Jack wearily. "And I think we'd be on a hiding to nothing, even if we knew. The Clump isn't an area of outstanding natural beauty, nor a conservation zone, nor anything except a chunk of overgrown woodland."

"Jimmy and some of his friends cleared most of the brambles. There were some bluebells last spring! People were just starting to go in there again."

A Mercedes with darkened windows swept past, heading for the security gates which fronted the Manor grounds.

"Whoever's living there is up to no good," pronounced Caitlin. "Gates, cameras, prowling guards ....."

"The press release said it was a rehab clinic," Jack offered. "That would make sense. If they've got celebs on the premises, they'll want to keep everyone away."

"Celebs!" Caitlin's voice dripped contempt. "What would a rehab clinic want with Wickens Clump?"

"Er ..." began Jack, when a new voice suddenly said:

"Mr. Moffat? May I have a word?"

"Oh, it's *you* again," sniffed Caitlin. "Wasn't my information good enough for you?"

"I have to extend my enquiries," said the newcomer, a thin greying man in a sharp suit.

"Then I'll be on my way." With a final black look, Caitlin stumped off.

"Jack! Dinner!" yelled a peremptory voice from within the Moffat household.

"You're a difficult man to pin down," said the stranger. Jack eyed him suspiciously.

"Are you the person who's been leaving messages at the newspaper?"

"I am. I'm seeking information regarding the whereabouts of Laura Meredith, also known as Laura Gilcoyne."

"If you've talked with Caitlin you're bound to know that my Aunt Margaret was Laura's unofficial foster mother for several years."

"Unofficial?"

"It was in the Sixties. Things were more free and easy back then. And since this arrangement began and ended before I was born, I don't see what help I could possibly be."

"You did meet her," persisted the man.

"Once, in 1996. She turned up for a couple of days with her second husband."

"Not husband, since she's still married to Peter Meredith," said the suit. "Do you know this person's name?"

"Has Laura done something wrong?" countered Jack, edging towards his front door.

"Not to my knowledge, except perhaps to choose the wrong companion. I believe he was known as Denny while living locally. What were your impressions of him?"

"Quiet, academic, good with animals," said Jack after a pause. "Definitely not a criminal type, although he did get himself arrested at Snelsmore Protest Camp."

"Jack!" A young woman appeared at the door.

"Coming, Phaedra. You'll have to excuse me, sir."

"Of course." A bony hand proffered a business card. "Do call me if you remember anything else which could help us find Mrs. Meredith. There could be some remuneration involved."

"Goodbye," said Jack firmly, and shut the door. After dinner, when Phaedra had settled down to watch soaps, he went up to the attic. Examining the business card for the first time, he found it displayed a mobile number and nothing else. He suspected, though he hadn't thought to ask, that the mysterious caller was something to do with Cheveney Manor.   Frowning, he lifted a box and placed it near the window: and in the fading sunset, re-examined his aunt's souvenirs of Laura – mostly photographs and cassette tapes. There was a letter too, which he'd inherited along with the deeds to Margaret Moffat's cottage. In it, his aunt besought him to give Laura shelter if she ever returned to Cheveney. "With her loved ones gone, she may never come back," the letter concluded. "But if she does, she'll be in need of a friend."

At length Jack replaced the box. "Where are you, Laura?" he murmured to himself. "Who's looking for you? Why?"

The Mercedes which Jack had noticed earlier was now parked outside Cheveney Manor. Its sole occupant had just enjoyed an equally solitary meal in a wood-panelled dining room, presided over by ancestral portraits and discreetly positioned security cameras. Having pushed aside his plate and dabbed his thin lips with a linen napkin, the diner picked up the house phone and ordered coffee and brandy. Four hours had passed since his arrival.

Eventually he went to the French window, keyed in a release code and stepped outside. A nocturnal hush pervaded the expanse of lawn. To the west, a crescent moon had almost set. To the east, the dark bulk of Wickens Clump obscured the horizon. But to the south, stars gleamed across distant fields.

Returning indoors, he lifted the phone again. "Is Preece still awake? I'd like to visit the observatory."

"We thought you might ask that, Sir John. He'll be down in a moment. I'll notify security of your intentions. You won't want any light pollution."

"Thank you." Sir John Cheveney put on his jacket and waited. The astronomer, Preece, duly appeared; the two men walked to a side exit and into the grounds. Aware that Sir John knew the way, Preece fell into step behind him.

The small observatory, little more than a folly, stood in the centre of the south-facing lawn. Preece, remarking that the skies had cleared quite nicely, opened the door and made some minute adjustments to the 15-inch reflector. There was only one object in the night sky of current interest to Sir John, and it had already been under scrutiny from this very location.

"I have it," Preece said after a few moments, and stood aside to let Sir John peer into the eyepiece at an insignificant point of light. "That's the best I can do. It's a bit too far south to observe comfortably. Of course, we'll have the latest digital imagery available at our briefing tomorrow."

"I don't doubt it," replied Sir John. "But given the circumstances, I wanted a preview. Are you sure this is the one?"

"Absolutely. You're looking at HD 200156 in the constellation of Aquarius, home star of the planet Celestra."

For a moment, neither man moved. Then Sir John turned to leave.

"Have all available data brought to the meeting."

"Of course, sir."

"And will our asset be present? My clients are most anxious that I see him face to face."

"He'll be there," said Preece.

The next morning, Sir John, immaculate in a charcoal grey suit, entered a conference room where several shirt-sleeved men awaited him. No introductions were made, as they had all met before. There was Joel Bartlett, the estate manager, and an accountant named Little, whom Sir John detested. Preece was there, as was Harmsworth, the investigator who had been asking questions in the village. Further down the table were two engineers, a secretary, and head of security Rod Tallifer.

They waited in near-silence. At one minute past ten, a young blonde nurse entered the room.

"Well, Ann, where is he?" demanded Bartlett.

"Where he always is," the girl said wearily. "In the gym. He says he'll be along when he's ready and not before."

"Tallifer, fetch him," Bartlett ordered. "But be polite."

"Aren't I always?" smirked the security chief, and left the room. Ann hastened after him. Presently they returned, escorting a dark-haired, dark-eyed man of around forty. He wore a white t-shirt, knee length shorts, trainers, and a resentful expression.

"Roegin," said Bartlett, "this gentleman is Sir John Cheveney, Baronet."

"Does that amount to something?"

"Try to be more civil," admonished Harmsworth. "Sir John donated his estate to our cause. And if he hadn't spent thousands of his own money on your medical treatment, I doubt if you'd be here now."

Sir John nodded courteously at the newcomer. "Your full name, I believe, is Roegin Drice-Tressa, and you are, or were, an agent of the Eldorian Covert Ops Division?"

"If you know, why ask me?"

"We've met already," continued Sir John, "though you won't remember. The last time I saw you, you were in an induced coma with grotesque swellings all over your body. You and your fellow operatives carried a dormant pathogen which, so I understand, was designed to activate after two years and kill you all. Unless, of course, it had been neutralised on the completion of your mission."

"It kept us loyal," Roegin said tonelessly.

"It also presented a unique challenge to my medical team. Fortunately, your will to survive was extraordinary."

34

Roegin, slightly mollified, settled into the nearest chair. "And because I'm conveniently alive, I suppose you want to interrogate me? Again?"

"I'm aware that you've co-operated with us in the past, but today is somewhat different. These people would each in their own way have facilitated the Eldorian Alliance, had it come about. I represent the UK investors. We're here to pool our information and try to form the clearest possible picture of what went wrong and why. As you can see, there are no cameras in this room, and there will be no electronic record of our conversation. Wireless signals are blocked throughout the building – but I'm sure you already know that. One shorthand account will exist, to be destroyed as soon as I've made representation to our backers."

The secretary scribbled in her notebook. Little cleared his throat.

"As you can appreciate, Agent Roegin, the bullion delivered by your empire was swiftly converted to our currency. Such large sums of money are proving difficult to conceal. We need to know if there is any realistic possibility of contacting your government, to discover why the landings never took place and if they're ever going to happen."

"And *I'd* like to know why the Senate abandoned us," Roegin said with a rare hint of emotion. "Ann says I'm the only survivor. Is that right?"

"To the best of our knowledge, you are," said Sir John. "The other countries in the pact have intimated that their visitors all died. Mind you, that's what *we* told *them*. For your own safety."

"So you decided to hide me in plain sight?"

"Hardly that. If there were to be a kidnap attempt, you'd see how well guarded you are. The same applies to an escape attempt."

"Roegin needs frequent injections to maintain his health," Ann put in swiftly. "He knows his best hope of a normal life is to work with us."

"Then let's begin," suggested Harmsworth. "Roegin, how did your people first hear about the Celestrians?"

Some of the listeners had heard the story already, but Roegin, with his usual air of reluctance, told it again: how a crippled Narvellan colony vessel had been found drifting at the edge of the Eldorian system; how the would-be colonists, who had never set eyes on Celestra, had nonetheless eulogised the planet for granting them FTL travel and an escape from their doomed homeworlds; how the fleet's guidance crystals had failed because they hadn't been mined but mass-produced in a hurry.

"What did I tell you, Bartlett?" exclaimed one of the engineers. "See what happens when you push for results -"

"Not now, Frank," Bartlett said irritably. "You'll get a chance to speak later. Go on, Roegin."

"Our leaders were furious. Our first alien contact, smart technology to vastly improve hull safety on our ships – but no FTL. Not a single intact crystal."

36

"What happened to the Narvellans?" asked Sir John quietly.

"It was said they died in a suicide pact. I was only a child at the time so I accepted that. Later I assumed they'd been killed."

"And why do you think that was?"

"They knew nothing of value. They were ordinary people, not mission trained. But they had psi ability which our scientists wished to study."

"I don't think we need to go down that road," Harmsworth said blandly. "Let's move on. How *did* you solve the problem of the crystals?"

Roegin glared at him. "You do realise that if my people ever turn up, they'll probably shoot me as a traitor for discussing this? I'm still an agent of my government and as such, duty bound to protect their secrets."

"Do you believe they'll turn up?"

"No. If they could, they'd have been here. The Earth-Eldor alliance was crucial to them."

Harmsworth steepled his fingers. "So you were ordered not to discuss the Narvellans because it showed your empire in a bad light?"

"I wasn't given reasons." Roegin paused, deliberating. "You might as well hear the rest of it. Of course, if any representatives of the Empire *do* come calling, I'll say you coerced me."

"Naturally."

Roegin took a slow swig of water, playing his audience. "Five years later, a Narvellan reconnaissance craft entered our system. We were still testing the damaged star drive and they'd detected it. We knew enough of their language to bid them welcome. The two men were met with an elaborate deception, calculated to separate them from their vessel and each other. They had a fully functional FTL drive and we intended to take it at all costs."

No-one spoke, but one or two frowns deepened.

"Would any of your governments have behaved differently?" Roegin enquired, icily polite. "I don't think so. I've read a lot while I've been convalescing and I know you people extremely well."

"Go on," said Bartlett steadily.

"We also thought we'd have instant access to Celestra. The older crewman, Axmiol, had been in charge of the Narvellan refugees there - and his young companion was his lover. If we'd threatened to harm the boy, Axmiol would have told us anything to protect him."

"Are you asking us to believe this boy wasn't tortured?"

"Yes, because he wasn't. Our emperor, may he rot in Ebbondrear, took a fancy to the pretty lad and adopted him as his favourite. No-one dared lay a finger on him, and Axmiol promptly clammed up. The only thing we got from either of them was a working knowledge of the Celestrian language – and since Axmiol had smashed the ship's communicator to very small pieces, we were no better off. So, we had to make do with exploration. Our factories were churning out spacecraft as swiftly as they could, but we still thought we were facing an interminable quest. And so we might have been, if we hadn't chanced upon Earth."

38

"Thank you, Mr. Roegin," Sir John said graciously. "We'll return to you shortly. This seems an appropriate time for Mr. Preece to explain to this committee exactly where Celestra is."

Preece handed round some photographs and diagrams. "This is HD 200156. It's a yellow-white dwarf star in Aquarius, distance from Earth 354 light years. It's spectral type is F5v, hotter than our sun, which means the habitable zone will be further out. According to Eldorian intel there are six planets in the system. We don't have independent confirmation but we should soon detect them by occultation. I, for one, would like to see where our messages are headed!"

"That appears to be your cue, Frank," said Bartlett to the senior engineer. "Let's have your report on those crystals, and why they're taking so long to develop."

"I'd like to know that too," Little put in. "You've already exceeded your funding by sixty percent."

Frank bridled. "The process can't be hurried."

"Then, for the record, would you describe this lengthy process?" asked Sir John.

"Preferably in terms we can understand," added Little.

Frank cleared his throat. "To make a substitute crystal, we first had to find its composition. We were hampered by the scarcity of original material to work with - every time we had to crush or fragment any aldacite, we had to obtain permission and explain why we needed to do it."

"And why did you?"

"To discover the element percent composition by mass. We examined a minute quantity of powdered crystal under a scanning electron microscope, which causes the scanned material to emit x-rays. These can be analysed fairly easily as each element has a characteristic frequency."

"Do get to the point."

Frank helped himself to a page from the secretary's notepad and sketched a quick diagram. "This is the structure of aldacite. Each ion has eight equidistant nearest neighbours arranged at the vertices of a cubic co-ordination group, similar to caesium chloride or metallic sodium. Not particularly significant and not particularly rare. So, we mixed some related compounds together, added an aldacite fragment to seed the mix, then fused it in a furnace. Edgar -" he indicated his colleague – "is in charge of the furnace. He'll explain the delay."

Edgar took over reluctantly. "The mixture has to be crystallised slowly by dropping the temperature degree by degree. Unfortunately our first attempts were unsuccessful as the seed crystal dissolved in the melt and its influence appeared to be lost. So we modified our template of similar crystal forms, and tried again. Several times. In fact, more than several." He glanced apologetically at Frank.

"We now have what appears to be a stable crystal," Frank concluded. "But in view of what we've heard today, we need to study it over a period of months to see if it converts or degrades. So far, we've only had weeks."

"The Narvellan disaster can be disregarded," said Bartlett. "We're not trying to build a spacecraft, only a communicator. If our attempts fail, no-one's harmed. But we're hopeful. Thanks to our friend Roegin here, who had the good sense to make contact with us *before* he fell ill, we were able to retrieve vital components from his HQ – or what was left of it."

Roegin nodded an acknowledgement. He'd known Control had a direct link to Eldor, as opposed to the comsat-dependent transposers used in the field. The Senate had forbidden overt use of the technology until after the alliance, but clandestine exchanges were inevitable.

"We now have transposer co-ordinates for Celestra *and* Eldor," Bartlett was continuing, "although of course it will be Celestra we try to contact. Mr. Roegin, would you explain the reason for this?"

"Again?" Roegin asked wearily.

"For the minutes of this meeting. If you wouldn't mind."

Roegin sighed. "After we discovered Celestra it was decided to set up a base there. We followed all due process and the Celestrians appeared to accept us. After about a year our Earth expeditionary fleet arrived on Celestra for a short stay before proceeding. Due to the immense distance involved, and the keening emitted by our stardrives, a period of rest seemed sensible. We, the agents, were finally told the fleet was on its way and ordered to report to our assembly points – which in my case was Control. One of the personnel had

41

friends on the Celestrian base and they patched through a local radio transmission describing the departure. We thought we'd be on our way home in a couple of hours. And then, unbelievably, the Celestrians launched an attack with weapons we never knew they had."

"What type of weapons?"

"A ray which dissolved its target so completely that no energy trace was left - "

"That's not possible," objected Frank.

"I'm only relating what I heard. Then there were mines, tractor beams – and all we had were pulse cannon and a protective shield of Celestrian design."

"If it was their design, you should have known they'd have the means to counter it."

"Yes, we should. We were complacent. The truth is, we regarded the Celestrians as a bit of a joke. They were …. well, I suppose you'd call them hippies. Sex and music, music and sex – that's all they cared about. They ran their world on a shoestring, with minimal productivity. We just didn't see them as a threat. Anyway, they managed to destroy most of our fleet. Soon after, our troops reported that the base was also under attack. That was the last we heard from Celestra. Over the next few days, we made repeated calls to the Eldor homeworlds; sometimes they answered, mostly they didn't. The Senate knew of the attack but the general public hadn't been informed. By this time we were aware of our predicament, and demanded rescue. The Senate said there were no available spacecraft. But then we heard the Celestrians were repatriating survivors, sending them back in their own vessels – so there had to be *some* spacecraft. None arrived. And then all contact with the Eldor system was lost."

"Do you think the Celestrians attacked your Empire?"

Roegin shook his head. "They were under-resourced. And underpopulated. There are three Eldorian homeworlds, remember."

"Underpopulated?" enquired Harmsworth. "Despite all the sex, drugs and rock 'n' roll?"

"So I heard. I was never there." Roegin thought this detail unimportant. "If there *had* been another battle, it would have been prolonged and messy, and this silence was too sudden. A geek at Control thought they'd done something to the communications portal, and maybe FTL as well. So, your transposer experiments *have* to be directed at Celestra, because only they can answer your questions. Now, if we're done - "

"Not quite yet, Mr. Roegin, " said Sir John. "We've saved the most interesting part till last. We now come to the question of why we're here in Cheveney, and why Wickens Clump is so meaningful to us. I believe you have some of the answers."

Surprisingly, Roegin looked quietly amused. "I was sent here with a junior colleague to investigate the reported sighting of a Celestrian spacecraft. Control said there were still traces of aldacite in the vicinity, so we took a room at the Green Man and waited."

"What year was this?"

43

"Early 1996. We'd no idea how to recognise a Celestrian when we saw one, but orders were orders – find them, take them alive. We didn't get much sleep as a drunken couple in the next room were having noisy sex all night – and these, to our incredulity, turned out to be our targets."

"Now there's a surprise," remarked Harmsworth. "How *did* you identify them?"

"The woman had a remote enabler of Narvellan design and was waving it around in the bar. Then they realised who we were and made a run for it. We chased them into Wickens Clump."

"And?"

"And lost them. They were following some rabbit trail so they must have known the woods pretty well. When they used the enabler we tracked the signal, but by the time we caught up, the spacecraft was sitting in a glade and they were inside. Control notified our orbiting contingent to pursue them when they took off, and gave us an earful for botching the assignment. Apparently there'd already been an attempt to catch one of their craft and they'd left us standing."

"Oh?"

"Yes, your world seems quite a tourist spot. Anyway, they weren't as speedy this time. They led us to Celestra and suddenly I and my idiot partner were heroes. That's when we discovered our amorous couple were the First Citizens, Idenion and Laura. I still don't know why they were here."

"But *I* do." Harmsworth produced a folder and threw it on the table. "Laura, full name Laura Gilcoyne, is English."

44

"Gods!" Roegin exclaimed, enlightened rather than astonished. "I should have guessed!"

"English through and through," continued Harmsworth. "Cheveney was her home. Birthplace, Islington. Parents, Jane and Philip Gilcoyne. Her father sold insurance, her mother was an entertainer. Both were killed in a car crash, 1962. Laura, then aged twelve, was adopted by her bachelor uncle Nathaniel Gilcoyne, of this village."

"That sounds a bit casual," ventured Ann. "Why wasn't she fostered?"

"It was fifty years ago, my dear," Harmsworth said patronisingly. "Nathaniel was financially secure, and that was sufficient. Laura seems to have been raised by the cleaning lady, when she wasn't at boarding school.

"In 1966 we start to see gaps in her history. She caused a local scandal by leaving home at the same time as her boyfriend Jimmy Stretton. She came back after three days, and was seen around the village for three weeks or so in the company of a longhaired boy known only as Denny. Idenion, or so I surmise. She then disappeared again, for a whole year this time. Then she turned up as vocalist with a psychedelic rock band, the Celestrians."

Raised eyebrows greeted this nugget of information.

"They were English," Harmsworth supplemented. "One of the women, Melanie Palmer, maintains a website dedicated to the band which broke up after a couple of years. I spoke with her briefly; she said Laura thought of the name."

"No surprises there, then," said Little.

"The next part of the story *is* a surprise. Laura married an accountant, Peter Meredith, and returned to Cheveney."

"You've become a font of knowledge in the space of a week," observed Bartlett. "The last I heard, you'd contacted Jimmy Stretton and received a two-word response – the second word being 'off '. Who's your informant?"

Harmsworth smirked. "Caitlin Stretton, Jimmy's mother. A bitter old woman who blames Laura for her son's estrangement. She has a remarkable memory. Incidentally, I traced Peter Meredith, who asks to be notified if Laura shows up again. He's been searching for her ever since she ran off with Denny, emptyhanded, in the autumn of '77. And that, apart from her brief encounter with Mr. Roegin in 1996, completes her history."

There was a moment of silence round the table as these revelations were digested. Then Sir John said:

"It seems we underestimated the importance of Wickens Clump. I would like to thank Mr. Harmsworth for his enlightening work. We now know that there has been a Celestrian presence in Cheveney for decades, perhaps longer; and we have ample proof, if further proof were needed, that our requisition of the Clump was strategically correct."

"But surely," ventured Preece, "they won't come back here after what happened last time?"

"It's Laura's home," Sir John answered patiently. "She's already shown she can't keep away. I can identify with that."

"And," Roegin added unexpectedly, "since they've neutralised Eldor, they'll think the Cheveney threat no longer exists. I recommend you maintain your watch if you want to make a capture. And now, if nobody minds, I'd like to get back to my work-out."

"Very well, let's wind this up," said Bartlett. "We'll reconvene in a month. That includes you, Frank, *with* your crystals."

"It's too soon," insisted Frank.

"September the fifth, and not a day later. There'll be no written confirmation so please ensure you all remember. Thank you for your cooperation, Mr. Roegin."

"I can assure you my motives were entirely selfish," said Roegin, insolently polite. Later, in his quarters, he and Ann shared a bottle of wine and watched the evening news. Buildings blazed in Tottenham as rioting youths claimed the streets.

"Just like home," Roegin murmured. "Your people needed that alliance just as much as mine did."

"And now we have to manage by ourselves," Ann said despondently.

Roegin fielded the remote and turned off the TV. "Don't frown. You'll get wrinkles."

"And you care about that, do you?"

Roegin shrugged.

"Do they listen to us – in here?" Ann went on hesitantly.

"I sweep this place for bugs every day. I find them, destroy them; they plant more and I find those too. It's a game we play. So, at the moment, no, we won't be overheard. But they know we have sex, if that's what you're wondering. That's why you've been kept on, after all. Comfort for the prisoner. Now, what's on your mind?"

Ann refilled her glass carefully. "Why did you call your late partner an idiot?"

Roegin swore inwardly. He'd been so exasperated with the English and their endless questioning that he'd let that comment slip. Trust a woman to pick up on it. Well, maybe it didn't matter anymore. "Buuth was a hothead. Not long after we first arrived he killed someone – a harmless UFO fanatic. I helped get rid of the body."

"Have *you* ever killed anyone?" Ann asked, emboldened.

"Not on Earth. At home, yes, when it was unavoidable. There was a war on. There was *always* a war on." Roegin finished the wine. "Now shut up and come to bed."

"I'm not one of your rec girls," she retorted. "Ask me nicely."

"Please," he offered. "And no more questions about Buuth. He *was* an idiot but I liked him. And if I'd let him be caught and sent home, he'd still be alive."

Once again Ann allowed herself to be drawn into his confident yet noncommittal embrace. He didn't care about her but he made her feel less alone. She too was a captive of Cheveney Manor.

"One more question," she ventured when they were lying sated but no less discontented.

"No," said Roegin, turning his back.

"Not about you."

"What, then?"

"The Celestrians. What were they *doing* here when Laura hooked up with them? What did they want with her?"

"Her voice. Celestrians can't sing. We always wondered why she was the only one who could. As for their presence here ..." Roegin smiled into the darkness. "We recorded one of their stage shows and Control got hold of a copy. Earth songs, though I didn't know at the time. They're stealing your music!"

Ann feigned outrage. "What a cheek! Someone should report them to the PRS if they turn up again."

"Is that a branch of your Secret Service?"

She suppressed a giggle. "Performing Rights Society."

"Well, good luck with that," said Roegin, and fell asleep.

Chapter Two

Tarlion lyr Tarlatine nyl Lydion surveyed his class. "And finally, here's a tale from Celestra – the home of my father Lydion. Like so many of my other stories, it comes from the journal my late mother kept.

"In a star system far from here is a planet called Myrma, where the people live in brightly-coloured tents and herd huge beasts called skang. When Celestra's First Citizen Idenion was a young man, not much older than *you* are, he and Lydion visited Myrma to enjoy the natives' legendary hospitality. Outdoors in the firelight, they drank and feasted and basked in the attentions of the local women.

"The day had some kind of religious significance, and presently Nal, a beautiful young priestess, announced by word and gesture that she needed a companion for the night: one who would help her celebrate the Ancestor. She led a half-grown skang round the assembled men, as traditionally the beast would make the choice for her. On reaching Idenion, the skang meekly lowered its great head into his lap. The priestess had the creature in a choke collar, which might have had something to do with this.

"Idenion was nervous and sought Lydion's advice, only to find he was – er - busy elsewhere. Reassuringly, however, it soon became clear that his role in the ritual was … exactly what you're all thinking it was."

The class giggled.

"Later, Idenion awoke on the bed of skins which he and Nal had shared, to find himself alone and with an urgent need to pee. But where could he, exactly? The Temple of the Ancestor was the most sumptuous dwelling in the village, with wooden walls and intricately woven matting over the entire floor. Idenion unlatched the door and peeked outside, only to be confronted by the skang beast, which snorted and stamped. So in desperation he went to a large shallow urn which Nal had been dancing round, and relieved himself into it, taking care not to splash the rugs. Then he went back to sleep.

"At dawn he was rudely awakened by an enraged Nal, who screamed and beat him with her fists. He hastily retrieved his trousers and stumbled outside, only to be confronted by most of the village menfolk, who had armed themselves with stones, sharp potsherds and large sticks. Lydion appeared, irritated and half dressed, demanding to know what in chaos Idenion had done.

"At this point in the story I must explain that my father's linguistic skills were deficient to the point of non-existence, even with a language as basic as Myrma's. But on realising the gravity of the situation, he rose to the occasion as best he could. Haltingly, he explained to Chieftain Gej that Idenion was young and untutored in Myrmian ways, and promised not to bring him there again. When a stony stare was the only response, he then offered to return with exotic fruits and fine wine.

"Gej remained unmoved, as did Nal, and for a moment Idenion's fate seemed inevitable. Then, suddenly, the skang ambled toward the miscreant and licked his face.

"Gej took this as a sign. After a short discussion with Nal, he beckoned a young man who proceeded to draw, in a few lightning strokes, an amazing likeness of Idenion, using a scrap of hide and a plumed feather dipped in vegetable ink. The drawing complete, he instantly started on another. Lydion knew what that meant. Runners would be sent to all the tribes, bearing the sketches and warning everyone against the blasphemer. Idenion wouldn't be safe anywhere on Myrma.

"At last Gej signalled the villagers to stand down, and issued some terse orders to Lydion. He was to send for his flying house and remove Idenion forthwith. Lydion hastily summoned the orbiting spacecraft and shoved Idenion on board before Gej could change his mind. And from that day on, my long-suffering father could only set foot on Myrmian soil if he arrived with gifts. Fruit, wine, and a certain green potion called starfire – which he'd been unwise enough to share on a previous occasion. Gej had long nurtured an ambition to become tribal shaman. Now, thanks to starfire - and Idenion's social blunder - he'd be the very best."

Tarlion paused, surveying his slightly bewildered class. "I've described religions to you before," he continued with sudden seriousness. "This tale illustrates why they're best avoided. One innocent mistake led to a terrible misunderstanding which could have cost Idenion his life. The

Myrmians worship their own forbears, and when an important person dies, his bones are ground to powder and mixed with clay to form a pot. Thus imbued with the spirit of the ancestor, these pots become sacred objects. No-one may eat or drink from them, and as for –"

At this juncture, Councillor Myrig entered the room.

"So, young ones," Tarlion concluded hastily, "if you should ever travel to primitive worlds, remember this tale and mind your manners. Class dismissed."

They departed, laughing.

"Are you here to find fault with my lessons?" Tarlion asked Myrig guardedly.

"Your stories are a little too colourful, but using them to conclude a seminar does at least guarantee a full attendance," conceded Myrig with an indulgent smile. "But I'm not here to discuss your teaching methods. Please accompany me to my house. We need to talk."

"Why? What have I done?"

"You're in no trouble. But the matter requires discretion."

Tarlion tried to keep pace with Myrig, but it was almost dark and he didn't have the Narvellan's night vision. The infrequent street lamps and the occasional lighted window were of little help, and he stumbled several times on the rough road.

Myrig, troubled, waited for him to catch up. It was no secret that Tarlion considered himself more Celestrian than Narvellan, although his genetic disposition favoured neither race above the other.

When younger, he'd persuaded his kindly stepfather Bydlor to teach him all the Celestrian he knew, and had even approached Myrig with the same request. He'd become quite proficient. Then he'd suddenly abandoned his studies and gone sailing up and down the nearest coast, demonstrating his self-sufficiency and inherently restless nature.

Like his father he was a teller of tales, but unlike Lydion, could switch effortlessly between languages. The colony had begun as a motley selection of all Narvellan classes and dialects, and these variants still persisted. Tarlion had taken each one, even the archaic and formal High Narvellan, and created a seamless blend of styles which his students admired. This, Myrig believed, was the linguistic future of New Narvella.

Naturally Tarlion had been in relationships. But not many. Women saw him as a diversion, a distraction, just as his lessons were. There was an air of impermanence about him.

Myrig didn't speak until they were seated in his study with a glass of local wine each. "Did you realise today was the twenty-fifth anniversary of our landfall?" he inquired at last.

"No, I didn't," Tarlion said without much interest.

"But you do recall, I hope, that the Conclave of Elders - your stepfather included – ruled that it would be twenty-five years before we could be sure of our future here?"

"I've heard it said."

54

"I've just come from the assembly rooms. Today, New Narvella ceased to be a colony and was redesignated our homeworld. And with it came some decisive new edicts." Myrig leaned forward, intent and serious. "Do you still wish to go in search of your father?"

"More than ever." Tarlion promptly shed his mask of indifference. "Bydlor said I should wait and see if I grew out of it, and for his sake I really tried. But every time I look in the mirror, every time I collide with something in the dark, I'm reminded of that heritage you've all been telling me to ignore. I want to ask for volunteers – just one or two of my students - "

"Stop." Myrig's voice was severe. "Do you really understand them so little? Your stories are legends to them, not history. Fantasies. Entertainments. If you confronted them with the cold reality of space, they'd be terrified."

"Can't I at least ask?"

"We're not a spacefaring species, Tarlion. We did it once only, and it was catastrophic. Celestrians, on the other hand, have a long history of space exploration. That's what drives you. I always disagreed with Bydlor. Stay here and you'll become embittered and resentful."

Tarlion stared at his mentor in amazement. "You're saying I should go?"

"That's why I invited you here." Myrig drained his glass. "A resolution was passed today, concerning our space fleet. It's to be broken up."

Tarlion swore softly. "So they're finally going to do it, are they? Why now?"

"Some scientists in North Town have found a way to reverse-engineer theridolyte, turn it back into therite. An explosive like that would transform our building programme, and the salvaged electronics would enhance our standard of living. By the time the components wore out, we'd have the industry to create more."

"I see. You've got it all worked out."

"I don't support the plan," Myrig said patiently. "But one opposing voice will change nothing. I'd rather show my disapproval by helping *you*."

"How?"

"For a start, I could supply entry codes to some of the spheres. You'd then have to run a diagnostic to make sure the systems were still functional."

Tarlion blinked. "Er – right."

"Is this conversation moving too rapidly?" Myrig asked.

"You startled me, that's all. You're not allowing me to read you - "

"Under the circumstances that wouldn't be wise. Now if I remember rightly, you've operated spheres before?"

"Yes, I was in the planet-mapping team. Before the Conclave grounded everything."

"Excellent. You'll know your way around the control systems." Myrig produced a weary smile. "I've no real worries about viability. If the crystals are intact, everything else will be. But I'd be failing in my duty if I didn't remind you of the dangers you *will* face."

"The Eldorians?" queried Tarlion.

"The Eldorians were never interested in us," Myrig declared. "Only as a source of information, and they'd already exhausted that. It was the Celestrians they wanted."

"You believe they may have found them?"

"It's a strong possibility. But I'm equally sure the Celestrians will have dealt with the threat in their own inimical way. *Your* problems are purely practical. I can't supply the galactic coordinates for Celestra, because Axmiol expunged them from our records. I can give you some idea of the direction, but unless you detect their transposal markers you could face years of searching, of replenishing your supplies from planets you happen across. And you'd be alone. Completely alone."

"I still want to do it," Tarlion said quietly.

"That's the answer I was expecting. So, at dawn, we'll take a buggy to Touchdown Valley and find you a suitable sphere. We'll have to hurry to avoid discovery, though I don't imagine the asset-strippers will put in an appearance for a few days. First, everything will have to be catalogued."

"Of course." Tarlion smiled - a slow, impish smile like that of his father. Myrig recognised it and became sombre.

"You do realise that if your mother had lived, we wouldn't be having this conversation? She loved you so much. It would have destroyed her if you'd left."

"Would it?" countered Tarlion. "I think she'd have wanted me to go. I'll see you in the morning, Myrig. I hope you don't change your mind. Oh, and thanks. For believing in me."

Surprisingly, the elderly man embraced him. "If only my son had been more like you."

Walking carefully home, Tarlion allowed himself one brief flight of fancy. This was like the tale of Clemoridys, which he'd heard from Myrig himself. First Citizen Tralvar had helped the poet Idenion to steal a sphere and rescue the woman he loved. But there the similarity ended. There was no programme crystal to guide him on his way, and no beautiful girl waiting at journey's end, wherever that might be.

**

The neatly assembled rows of spheres stood on the rock and shingle of a dried-up watercourse, the river having found a lower level. When Tarlion and Myrig arrived, they very quickly realised they'd acted none too soon. Some of the spheres had already been stripped of their logic systems and crystal arrays. Obviously the decision of the Conclave had been foregone, and the salvage teams weren't waiting for an inventory.

Myrig found a sphere that looked intact, then insisted on running a full diagnostic to ensure nothing was missing. They stowed the non-perishable food he'd provided, and Tarlion shoved a change of clothes in the locker. He'd brought nothing else.

"How long will this take?" he asked, then yawned. "Sorry. I was awake all night." He moved to the open hatch, scanning the horizon.

"A few nerves are only to be expected."

"I wasn't nervous, not really. Just wondering what will become of this place once I'm not here to stir it up."

"You needn't fear for us, Tarlion. You think we haven't rid ourselves of the bad old days, but I sincerely believe we have. We've no class structure anymore, no elite, no elite-wives, and the Directress girls can walk freely and use their talents without obscuring their other senses. Soon the old guard, including myself, will be gone; and once no one can recall life before the solar flares, society will evolve in directions I can't possibly foresee. I have great hopes for this modest little colony."

"If I find Celestra," Tarlion said slowly, "what message should I deliver on your behalf?"

Myrig sighed. "In the end it will be your decision, but my opinion – for what it's worth – is that there can never be harmony between our peoples. We asked for their help, they gave it, and we betrayed them. They won't want reminding of that."

"I see."

"We took a decision to isolate ourselves and I'm reasonably sure they'd respect our wishes, but take no chances. Destroy your flight log."

Before Tarlion could frame a promise, there were two interruptions. From the control deck the system shrilled its readiness; and in the distance he spied the dust cloud of an approaching vehicle. "Myrig, my friend, we've got company."

"I'm surprised it took them this long."

"Trust the Conclave to spoil my farewell speech. I'll make this brief. Out you go, Myrig. Clear the ramp. Celestra here I come!"

***

The Lyricon, Alda Mexa, 6.5.7.4030

"He's done it again, Guildmaster!" Bekta, the most vociferous addition to the junior scolia, was airing her feelings as only she could. "He made us go all wrong 'cos he's too *loud*!"

"*And* he was out of phase," added Arcto, the eldest of the group.

"I wasn't out of phase," yelled Esclevon, the object of their complaints. "You weren't keeping up!"

"Quietly now," advised Guildmaster Lann, privately wondering if he was the best choice to teach these ebullient youngsters. He appreciated their talent but was far happier with older students. He'd only taken charge of the Lyricon beginners as part of the city-wide assessment of scolia-sensitives, and as a favour to Nefyrra, who at that moment was monitoring proceedings from the back of the rehearsal room.

At last the children stopped arguing amongst themselves and re-focused on their tutor.

"That's better," said Lann. "Bekta, it isn't accurate to say that Esclevon is too loud. He over-resonates. And he wasn't out of phase, Arcto; you were out of phase with one another. You're all advanced for your age when it comes to forming a lattice, but you *are* still young and there are bound to be imperfections at first. You need more practice."

"I've got a headache," said Bekta sullenly. "Too much over-resonance." She glared at Esclevon.

"Very well, let's break for lunch," Lann said. "Back here in one ild. We'll practise your keyboard skills next. Esclevon, your playing is excellent and thus you're excused for the afternoon. Nefyrra has an assignment for you."

Esclevon looked apprehensive.

"Don't you want to know what it is? Off you go, she's waiting!"

Esclevon approached Nefyrra awkwardly and stood scuffing at a worn tile. "I'm sorry I shouted in class, Custodian."

"No need to be so formal, Vonnie. You can call me Nefyrra or even Grandmother."

"I don't like reminding the others that you're family," Esclevon said candidly. "They say I'm your favourite. And please don't call me Vonnie! I'm too old for that now."

"How old *are* you exactly?"

"I'll soon be seven. Grandmother Laura says I'm eleven."

"Laura still applies the Earth years to everything and everyone," Nefyrra said with a wry smile. "Shall we continue this chat in my study? The matter I wish to discuss has nothing to do with your classmates. Don't worry, I'll feed you."

"Am I in trouble?" asked Esclevon, stumbling up a step as he followed her.

"No," Nefyrra said emphatically. "You're not."

In the elevator he stared at his feet, avoiding her gaze. Clemis and Trevone's firstborn, so like her late father Tralvar in his youth. The musicality, the awkwardness, plus the unruly hair, all matched the retraces given by Tralvar's peers and by Tralvar himself. Far from indulging the boy, Nefyrra had often overcompensated by being harsh with him. She suspected Lann had too.

"I haven't seen your mother for a while," she said after he'd finished his second bowl of soup.

"Neither have I." Esclevon mopped the bowl clean with half a grain cake.

"But surely you're living with your parents?"

"No, I'm in one of the dorms on Lateral Two. There are some dancers, apprentice masons and two of the older scolia to keep an eye on us. I like it. They're all from other city states so it makes me feel I've travelled."

"I see."

"I go home on rest days, or I go to Laura and Idenion at the akron. I like it there too. Idenion helps me with my general studies and Laura tells me about Earth."

"I can't believe Clemis has lost interest in you," Nefyrra said, frowning. "She loves children. She's still a nursery nurse, isn't she?"

"Yes, and sometimes she helps Dr. Escir with the neonates. She didn't neglect me, Nefyrra. Just the opposite. She'd never let me *do* anything."

"Ah." Nefyrra was beginning to understand.

"Father's upgrading the Alda Six scanner and I wanted him to take me there. But mother wouldn't

62

hear of it. And she wouldn't let me go to Scapirion with cousin Kalyx in case I fell through the ice. And when I went skinny-dipping at Lake Holpen with some of my class, she had to come and watch. It was so embarrassing!"

"So who has charge of you now? Officially?"

"Still my parents, I think."

"Right," said Nefyrra decisively. "I'm going to have a word with my son. I want to send you to Tafret on a study course and your mother isn't going to prevent it."

"Tafret? The relayist school?"

"They do more than relayist training now. The tutors help gifted children who are having difficulty processing their abilities. I want to see how you perform in a lattice with others like yourself and others who are too loud, as your friends call it."

A trace of hope awoke in Esclevon's eyes. "Others like me?"

"Yes, Vonnie. There *are* others like you, and you shall meet them."

"I wanted to ask ..." Esclevon faltered.

"I wanted to ask Guildmaster Lann, only he's always so busy keeping order ..." He paused again, and this time Nefyrra merely waited for him to continue. When he did so, the words came in a rush. "Why are there only eight people in a lattice? We've had large scolia groups at the Lyricon, in shows, so why can't we have a lattice of sixteen or twenty four or even bigger? It could be as big as a city!"

"You've studied elementary resonance theory, haven't you?" Nefyrra asked gently. "Everything

63

is subject to the rule of eight. The octave, aldacite, transposal portals -"

"I know. We could still have groups of eight, but linked. Linked by the loud ones, like me."

"Linked how?"

"I'm not sure. I haven't developed the idea. But maybe a ground base, a drone, like the Zarf Dance? A resonance, not a note. A carrier wave." He faltered to a stop.

"Where is your father now?" Nefyrra asked abruptly.

"Still on Alda Six."

"Then I'm putting through a call this very day. I think you should go to Tafret as soon as possible, and tell Nohal of your theories."

"First Relayist Nohal?" breathed Esclevon.

"Don't worry – he's a kindly, approachable man. Laura and Idenion recently went to see him about setting up entrainment centres for the talented young. Tafret can't handle everyone. But I think Nohal's going to be very interested in *you*."

"Perhaps he'd think I was a nuisance with silly ideas."

"Vonnie, I know you don't have confidence in yourself yet, but that day will come."

"When I've stopped falling over my own feet."

"I was the same as you," Nefyrra said softly. "You're going to be tall like me – or even taller – and at the moment your hands and feet seem too large for the rest of you. That will change as you grow. Believe me, it will. Now, are you willing to enrol at Tafret?"

"Yes. Yes I am."

"Then let's go and find a transposer. We'll *both* speak with Trevone."

***

The Ephren Estates, Patieron City, 12 Empire years after sequestration

Ymer Coll-Preda, survivor of the Ninth Eldorian Expeditionary Force, alighted from an aircar outside Lord Ephren's mansion and handed his credentials to the armed detail which awaited him. Then, displaying a confidence he did not feel, he proceeded with his escorts to a spacious reception room. The twin dagger insignia of House Patieron was everywhere, from the stained glass windows to the cushions. The soldiers stationed themselves outside the double doors.

Ymer moved further into the room, then paused in momentary surprise. A youth in his late teens rose unhurriedly from a wing-backed armchair and came forward to greet him.

"Welcome, Master Technician. I am Veylis Pervain-Opna. Lord Ephren is indisposed and bids me receive you. May I offer you some wine?" He ushered his guest to a chair opposite his, dismissing two burly manservants.

Pervain's bastard son, thought Ymer. Shaping up nicely, or so I hear. I wonder if he's as devious as his father? "I'm honoured to meet you, Freelord. I bring significant news from Project Reclaim. In view of the sensitive nature of this work, Lord

Ephren advised me to deliver the update in person rather than risk having it intercepted."

"A wise precaution, since Patierade scientists have their own version of the project. Sympathy for their cause has increased and it would not auger well for House Patieron if they beat us to a result."

He spoke with the assurance that came with his title, but the meticulous elocution lessons he must have received hadn't quite cancelled out the provincial accent. Possibly by choice. Ymer began to like him.

"The Freelord may be aware," he began carefully, "that we've been studying the orbiting devices retrieved from the planet Dral."

"And I'm also aware the Celestrians placed these devices. Continue."

"By taking operable components from each unit and adding some materials of our own, we've succeeded in restoring one to working order. We've studied the resonance it generates and have negated it – although of course the Dral prison array was a primitive forerunner of the Transfix which surrounds us now."

"A prison is a prison, whether it's the breadth of a planet or ten light years wide," pronounced Veylis. "And you believe the Dral artefacts and the Transfix share the same operating principle?"

"I realise how unlikely that sounds, but the Celestrians often draw on their past technology. The sphere-shield plans we stole from them, for instance, were based on ancient tech. I worked on those plans, so I should know."

Veylis looked unconvinced.

"I'm not saying we can take down the Transfix here and now. It has a very complex harmonic, some aspects of which have still to be mapped. Our other problem is that some of my team, especially those who studied under Habbon Mol-Varna, think we've made only a partial reconstruction of the Dral array – that each device produced a different, complimentary resonance. We've no way of telling. But we're reasonably hopeful that our submediant emitter will puncture or disrupt the Transfix. We need to augment our equipment, then take it to the boundary and make the attempt. We need the Senate's permission and – forgive my plain speaking – Patieron funding for this next phase."

"You shall have it," Veylis replied instantly, "on two conditions: that you have an armed contingent standing by to cross the boundary should your attempt be successful, and that I am the appointed leader of this task force."

"You, Freelord? Would Lord Ephren sanction that after losing your father?"

"I haven't yet finished my military service, Ymer. I think Ephren would prefer me to take my chances off-world amongst trusted men than be targeted by Patierade extremists closer to home. But, I shall discuss it with him first. I think he'll see the sense in it."

"Let's hope so."

Veylis poured more wine. "Ephren is a changed man. He made Pervain fight for everything he wished to achieve. With me, he's generous to a fault – as are most grandparents. My request will come as no surprise to him. He knows I've been teaching myself Celestrian from my father's effects."

"In that case -" Ymer raised his glass. "To Project Reclaim. I look forward to serving with you."

Veylis smiled broadly. "To Project Reclaim – and the end of Celestrian oppression!"

***

The Akron, Alda Mexa, 8.8.7.4030

"How's it going?" asked Laura, peeping into Idenion's cluttered study. "Have you found anything interesting?"

Idenion, half hidden behind a stack of Alendis' files, smiled ruefully. "If you'd asked me that an ild ago I'd have said no – just endless speeches full of meaningless platitudes. I can't believe I was ever taken in by him."

"You were young," Laura said softly. "And he was very charismatic."

"Yes. Well." Idenion shuffled some papers. "I finally found some of his earlier writings. If Tralvar hadn't imposed his own particular brand of chaos on the collection I wouldn't have gone near all that propaganda. Anyway, listen to this …". He positioned a fragile sheet of paper under a magnifying screen. "Placing our infants near ageing minds, on the assumption that they will absorb good character, is instead stultifying the talent they were born with, and is leading to the stagnation of our society."

"That's what Geffin believed," Laura exclaimed. "Sorry, go on."

"Instead, children should be raised in creches, to absorb from one another, to grow and evolve freely."

"That's what we're doing now," Laura said, more quietly this time. "Are we getting it right?"

"According to this, we are. He goes on to say ..." Idenion blinked several times and adjusted the page. "It is my contention that every child is born a scolia-sensitive. It is with reluctance that I use this popularised term; no other exists at this time. The call to the scolia, which is resonance-based communication at its most basic level, hints at the perfectibility of a medium which we have scarcely begun to explore. Complex information or knowledge could be communicated within this unrefined wave-form.

"An unpopulated lattice has similar qualities: a resonance which can heal or destroy, or, if a sufficient number of sensitives is linked, to carry the mind to a higher plane of perception. To restrict the lattice to the performance of music is an abuse of our true ability ..." Idenion switched off the screen light. "Usual rant follows. We should unlock the full power of our minds, and so on, and so on."

"Right," said Laura briskly, "I'm taking over. You're giving yourself eyestrain. Which files have you read?"

"These. And those on the floor, and that pile in the corner. Don't forget, we're looking for anything that would suggest he put his theories into practice. Research, experiments -"

"Then shouldn't we discount the early writings? If he'd tried to change the way children were nurtured he'd never have made First Citizen."

"No, we have to read it all. An attempt to enhance the lattice, for instance, wouldn't have been considered suspect. In fact, it might have increased his popularity. Are you sure you can spare the time for this, Laura?"

"Yes – now go and relax. When did you last eat?"

"Not for a while."

"Then go," said Laura firmly.

Idenion acquiesced, but reappeared very soon in a state of suppressed excitement. Laura looked up reproachfully.

"You never made it to the kitchens, did you?"

"Afraid not. But this is important!"

"It always is."

"This time it *really* is. Kalyx has just called from Scapinon."

"Oh?"

"He called because he'd just heard from Habbon at the Alda Four dig. They've found a scattering of data crystals. Habbon was absolutely right – there *was* an ancient settlement there and the Narvellans built over it."

"Does anyone know what's on these crystals?"

"It's an alphabet. A teaching aid for very young children. And it's threefold: an object, the spoken name of the object, and the name written onscreen. They don't yet know how complete it is but Habbon is convinced it's the key to deciphering the time capsule diaries!"

"Your very own Rosetta Stone," Laura breathed.

"You can tell me what that is later. The crystals will have to be treated with great care – they weren't preserved deliberately like the others. Scapirion has the best resources so that's where Habbon's sending them. That's why he spoke to Kalyx. And he wants the decryption teams assembled again, which is why Kalyx called *me*."

"Do you remember who they were?"

"No, but I'm sure Lann and Nefyrra do. I must notify them at once. That pre-Impact jumble in the time capsule wasn't the real message, Laura. That's still waiting for us!"

Chapter Three

Clemis and Nefyrra sat side by side in Tafret's amphitheatre. It was modest compared with the Lyricon, and had a retractable awning in place of a weathershield. But the architecture was graceful, boasting the same perfect acoustics as its counterpart in Alda Mexa.

The resident scolia had just performed. They were accomplished, but, Nefyrra thought privately, lacked the Lyricon scolia's edgy brilliance. Their lattice had been excellent though, perfectly balanced and well sustained. After the interval they'd play again, and this time their lattice would be enhanced by young students from Nohal's academy. Esclevon would be among them.

"I can't believe he's ready for this," said Clemis in a mixture of pride and apprehension. "It's less than a span since he enrolled!"

"Nohal's amazed at how fast he's progressed," Nefyrra answered a little distantly.

Clemis was silent for a moment. "I'm sorry I sounded off at you for sending him here. You were right. Trevone was right."

"And have you apologised to him too?"

"No need. Idenion calmed me down before I could reach a transposer." Clemis grinned ruefully. "When Trevone gets back from Alda Six I shall be extra nice to him, to compensate for the row we never had!"

"What changed your mind about Vonnie?" Nefyrra asked gently.

"Vonnie did. Have you ever seen him so confident, so positive? For the first time he's with kids like himself. Nohal's even given him a couple of sessions on the retracer, to study his output. I thought he'd be scared of it but he isn't. And the kids love the prill! They've adopted a plant each and are responsible for its upkeep. Vonnie's named his Pretty, because it isn't. Oh, look – the scolia's back. Now we'll see what this new improved lattice is all about!"

The children formed a broad circle around the scolia players – not, as Esclevon had explained, that they needed to. It was just for effect. Once more the lattice sprang into existence, a perfect eight-point figure imbued with the music's form and meaning. Then, suddenly, to the surprise and delight of the audience and half of Tafret, the enhanced lattice surrounded the first and augmented it with dazzling precision.

Nefyrra marvelled at the strength of it. No stray thought or other distraction was going to make this resonance decohere. And she also knew that it could carry much more than the scolia was putting into it.

+I can read Vonnie's autograph in there+ Clemis informed her.

+How can you, when I can't?+ Nefyrra inquired. +You're not scolia+

+I'm his mother+ Clemis answered succinctly.

Afterward, once they'd disentangled themselves from an excited Esclevon and several of his friends, they went to dine with Nohal.

"I'm pleased you liked the performance, Custodian," he said cordially to Nefyrra. "I'm still discovering what the children's limit is, and how long they can sustain it. Once I have, I can start planning additional outlets for their talents. At the moment, as with all new innovations, we're still finding our way."

"You've made an illustrious beginning," Nefyrra assured him. "And the Lyricon scolia will be at your disposal once the Peisistrata is over."

"I'm sincerely grateful," Nohal said. "Tell me, Clemis, did you ask Escir's opinion about this wellspring of new abilities?"

"He says anything to do with perception is beyond him," Clemis answered, "but he doesn't discount the possibility that removing the birth restrictions has somehow kickstarted our evolution. He confirms the new generation's healthier, with an increased weight at birth. The good news is, he's offered to work with you on standardising brain activity measurement. I explained that we'd only measured brain waves electronically since the first retracer was built."

"You're a good negotiator, Clemis," said Nefyrra approvingly.

"Well, I *did* ask Ailsi to put in a good word for Nohal," admitted Clemis. "My birth mother's always been a force to be reckoned with!"

They continued to plan musical activities between Alda Mexa and Tafret until the daylight began to wane. "Time to go," Clemis said reluctantly. "I'd better round up Vonnie. I promised I wouldn't leave without saying goodbye in person."

"I'll wait for you here," said Nefyrra after a slight pause. "I just want to finalise a couple of things with Nohal." Then, once Clemis had gone, she went on swiftly: "I wanted a quick word with you about my weathershield operator's daughter. "Tonor *did* bring her to see you?"

"He did. He had concerns."

"I told him he'd be wasting his time and yours. Was I right?"

"As far as the Academy goes, yes. There was no point in running the usual tests. Tonora has no aptitude for music, and with her lack of projection she'll certainly never be a relayist. But she can detect resonance patterns in objects and to some extent read the future of a pattern."

"Exactly what I thought you'd say. All the Lyricon staff knew she was resonance-sensitive. She was a difficult baby, would never settle, and Tonor sometimes brought her to work to give his wife some peace. Tonora always fell blissfully asleep as soon as he started the shield."

"Interesting," mused Nohal. "But it's the pattern recognition that worries Tonor, as I'm sure you know."

"He's being silly," Nefyrra said dismissively.

"He's being conventional. He thinks Tonora's abilities are just a tiny bit sinister. She's several times told people when their patterns will stop. When they'll die."

"Which is precisely why I wanted Clemis out of the way before we discussed this. If she overheard, Ailsi would find out and then the whole city would know. I don't want Tonora thinking her talent's something people will shun. She's growing up to be a bright, well-adjusted girl. She just needs a lesson in tact."

Nohal's craggy face crinkled in a smile. "And if you were to provide that lesson, how would you phrase it?"

"I'd start by telling her about the Narvellans and their Directresses, and Sijek, and Lydion. And about Eketa and Xorian on the Gloriana, reading a pattern's future *and* its past."

"Just to show she isn't the odd one out?"

"Yes, exactly. But then I'd say that people don't always want to know when their pattern will end – even if they say they do. So for the sake of the ones who don't, it might be better if she stopped mentioning it."

"And will you suggest a career in healing?"

Nefyrra looked surprised. "No, that isn't what she wants. She wants to be Tonor's apprentice, train as the next weathershield op."

"Is that feasible?"

"More than feasible, given her affinity with the equipment. And it's high time Tonor had an apprentice. He isn't much younger than Idenion!"

"It sounds as if the child has designed her own future." Nohal poured himself a measure of liman. "Very well, Nefyrra, talk to her. I'm sure Tonor will be happy with the result."

6.1.1.4031

His dreams no longer sustained him. Patterns of resonance, varied and intrusive, pummelled his reluctant consciousness. Mechanically he identified their origins: the familiar, almost comforting thrum of the planet beneath him, the boom of the distant sun, the fixed harmonies of the outer worlds and their moons. He'd often used these three sources as a base line, a place to retreat to when his calculations had taken him to places he'd rather not have visited. Yes, he'd been scared, but the work had to be done. The Eldorians had to be contained. And he –

Was dead. Murdered. His work unfinished. He'd failed, and the Eldorians had triumphed.

+You didn't, and they haven't+ said Sarune. +I watched your Cadence device being tested+

Resignedly he focused on her. +Oh, chaos, I thought I'd dreamt you+

+How ungallant of you, Lydion. And after I've spent over seven years shoring up your pattern+

+Seven years? Then I'm forgotten as well as dead. Well, Sarune, what would you have me do for the *next* seven years? I could try making passionate pattern-love to you, if such a thing exists+

+Still the same lamentable sense of humour, I see+

+And that irritates you, doesn't it? I'll bear that in mind. It might just stop me going crazy. In the meantime, tell me how the Eldorians were defeated. I want to know who finished my project and why it's called Cadence+

She challenged him to read her, believing he'd refuse out of distaste or unfamiliarity with his powers. But Lydion responded, partly due to the hint of coquettishness in the invitation – something which possibly only he could have detected – and partly due to the significance of the information. The exchange was more rapid than he'd ever experienced, but he coped well, calmly absorbing the facts without pausing to comment.

It wasn't easy. Some events, portrayed by Sarune through the filter of her unique Synectic consciousness, needed interpretation before he understood. On his homeworld octals passed, but unlike before, he was aware of the passing time. He'd done with hibernating. There was no solace in it.

Sarune took him beyond the end of the short, desperate battle to the reunification with Scapirion and the raising of the time capsule.

+So Pervain's dead+ was Lydion's predictable remark after she'd finished.

+Fortunately for you. You'd have spent a fruitless and frustrating time planning a revenge you could never enact. I know, I've been there+

+Then I must defer to your greater experience+ Lydion responded with thinly veiled sarcasm. +In any case, I'm more concerned with my transposal dampener and what this Scapirian girl did to make it sound a harmonic when activated. It shouldn't have made any sound at all. The t-space resonance had to be completely locked off, so that any prompt from a transposal Drive would have nothing to key into+

+Sorry, you're losing me. I don't do transposal theory+

+Then let me *show* you. There, right there, is the region we call t-space, underpinning our normal dimensional space. See? We're kind of bolted onto it, or it to us. There are actually several t-space realities. I created a resonance buffer to link with each one and block it, then reinforced the block with a series of rests or null-points. Only I hadn't finished reinforcing it. If Ruvrin used a wave antiphon to secure it, the dampener would have worked, but not so well. That harmonic of hers offers a way through, though I'd have to see the schematic to determine the risk+

+Impractical, given your circumstances+

+Quite. Well, we can only hope it holds. If t-space weren't such a menace to work with I'd have finished the calculations long ago, and we wouldn't have this problem. Any one of those other dimensions would have been a joy to arrange. See them, Sarune? Calm, stable, no storms, with as many folds and strands as a resonance engineer could wish for. And look at those bubble universes, some of them here and gone in a single moment. And did you see - +

+Lydion, stop. Stop!+ Sarune seemed almost distraught.

He signalled irritation. +What's wrong?+

+I can't see what you're seeing. Your perception of the universe isn't like mine+

+But it must be. You evolved me+

+I *marked* you, then neglected you. You did it all by yourself. I can't perceive your folded dimensions, let alone any bubble universes. And t-space to me is only a perturbation without detail+ She paused ruefully. +I totally misjudged your race's potential. To think that someone like you, with perception that was little more than basic - +

+Thanks!+

+ - could ever achieve such vision. I'm envious. Don't shield – I shan't strike at you. You didn't ask for any of this, as you keep reminding me+

+Tyvian would have been a better choice+ Lydion answered sombrely. +He'd have been enthralled. What you did to him was unforgivable+

+It wasn't me+ Sarune replied earnestly. +Read me if you think I'm lying. You're strong enough now+

+I think I might just do that+ Lydion scanned the memories she offered, seeing again the Synectic over-mind as it had once been. It wasn't pleasant, but he persisted until he had his information.

+I was angry with Tyvian for spying on us+ Sarune supplemented, +but I only wanted to mark him, just as I'd previously marked *you*. He was old and frail – we wouldn't have had to wait long to draw him in. It was Arbros, our founder, who wanted him dead. In those days I wasn't strong enough to challenge Arbros. Later, I was. I eradicated him and took command+

Lydion had to be content with that. He spent perhaps a day studying his surroundings, then typically grew restless. +This is all very well, Sarune, but how long am I supposed to hover above my homeworld like some redundant satellite? Where's the meaning? Where's the excitement? If this is all you have to offer, you can give me the Arbros treatment right now!+

+You can't possibly be bored, Lydion+

+Can't I? Sorry I'm a bit lacking in profound thoughts, but that's the kind of man I am. Was. I know – you could tell me how you transposed. That must have been an effort, since you can hardly sense t-space+

+What nonsense is this? We can't transpose. If you so much as put one tendril into t-space you'd be torn to shreds+

+Then how did you get here? You were on Ipsa+

+After the explosion, the reducees who worked on the base were still alive. I simply occupied one of the damaged minds, and kept quiet. As it happened, my choice was the brother of Directress Passik, and at her request he was sent to Ilonna+

+And then?+ asked Lydion ominously

+Ah, here come the recriminations. I killed my life-bonded's child, I nearly killed Dena+

+Well, didn't you?+

+My mistake,+ Sarune began carefully, +was in leaving my unwitting host too soon, instead of resting and building my strength. I still had a nebulous bond with my partner Chisrin but I thought it wouldn't matter. It may interest you to know that the other Synectics had their life-partners disposed of. I merely had Chisrin sent away. So then it began – I was dragged into the psyche of my dying husband, then his unborn child, then Dena. I was too puny to free myself. And I was terrified of what would happen when I did. Something similar could have happened to you. I spared you that+

+I hope you don't expect me to thank you. Not when it's your fault I'm here in the first place+

+Don't, then. You'll do as you please, just as you've always done. You've no conception of what it's like to have your entire life mapped out for you, every decision made for you. I was to be a Directress, but the training was unbearably restrictive. So I sidestepped into marriage, only to find myself in servitude of another kind. Even the other Synectics considered me subordinate to them, despite my being their unifying force. Such was Narvellan society+

Lydion, still intuitive as ever, saw through the bitterness to her proud but unfulfilled spirit. +Much was denied you+ he answered. +That's all too clear. But I still can't see why you'd let your youth and strength be shrivelled away for the sake of that vile experiment. You were an attractive woman+

The comment took Sarune by surprise. +Was I? How would *you* know?+

+The impress disc you gave Chisrin. I didn't see it in operation, but Dena did and so did Laura. They said you were beautiful+

+Impress disc+ Sarune repeated slowly. +I don't recall one. It couldn't have been important+

+Chisrin thought it was+

+*None* of my pre-Synectic life is important+ Sarune answered dismissively.

82

Lydion discovered he could still shiver. She's forgetting, he thought to himself. Is it deliberate – or inevitable? I can't let that happen to *me*. I won't. It's what I am. It's *all* that I am. And if I find I'm losing any of it ..... well, there's always t-space.

+Plotting something?+ asked Sarune suspiciously.

+Yes, actually. Since your past wasn't much fun, how would you like to share mine? I'm going to review it, to give myself some perspective. You're welcome to join me+

+Do you *need* an audience?+

+It's what I'm used to. Give it a try, Sarune. You might enjoy it+

+I doubt that. But I brought you here, so I suppose I must indulge you+

+Good. And when I'm done, I'm going to find what passes for adventure round here. Whether or not you tag along is entirely up to you+

Eldorian space, somewhere near the Transfix

"Disengage Drive," Ymer instructed. "Proceed on auxiliary power, cautiously. Cautiously I said! I know you're eager for action, Veylis, but if we so much as touch that thing we'll be dead in space."

Veylis peered over Ymer's shoulder. "Scanners aren't registering it. How are you determining our position?"

"It has a faint EM signature, similar to cosmic background radiation. That's what we thought it

83

was at first. Once we knew its origin we were able to quantify its position and depth. Listen." He touched a key on his armrest. Veylis listened intently but could only hear white noise. "Don't worry, the computer has its range. We'll soon be at the planned coordinates."

"How deep *is* it?"

"It isn't. Under different circumstances, and at this speed, we'd be through it in a couple of zytl."

"Then why can't we shut down our systems and drift through?"

"It's been tried," Ymer said laconically. "Even when the Drive's inert the crystals can still respond to the Transfix's properties. After that, they're so much junk. Right, we're here. Where are the others?"

"Adopting their assigned formation. Four groups of two."

"Good." Ymer touched another control. "Reclaim mission, this is team leader. Power up your emitters and stand by."

They responded one by one, their voices muzzy through the blanketing static.

"Reclaim Seven, repeat. There's an echo."

Veylis was suddenly tense. "That's no echo – we've got company. Tell everyone to stay off the radio while we run a trace."

They didn't need telling. The intruder spoke again, more distinctly. Ymer could still make no sense of it.

"Patierades!" said Veylis furiously. "I know their dialect."

"Maybe it's just a recon," Ymer ventured. "There they are, almost out of detector range. Only two of them. Five stellar units away."

"Which means they won't hear our short-range transmissions for another fifteen zytl." Veylis held up a hand for silence as the voice spoke again. "I knew it – they're here for the same reason *we* are. They're running checks." He paused again, frowning. "What in Ebbon's name is a node destabilizer?"

"I'm not sure," Ymer said helplessly.

"Well, whatever it is, they're going to use it on the Transfix. Don't just sit there – give the order to fire our submediant array. Take that thing down!"

"We need to align the tonality - " began Ymer.

"Align? What for? We can't *miss*. I won't let the Patierades steal our glory, Ymer. As your Freelord I'm commanding you to give that order. Now."

The eight spheres fired their emitters. Simultaneously, the two Patierade craft fired theirs. In far-off Cheveney Manor, Frank switched on his newly constructed transposer. And on Alda Six, Trevone activated the restored and enhanced deep space scanner.

***

7.3.1.4031

+Hey, I could get to like this!+ Lydion was lazing above the Lyricon, his pattern spread wide to mirror the dimensions of the lattice beneath. The

85

concert was the third in a series featuring the pick of Nohal's academy and the Lyricon's junior masterclass. +They're improving, aren't they? This one's halfway toward Lateral Two. A lattice for the masses! Wonder if it'll affect the recording industry? You know, I never bothered much with lattices when I could *hear* music. But now, it's something to be admired.+

+And more proof that I was completely wrong about you people. Those children are on their way to becoming something amazing+

+And they don't need to be dead to do it!+ Lydion pointed out with a degree of satisfaction.

Sarune changed the subject. +You're spreading yourself too thin+

+Says who?+

+Me. I've studied the optimum form for our patterns. The more you dissipate yourself the more at risk you become from unexpected energy bursts and stray particles. You should maintain a dimension equivalent to your corporeal form, or even a little smaller+

+Oh, never smaller!+ Lydion reluctantly detached himself from the fringes of the lattice. +I'm tired of being bunched up. Where's the harm in drifting along with those kids?+

+They can't sense you, Lydion+

+Of course they can't. They're much too focused. Anyway, it would be rude of me to interrupt lattice work+ He resumed his former shape. +Happy now? How about some more memoir?+

+Can we leave it a while, please? I'm finding it too ....+

+Titillating?+

+Repetitive. Shouldn't you be above this sort of thing?+

+You're hard work, Sarune+ Lydion was suddenly serious. +Without the framework of our former lives we'd have nothing. We're not an advanced lifeform – we're not *any* kind of lifeform. We can't reproduce; and according to you, can't communicate with anyone save ourselves. We're an echo, a remnant, a – *what was that*?+

Sarune, who had reacted instantly and defensively, uncoiled herself. +Are you damaged?+

+No, just dazed. Give me a moment or two+

+If you'd still been splayed across Lateral One, you'd have been much more than dazed+ she remarked.

+Yes, yes. Point taken. I won't do it again+ Lydion refocused with care, reading the evidence left by whatever had struck them. +This isn't good, Sarune. That bad resonance was the equivalent of an aldacite backlash, transposed. It's as if every active aldacite crystal tried to link with every other, no matter how distant+

+As in entanglement?+

+Aldacite *is* entangled to a lesser extent. It's how transposal works. But this wasn't ordinary transposal – it didn't use t-space but another dimension+

+One that you can see and I can't?+ Sarune inquired sarcastically.

+Put simply, yes. Read around you carefully, before the residue fades. There's a scar at the egress point. The energy surge that glanced off us was directed at Communications. And that one, more distant, at Treva. And a third at Alda Six. There are hints of others too far off for me to read+

+But where did it originate?+

+That's the bad part. There was an interrupted harmonic in that resonance, man-made. I think someone tried to take down the Cadence, someone who didn't know what they were doing, and this was a side-effect+

+Do you think they succeeded?+

+That harmonic must have come from inside the Cadence zone, so yes, it's been perforated. I designed it to reseal itself if that happened, but I'm not sure how long the breach would have lasted. Maybe something more substantial got through. I have to speak to someone about this!+

+That might prove difficult+ Sarune reminded him.

Lydion grew agitated. +I said, I *have* to! They're going to need my help. How thoroughly did you *try* to make yourself known? After all, your average Celestrian wouldn't have been too pleased to find you were still around!+

+I tried+ she answered evasively.

+Your people or mine?+

+Both+

+But you spoke to Idenion when he was trying to save Dena+

+I was in her body. If you can find another identical twin out of his skull on starfire, whose

88

sibling happens to be dying, go ahead and occupy her mind. You might make contact for an isk or two+

+Discord's dreams, Sarune, don't be so negative! I'm going to make the attempt. I'll start with Nohal at the retracer lab+

+You'll be wasting your - + began Sarune, but Lydion was no longer there. For one absurd moment she thought he might have added teleportation to his new range of abilities, but given his unruly persona, that was highly unlikely. He'd simply moved very very fast. Something else she couldn't do.

At Tafret, Escir had just delivered a prototype brainwave monitor into Nohal's safekeeping. "Sorry this is a bit rudimentary. I was hoping to give the scolia-tech a general idea from the heart monitors Eldor supplied, but I'm afraid none of them work anymore. The Alda Mexa healers are useless with machinery."

"They prefer more intuitive methods, I imagine."

Escir grinned. "I just leave them to it these days. The younger generation needs me more. Now, each of these electrodes has to be attached to the scalp. At the moment we're using adhesive, but that's not very kind to one's hair, so a couple of scolia-tech girls are working on an ultra-fine theridolyte net with the electrodes embedded. It should then ripple shut in the form of a cap, ensuring good contact. Sensors will ensure nothing hurts or fits too tight."

"A device like that could transform my sorry efforts!"

"You're too modest, Nohal. Lann tells me you've identified the four basic types of brainwave."

"In a strictly observational way."

+Nohal!+ Lydion interposed himself between the two men. +Nohal, please focus on me+

Nohal went on talking. " – and of course, scolia work requires the highest level, peaking at sixty cycles per isk -"

+Nohal?+

Still no acknowledgement.

+Right! No more politeness. I know you screen out ambient chit-chat when you're busy, but I'll have to cut in - + At this point, Lydion's thought processes stalled, and the sense of coldness he'd felt at discovering Sarune's memory loss came rushing back tenfold. Unaware, Nohal and Escir continued their conversation.

Belatedly Sarune arrived. +Lydion?+

He stirred, recovering. +I can't read them, Sarune. Not even Escir, who can't shield. *Why* can't I read them? Will it be the same with everyone?+

+I'd have warned you if you hadn't taken off+ she answered gently.

+You told me you couldn't communicate!+ he blazed. +I took that to mean you couldn't converse. You didn't say you couldn't read anyone!+

+I'm sorry I waited so long to tell you. When you stopped basking in the cosmos and turned to lattices and the like, I should have explained. I didn't foresee such a pressing need to contact your people+

Lydion tried to calm himself. +I assume you *can* explain this?+

+I have a theory. You'll probably shoot it down+

+Try me+

+I believe+ Sarune began carefully, +that in our present state our perception – which forms the greater part of us – is out of phase with everyone else's+

Lydion was suddenly insightful. +And it isn't just our perception, is it? We're slightly out of phase with this reality. Me especially, because I can see other dimensions and you can't. I take it we can't engage with the prill?+

+I tried years ago. No contact+

+Then, Sarune, I have a problem. Unless I can notify someone how the Cadence was wrongly set up, and how to fix it, Escir's burgeoning new generation won't last very long+ He scanned the vicinity. There were no idle conversations, no relayists practising their craft, nothing local. Just the ever-present natural and cosmic resonances that had obscured the lack of telepathic chatter.

+Lydion - +

+I perceived the lattice+ he mused, unresponsive. +Why? Why did I? Because … because … the lattice is greater than the sum of its parts. A broader telepathic spread. We all differ. So it's quite possible that I can make contact with someone, somewhere. I'm going to repeat a question I asked earlier, because I think you were being less than honest. How rigorous were your attempts at making yourself known?+

She hesitated.

+Exactly. You were scared, weren't you? Scared of being attacked, of being trapped again. Admit it+

+I approached a cross-section of people in various locations+ Sarune replied defensively. +I then drew my conclusions based on a total lack of success and the complete absence of background emanations.+

+How many individuals did you approach?+

+Plenty+

+*How many*?+

+Hundreds. Maybe a thousand+

+A thousand+ repeated Lydion in something resembling triumph. +There are six million people on this planet. You didn't apply yourself+

+No, I didn't+ she retorted, recovering. +The need wasn't there, not then. And besides, I wasn't completely alone. I had you. Yes, Lydion, you! Ever since Eluthia. I could have revealed myself any time I wanted, but I stayed out of your life and supported your illusions+

+Tarlatine+ Lydion uttered the name just once, then pushed the thought away. +Let's not go there. Here's what I propose. We'll split up to save time and make a search based on mindset. We can ignore the ultra-disciplined types like Nohal – I've already proved that won't work. We'll concentrate on resonance-sensitives, creative and meditative minds+

+Just those?+

+Not quite. From what you were telling me, reducees seemed particularly attuned to your output. If any of ours survive, they could be the answer+

+You seem to have it all mapped out+ Sarune was back to her usual sardonic self. +I have to admire your enthusiasm. Wait till ennui sets in+

+Just *do* it, Sarune!+

+Any idea where I should look?+

Lydion searched his memory. +Try Corayn. Most reducees ended up there. The healers brought a group of them to the Lyricon once, hoping the lattice might – chaos, why didn't I think of him earlier? Tonor!+

+Who?+

+The weathershield operator. I was nearly dead, he was asleep, and -+ But Lydion was already out of range, hurtling back toward the Lyricon.

Sarune let him go. She couldn't keep protecting him. He was still vulnerable, still governed by the recklessness that had typified his life – but he was now too strong to be encircled. If she still had the resources of the Synectic net she could have reined him in, prevented him from throwing himself about and squandering his precious energy. Or, to make her presence known to the Celestrians, she could have taken control of someone or even used telekinesis to write a message on a wall. Not anymore. In this particular endeavour, she and Lydion were alone.

***

Deep space scanning array, Alda Six.

"Attention, team," said Trevone. "I now have the damage reports from all sections and it isn't as bad as I first feared. The circuit breakers prevented a cascade failure, so what we're looking at is localised burn-out in the main system and one of the back-up units. Plus some minor damage to the array itself. Nothing too serious, but it does man we'll be here for another octal or two."

Groans of protest followed this statement.

"I know, I know – it was the worst possible luck for a massive EMP to hit us just as we went live. But until we know what caused it, we should spare no effort in restoring this facility to operational status. It's our first line of defence, and until I know otherwise I'm treating this anomaly as a hostile act. I want surveillance at one quarter power by the end of the day. The longer we're blind, the worst it might be for us. I shall be running a diagnostic on the overload and I'll want to convey my findings to Treva and Alda Mexa as soon as I'm done, so please ensure you prioritise repairs to our transposer. That's all for now – and thanks again, everyone, for your swift and organised response to this event."

***

Tarlion's journey wasn't as random as Myrig had believed. Safely in a parking orbit round New Narvella's planetary neighbour, he'd thoroughly familiarised himself with the sphere's logic system

94

before setting the parameters for his search, his calm, patient approach to the work echoing his late father's methods. Although he didn't know Celestra's location, he had some fairly good clues. He knew, for instance, exactly where Old Narvella was – near the edge of the galaxy's spiral arm, in an area where stars were few and scattered. He also knew that a thousand light years – Celestrian years – separated its faltering star and Celestra's sun, and that Alda lay in an area replete with stars. Therefore he'd restricted his search to the centre of the galactic arm, adjacent to Old Narvella's position. Next he'd excluded everything but yellow-white dwarf stars with planets. It would cut the odds by at least fifty per cent.

Now, he wasn't so sure of those odds. Planets! He'd never imagined there'd be so many. At first he'd tried to maintain a sensible sleep cycle, but as the enormity of his task dawned on him he'd spent every possible moment hanging hollow-eyed over the logic system, checking and re-checking the transposer modes for any sign of communication, searching in vain for stardrive markers. His food supply was two-thirds gone, the atmosphere had been filtered so many times that impurities were beginning to creep in, and he didn't dare think about the recycled water, which he was doing his best to ration. His clothes were in need of a real wash instead of the particle scrub which left a build-up of sweat.

And this was after barely a season. Sooner, rather than later, he'd have to make landfall. Sighing, he resigned himself to staying out of transposal even longer than he had been, scanning for planets with water and a breathable atmosphere. He wasn't surprised at the number of arid rocks he encountered.

Then his luck appeared to change. The permanently vigilant radio, which he'd programmed to ignore cosmic static and pulsars, locked onto a new signal source. Intermittent, unintelligible, but an unmistakeable sign of civilisation. The system of origin was seventy-five light years distant, in a region he'd almost missed as being outside of his parameters. Hopeful for the first time since his journey started, he engaged the Drive. And, during the brief interval of transposal, went to have a much needed shower.

When he emerged, viewed the blue planet of his destination and heard the brash miscellany of its broadcasts, he was in no doubt where he was headed. This was the world Idenion had dared to visit: the Clemoridys planet, Earth. Which meant Celestra must be within a day's transposal – but in what direction? He checked yet again for markers and transmissions, and instead of the usual negative result, detected a solitary active transposer.

Then, suddenly, he was in trouble. The transposed message was from Earth. He heard a voice say "Celestra". Then the communications panel erupted in a cascade failure. The logic system folded and the lights died, leaving him in smoke-filled darkness.

***

Cheveney Manor, 5.9.2011

"Is it working, Frank? Well, why don't you say something to our Celestrian friends?"

"*Me*? I'd sound like a prat. This was your idea, Bartlett, so *you* do it. Or shall we ask Roegin?"

"I'm not sure that's wise. Didn't anyone write a speech?"

"Give me the microphone," said Sir John. Then, after a moment to compose himself, began: "This is Cheveney Manor, England, calling Celestra. We know you understand this language. We wish to speak with your First Citizens on a matter of political sensitivity. Please respond."

Everyone waited. Then a faint odour of burning rose from the makeshift gadget. Frank cut the power and cautiously opened the side to reveal an array of blackened and useless crystals.

"Nice one, Frank," said Tallifer.

"I don't know why it did that," Frank said lamely. "Do you think they heard us?"

"If they did, they know where we are," said Sir John calmly. "Replace your crystals, Frank, and we'll try again later. In the meantime I recommend patience and vigilance."

***

With the air purifiers at maximum, Tarlion laboured to make repairs under the insufficient glow of an emergency light bar. He'd taken interchangeable circuit cards from the refrigeration

97

unit, the music player and – after some deliberation – the hygiene cubicle. It was imperative to restore full function to the transposer and logic systems in order to study what had happened. Just before the power failed, something very odd had appeared on the monitor, something to do with that message. He only hoped it was retrievable. "This is weird," he murmured aloud. "Talking to yourself again, Tarlion? Another reason for a change of scene. But it *is* weird. The message wasn't intended for me, so why did I hear even a bit of it? Transposers don't work like that."

Had the signal reached Celestra? Unlikely. There'd been much degradation in the content. But the transposer beam itself, and its target encode, had probably fared better. He was counting on that.

At last, with power restored, he coaxed the logic system into grudging response – and then stared in bewilderment. It was as if someone had mapped every active aldacite source in the quadrant, and then joined up the dots. His spacecraft was one such source. No wonder everything had shorted out – the energy surge must have been colossal.

But whatever it was, it had gone, and he had his information. Not only the correct encode for Celestra, but its location as well. Elated, he programmed the Drive.

His joy was short-lived. There was a keening sound from somewhere under the floor, and the sphere shook a little. The Drive failed to engage. Tarlion cursed himself for not realising that all the onboard systems could have been damaged by the surge, not just the ones under his nose. Hardly daring to look, he unfastened a panel beneath the guidance controls and peered at the auxiliary array. Three of the power nodes were unlit, leaving five. This, like the Drive, was beyond his ability to repair. With those power levels he might make landfall, but nothing further.

Behind him, the transposer gave a peremptory beep. Disbelievingly he scrambled back to the diagnostic screen, which foretold the imminent failure of several more crystals – the ones he'd just replaced. "No, no, *no!*" he yelled. The cabin's dead acoustics took his cry and stifled it. Hastily he copied that day's flight log to a file, added a few hurried sentences in his own voice, then transposed the file as a data burst. He briefly glimpsed an auto-response from the Celestrian receiving station before the screen sputtered out.

He glanced at the still-open thruster array. One of the five nodes was flickering. "So what's next on the malfunction list?" he asked himself. "Life support? Hull integrity? You're out of options, Tarlion. Stop dithering and land this death trap. You can do it."

The sphere hurtled earthwards towards the origin of the aldacite signal.

***

"Gods, that was rough! Veylis disentwined himself from the co-pilot's seat. "What's our status, Ymer? Did we make it?"

Ymer didn't speak until he was sure. "Yes, we've broken through."

"Don't sound so pleased!"

"The Transfix has closed up again. Do you realise that? We're stuck out here!"

"Of course." Verylis was unperturbed. "I saw the rift resealing itself and ordered you through it. My decision. Now, did anyone follow our example?"

Ymer checked the scanner. "Reclaim Two and Four. No sign of Three; Razel was always slow on the uptake. And none of the second group seems to be here. Uh oh."

"What?"

"Look. One of the Patierade spheres. He's keeping well away from us."

"He'd better," said Veylis sourly. "Run your checks. I'll keep an eye on him."

Ymer began an internal scan of the baffles protecting the vulnerable crystal arrays. He knew the two other Reclaim crews would be doing likewise as per their pre-flight briefing, and he assumed the Patierades would be similarly occupied.

"Checks complete," he said at last. "Only minor damage. Now we can move forward."

He radioed the rest of his team. Their spacecraft, too, were unscathed – a tribute to the mission engineers. Then, under the disapproving eye of Veylis, he addressed the silently waiting Patierade vessel.

"This is Ymer Coll-Preda of Project Reclaim. Kindly identify yourself."

"I am Fley Dhuvin-Mytyl."

There was a smothered gasp from Veylis. Ymer waved an arm to shut him up.

"I have one technician, non-military, on board with me," Fley continued, his authoritative voice carrying clearly above the background static. "Tell me, Captain Ymer – do you have any contingency plans for the situation in which we find ourselves?"

"Explain," said Ymer, to buy himself some time. He wasn't about to say he hadn't.

"You believed, did you not, that the Transfix would either be untouched or permanently destroyed?"

"He's no business interrogating you," said a voice from Reclaim Two.

"Under the circumstances I believe he has," Ymer said, regaining his composure. "This *is* an unprecedented situation and we should maintain transparency. As I'm not a scientist I did *not* foresee this outcome. Did *you*, Fley?"

"My colleague did."

"Then what do you propose we do?" Ymer demanded.

"We all have the same objective: to find the Celestrians and persuade them to take down the Transfix. I suggest, then, that we temporarily put aside our differences and work together."

"How, exactly?" asked Ymer. "The Celestrians have superior firepower. If we went in with all guns blazing we wouldn't last five zytl."

"We should confer," said Fley after a pause. "There is a planet two light years away which was once assessed for colonisation."

"By Patierades?" inquired Ymer.

Fley ignored the question. "I suggest we land there and continue this discussion in a more congenial setting. Sending co-ordinates."

"Lead on," Ymer said resignedly. There was no other choice.

"You didn't tell him about me," observed Veylis when they were underway.

"He'll find out soon enough. This is going to be a very tricky meeting, so please be diplomatic. You do represent your House."

"Indeed," agreed Veylis. "I think I can manage to be civil. It isn't every day I get to parley with the sub-commander of the Patierade Free Territories."

Chapter Four

Cheveney Manor, 5th September 2011

Roegin remained in the gym all evening, pounding the punchbag in a cold fury. There was a fresh cut on his forehead. Outside a thunderstorm raged, matching his mood.

At nine-thirty Ann looked in. "Roegin."

He carried on punching.

"Roegin, stop. This is all about Rod, isn't it? Why do you keep picking fights with him? He'll always beat you."

"Maybe next time he won't."

"There doesn't have to *be* a next time!"

"Doesn't there?" Roegin picked up a towel and mopped his face. "Tallifer doesn't like me and I don't like *him*. Bartlett's a fool to trust him."

Ann sensibly changed the subject. "Shall I see if there's any dinner left? I could have it sent up."

"Not for me. I'm going to crawl into bed – alone – and forget about today."

She accepted the rebuff without protest. "Don't be too disappointed in Frank. He's got more crystals and he'll try again once the weather settles down."

"It should have worked." Roegin's voice was uncharacteristically raw. "We had the schematics from Control. It *looked* right. I really thought there was a chance of – "

An odd thump from outside made him pause.

"A chance of?" prompted Ann.

"Did you hear that?"

"It's just the storm." She laid a hand on his arm. "You're all keyed up. Shall we have a drink together at least?"

Roegin shrugged her off, strode to the nearest window and hauled up the blind. "Put the lights out."

"Why? What's wrong?"

"Lights! Now!"

She obeyed, uneasy in the sudden darkness. The shape of the large window became palely visible, outlining his tense silhouette.

"Ebbon's blood!" he breathed. At the far end of the lawn, illuminated fitfully by sheet lightning, was a small white hemisphere, identical in size and shape to the spacecraft which had brought him to Earth years before.

Ann stumbled to his side. "Oh, Roegin! It *did* work! They're here!"

He shook his head as if to clear it. "No. Something's not right. It's too soon."

"But you said they could be here in a couple of hours!"

"Yes, but – they wouldn't. Not without an investigation. They're not that naïve."

"Aren't you going down there?"

He smiled at her in the half-light. "Have you forgotten I'm a guest in this house? As a guest, I need to be invited."

Figures were already swarming toward the alien craft. Seconds later the door to the gym crashed open to admit Tallifer.

"Roegin, you're wanted. Now."

"See what I mean?" Roegin sauntered toward the security chief. "Ann, stay indoors. Some of those goons could get trigger-happy."

Tallifer gave him a shove down the corridor. "Try to run away and I'll shoot you myself."

Roegin merely glared. Neither man spoke again until they reached the garden entrance; then Tallifer tossed Roegin a yellow kagoule and said:

"Here, put this on. Sir John won't want his prize asset catching cold. Just think, there might be two of you after today!"

The worst of the rain was over. As Roegin approached the sphere he became aware of two things: the craft had a distinct tilt, and there was a long furrow in the grass where it had skidded to a halt. This had been a forced landing.

"I assume you didn't capture anyone?" he inquired of Tallifer, who scowled.

"Nah. Whoever it was did a runner while this lot were faffing around breaking out the small arms. But we'll get him. And his pals, when they come looking for him."

Bartlett was shouting at his men. "Stop waving lights around. We don't want nosy villagers taking pictures. Where's that idiot groundsman?"

"Out getting pissed," someone yelled back. "It's his birthday!"

"Well, find him. Tell him we need a tarpaulin over this, pronto, before the sky clears and gives every spy satellite the photo-scoop of the year. Ah, Roegin. I believe you're familiar with these – conveyances?"

"Only as a passenger."

"Well, come and see what you make of this hatch. We can just about squeeze through but it's obviously jammed."

They clambered inside.

"I understand this, at least," Roegin said. "From our safety drill. The hatch is made of a smart alloy which unseals itself on demand. Melts apart."

"Melts?"

"That's what I said. It wasn't very reassuring to know that some goo was the only thing between me and outer space. Anyway, we were told that in the event of complete power failure or sudden impact, the alloy would revert to its default setting. Rigid. To get out you have to open a side panel - "

"Already open," said Bartlett, shining his torch.

" – and move this key back and forth."

"Clockwork. Now I've seen everything."

"Impervious to power drain, cosmic rays, you name it," continued Roegin. "It generates just enough charge to crack the door seal. Once that's done, there's a lever to crank it open. It should be … under that missing floor tile."

"No tile, no lever," said Bartlett. "So our fugitive has a weapon and a jemmy. Resourceful." He surveyed the cabin in greater detail. "Bit of a mess."

"You didn't let your men throw the evidence around?"

"No, and I don't intend to. We're the first in here." Roegin found Tarlion's discarded light bar. The additional radiance, plus his keen observational skills, soon allowed him to piece things together.

"Careful where you're walking, Bartlett. There are burnt out aldacite crystals all over the floor. And the greatest concentration is right here, next to what I believe to be the ship's computer and communicator." He held the light higher. "See? Panels open, components stripped out. He was trying to keep the essential systems going. I think that whatever killed Frank's radio also wrecked this spacecraft."

"At the same time?"

"It fits. Our traveller hadn't been near his homeworld in a while." Roegin had found some torn packets and a trail of crumbs. "These look like rations."

"But what was he doing here?"

Roegin shrugged. "Surveillance? Stealing music?"

"And he heard our message."

"Maybe. Or maybe he was heading for the one contact point he knew."

"Oi, Bartlett!" Tallifer bellowed from outside. "What are you two doing? Don't we get the guided tour?"

Bartlett stuck his head out of the hatch. "Sorry boys, this has to go to forensics. Have the low-loader brought round – we'll ship it to Frank's factory at dawn. And where's that tarpaulin?"

While he was talking, Roegin made a quick inspection of the sleeping area. Finding Tarlion's sweat-stained, tattered clothes, he shoved them into the kagoule's capacious pocket. Tallifer's bound to bring his dogs in here as soon as we're gone, he thought. Well, his job just became a little less easy.

"Find anything else?" called Bartlett.

"More of the same," Roegin said casually. "These systems are toast, and I imagine the hyperdrive is too. Otherwise, our Celestrian wouldn't have abandoned it. They have rules about that."

"So he's in the same situation we are," Bartlett said with a dry chuckle. "That might make him show his face. Well, there's nothing more to be done here. Let's go."

Tarlion was closer than either of them realised. As soon as the sphere had stopped moving he'd thrown himself at the hatch, cursing its leaden response to his attempts at cranking. He wasn't used to reading nonconversants but he'd known hostility when he sensed it. So, as soon as he was able, he'd leapt from the craft and raced for cover, instinctively keeping hold of the hatch releaser. The Earthers were in a bunch toward the perimeter of the site they were guarding, so he'd run the opposite way toward a small domed building he'd glimpsed before the scanner cut out. It was in the centre of this lawn or field – but where *was* the centre? And why in chaos couldn't he have inherited night vision?

A fortuitous flash of lightning had come to his rescue. Soaked to the skin, he'd reached the observatory, forced the door and tumbled inside. It had taken him a while to find a light source. He'd been looking for a switch or toggle, not a cord. When at last a dull yellow light revealed his surroundings, he saw the telescope and smiled broadly at a choice well made. No-one would disturb him on a night like this. He now had plenty of time to read those around him and plan a strategy.

He'd soon grasped the situation. These idiot Earthers had tried to make allies of the Eldorians – and it didn't take much imagination to guess how *that* would have turned out. Somehow the Celestrians had managed to prevent it – and now the Earthers were trying to make contact with Celestra in hope of preferential treatment.

So all he had to do was learn the language, stay out of trouble and stick around to protect whoever Celestra sent to pick him up. It was beginning to sound like one of his father's stories, and Tarlion was determined to do it justice.

The Earthers thought he was Celestrian, and that gave him an advantage. He'd just read the overseer, Bartlett, telling his men to search for a slightly built pale stranger with fair hair. Tarlion was tall and athletic, with his mother's wavy black hair and his father's grey eyes. His skin tone had neither the Celestrian pallor nor the deep gold of Narvella, but a mixture of the two: pale gold, tanned by New Narvella's summer sun.

Exploring further, he found a folding chair, an old coat and half a pack of biscuits. Near the chair was a pair of knitted shoes, soft and fluffy, with a thin electrical wire attached to each one. There was seemingly nothing to plug the tiny connectors into, which was a pity, as they were obviously designed to give heat. But they'd suffice until his own shoes dried. Draping his wet shirt over the telescope casing, he put on the coat and slippers, sprawled in the chair and began to eat the biscuits. He'd spent the night in far less congenial places when at sail on New Narvella.

And all the time he was reading the occupants of the big house – in particular, the Eldorian. Roegin still had to frame his English carefully, which made him an excellent if unwitting tutor.

When Roegin was asleep Tarlion switched his attention to the CCTV operator in the basement, studying the various screens through the man's eyes, noting that the perimeter cameras all faced outwards, while those placed around the manor walls only showed their immediate vicinity. It wasn't thought necessary to scan acres of lawn – although the area would be instantly floodlit should any movement be detected. Best, then, to stay put until daylight. Everyone was convinced their quarry had already made his escape, which should operate to his advantage.

But it still wouldn't be easy. He'd doubtless have to compel or delude one or more of his nonconversant foes, and while he was sure he had the ability – his father certainly did – he'd never had cause to put it into practice. A trial run was needed. He soon realised, however, that inducing the CCTV man to scratch his head and touch his toes wasn't proof of anything. He needed to persuade someone to act against their nature, or, at the very least, disobey orders. And, having mentally roamed the mansion in search of another insomniac, he found the very person he needed: Little, the accountant, poring over spreadsheets. Tarlion was soon furious.

"You traitor!" he muttered aloud. "You're handling Eldorian money, bribe money, all set to broker that alliance if talks ever resume. I don't suppose that's *all* their investment but losing it might just hinder the cause."

The Earther financial system was complex, not at all like the simple currency of New Narvella, but Tarlion soon understood that the Eldorian funds had to be constantly switched to avoid detection. Accordingly, he set about convincing Little that the money was better off where it was. It wasn't as difficult as he expected. Little had the utmost faith in his abilities but scant regard for his employers, who in his opinion lacked the resolve to see the conspiracy through.

Tarlion now had something to build on. +It's obvious+ his and Little's thoughts said, +that after today, things will come to a head. Do I really want to meddle with these accounts when the whole project's about to go pear-shaped? Far better to step back and get ready to bail+

There. It was done. Or rather, *not* done. Little continued to stare at the figures before him while Tarlion grabbed a sketch pad and pencils from a chart table and laboriously transcribed the symbols. They might be useful to the Celestrians, assuming anyone was going to turn up.

Finally Tarlion sent Little to bed and, newly confident, duped the CCTV operator into disabling the motion sensors for three minutes. He then strolled outside to answer a call of nature, returned to his chair and settled down for a doze.

At daybreak, the rumble of heavy machinery plus some shouted instructions indicated that the sphere was about to be removed. Choosing his moment carefully, Tarlion waited until the driver was conferring with the men at the gate, then walked unhurriedly toward the low-loader.

The sphere had been securely braced at an angle to accommodate its width, covered in layers of opaque black material to disguise its appearance, then tethered to the trailer. A final layer of the black sheeting had been thrown over it and tied to the vehicle, creating a tent shape.

"… not even sure that's legal," Tallifer was saying.

"Best we could do at short notice."

"Well, if anyone asks, tell them it's a fairground ride. Here's your route. Stick to it. Stay off the motorway."

One man had been left on guard. He looked up from his mobile as Tarlion approached. "Who're you? The gardener?"

+Forget you saw me+ Tarlion instructed, then mounted the trailer and concealed himself under the folds of PVC.

Moments later the driver returned and they were underway. Tarlion waited until the lorry was negotiating a tight turn on the outskirts of the village, then stepped smartly off and hid behind a tree until the road was clear.

Immediately, a sense of loss descended on him. The sphere was only fit for the scrap heap, but it had been his home and his best hope for the future.

Now he had nothing but his wits to help him survive.

He'd reluctantly abandoned the coat in case someone recognised it, and this had left him with a possible problem. Having seen the drivers' and security guards' attire, he was beginning to think that he was under-dressed. If so, he could become the target of ridicule or outrage – just the kind of attention he didn't need.

Most of the villagers were, he divined, still asleep. He trudged along the narrow road, despondent and increasingly thirsty. What would Lydion do? he asked himself. Find a woman, I suppose. Sorry, father of mine, but I don't think your universal solution's going to work this time.

A distant figure hove into view and he tensed. Moments later, he almost laughed in relief. The young man approaching at a steady jog-trot was dressed exactly as he was, in a sleeveless shirt, shorts and canvas shoes. There was one difference however – the white wires trailing from each ear and leading to some kind of music device. Tarlion perceived a little of the music in question. It had nothing to commend it. The Earther's thoughts were equally shambolic. "… last time I go backpacking with Des. I turn my back for one minute and he's let some scumbag steal my Blackberry. Need to get away this year, abroad, anywhere. Rent the flat to some tourists like Leanne did and disappear for a month …"

The jogger pounded past Tarlion without sparing him a glance, and the street was deserted again. Tarlion wondered if he should also move on, or simply sit at the roadside and wait for signs of life. Suddenly a slithering crash from close at hand make him jump violently. In the yard of the nearest building, a woman of about his age was about to tip a second load of bottles into a chute.

"Sorry, did I startle you?" she called. "Just recycling the empties."

"Wait!" said Tarlion hastily before she could retreat indoors. "Could I ... er, that is, please could I ..." He didn't have a chance to read her in any detail, but her surface thoughts said hostelry, customers, long day ahead. "Could I please have a drink of water?" he concluded, sounding more desperate than he'd intended. He had to do better than this. She'd think he was a vagrant or a thief.

But Kelly Thorogood, landlady of the Green Man, knew trouble when she saw it. And she wasn't seeing it now. "What happened?" she asked sympathetically. "Did your car break down?"

"No, I was backpacking." Tarlion held her gaze in what he hoped was an earnest expression. "I put the pack down for less than a minute and it was gone. My clothes, money, Blackberry, everything."

"Did you tell the police?"

He made a helpless gesture. "Nothing to tell. I saw nothing."

"Where *was* this?"

He pointed vaguely. "The motorway."

"You've walked all the way from Cheveney Services? No wonder you look exhausted. Come on in. I'll get you that drink and you can freshen up. I expected you're hungry too?"

"Yes." Tarlion continued to look helpless, as it seemed to be working. He sat down at the table she indicated, too tired to notice his surroundings in much detail.

"I'm Kelly. What's *your* name?" his rescuer asked, setting a tall glass of lemonade in front of him.

"Tarlion," he replied hesitantly, wondering if he should have made something up.

"Leon," she repeated. He instantly realised that "Ta" was a thank you for the drink, and "Leon" was a name she recognised. Leon it is, then, he thought wryly, and drained the glass.

She cooked bacon and eggs, which he bolted without waiting to see if he liked the taste. But he did remember to thank her.

A door slammed nearby and he gripped the table.

"Edgy creature, aren't you? That'll be Debs, my cleaner." She paused. "Leon, is there something you're not telling me?"

Tarlion stared at the tabletop, fully believing he was about to lose her sympathy. "I can't hitch a ride home. That's what you're thinking, I imagine. I let my flat to some tourists for a month."

"I see." Kelly tried to look severe, then suddenly laughed. "OK, here's what I'll do. The brewery lorry will be here any time and so will my senior barman, so if you don't want people to think you're a gentleman of the road, I'll need to spirit you away. There aren't any guests at the moment, so I'll put you in the en-suite. Hang the Do Not Disturb notice on the door, have a shower and a kip!

I reckon you'll buff up nicely. We're not busy on a Tuesday so once the lunches are out of the way I'll run you into Newbury and we'll hit the charity shops."

"Second-hand clothes?" he asked slowly.

"Of *course* second-hand! Oxfam's finest. You can pay me back later. For the time being, ditch that threadbare old shirt and put this on." She yanked a t-shirt from a drawer. "The bar staff wear these. Like him?"

Tarlion wasn't sure. Under the caption of "The Green Man" was a picture of a small skinny humanoid with huge eyes and two antennae.

"The mythical Green Man's a bit scary so we thought people would prefer a cute little alien," Kelly explained.

"Are aliens green?" Tarlion inquired.

"Well, just between you and me, I've never actually *seen* one. Have you?"

"No," said Tarlion. "Never."

***

Tonor was purging the weathershield projector coils – not his favourite task. He worked swiftly and efficiently, as befitted the leading weathershield operator on the planet. The citizens respected him: his presentations were colourful, reliable and flawless – exactly what the concert organisers asked for. But he didn't have Lydion's intuitive flair, and he knew it. Even now, he sometimes had the feeling that Lydion was looking disapprovingly over his shoulder.

116

+That's because I am!+ Lydion responded forcefully. +Chaos, Tonor, pay attention! If I can read you – and I can, though it's like trying to focus through silt – then you can read *me*+

But Tonor merely hunched down and continued his work. Lydion kept attempting the all-important breakthrough, fuelled by anger and exasperation in equal measure. He maintained that anger, as at the back of it lay despair. And he wouldn't give way to it.

+Tonor, this is important. To all of us. Couldn't you make just one effort … *don't you dare close off!* +

A small hand touched Tonor's shoulder. "Fa?"

He smiled wearily. "Hello, Tonora. I wondered when you'd show up."

"Fa, why are you ignoring your friend?"

"Er – what?"

"You're always saying how much you miss him, and now he's here you won't talk to him!"

Lydion, incredulous, confronted the child-pattern. +You can *read* me?+

+Yes, of course+

"Oh, thank harmony. Now listen – this is very very important. Tell your father that someone's broken through the Lydion Cadence. There must be some Eldorians on their way here. Repeat that back to me: Lydion Cadence. The breakout is what caused all the crystal damage. Tonor needs to get word to the First Citizens+

Tonora dutifully repeated this. "Lydion's very worried," she added.

Tonor looked perplexed, then irritated. "Tonora, stop this at once. Lydion died years ago."

"Yes, but his pattern didn't. He's saying it's complicated, that he'll explain later, after you've delivered that message."

"I'm going to be very cross with you in a moment," Tonor said ominously.

"He says," Tonor persisted, "that he never called it the Lydion Cadence. That was Ruvrin. *He* called it the transposal dampener."

Tonor's anger faded, to be replaced by unease. The term didn't exist in resonance theory, but it did make sense. Not that Tonora would know, as she'd had no tuition yet.

Lydion pursued his advantage. +Quote me+ he instructed. +Hurry, while he's dithering+

Tonora drew herself up importantly. "Must I tell this innocent child about your escapade with Prahina The Undefeated?" she recited with great care. "Who was that, Fa? A warrior maiden? Did you fight her?"

"All right, Lydion, enough!" Tonor held up his hands in surrender. "Where are you?"

"He's behind you," said Tonora. "He says you can perceive him if you really try. Copy me, Fa. Copy me."

Tonor tried to mimic his daughter's perception – oblique, almost off the spectrum, tightly focused. It was an effort, and made his head spin. Tonora's thoughts danced ahead of him.

+Here he is, Fa! Here! Here!+

And gradually, though he could still see only normality, he began to sense the warm, amused,

118

unmistakeable mindset of his friend. A flood of his own emotion broke the contact. "Oh, chaos, Lydion!"

"He says, enough of the drama," Tonora said pertly.

"Sorry."

"He also says, take Nefyrra with you to see the First Citizens. She'll help them believe your story."

"Why should she?"

"When Lydion was a person he could see patterns, like I do," Tonora said. "He was scared so he only told Nefyrra. And she told *me*."

"I'll … go and find her," Tonor stammered, increasingly confused.

"Lydion wants to stay here and talk," said Tonora. "Is that all right, Fa? He just wants to know more about me. And he wants you to hurry."

"All right!" Tonor was halfway to the door. "Enjoy your chat. And Lydion – that doesn't include my private life. Understood?"

Left alone with the young resonance-adept, Lydion gently quizzed her on the extent of her fledgling powers. He was intrigued to learn that she could read something of a pattern's future. According to Sarune, the Earther women of the Gloriana could do just that, albeit with the help of empathetic software. +How far into the future can you read?+ he asked.

Tonora pondered the question, head on one side. +I'm not sure. I'm not very good at that part of it, though I'm getting better+

+So you can't tell me when my pattern ends?+

Tonora was suddenly dubious. +I'm not supposed to say. People don't like me telling them+

+I'm not people+ Lydion pointed out reasonably. +And I really would like to know. Please?+

Obediently, she concentrated. +I'm sorry, I can't see. It isn't yet+

+But it does *have* an end?+

+Yes+

+Sure?+

+Yes+ Tonora wasn't happy at this line of questioning.

+Then can you tell me *where*?+ persisted Lydion, and the girl's face brightened.

+That's easy. Here+

+Here on Celestra?+

Tonora gave an exaggerated sigh. +No, silly. Here. Your pattern ends here, in this room!+

***

Alda Mexa, 2.6.1.4031

"Kalyx, Prefect of Scapirion, calling Idenion at the akron listening post. Are you still there?"

"Just about. It's very late. I let the duty operator go home."

"Sorry about the delay. We're down to three working transposers and they've been in use all day. Preparations for winter. We're still experiencing EM interference across the radio spectrum."

"Same here. And Communications just had a call from Trevone on Alda Six. They're getting it

120

as well. Trevone thought it might be their equipment at fault. They've only just powered up after that crystal meltdown. Anyway, what's the news?"

"Good. The kid eventually managed to relay all Lydion's instructions to Ruvrin, who says she can see where she went wrong with the Cadence. As soon as she's done the maths we'll have Treva adapt the spheres we used previously. They'll then carry out a partial rendition as before. And with Lydion around we'll know at once whether we've got it to rights!" He paused. "It feels so weird, saying that. I can't believe what that Synectic creature did to my poor uncle. As if he hadn't suffered enough!"

"If she hadn't marked him all those years ago, he wouldn't have created the Cadence and we'd have had no way to contain the Eldorians," Idenion reminded him. "At least everyone now believes I fought with Sarune the night Dena nearly died. I knew I wasn't hallucinating!"

"Lydion also says," Kalyx added, "that we shouldn't be in too much of a hurry to upgrade the Cadence. Someone got out, and we don't want them permanently on our side of it."

"We've had a top-level meeting about that," Idenion said. "We don't think many Eldorians escaped, otherwise they'd have been all over us by now. But we're expecting contact soon, and I've given orders that every sphere carrying the dispersal engine should be readied for service."

"We have three based at Ninka," said Kalyx. "I've already put them on alert."

"Where's Sarune now?" Idenion asked uneasily.

"Staying out of my way, I hope. According to Lydion she's off looking for an adult she can speak through."

"I take it Tonora's free to come home now? Her father's getting anxious."

"She and her mother will be leaving for Alda Mexa tomorrow," Kalyx assured him. "Lydion too, probably. He won't let that child out of his sight – if sight's the right word."

"You can hardly blame him," Idenion remarked, then paused at the sound of a commotion. "Kalyx? What's going on?"

"Habbon's just turned up -" began Kalyx.

"Yes, and he needs to talk to Idenion," said the elderly scientist testily. "Out of the way, my boy."

"Don't 'my boy' me! I'm the Prefect!"

"Well, at least you had the sense not to call yourself First Tech," Habbon retorted. "Idenion, this is urgent. I intend to be on tomorrow's transport to Alda Mexa, and once you have word of my arrival I want you to convene an emergency meeting of the Administrators."

"Another? I've just dismissed all eight of them!"

"Yes, another, and make sure you *and* Laura are present."

"Is this to do with the time capsule decryption? You'll have to give me a good excuse if I'm to recall everyone."

122

"Very well: try this for size. The meteor strike that destroyed your first civilisation wasn't an accident. It was an act of war."

"That's startling news, but how is it relevant to us today?" Idenion queried mildly.

"Because the perpetrators have never been identified," Habbon said carefully, as if explaining something to a backward pupil. "Your society, your history, owes its existence to their aggression. Is that relevant enough?"

"All right, I'll summon everyone back," Idenion promised. "But some might not turn up. Two are supervising building projects and the third just left for Treva. That leaves Sheyell, Ansela and Dessin – and Trevone on a transposer link. Enough to pass resolutions, if that's what you think it will come to."

"I do."

"Understood. Bring your evidence to the akron at noon plus one. Idenion out."

Habbon exhaled gustily. "I really didn't think he'd agree. Not on the strength of what I told him."

"There's more, isn't there?" asked Kalyx quietly.

"There is, my boy. I suppose you've been reading me?"

"Reading *you* is like trying to find something in the Alda Mexa archive," Kalyx answered with a thin smile. "I'm defeated before I start. But something's up. Your team's been shielding all day, even when off duty. And then Ruvrin started doing it too! So, spill."

"We asked Ruvrin's opinion. We also asked her to be discreet and not start a panic. Now I'm asking you to do the same, at least for the time being."

"I'm listening."

"The ancients wrote about worldwide disruption to their communications a few days before the meteor hit. They couldn't determine its cause. Neither can we."

"I thought it was sunspots."

"Not according to your experts. Nothing seems to be generating the interference. Tiny EM sources appear briefly and randomly, as if there's some form of transposal at work."

"Did Lydion have anything to say about these mini-sources?"

"Not much; he's been busy with the Cadence. But he was adamant that they first appeared just after the Bad Resonance, as he calls it. Our communications weren't affected straight away. The ancients say the same: a gradual worsening of static on all bands, followed by a sudden cessation. And seven octals later – bang."

"And that's why you called the meeting? You think history's repeating itself?"

Habbon bowed his head. "I hope I'm wrong. But in my opinion someone or something's taken exception to that resonance event, and they're on their way back to finish what they started."

"But why attack the ancients in the first place? Doesn't your chronicler have anything to say about that?"

"He does, and we're still translating it. By tomorrow I should have something definitive to tell the Administrators. Come with me if you want."

"I think I'd better. Thanks for the heads-up, Habbon. I'll leave Ruvrin in charge till I get back."

***

3.6.1.4031

"So to summarise your theory, Preceptor Habbon," said Idenion, "you believe that whatever destroyed our first civilisation has returned, reawakened – if I may use that term – by the adverse resonance event we recently witnessed."

"That is my belief."

"But you implied we were to blame for the meltdown," Sheyell objected. "We weren't. It was the Eldorians, trying to break through the Cadence."

"We *set* the Cadence," Dessin pointed out.

"Is Lydion - " Laura stumbled over the name and started again. "Is Lydion sure the Eldorians triggered the resonance?"

"He says that's part of it," Habbon replied. "We've since established that Alda Six came back online at the same time, and the sudden surge of crystal activity might have worsened the event locally. He also said something else must have been present to triangulate the event, trap it if that makes sense. Otherwise the effects would have dispersed into t-space and been lost."

"So we don't know what its boundaries were," said Dessin. "Therefore, we don't know what damage it's caused."

"Very well, let's concede that some of the fault lies with us." Kalyx was anxious to move the discussion forward. "Habbon, you hinted yesterday that the ancients knew why they were targeted. Can you elaborate on that?"

"I can. My translation still needs refining, but basically, your ancestors were experimenting with a new type of FTL, one which didn't involve exposing ships and crew to the rigours of t-space. I haven't deciphered their maths yet, but I believe the dimension they substituted is one of several adjacent to ours. What the scientists didn't take into account was the damaging effect transposal has on any space it utilises. With t-space it hardly matters, as it's such a primal dangerous mess. But the substitute was doubtless more vulnerable. Perhaps it was inhabited. The chronicler believes it was."

"Did he say if the hostiles made any attempt to communicate, prior to the bombardment?"

"None that could be understood. He thought the radio interference might have been a language, but no attempt was made to study it retrospectively."

"Trevone, are you hearing all this?" Laura asked.

"Every word," responded Trevone via the Alda Six transposer. "And to think I was just about to start for home!"

126

"I'm so sorry," Laura said contritely. "But until we know what we're up against I don't want to rely on automated warnings. We need you there."

"I agree. And I also agree, by the way, that it would be a waste of time and resources to repair the communication satellites that were damaged in the meltdown. If Celestra's attacked they'd be the first things an invader would take out. We'll have to construct more transposers instead."

"I'll pass the instruction to Treva," Idenion said, "just as soon as we've finished our conference. Assuming the worst happens, how many dispersal-enabled craft and skilled pilots do you have out there?"

"Three spheres, and two veterans of the Eldorian battle. Three if you count myself. Not many, I know, but we thought we'd only have a few Eldorians to worry about. If anything gets past us, you'll have Zanna and Plinn in Ninka – they practically invented our battle tactics - and Ibri and his team in Treva."

"And I'm sure Space Tech will lend a hand," Dessin put in.

+Your pardon+ The interruption was discreet but compelling, and they all fell silent. Relayist Kyrin wouldn't have ignored city protocol unless the matter couldn't wait. +The Warden of Kest has been trying to reach Idenion for over two ilden. He's just called Communications and they're waiting to copy you over+

"Kest? What do *they* want?" muttered Dessin.

"A service engineer," Kalyx suggested. "Their transposer needs a new wick!"

127

"Shh!" ordered Sheyell with a glare.

"I'd better respond," Idenion said resignedly. "Sign off, Trevone. We'll keep you informed."

"Understood. Trevone out."

The transposer immediately reactivated with a visual from Kest's shabby spaceport. To everyone's surprise, the habitually pompous Warden looked abashed.

"First Citizens, permit me to dispense with formalities as enough time's been wasted already – and I'm not referring to this afternoon. He swallowed noisily. "You may recall that our deep space transposal array was the only one to escape damage during the meltdown."

"You were offline," said Kalyx.

"Well … yes, we were. And a number of messages – stray messages which found their way to us because ours was the only portal – were shuffled into a reserve store and not discovered until today. Among them was this." He closed a switch. Amid a wash of static a young man spoke swiftly and urgently.

"My name's Tarlion, son of Lydion, and I'm looking for my father. My spacecraft's systems are failing and I need help. I'm close to Laura's planet, Earth, and I believe I can make landfall. There's been transposer activity in a single region, so it makes sense to head for that. I'm sending a data packet of my status, location and projected landfall coordinates."

There was a stunned silence. Idenion recovered first. "How long have you had this recording, Sevet?"

128

"Since meltdown day, 7.3.1. Nearly three octals."

Three octals!" Laura had found her voice. "He's been on Earth for three octals?"

"If he made landfall," said Kalyx unhelpfully.

"Send the additional data to Communications," Idenion instructed Sevet. "We can't process it here. And Warden - "

"Yes, First Citizen?"

"If your staff can't be more vigilant in future I shall have to draft in replacements."

"My humblest apologies, First Citizen. May I assure you of my best - "

Kalyx leant forward and cut him off. No-one offered a reprimand. Moments later the communications tower signalled. "Idenion, it's Daphos. We've got the data. Sorry I

had to ask Kyrin to crash your conference."

"You did right, Daphos. Extract everything you can from those files and report your findings to me as a matter of urgency."

Laura tugged his arm. "We have to mount a rescue. We need the information *now!*"

"Wait, Laura, wait. Daphos, would a preliminary scan tell you anything?"

"Already on it." The technician's calm voice soothed Laura's agitation a little. "There's no doubt his spacecraft had a cascade failure. It looks as if the resonance event caught him. Spacial co-ordinates place him close to Symerid Three, so he was right about that."

"Can the transposer activity be detected?" asked Idenion.

"I'm searching. Some of the files are corrupted."

"First Citizens," said Sheyell into the brief silence, "may I remind you that we're on a possible war footing? This is no time to consider rescuing lost adventurers."

"That's my cousin you're talking about!" objected Kalyx.

"And I for one won't write him off," snapped Laura. "You're out of line, Sheyell."

"We agreed to stay away from Earth," Sheyell persisted.

"Perhaps we should put it to the vote," Dessin suggested more mildly. "Once we know where he landed, that is. We can't search an entire planet for him."

"I've found it," said Daphos, on cue. "Well, half of it. I've no record of what he heard, but the landing co-ordinates are as follows."

He read them out. They were startlingly familiar.

"Cheveney," said Idenion. "Someone's using a transposer in Cheveney."

Everyone looked at Laura. "The Eldorian spies," she hazarded. "One or more of them must have survived, or their technology did."

"Maybe you should've checked after you blew up their comsat, Daphos," remarked Kalyx.

"I did, several times! There was nothing. And in any case, what could they do except send futile messages?"

"And there you have it," said Habbon. "The third side of Lydion's triangle. A botched attempt at communication, probably made by Earthers."

"Why Cheveney?" asked Dessin.

"Never mind why," said Laura impatiently. "Whatever's going on, Tarlion will have blundered straight into it – so it's even more important that we find him *and* his spacecraft!"

Idenion took the point. "New instructions, Daphos. Put all routine tasks on hold and start that analysis now. Get your entire team on it. In particular, we need to know the exact condition of the Drive, whether landfall was even an option, and if so, how much of our science might remain."

"Understood. I'll update you in one ild."

Idenion swung round to face the others. "I want all those present to know that I *will* sanction a visit to Earth, to be undertaken by Laura, myself and a third crew member. Our objective will be to retrieve Tarlion if he's alive, and to remove or neutralise our technology. Are we all in favour, or should I ask Trevone for a deciding vote?"

"We all agree," said Sheyell grudgingly.

Ansela raised her head. "May I speak?"

"The chair recognises Archivist Ansela."

"I *am* in favour, but on one condition."

"Namely?" Idenion asked.

"You can't both go. Not after your narrow escape last time."

Idenion looked uncomfortable. "I'd be the first to admit that our last expedition was ill-advised and hasty. But we thought Clemis was in danger."

"No-one except one Communications tech knew where you'd gone. First Scientist Jarras couldn't cope."

"That won't happen again. Everyone will know where we've gone and why."

"And Trevone isn't the type to panic," Laura put in.

"You are our leaders," Ansela said insistently. "People look to you for stability and reassurance in precarious times such as this. One of you must stay."

"Much as I hate to pass up an opportunity to be in charge," said Kalyx, "Ansela's right. A reassuring presence is essential, and that means you, Idenion. Laura spent years in Cheveney, and you've been there how many times? Three. And the second visit was over in an afternoon."

"So who's coming with me?" asked Laura. "He or she will need Idenion's flexibility with languages, and ideally be a graduate of Space Tech."

"Daphos," said Dessin and Kalyx simultaneously.

"Clemis," said Idenion.

Laura stared. "You're not serious?"

"We can't spare Daphos from his duties. Clemis can speak English and Eldorian, has studied at Space Tech and can handle a sphere under battle conditions. She'll give you all the assistance you need."

"It *does* make sense," said Laura slowly. "She'd jump at the chance, I'm sure. As long as she only does the setting down and picking up."

"Won't you need a conversant to help you find Tarlion?" asked Kalyx, blissfully tactless.

"It's not easy to locate anyone in a crowd of Earthers," Idenion said. "I should know. If Tarlion survived he'll find *us*. He'll be close to Wickens Clump, keeping a quiet watch."

Chapter Five

"Pick a card, any card!" Tarlion had to raise his voice to make himself heard about the amplified bouzouki music. Loud guffaws came from the lounge bar, and Phaedra Moffat noisily stacked dirty dishes.

The teenaged girl that Tarlion had addressed, one of several clustered round him, drew a card from the deck in his hand.

"Look at the card, memorise it and put it back. Don't let me see it."

She obeyed. Tarlion then handed her the entire deck.

"Shuffle it. Take as long as you like. Now, give me the cards." He fanned them out. "And there's your choice. Ten of diamonds."

"He's right *again*!" enthused a second girl. "Let me try, Leon. You can't keep on getting it right!"

"I can."

A third girl slid her arm in his. "Tell my fortune, Leon."

"Again, Sandy? I told it yesterday. And last week. Nothing will have changed."

She smiled coquettishly. "Then I'll tell everyone what I know about *you*."

"Please do."

"You're a male model and that's an all-over fake tan."

"Leon!" hollered Bill the senior barman, and he excused himself with a theatrical flourish.

Kelly had been watching through the serving hatch. Phaedra dumped the last of the plates and paused next to her.

"*Where* did you find him?"

"I told you, he just turned up."

Phaedra began loading the dishwasher. "You don't sound very pleased. He's quite a crowd-puller."

"He's a novelty, that's all. He only knows one or two card tricks. And once Sandy Jennett realises he isn't going to fall for her, she and her friends will just drift away. It's your Greek nights that keep this pub going."

"Oh, I don't think that's true."

"It is. We've lost all the trade from the manor since that secretive lot took over. I can't understand Sir John – he was always so involved with the village."

"Maybe *he's* running out of of money too." Phaedra took off her apron. "Right, I'm off. I'll send Jack over on Sunday morning to help with your tax return."

"You two should be running this place."

"So you've said. I wish we could afford to buy you out. Jack would quit reporting tomorrow, given half the chance. They won't let him write the stories he wants."

"I hope he isn't thinking of moving on."

"No, no, he loves the village. He just gets annoyed with his job. He was so full of optimism at uni – he was going to be a political columnist or a foreign correspondent." She giggled suddenly. "And I was going to be a Goth fashion designer. We settled for what was achievable."

"As we all do," said Kelly with a tiny smile. "Night, Phaedra."

"Night."

Tarlion was tired. Trying to make himself understood in a roomful of nonconversants always gave him a headache. He mooched about collecting glasses, glad that Bill had turned off the music before leaving. Reaching out clumsily, he sent a tumbler flying – and involuntarily used his mind to arrest its fall. He fielded it in haste, and was about to move on when a voice at his elbow said:

"Interesting trick."

Tarlion went cold as he recognised one of the gatehouse heavies. "You mean with the cards?"

"I mean with that glass."

"It bounced," said Tarlion unflinchingly. "I was lucky. Breakages come out of my wages."

The guard circled him. "Were those girls right? Is that a fake tan?"

"It's real." Tarlion again tried to move away, convinced he'd blown his own cover.

"Humour me, Leon, if you will," said his adversary. "Sing to me. Anything you like."

Tarlion tried to react as an Earther would. "Why the hell should I?"

"Please. I insist." The guard had produced a mobile. "Or should I call the manor for back-up?"

Kelly appeared from the kitchen. "What's going on?"

136

"This – gentleman – has requested a song," Tarlion explained. "But since his looks don't inspire me, I'll serenade *you* instead." Then, to Kelly's bewilderment, he sang two verses of "The Gypsy Rover," imprisoning her hand as he did so. He didn't know all the words and his voice was nothing special. But it *was* a voice.

When he turned round, the security man was gone. Kelly ushered out a couple of stragglers, bolted the main doors and returned to Tarlion, who was waiting irresolutely.

"Look – I'm sorry about that," he began.

"I'm not," said Kelly, and kissed him.

***

Following the buffeting they'd received in escaping the Transfix, the four Eldorian spheres had made landfall on the planet indicated by Fley. Two of the craft needed repair before lengthy transposal could be undertaken, so the engineers had rigged a temporary shelter and set to work, cursing the endless twilight and incessant drizzle. No wonder this place had been passed over by the colonial survey teams.

Keska Fley-Talt emerged from one of the damaged spheres, her short dark hair tousled and her face grimy. She wore the uniform of a Patierade soldier. Two of Ymer's contingent eyed her disparagingly as she strode past; they still felt ill at ease in the presence of a woman dressed like a man and doing a man's job. Ymer, having lived on Celestra, had no such qualms – particularly since he'd realised that without Keska's expertise, they'd still be inside the Transfix. Without the node destabiliser she'd perfected, the Patieron device would have been useless.

"All done!" Keska greeted him. She spoke Standard with no trace of a Patierade burr. "One of the coils was fractionally misaligned, so the field modulation was out by two per cent. You'll notice the difference when you transpose."

"Does this mean we can leave this mud-bath? inquired Ymer.

"Not just yet. Father and Veylis are still talking."

"They've been talking since the day we arrived, and Veylis chases me off every time I try to cut in. You were with them to start with, so isn't it time you enlightened us?"

"Two lenders from opposing nations have met on neutral territory," said the girl blandly. "I stayed to ensure they didn't try to kill each other."

"And you could have prevented that?"

"Don't underestimate me, Captain Ymer. I've worked hard to ensure this meeting took place and I wouldn't have let any misplaced male pride jeopardise it."

"Right," said Ymer slowly.

"You didn't think it was a coincidence that we made our attempt on the Transfix when *you* did? We had intel; we knew you'd be there. And I was so sure as I could possibly be that the Transfix would heal itself and shut us out. I knew we'd be obliged to collaborate and saw it a rare opportunity to build bridges."

"And Fley agreed with you?"

"He took some convincing. He was dismayed that we were the only Patierade craft to make it through, which explains his early hostility." Her expression softened. "We had no idea Veylis would be here. That made all the difference."

"How, may I ask?"

Keska poured herself a hot drink from an urn. "I and my fellow researchers are trained to study formations," she began, seemingly ignoring his question. "Not just in stellar resonance but in society too – and something about the evolution of the civil war didn't make sense. It's too self-sustaining. We believe someone, some organisation, has an interest in prolonging the war, and we've begun collecting evidence."

"Are the Patieron generals aware of this possibility?"

"Maybe. But why should they investigate when they're always one step away from winning?"

"Always one step," Ymer repeated thoughtfully.

"I see you've taken the point. But the time I'm able to return home, my team should have enough data to start naming names."

Ymer looked unconvinced.

"For now," Keska went on, "I'll give you an example. Freelord Pervain left two bastard sons, but only one could inherit his title. The other had to meet with an accident."

"Everyone knows that."

"But not everyone knows that Lord Ephren wanted the younger boy, Chel, as his successor."

"*What?*"

"Think about it. Chel was born into a rigidly Patieron household, and was young and malleable. A blank slate. Veylis was more than eight years old and his mother Opna was trouble. She'd already stung Ephren for money, and she had no political affiliations." Keska paused for emphasis. "My father's agents uncovered a plot to kill both boys and blame it on the Patierades. Leaving House Patieron with no heir would have guaranteed another twenty years of bitter fighting. We were too late to save Chel but we rescued Veylis and his mother and took them to a safe house. *Our* house."

"And that's where she met me!" Veylis had approached unnoticed. "She'd been told to keep away, but how do you restrict a curious six year old?"

"I didn't think he'd any right to be there," Keska grinned. "I bit him, and he pulled my hair. We were best friends after that."

"For one day only," Veylis said soberly. "Fley's personal guard took Mother and me to a rendezvous point and Ephren picked us up."

"Veylis remembered me as soon as he saw me," Keska said proudly. "Now perhaps you'll see why he and Fley had so much catching up to do."

"We can now go to the Celestrians and show them we've begun peace talks." Veylis spoke with enthusiasm. "They need a good reason to dissolve the Transfix. I can't think of a better one."

"One step at a time," Ymer said amusedly. "You've discovered some common ground and I daresay the Celestrians will take note. But for now, let's see how my men react!"

***

"We're here, Laura," said Clemis. "Maintaining geostationary orbit above Cradle of the World."

"Wickens Clump," Laura corrected her automatically. Then, seeing only the crescent Earth on the scanner, "Are you sure?"

"If you still don't trust my piloting," Clemis said with a lofty grin, "trust the computer experts who've been upgrading this programme over the years. I'm simply following it. Now, are you ready?"

"Yes," said Laura unhesitatingly. She wore a grey one-piece suit and lightweight boots, and carried only a communicator and an air of determination. "Now remember the drill. As soon as we touch down, I'm out; and as soon as I'm out, you're gone. Return to this orbit and stand by. I'll make contact every two ilden to start with. If for any reason I don't, wait one day, then call Alda Mexa for instructions. Do *not* come looking for me."

"Understood," said Clemis, keying in the landing sequence. "Take care, mother."

Moments later, Laura descended the ramp into a late September morning. It was warm, even hot, and she briefly wondered if Daphos had miscalculated the date. It was supposedly the 30th of September, 2011. To her unaccustomed eyes, the

141

Clump looked less wild than before, as if someone had made an attempt to clear the undergrowth but given up. She found the trail she normally used, leading to the southern end of the village, and started walking.

Concerned only with the change in gravity, she sensed, rather than heard, the sphere lift off. For a moment she felt nervous, then chided herself for being silly. This was Wickens Clump. What could possibly be wrong in this much loved place? Soon afterward, she knew.

A high wooden hoarding, the type used on building sites, blocked the way out and extended in either direction as far as she could see. Surely no-one was planning to build here? Indignant now, she began to follow the line of the barrier. If it had no break then she'd have to ask Clemis to get her out. Not a good start to the mission. Once, she reflected, I might have been agile enough to climb over that. But not anymore!

She'd almost reached the northern edge of the Clump when the fence ended abruptly, to resume further on. Venturing through the gap, Laura recognised the Georgian elegance of Cheveney Manor. Bewildered, aware that she might be trespassing, she moved hesitantly forward into the grounds. Her fingers touched the cool surface of the communicator in her pocket.

Suddenly a hand gripped her shoulder. "Going somewhere, love?"

She whirled. A security guard, with the Cheveney coat of arms on his cap and jacket, regarded her insolently. "I'm … sorry," she began awkwardly. "I lost my way in the wood …"

He smirked. "Did you now? Laura Gilcoyne, if I'm not mistaken. We've been expecting you."

Incredulous at hearing her name, she froze just long enough for him to believe she'd be no trouble. Then she ran. It was undignified and futile, as she was sure he'd easily catch her, but it was her one chance to get rid of the communicator. She'd misjudged the Cheveney situation completely.

Instantly breathless, she made for the orchard on the south side of the estate. She and Jimmy had gone scrumping there as teenagers, and known all the ways to dodge the elderly gardener. Perhaps some of those ways survived.

The guard wasn't following. Glancing round, Laura saw him talking on his radio – which probably meant she was being headed off.

The orchard looked no different, but the boundary wall was topped with coils of barbed wire and evenly spaced surveillance cameras. The side gate had been bricked up. Aimlessly she turned back toward the manor, moving ever closer to it, still trying to dispose of the communicator but seeing nowhere to conceal its pristine whiteness. Through the trees she glimpsed her pursuers, five of them, fanned out across the lawn. They weren't hurrying, merely strolling. Which, she decided, was insulting. It also meant there was no escape – not that escape had been her objective. She had to find out if these people had Tarlion.

"Mrs Meredith!"

A short grey-haired man in a donkey jacket had appeared in front of her. Posed for flight, she hesitated. She didn't recognise him, not after thirty years, but something in his voice stirred an echo.

"*Darren?*"

"*Not* Darren, not anymore!" He hurried her toward the temporary cover of a lean-to containing motor mowers. "I'm Jonathan Stone, head groundsman. And I need your help."

"*My* help?"

"They've got an Eldorian in there, but I'm not allowed in. He knows what happened to my best friend Chris. The missing person, remember?"

"Jack had a poster," Laura said, more bemused by the second.

"Hah!" said her companion dismissively. "Jack Moffat could blow the whistle on all this, but he won't try."

"Jack's *here*?"

"Yes, in the village."

Laura peered outside. One of the searchers was twenty yards away. "OK, I'll find out what became of your friend - "

"Thank you. It's for his mum. She wants closure."

" – but you must do something for *me*." She placed the communicator in his hand and closed his fingers round it. "Take this to Jack. Tell him I'm here, tell him to keep this till I collect it."

"I can do that."

"Good. Now call the goons and hand me over."

Darren – or Jonathan as he now styled himself – obeyed with enthusiasm. "Mr Jellicoe, over

144

here!" he yelled, grabbing a pitchfork to add effect. "She's here! I've got her!"

Jellicoe appeared in the doorway. "Well done, Stone. Now get back to work." Then to Laura, "Why did you run? We nearly set the dogs on you!"

"I thought you were the police," she replied coolly. "There were issues, the last time I was here. Forgive the misunderstanding. Shall we go?"

"Not that way," said Jellicoe, moving to obstruct her.

"This leads to the front door, doesn't it? Then that's where I'm going. I'm the representative of another world and I don't propose to use the tradesman's entrance. I'm here in response to Sir John's message."

It was an inspired guess. Jellicoe looked astonished. "You *heard* it?"

"Of course, and we attempted to reply. There appeared to be some technical problem."

"Then you aren't here because of the crashed spacecraft?"

Laura affected a frown. "I know nothing of that. If some itinerants took it into their heads to visit you, they did so without clearance. Is Sir John here?"

"I believe he's been sent for."

"Good." Laura had reached the steps to the portico. "In the meantime I shall meet with your senior staff. I hope there are refreshments on offer."

"I'll speak to the caterers," said Jellicoe impassively. "Would you like a full English breakfast?"

"Just egg on toast please. And some chocolate. Cadbury's."

A thuggish guard in shirtsleeves was slouched against a pillar. "Well, well," he said disparagingly. "The elusive Miss Gilcoyne. Sir John was absolutely right – you couldn't stay away from home sweet home!"

"And you are?" Laura inquired frostily.

"Rod Tallifer, head of security."

"Fine. Now take me to whoever's in charge of *you*."

This wasn't necessary as Bartlett emerged from the gloomy hallway, pulling on his jacket. "Miss – Mrs – Gilcoyne. We didn't expect a visit from you in person. I'm sure you must realise there are a great many questions we need to ask."

"I've plenty of my own, Mr - ?"

"Bartlett. Project Leader. First, as I'm sure you'll understand, we have to ensure you're not carrying any harmful devices. A female member of staff will search you. Then, once you've taken breakfast, we can initiate talks."

As long as *they* do the talking, Laura thought. For starters, I want to know all about this crashed spacecraft. It has to be Tarlion's. And I'll insist on meeting their Eldorian prisoner, as I'm sure he'll have some enlightening comments.

She only hoped she could maintain her composure well enough to fool these people. And above all, she hoped Clemis would obey orders and not come looking for her when she didn't check in.

Jack, working from home and trying to turn user-generated content into something interesting

146

for his column, wasn't in the mood for visitors. "What is it this time, Darren? I've told you before, if you have a sensible story, email me."

"I don't go online. And the name's Jonathan."

"Sorry, forgot."

"Try to act as if you don't know me. Could I come in, please?"

"Not if I don't know you."

"Jack!"

"Five minutes." Jack marched him into the kitchen. "Start talking."

Darren drew a deep breath. "I've just seen Laura Gilcoyne taken captive by Sir John's security men."

Jack stared. "*What*?"

"She came walking out of Wickens Clump and one of the guards grabbed her. She got free, ran away – and they let her run. She was looking for the side gate, but of course that's gone. I know this is a bit hard to swallow, but – "

"No. No, it isn't for once," said Jack, remembering the investigator who'd accosted him. "Someone was asking questions about her a few weeks back."

"There's more," said Darren. "Before she was caught, she gave me this." He drew something out of his pocket. "She asked me to bring it to you. You're to keep it until she comes for it."

Jack, increasingly bewildered, examined the object Darren had placed on the table. It was square, white, featureless, and about half the size of a bathroom tile. "What *is* it?"

"I was hoping *you* could tell *me*."

Jack attempted to take charge. "Is Laura in any immediate danger?"

"No," Darren said positively. "She's important to them. Look, I'd better go. I'm supposed to be getting cigarettes for the gate crew."

"Darren, hang on. You haven't said – "

The back door slammed.

"- how she got *into* Wickens Clump." Jack finished the sentence aloud before returning his attention to the little tile. Something was nagging at his memory – and suddenly he was back at the Snelsmore protest camp, with screeching chainsaws and eco-warriors yelling insults at bailiffs and police. Laura's husband, under arrest, had broken free long enough to lob something that whistled past Jack's ear.

"Laura! Catch!"

Another white tile. Or maybe the same one. Jack picked it up, examined the identical surfaces, shook it and squinted at it. He was none the wiser. But whatever this was, Denny hadn't wanted the police to find it and Laura hadn't wanted the manor militia to see it. As for Laura herself: he cogitated a moment, then retrieved his mobile and dialled a stored number. "Jimmy Stretton? It's Jack Moffat here. No, it's not about your mother. Something strange has just happened and I thought you'd want to know."

***

"Trevone! How lovely to hear from you!" Clemis, nonchalantly seated at the sphere's main console, was surprised and just a little wary.

"My best girl, I'm *not* checking up on you."

"Of course you're not. Well, keep it short. I'm supposed to stay off the transposer in case Laura wants to speak to me."

"I know, and I'll be quick. I just thought I should warn you that the EM interference stopped a few ilden ago – and I don't need to remind you what that ancient text said. A few octals, then the meteor impact. We're on maximum alert, scanning for anything that shouldn't be there. So, when you're ready to return, call us first. We've no idea what you might be running into."

"Understood."

"Do you know how long you'll be?"

"No idea. Laura said she'd make a report every two ilden, but I've had no word from her since I set her down. That was over six ilden ago."

"Are you tracking her communicator?"

"It isn't active, but its theridolyte signature places it somewhere in the village."

"She probably can't get time alone. Give Idenion a call if you get really concerned. What are you doing to amuse yourself? Listening to Symerid Three's music?"

"Yes, and trying to improve my Ing-lish."

"You're not to land. Idenion said so."

"And I won't, Trevone, unless he tells me otherwise."

"What about the space junk?"

"Proximity detectors are on and ready to trigger the repeller field you and Daphos designed ten years ago. Stop fussing. If you want to worry about anyone, worry about Laura. I wish she'd tell me what she's doing!"

***

Sir John, the embodiment of old-world courtesy, poured tea into a bone china cup and handed it to Laura. "I'm sure you must realise that extensive if covert arrangements were in place to welcome our new allies the Eldorians – a meeting that, due to Celestra's intervention, never came about. The transmitter we constructed, the message we sent, was an attempt to discover why you prevented it, *how* you prevented it, and if there can ever be friendship between Celestra and Earth."

"The Eldorians would not have been your allies, any more than they were ours," Laura replied. "Consider their level of technology. They didn't need you. They *did* need an enemy to unite them."

"Are you saying you acted to protect us?"

"Yes that's exactly what I'm saying."

"And you restrained them how?"

"That's classified. And even if it weren't, I'm not qualified to explain."

"You just sing."

"Exactly, Sir John. I just sing." Laura didn't mention the third part of his question, and neither did he. He excused himself and went out, leaving her with the tea tray.

Bartlett and Tallifer had heard the exchange. "She's stalling us," Bartlett said. "She miscalculated, and now she's waiting for reinforcements."

"She doesn't give a toss about your message, John," declared Tallifer. "She wants whoever was in that wreck."

"I'm inclined to agree," Sir John said quietly.

"I could find out."

"Indeed you could - but at the expense of everything we've worked for. We'll follow Bartlett's suggestion and put her with Roegin. I'm sure we'll learn something from their conversation."

"Intergalactic insults. I can't wait."

"You won't have to. Take her to the first floor guest suite and send Roegin in. Station a guard in the corridor. I'll call surveillance and have them copy the audio feed to my office."

A little later, Laura was exploring her new surroundings when she heard the apartment door open and close. She turned, then gasped. "Hell's teeth, it's *you*!"

"Hello again." Roegin sauntered forward with his customary bold stare. "It's been a while."

"You were at the Green Man," she said, defensively polite. "How long's it been …?"

"Fifteen years. I'm flattered you remember me."

"I was in fear of my life. It tends to sharpen the memory."

"We weren't trying to kill you," Roegin answered, amused. "We were curious to know why you were here."

"Some things never change," Laura returned coolly.

"Apparently not. Would you care for a drink? I'm sure the cabinet's fully stocked."

"Just lemonade, please."

He brought it to her, poured himself a Scotch and joined her on the window seat. "Lovely view, isn't it?"

"You must be sick of it. Why don't you skip the pleasantries and introduce yourself properly?"

"My apologies. I'm Roegin Drice-Tressa, solitary representative of Eldor on Earth."

She studied him, trying not to look him in the eye while she did so. He seemed uncomfortable in a suit, and he'd cut himself shaving. Suddenly he seemed a lot less threatening. "Did they send you to interrogate me?"

"Sort of. I told them I'd only ask the questions *I* wanted to ask."

"Then fire away."

"Dammit, Laura, you *know* what's most important to me! What did your people do to the Eldor homeworlds? Why couldn't we contact them?"

"We didn't wipe them out," she said gently.

The relief in his face was immeasurable.

"We have a device called the Cadence," she went on. "It - "

"Before you give away any trade secrets," he interrupted, "you should know the room's bugged." He ran his fingers under the windowsill, removed a small bauble and crushed it. "There'll be others. I could search."

152

"There may be no need." Laura smiled at him. "Do any of our captors speak Eldorian?"

"No, of course not. We didn't use it in front of Earthers."

"In that case - " Laura switched languages. "We can have a full and frank conversation, secure in the knowledge that it will be completely private."

"Ebbon's blood!" Roegin bent his head over clenched hands and didn't move for over a minute. Laura thought she saw a stray teardrop on his eyelashes. "Sorry. I didn't expect that. Now you'll think captivity's turned me soft."

"How long is it since you've heard your own language?"

"Eleven years." Roegin gazed at her searchingly, and this time she didn't look away. "You speak it very well. Why go to the trouble?"

"I had to convince the expeditionary force that I was telepathic."

"Oh, I see." He continued to stare. "I'm beginning to realise what a resourceful woman you are."

"Just doing what I had to." Laura finished telling him about the Cadence, which didn't take long as she knew nothing of the science.

"So you gave the Empire room to grow," Roegin commented. "That was fair."

"Do you have family at home?"

"Yes. Is this where I'm supposed to fall at your feet and beg you to turn off that musical forcefield? Don't worry, I'll save you the embarrassment. Naturally I want to go back, but not because of family ties. For years I've dreamt of the day when I take down the Senate – or die trying."

Laura waited.

"I told Sir John's committee that the Senate abandoned the Covert Ops teams, but I never said why. The truth, Laura, is that we advised against the Earth-Eldor alliance. We surmised it would turn into war and we didn't think the Empire could contain this world. We also thought that involving Celestra would weaken us."

Laura wished she could tell him how accurate those predictions had become, in another time.

"Can you imagine what would have happened if we'd gone home after the battle? We'd have been proved right and the Senate would have fallen. So, they left us. But they weren't just glossing over their mistakes. They never intended to extract us." His anger, seldom far from the surface, had acquired more of an edge. "We carried a pathogen, as you know. We needed an inhibitor shot every two years to keep it dormant – and we'd run out. A supply problem, we were told. A bad batch. But not to worry – the Tenth would soon arrive. By the time we were called to our assembly points, half of us were displaying symptoms. I've often wondered if the rest would have been gunned down. No way of proving that, of course."

"Can you prove *any* of your story?"

He shook his head. "Everything was trashed. I was hoping *you* might have kept something."

"Such as?"

"Communiques, orders. We managed to stall the launch date several times."

154

Thus enabling us to complete our superweapon, Laura thought wryly. She didn't say it. She wasn't sure of Roegin's motives yet. Instead, she apologised. "We could have made an effort to rescue you, if we'd had more time. We should have *made* time. But we had to repatriate what was left of the Tenth, and get the Cadence set up. With no spacecraft here, and without a theridolyte signature to guide us, we'd have stood little chance of finding you."

"The homeworlds could have told you where to look. I'm assuming they didn't."

"No, they didn't," Laura said slowly. In retrospect, it seemed odd.

"Your turn," Roegin suggested. "A confidence for a confidence. Tell me something you didn't tell Sir John."

"Shortly before I left," Laura said after a moment's deliberation, "we had cause to believe the Cadence had a weakness, and that one or two Eldorian craft had broken out. They haven't approached us yet, but whatever the outcome when they do, the Cadence will have to be recalibrated. Which, so I'm told, will require a brief shut-down."

This time, Roegin's expression gave nothing away. "What was the *real* reason you came back?" he asked quietly.

"Roegin," she began helplessly.

"I know. You can't share it till you know me better. If I told you what happened three weeks ago, would you trust me enough to fill in the gaps?"

"Tell me, and we'll find out."

Sparingly, but with a spy's attention to detail, Roegin described the state of the crashed spacecraft – especially the squalid cabin.

"Oh, chaos, poor Tarlion!" Laura spoke his name before she could stop herself.

"Relax," advised Roegin. "Even if they're recording us, they can't translate."

"They could ask you, later."

"In which case I shall mislead them, not for the first time. Now who's Tarlion and why was he on the verge of starving to death?"

Laura sighed. "He's half Celestrian, half Narvellan, born to a Narvellan woman after she'd opted to join their colonial fleet. He must be about thirty by now. Out of the blue we had a message from him: he was hoping to meet his father. I'm willing to bet he stole that sphere. And because the Narvellans had dispensed with our co-ordinates, he made the journey with only star-charts and a great deal of hope. He must have been in space for months!"

"Gods! He doesn't lack nerve."

"And he so nearly made it. He'd found our location: just one transposal hop and he'd have been home. I *had* to look for him."

"Actually," said Roegin with a slow smile, "I think I know where he is. There's a new barman at the Green Man, calling himself Leon. He was apparently seen levitating a pint pot, but averted suspicion by singing."

Laura smiled too. "What a survivor!"

"Only just. He left some dirty clothes in the sphere, but I smuggled them out and burnt them before Tallifer's hounds had his scent."

Laura stared. "Why would you do that?"

Roegin shrugged. "To help a fellow exile and to spite Tallifer. So, what's your rescue plan? How do you contact your castaway?"

"I don't have a plan. I was hoping he'd find *me*."

"But you do have back-up in case of trouble?"

"Yes. My daughter."

"And?"

"Just my daughter."

Roegin made a derisive noise. "And these are the people who defeated the Three Worlds!"

"We'd no idea Cheveney was such a hotbed of intrigue," Laura said in justification. "We thought someone was fooling around with discarded tech. My daughter's very capable, Roegin. By now she'll have realised something's wrong. Help *will* arrive."

The inscrutable stare was back. "And then?"

"I'm not leaving you here. We'll take you to Celestra."

"So I'd still be a prisoner?"

"No, you wouldn't! Other Eldorians have claimed asylum; you can too. And eventually, when we upgrade the Cadence, we'll be able to send you home. You'll get your chance to overthrow the Senate, if you want to take it."

***

"Ann!"

157

She paused halfway along the corridor to Roegin's suite. "What do you want, Rod?"

Tallifer smirked. "Relax, frosty-face. This isn't an attempt on your virtue – such as it is." Using his pass-card, he propelled her through Roegin's door and closed it firmly.

"Why are we in here?"

"I said, relax. Lover-boy's still romancing Laura. And we're in here because he'll have dealt with the surveillance as usual." He paused, letting go of her arm. "I've had word from my contact. In view of recent developments, namely our new guest, the Syndicate wants to bring the operation forward to Sunday night."

"This coming Sunday? Are we ready for that?"

"We'll have to be. And there's been another change of plan. Instead of Roegin, they'll be taking Laura. The runaway too, if he turns up. But he's not important: this is all about leverage."

"But surely – "

"You heard what Laura said before she pulled that language trick on us. The Celestrians have blocked communications with Eldor, so Roegin can't help us in that regard. If we have Laura, Celestra will have to end the blockade or else."

"I won't leave Roegin."

"Do you want to get out of here or not?" Tallifer snapped. Then, more quietly: "Maybe I haven't made myself clear. The Syndicate doesn't like loose ends. Roegin's no further use, *and* he's disaffected. They won't let him live."

"Rod, you promised!"

"I promised you a way out and you still have that."

"You can't let them kill him!"

"Get real, Annie. He doesn't even *like* you. And if you're thinking of warning him, maybe I should tell him you've been giving him placebo injections for years."

She hung her head. "Those were my orders, and you know it."

"Look," said Tallifer in an attempt to sound reasonable, "I'll have another word with our man. See if we can fix this. We need you on board for this op. We're counting on you, Ann."

"This is moving too fast for me," she said miserably.

Tallifer smiled unconvincingly. "Just do as you're told and you could be a free woman next week. Deal?"

"Deal." Her reply was scarcely audible.

Tallifer left her in the apartment, collected a pre-paid mobile from his room and strolled to the gate-house. Inside, a noisy card game was in progress. Pausing by the lighted window, he dialled a number and waited.

"Pavel? It's Rod. We have a problem with the nurse."

Chapter Six

Alda Mexa 4.1.6.4031

"It's about Lydion," said Tonor over the transposer. "I don't want to complain - "

"But you're going to," Idenion surmised wearily. "Couldn't this wait till morning? Why are you calling so late, anyway?"

"I've only just finished work at the Lyricon. Before that I was at Tonora's school, and before that - "

"Never mind. What's the problem?"

"Well ..." Tonor floundered a little. "Lydion was my mentor and I owe him, and I realise this half-existence of his must be a nightmare for him, but he mustn't monopolise Tonora as he's been doing. I know the Cadence needed correcting, and that was important, but now he has to see that Tonora's routine and schooling have to come first. Couldn't you speak to him?"

"And how do you propose I do that?"

"He hears what we say."

"If he's around. And the only way I'd know that is if you sent Tonora with him to *tell* me."

"Well, it's got to stop," Tonor said lamely. "Where's Sarune? Can't he talk to *her*?"

"I haven't a clue where she is. And before you say it, I don't like the idea of Sarune prowling around the planet any more than you do, but it's just possible she'll find others who can read Lydion and herself."

160

"But that could take octals. A year, even. Can't you just - "

"Tonor," Idenion said irritably. "It's half after nadir, I've had people underfoot all day and I can't leave this transposer and go to bed until I've made four more important calls. Must I remind you that we could be under attack any day now?"

Tonor looked crestfallen.

"If there's any distancing to be done, Tonora has to do it herself," Idenion went on. "If she won't listen to you or your wife, involve a teacher. Or Nefyrra, even. Someone she knows."

Tonor brightened instantly. "That's a marvellous idea! Nefyrra and Lydion were great friends, weren't they?"

"Eventually."

"Then *she* could talk to him. To them both. I'll get straight onto it in the morning. Thank you, Idenion."

Idenion gazed with some relief at the blank screen. "So now I can add life counsellor to my list of accomplishments," he said to himself. "Right, who's next? Nohal, I think. At least he won't give me a hard time."

It was early morning in Tafret but Nohal was already on duty and preparing the day's work. "How can I help you, First Citizen?"

"I won't keep you long. I'm sure you're aware that Alda Mexa's population is rapidly increasing, and that means more work for the relayists. We've created some extra places in the chain, and so far everyone's coping, but I'm starting to worry about Kyrin. He's channelling the akron load singlehanded – and that load's increasing by the day. He's so pivotal to our communication routes – *too* pivotal. We don't know what we'll be facing in days to come and I don't want one single individual to carry so much responsibility."

"Have you spoken to him?"

"Yes, but you know Kyrin. He said he was fine. I offered him an assistant and he turned me down flat. Said he'd always worked alone."

"What would you like me to do?"

"Choose someone you can trust to step in if there's a crisis. Train them for the post."

"And if Kyrin finds out?"

"Oh, he's bound to eventually. There's no keeping secrets from *him*. But I hope he'll understand why I'm doing this. I assume *you* do?"

"Yes, of course. And feel free to refer him to me if he has any future quibbles. As a matter of fact, I believe I have just the person to assist him. He's from Virda, just like Kyrin. He may even be related, though I haven't checked. He has the same remarkable range, but isn't too accurate with content as yet. We're working on it. His name's Bridd."

"Keep me apprised of his progress. Thank you again, Nohal."

"My pleasure. And speaking of overworked people, you look in need of some rest yourself. Get some sleep!"

"Soon, Nohal. Soon." Suppressing a yawn, Idenion dialled an industrial complex in Treva. The night shift had started an ild ago, but no-one seemed in a hurry to answer the signal. The operator, when

162

he finally appeared, was suitably flustered to see who his caller was.

"Never mind the formalities," Idenion cut in swiftly. "I'd like you to check your manifest and tell me why Scapirion doesn't have the extra transposers they requested."

"I don't need to look," the young man said unhappily. "Our last two consignments of aldacite were diverted. Repairs to essential systems."

"Diverted by whom?"

"The Prefect."

"I see. I'll speak with him tomorrow. In case I can't locate him, see that he's informed that Scapirion takes priority. They're approaching seasonal shutdown and they need that equipment."

"Yes, First Citizen."

"And as soon as that order's fulfilled, you're to send three additional transposers to Alda Six, with enough spares to maintain them for a year. I'll send printed confirmation to you *and* the Prefect. And I'll personally ensure there are no more diversions."

"Understood, First Citizen."

Idenion cut the connection and sat fuming for a moment. He'd given Treva too much autonomy and now he faced the prospect of taking it back. And that meant involving the Administrators. And *that* meant more meetings, more discussions, more time away from anything approaching leisure.

His next conversation, with a prill farm in Corayn, proved trouble free. He wanted production at maximum and the team leader was happy to comply.

"There's a theory," Idenion added, "that without exposure to their planet's natural predators, homegrown prill are becoming less robust. It might be an idea to introduce fresh stock from the homeworld."

"Consider it done," said the botanist.

Thankfully, Idenion made his last scheduled call - to the maverick engineer Ibri at Treva spaceport. "Sorry to keep you waiting, Ibri. Tonor and some time-server at Crystal Tech held me up. Since you won't look me in the eye, I take it there's no good news?"

"We gave it our best shot. We really did," Ibri apologised. "You know how I hate to fail. But we couldn't come up with a single working pulse-cannon from the stuff we stripped out of the Eldorian fleet. They'd all been burnt out in the conflict – and to be honest, some of my lads hadn't been too careful with the disassembly."

"I'm grateful for your efforts," Idenion said, desperately tired. Ibri finally raised his eyes from the circuit he was fashioning.

"Chaos, Idenion, are you all right? You look as though you haven't slept for an octal!"

"Thank you, Ibri, for that enlightening comment. At least your news has spared me one unpleasant duty."

"Oh?"

"Admitting to the Administrators that we've been trying to revive Eldorian weaponry."

"They didn't *know*?"

"I'd only have had yet another set of objections to veto. If things continue like this I'll go down in history as Celestra's second dictator!"

Ibri chuckled and signed off.

Idenion, though he was now free to quit the transposer, didn't do so. He hesitated a moment, then flagged up Clemis' code.

"Discords, Idenion, what is it this time? If it isn't you it's Trevone. I'm watching an Isles of Ing telecast. A dancing competition." She paused to let Idenion hear the short-range receiver. It didn't *sound* much like a dance, just a series of whoops and yells. On that evidence, Symerid Three's broadcasts were as noisy as they'd ever been.

"I'm trying to capture some of it for Ailsi," Clemis went on. "It's a cultural study!"

"Well, don't clog the logic system with too much culture. It still has to get you home. I take it you've heard nothing from Laura?"

"No. The communicator's at the same location, but it isn't switched on."

"How long's she been down there?"

"This is the evening of day two. Not *that* long, I suppose. Not if she's looking for Tarlion."

"Wait one more day. One more *Earth* day, that is. After that we'll need a plan."

Clemis muted the exuberant telecast and gave the transposer her full attention. "Sorry I sounded off at you, father. You're bound to be worried. And you look so - "

"*Don't* say tired."

"I was going to say lonely. You and Laura do everything together."

"I never thought I'd miss her so much nor so soon," Idenion confessed. "I shouldn't have pre-empted you just then. I'm sick of transposer conversations – perception rendered useless, always having to watch the person's face."

"Laura has to deal with that all the time," Clemis pointed out.

"Which makes her all the more phenomenal. Page me tomorrow, Clemis – and if you've still had no word, I *might* give you permission to go after her."

***

Deep Space Scanning Array, Alda Six

"Trevone! Trevone, wake up!"

He sat up blearily. "Ysara? Have I overslept?"

"No, it's only four ilden since you went off watch. I'm sorry to disturb you but we may have a situation."

"We *may*? Do we or don't we?"

Ysara paused to calm herself. "4029ALC36 has disappeared."

"So? Asteroids do break up."

"There's no debris. And I've – well, you'd better see this for yourself."

Trevone located his shoes and trudged after her, yawning.

Ysara led him to her workstation. "Alcine Heights catalogued this asteroid a year ago. It follows, or rather used to follow, a staple ellipse, taking it well within the orbit of Alda Four but

166

nowhere near Celestra. Two octals ago I noticed a variance, but it was still within acceptable limits." She switched to another image. "Jex has been fine-tuning the all-frequency array, and yesterday something odd turned up in the routine sweeps. See that EM trace? It's a small pocket of the interference that was swamping us."

"It's the same signature," Trevone agreed.

"And it's right on top of 4029ALC36, which is why Jex told me about it. I ordered a timed sequence and retrieved the data half an ild ago." She switched the display again. "Where the asteroid went, the signal followed. And now they've both gone. Only they haven't, have they, Trevone?"

"Oh, they'll still be there," Trevone confirmed grimly. "Just not where you thought they'd be. I'll need to re-position the array. Once it's aligned, search these coordinates for the signal." He tapped briefly on the keyboard. "I'll be back as soon as I can. If you find it, try and raise Ninka Observatory for confirmation. Alcine too, although it's the middle of the day there. I want to be absolutely sure I'm right about this before I tell Idenion."

***

Sarune considered herself the most patient of beings. She had, after all, devoted seven years to nurturing Lydion. But after just a few octals in the presence of ex-relayist Rinyi, she found her patience wearing thin. At Lydion's suggestion she'd visited Corayn, and had located Rinyi without much difficulty. That had been the easy part – she'd spent enough time with Narvellan reducees to know exactly what she was looking for. Erratic perception, almost off the top end of the scale with the lower register simply not present. He was working in the Corayn herb gardens, the last survivor of a dozen similarly damaged Celestrians. He could read her, which was good. And he was petrified of her, which was the source of her irritation. Finally, after what seemed like endless cajoling, she'd forced him to recognise that she meant no harm. Next, she began work on his defeatist mindset. Psychology wasn't her strong point but she did her best. +You have to stop thinking of yourself as a permanent victim. You started a riot, you took your punishment, and it's high time you moved on. Kyrin and Nohal have excelled at rehabilitating you. You're almost back to normal+ This wasn't strictly true, but she could apologise later. +Why spend the rest of your life picking flowers when you've a chance to make a real difference to your world?+ she went on expansively. +I've explained what Lydion has become. You must have heard about his wonderful inventions and how they helped defeat the Eldorian Empire. Well, suppose – just suppose – we need his help again. Wouldn't it be a privilege to interpret for him?+

+You said there was a little girl. Couldn't she do it?+

+She *has* been, but there's a limit. She needs rest and play+

+I'm scared+ Rinyi seemed genuinely distressed, otherwise Sarune would have given way to wrath.

+What of, Rinyi? You now know you don't have to fear me. And you're surely not afraid of Lydion?+

+No. I'm afraid of the Others+

+What others?+

+They were here. Everywhere, in their thousands. They mean us harm+

+When was this?+

+After the event which shattered all the crystals, they came. They studied us. They didn't know I could read them but next time they might realise+

+They're coming back, then?+ Sarune was still half-humouring him.

+The pickers teased me+ Rinyi went on, sensing her disbelief. +They said there were no others, that it was just radio interference+

+Chaos!+ Sarune was suddenly enlightened. +Did you tell anyone else about this, such as your supervisor, or Nohal?+

+No. I didn't want any trouble+

+I understand, but this is too important to keep to yourself. We can start by telling Lydion. And then, Idenion. You can't hide from this, Rinyi. You're needed. You may be unique in all the world!+

**

Cheveney Manor 2.10.11

169

On Sunday evening, the third day of her captivity, Laura was again shown into Roegin's presence.

"Well, look at *you*!" he remarked.

She was wearing a floral tea dress with a fitted bodice and short sleeves. A pair of beaded slippers completed the change of image. "I needed fresh clothes," she explained. "Something more suited to this heatwave. Sir John let me choose from his late wife's things. Isn't it sad that he can't bring himself to get rid of them?"

Roegin continued to appraise her. "Are those silk stockings? What else did he lend you?"

"I think I should leave that to your imagination," Laura said lightly.

"You know," Roegin went on shamelessly, "If I hadn't seen Harmsworth's dossier I'd never have believed you were sixty-one. You look so much younger. Must be that diet of music, drugs and free love."

"Clean air, fresh food and a happy marriage," Laura amended. "Your chat-up lines belong in the Sixties, Roegin."

"I'm the old-fashioned type." He patted the settee. "Sit down and tell me what you've been doing. I missed you yesterday. Where were you?"

"I was escorted to the gatehouse and shown the internet. The goons thought I'd be impressed. Tallifer asked me if I'd ever been online and I thought he was talking about cocaine!"

"And were you impressed?"

"Amazed." She switched languages. "But having seen what's going on in the world, I can categorically state that an alliance between Earth and Celestra is at least a thousand years away."

"Well said."

"They also gave me a CD of songs they'd downloaded from Melanie Palmer's website. My vocals for the rock band I was in."

"Pleasant memories?"

"No, just a reminder that I wasted a decade instead of staying on Celestra."

"I know how you must feel," Roegin said, instantly sombre. "I had a decade wasted *for* me."

"We should form a society." Laura helped herself to wine. "Or at the very least, an escape plan."

"Still no word from your bar-keeper friend?"

"He doesn't know I'm here, obviously." Laura stared out of the window at the far-off gate to freedom. "I found out it was the harvest festival today and asked if I might go to church. Someone might have seen me there, even if it was only Caitlin." She sipped her drink. "I liked harvest festivals. Hints of the pagan. I used to sing Harvest Home as a solo when I was a young teen."

"I assume they wouldn't let you go?"

"No, but Sir John sent Jellicoe to film the choir on his phone. It's frightening, the direction technology's suddenly taken. There'll be no turning back from it now."

"Why would you want that?" Roegin asked curiously.

"When I took Idenion to London in 1966, he sensed a number of latent telepaths. I thought – I hoped – that in several more generations the talent would emerge properly. But now, with these phones, there's no need for it. If I could come back in a hundred years, or fifty even, I might find cyborgs." She gazed intently at Roegin over the rim of her glass. "But I'm not coming back. Not after this."

Just then a caterer brought dinner, pausing to light standard lamps and switch on background music. The conversation ebbed. Outside, sunset deepened into twilight. Sir John's Mercedes moved quietly down the drive and was gone.

In the Green Man, Jack put the final touches to Kelly's tax return and left it for her to sign. Phaedra had just arrived to prepare bar snacks; she just missed Jack as he left via the back door and headed home. The bar-room was heaving with security men from the manor. Their contract had seemingly ended suddenly, with a generous hand-out which they were now eager to spend.

Jack was on his mobile as soon as he reached the lane. "Jimmy? Why aren't you here? Is an anti-fracking demo really more important than Laura's safety? Well, make sure it *is* only half an hour. Something's up: the security guards are all in the bar but I didn't see the chief or his pal Jellicoe. There's either been a change of personnel or they're going to move Laura. No, I haven't seen any activity near there, but Sir John's just driven by, going like a bat out of hell. Who've you got with you? Great. I'm on my way home now, but if I'm not in you know what to do. See you."

Tarlion, troubled, sought out Kelly. "I need some time off. Now."

"What? With the place like this? You're kidding, I hope?"

"A friend of mine is in trouble. I have to go."

"Leon!"

"I'll explain later. Sorry!" Tarlion dived out of the pub and ran after Jack, catching up with him as he reached his front door. "Jack, wait! I need to talk to you."

"Oh. Leon. Did I forget something?"

"No. Look – this is going to sound a bit weird, but I know that Laura Gilcoyne's a prisoner at the manor, and I believe you have something belonging to her."

"Have you been talking to Darren?"

"Never mind that now. Those men, the ones in the pub – they were bribed to desert their posts. We have to get Laura out as soon as we can, with or without your friends. That object the gardener gave you is a transmitter. If you let me see it I might be able to call for immediate help."

"You're right – this *does* sound weird." Jack unlocked the door. Tarlion pushed past him into the hall.

"Trust me, Jack, please. I feel responsible. She's there because of me."

"How do you make that out?"

"Because I sent a message and she replied to it in person. Can I see that tile, as you call it?"

173

Jack fetched it. "There's always been something unusual about Laura," he conceded. "The way she just comes and goes. Not to mention cryptic letters from my late aunt, tasking me to give her shelter. She always arrives with nothing. Just like you."

"You catch on fast." Tarlion held the tile between his thumb and middle finger, and squeezed the edges firmly. The surface flowed back. A display of lights shimmered across the tiny screen.

Jack simply stared. Before Tarlion could proceed further, a young woman's voice said, in Celestrian: "Finally! Where have you been, Laura?"

A brief terse conversation followed before Tarlion rippled the screen shut and pocketed the device.

"Do feel free to keep it," Jack said pointedly.

"Thank you, I will."

"What language was that?"

"I'll tell you later. It was Laura's daughter I was speaking to. She's going to meet me at Wickens Clump."

"Is that wise?"

"I've explained the situation and she'll be armed. Well, are we doing this or not? Come on!"

Jack didn't feel he had a choice. He'd be letting Laura down if he didn't go. But he was beginning to realise how little anyone knew about Leon – if indeed that was his name.

"It's Tarlion," said his companion. "Leon for short. Once I'm closer to the manor I'll know who's still around and where they are."

"And how will you do that? Can you see in the dark?"

"I wish!" said Tarlion bitterly. "I'll manage."

"I should have brought a flashlight."

"No, you shouldn't. It would draw attention, and until we meet with Clemis I'd rather not do that. Now is probably a good moment to tell you that Laura isn't the only one under house arrest. There's a long-term prisoner, a spy."

"So, no celebs. No rehab clinic."

"Afraid not."

Jack wanted to ask him how he knew, but didn't. Tarlion would doubtless promise to tell him later. "This is unreal," he said as they walked through the sultry dusk. "Who is this spy? What nationality? Is he dangerous?"

"He won't be any trouble. He just wants to get home."

"And Laura? Is *she* involved in espionage?"

"No. I told you, she was looking for *me*. She has a home and family elsewhere, and she's much loved. I have to put this right."

"You haven't told me how *you* wound up here," Jack said, none too hopefully.

"No," replied Tarlion. "I haven't."

They rounded a corner, and the upper storeys of the manor became visible in the distance.

"Come on, Leon, make this easy for us," suggested Jack. "Get your mojo working. Where's she being held?"

He sensed, rather than saw, exasperation. "If you don't keep quiet and do exactly as you're told," Tarlion said coldly, "you'll only be a hindrance. So you can either trust me to get things right, or go back to the village. For Laura's sake, I hope you'll stay."

"Do as I'm told, eh? You sound just like my old headmaster."

"Good. I'm glad I haven't lost my classroom authority."

"You're a *teacher*?"

"I was. Come on, let's find Clemis."

Jack shrugged and followed, temporarily turning his back on Cheveney Manor and the softly lit second floor windows. Laura, Laura, he thought. Woman of mystery – what did Aunt Margaret discover about you?

Oblivious, Laura put down her coffee cup, leant back and closed her eyes. For the first time in three days she'd been able to relax. Her head was almost touching Roegin's shoulder, but she didn't adjust her position. They were both at ease with one another.

"Nice perfume," he commented.

"It's Lady Cheveney's. Je Reviens. Roegin, I've been meaning to ask you something."

"Oh?"

"Don't be cross, but I promised a friend I'd ask. Do you know anything about the disappearance of Chris Edgewood?"

"Gods, must that keep coming back to haunt me?" Roegin stood up, dislodging her, and paced across the room. "My trainee partner Buuth – you saw him with me at the Green Man – caught Edgewood spying on one of our landing sites, and killed him."

176

"But *he* was no threat! No-one would have taken him seriously!"

"I know that and *you* know that, but Buuth didn't. And, so, since my mentoring was at fault, I helped dispose of the evidence. We dumped the body in one of the eco-warriors' disused tunnels, which later collapsed. A low point in my none too illustrious career."

"Would you be able to find the place again?" persisted Laura.

"Ebbon's blood, Laura, will you stop interrogating me! It was in another life!" He calmed himself with an effort. "Sorry. I didn't mean to shout. Maybe I – " The unfinished sentence hung in the air. "Laura."

"What?"

"Something's not right. Turn that piped music off, will you?"

She obeyed.

Roegin held up a hand for silence.

"I can't hear anything," she whispered after a moment.

"Exactly. Look." He pulled her to the window. "There's no-one in the gatehouse. It's in darkness. Noise travels, especially on a warm evening like this. For years I've listened to that bunch of morons laughing and swearing, and those wolfhounds of Tallifer's yelping because he keeps them hungry. Tonight, there's nothing. Where are the patrols? And where was Sir John off to earlier?"

"His town house?"

"Not with *you* here. I think he's been lured away. We've been set up, Laura. Someone knew

I'd be off-guard if they let me wine and dine you. And if you hadn't provoked me just now, I still would be. Why hasn't anyone collected the dishes? And where's Ann with my meds? She couldn't wait to break up our twosome the other day."

The lights of a passing car, travelling slowly up the lane adjacent to the manor, moved briefly across the darkened gatehouse and sentry post. The electric gate stood open.

"Does this mean we can just walk out?" asked Laura incredulously.

"It means someone wants us to think we can. Someone who's planned a quick getaway."

"But why haven't they just - " Laura stopped, unwilling to voice her fears.

"Drugged us, used tasers?" Roegin supplemented. "They'll have been told not to risk damage to an asset. You could have a bad reaction to those things."

"As could you."

"I don't think this is about me." Roegin opened the door a fraction. "No-one on watch. If I can get to my suite, I've some improvised weapons stashed away."

"But that's on the third floor! We need to get *out*!"

"Laura, I won't defer to you on this. Any moment, someone will give the go-ahead and some really nasty characters will charge right through that door. So will you please get your elegant backside up those stairs? *Now*?"

They ran.

Just beyond the open gate, a man in dark clothing spoke on his mobile. " ... no signal in or near the manor. Why weren't we told? Yes, everyone's in position. Do we have clearance? Copy that. I'll tell them."

"No you won't," said a sweetly feminine voice. The tiny weapon in her hand spat fire.

"Neatly done," observed Tarlion, closing the distance between them.

"Thanks. Remind me to turn off these image enhancers next time. I'm dazzled!"

In the brief lightning-flash Jack had glimpsed a petite blonde woman, wearing dungarees and what he assumed were night vision goggles. Once again, he had no idea what was being said. "Are you Laura's daughter?"

He sensed, rather than saw, a smile. "Yes. Later we speak Ing-lish together. First, we find mother."

"Right, boys and girls," said Tarlion, "let's get our sleeping friend off the public highway. Grab an arm, Jack."

They dragged the fallen agent into the gatehouse reception area which faced the lane. Tarlion risked putting on a desk lamp to examine the man.

"Narvellan stun tech, if I'm not mistaken," he commented obscurely. "He'll be out for hours. And his phone's a write-off."

"Any weapons on him?" asked Jack.

"None."

"Do you think anyone saw us?"

Tarlion and Clemis paused as if listening. "No," they said simultaneously.

"At least," Tarlion added, "none of the ops team." And he made a sudden dash through the door, returning almost immediately with a sheepish Darren. "This one's been shadowing us for quite a while."

Jack was incensed. "Darren, you idiot!"

"Jonathan."

"Whatever. You nearly got yourself zapped. I thought you'd gone, anyway."

"They threw me out, which was all the more reason to stay. I want to help save Laura."

"Fine," Tarlion said curtly. "Just don't screw up."

"And the Eldorian too," Darren rushed on. "I heard Tallifer say – do you know Tallifer?"

"We've met."

"I heard him say the Eldorian was surplus to requirements. We can't let him be harmed. I need to question him."

Jack looked from one to the other in disbelief. Eldorians? Narvellans? Was all the nonsense Darren had been spouting over the years *true*?

"You can add Celestrians to that list," Tarlion said. "Darren, tell Jack how many of this bunch there are." He indicated their victim disparagingly.

"Five two-man teams, including him," Darren said importantly.

"Why so many?"

"Six men to locate Laura and the Eldorian, and to deal with any other opposition. Two more are waiting in an SUV, parked in the spinney over there." He pointed due east. "And another two are at Cheveney Services with a replacement car."

"Now tell us how you know this," Tarlion said, smiling.

"I was listening till I was evicted."

"How, when you weren't allowed inside?" Jack was still only half convinced.

"Sir John's people got careless, started leaving windows open. And that climbing wisteria always needed pruning."

Jack finally had to accept that he'd been very wrong about Darren. "Leon, you seem to be in charge of this rescue. Shouldn't we make a move before the others start looking for their pal?"

"Agreed. Best route, Darren?"

"Try to remember it's Jonathan. The kitchen door's open. Matey came through it."

"Then let's go. Clemis, you're the eyes, so you lead."

"Just a minute," Jack objected. "We can't barge straight across the lawn. There are floodlights!"

"The control room's unoccupied," said Tarlion after another pause.

"Tallifer told them not to use any lights," Darren added. "He said the manor was a soft target surrounded by hard-core nosey parkers."

"True enough," grinned Tarlion.

Clemis adjusted her googles and set off, the three men following in single file.

"This is crazy!" said Jack in a stage whisper. "We've got one weapon against half a dozen scumbags, not to mention the redoubtable Tallifer."

"We'll cope," said Tarlion.

"Got superpowers, have you?" Jack asked sarcastically.

"I've one minor talent which has never been used in anger," Tarlion replied, utterly serious. "Phaedra says you were a keen amateur boxer at uni, so let's hope you haven't lost the skill. Now keep quiet!"

+Tarlion+ ventured Clemis.

+Yes?+

+I've located Laura. She's with the Eldorian. We could announce ourselves+

+Better not. Their reaction might give us away+ Tarlion frowned into the darkness. +Clemis, someone's on the move. We'd better hurry+

He broke step and rushed forward. Clemis followed.

"What ...?" began Jack.

"Run!" Darren hissed in his hear. "This is it, Jack. "We're on!"

182

Chapter Seven

"There's no possible doubt, Idenion," said Trevone. "The asteroid's under propulsion. It's following a spiral course, which is why we lost it for a while."

"How did you find it again so quickly?"

"Our short-range navigational programmes use similar vectors. Once I'd guessed what was going on, it was easy to compute the rest."

"Then these attackers, whoever they are, think like us?"

"It's probably coincidental. A continuous low acceleration transfer's an efficient way of getting the result they're after. A spiral, gaining speed all the way, then cutting sharply across the destination orbit – Celestra's orbit. If it's allowed to continue, it'll approach from the direction of the sun. You won't see it till it's too late. That's how they wiped out our ancestors."

"Be very sure about this, Trevone."

"I am. Alcine Heights have taken their own readings and so has Ninka. The impact probability is ninety five per cent. And it's large enough to cause an extinction, as before. I need your authority to use the dispersal engine on it, while it's still far enough away to do so safely. Otherwise we'll just be substituting one threat for another."

"Permission granted," Idenion said calmly. "And I want you to do this yourself. One clean shot. I don't trust anyone else to get it right."

"Understood. I'll tell the spaceports to ground all vessels until further notice. Can you get word to Clemis?"

"Yes, leave that to me. Inform me when the target is neutralised, and have the Alcine and Ninka observatories map the condition of the marker." Idenion, not as calm as he'd appeared, signed off and put in a call to Administrator Dessin. The unknown assailants would be expecting the meteor strike to decimate the planet, as before. What would they do when it didn't?

Idenion had never forgotten how the Eldorians had pulverised Ilonna. Not entirely trusting the Cadence to keep them contained, he and Dessin had set up meetings with Celestra's best engineers to devise ways of protecting the land and people. However insufficient those plans, it was time to bring them into operation.

Dessin, to his relief, didn't flinch when told of Trevone's mission. "What would you have me do?"

"I want you to contact each city state and check the status of the underground food silos. The construction will be finished by now, but they need to start moving supplies in. Don't bother checking with Scapirion – they've always had to live that way."

"Their seed bank's quite amazing," Dessin agreed.

"A pity we didn't follow their example. Next, speak with the team I commissioned to build and distribute small generators and storage batteries. I hope the work's complete – I've been too distracted to chase it up. If they've been slacking, lean on them. Alda Mexa could need that equipment more than most."

Dessin looked quizzical.

"Why us? Because our hydro-electric plant is a vulnerable target, and our solar collectors alone won't run the city. And a city without power can't defend itself."

"You're thinking this might turn into a siege?"

"I'm thinking we can't rule anything out. I just wish we had some operational pulse-cannon, something we could deploy at will."

"The dispersal engine's a formidable weapon."

"It is, but I'd be reluctant to use it after today. Too many risks, even with a single firing."

"Trevone won't let you down," Dessin said staunchly.

"He won't miss, but he can do nothing about the aftermath. That rock's a massive target. We've never dispersed anything larger than a sphere."

"Numerous spheres in quick succession," Dessin corrected him. "There'll be no permanent damage to space-time, you'll see."

Idenion, not quite believing him, tried to contact Clemis. There was no reply, but the sphere's transposer logged his call – meaning she wasn't in t-space. He assumed she was asleep.

Trevone soon reported back, confirming that the threat had been neutralised. "We're tracking the marker. It *is* closing, but seems to be forming an ellipse. If it continues in this manner it'll decline into a long trail rather than one hotspot. I think it's safe to allow spaceflight but everyone should avoid these coordinates until further notice. We'll need to go public with this now."

Idenion agreed. "Let the observatories make the announcement. Tell them to say the asteroid's orbit changed and we removed it as a precaution. Nothing else. We've dealt with it so there's no need to alarm anyone."

"I suppose not."

"And make sure Clemis knows about the contaminated area. Post an alert if she's still off-line."

"Understood."

That evening, Idenion reluctantly revisited the transposal post. Just one courtesy call to Dessin, he told himself, and then I'm having an early night. Wearily he began to flip switches. When the system immediately reconnected with Alda Six he suspected a malfunction, but a very worried Trevone assured him it wasn't.

"I've called you repeatedly for the past half-ild. Clemis, too. She doesn't answer."

"If she's sleeping she'll have blocked all signals except Laura's. Is that all you wanted?"

"No, Idenion, it isn't. I'm sorry to impose this on you so late in the day, but – there's another one."

"Another one," Idenion repeated blankly.

"A second asteroid heading your way. What in chaos should I do? We can't keep on using the dispersal engine!"

"Where is it?"

"Further out than the first one but not on a spiral trajectory. If the acceleration's continuous we have even less time than before. We need a strategy. Do you know how many asteroids are out here? Thousands!"

"I've seen them for myself," Idenion said tersely. "My instinct would be to get rid of this one immediately, but I'm no scientist. You need to talk to someone who knows about t-space markers."

"There's only me, and possibly Zanna. That was Earther tech, and it vanished along with the Gloriana."

"What about the data from the battle?"

"Gone too. We have a few data logs from our spheres, that's all. None of the observatories took readings after the conflict. Nobody thought of it."

"Great. Well, we *do* know that damage to space-time occurs when markers combine; so my advice, such as it is, would be to deal with this asteroid immediately, thus keeping the markers as far apart as we can."

"Understood. Stand by for updates. Trevone out."

Idenion wished he hadn't been called on to make that decision. He was, as he'd reminded Trevone, not a scientist. It was a straight choice – now or later – but it still meant he had a fifty per cent chance of being wrong.

***

Roegin's door stood open.

"A trap?" whispered Laura breathlessly.

"Maybe. Let me go first." He snapped on the lights and disappeared inside. A moment late Laura heard a cry of shock and anger, and ran in to find him kneeling beside Ann's prone body.

"Don't look, Laura, don't look. She's dead, and it isn't pretty." He picked up a housecoat and gently covered the dead face. "Oh, Ann, why didn't you leave with the others? There was nothing for you here."

Laura put a tentative hand on his shoulder. "Why would they murder one of their own?"

"Silly bitch tried to warn him," said Tallifer from the doorway. "Almost managed it, too."

"Warn him of what?"

Tallifer leered. "Sorry to deprive you of your new squeeze, Ms Gilcoyne, but Roegin's no longer a viable asset. Pavel here will escort you downstairs. Oh, and don't go looking for your weapons stash, Roegin. We found it. Steak knives, pepper, bleach – did you think you'd be fighting scullery maids? The cheese wire came in handy though." He glanced at Ann.

White with fury, Roegin launched himself at Tallifer, and the two men crashed through the door onto the gallery.

"Want a ringside seat?" Pavel murmured in Laura's ear. "Don't get your hopes up. Roegin will lose."

Laura was all too aware of that. Then, out of nowhere, Darren was there, leaping on Tallifer's back and trying to drag him away from Roegin.

Pavel had Laura's arms in a crushing grip. "The gardener isn't being much help, is he? Don't struggle, Ms Gilcoyne. I was ordered not to damage you but I can still hurt you."

188

She was dimly aware of sounds in the distance: shouts, footfalls, a vehicle screeching to a halt outside. Before her, Tallifer's massive fists rained blows on his two opponents. Then, inexplicably, he faltered, bellowed in pain and fell to his knees. Darren and Roegin exchanged bewildered glances.

"Stand away from him," her daughter's voice ordered: and there was Clemis, aiming her stun-pistol. Touched by lightning, Tallifer toppled gently sideways and was still.

Clemis then turned toward Pavel, but he kept Laura before him as a human shield and began inching toward the stairs. Then he suddenly released her, staggering back with his hands to his head. Clemis promptly fired again, then swore and almost dropped her weapon.

"Chaos, Laura, when will our dozy techs stop these things overheating?"

"Nice to see you too," she answered lightly.

A young man she didn't know bent to inspect the unconscious Pavel. Then he turned to face her, evoking a mingled pang of affection and loss. "Hello. I'm Tarlion."

"You have your father's eyes," she observed. "Plus a few Narvellan fighting skills?"

He grinned. "Psychokinetic cosh. I'm not much good at it. But Clemis and I make a great team!"

On the gallery below, Jack had just decked one intruder – much to his own surprise – but two more had him pinned in a corner. Then, to his infinite relief, Jimmy and another grizzled eco-warrior bounded into view.

"Okay Jack, we've got this."

"About time," he retorted, and slumped thankfully against a wall.

Jimmy was as good as his word. He and his friend Baz fought dirty, gouging and biting. The brief but furious bout ended when Baz slammed his opponent's head against the wall next to Jack.

"You all right, mate?"

"Just about. Where are Miggy and Devo?"

"Sorting out the two in the getaway car. They tried to do a runner but we blocked them in."

Darren appeared, limping a little. "Sorry I couldn't get to you, Jack. We had our hands full. Roegin's nurse is dead, and he's taken a beating."

"Is Laura all right?" demanded Jimmy.

"She's fine. She'd like to see you."

"Later," said Jack. "By my reckoning there's one more villain unaccounted for."

"Probably holed up somewhere," said Jimmy. "Why don't you take Laura and the rest of the party back to yours? We'll comb the place and make sure everyone's rounded up."

"We left one unconscious in the gatehouse."

"Right. We'll check the grounds too. Oh, and if you're going to call the Old Bill, wait till we're gone."

Darren organised some torches, Laura retrieved her boots, and the little group set off. Roegin had a bloodied face, a split lip and extensive bruising, but he insisted on walking unaided through the gate. "I've dreamt of this moment for years, and I'm doing this without anyone's help – even if I have to crawl!"

190

"Stubborn piece of work, aren't you?" Tarlion remarked.

"It's what kept me alive," Roegin answered, then stumbled. Tarlion caught him.

"Okay, we're outside the gate now, so put your arm round my shoulder. That's right. Let's go."

"I still can't believe we got out. I thought they'd have knives."

"Orders," Tarlion said succinctly. "Minimum force only. If they'd had knives the chances were they'd have been used, and on the wrong person. Laura's safety was paramount."

"And you've still no idea where the orders came from?"

"Not a clue. Pavel was the middle man and even he didn't know. The men at the handover point might have, but they'll be long gone."

"Did Tallifer ..." Roegin hesitated a little. "Did Tallifer kill Ann?"

"No, it was Pavel. The original plan was to dispose of you both en route, but Tallifer thought his new bosses were being a bit hasty. There was no guarantee that Celestra would accede to a ransom demand, and in which case you might still be needed. So he and Pavel set about framing you for murder. Later, Tallifer would have denounced you to the police, using your historic Earth alias. You'd have been remanded in custody long enough for the new syndicate to have second thoughts about you. If they were going to, that is."

Roegin was silent for a minute or so. "Thanks for your help back there," he said at last. "Aren't we supposed to be on opposite sides?"

"Well, technically. But Laura likes you, and that's good enough for me."

Once home, Jack slopped whisky into tumblers and handed them round. Laura located a first aid kit and began tending to Roegin's face.

Tarlion downed his drink in a couple of swallows. "I have to say goodbye to Kelly," he announced. "We had a bit of a … thing … and I can't just disappear. Here, this is yours." He tossed Laura's communicator in her direction and took off at a run for the Green Man.

"Hell's teeth, he's just like his father!" Laura said amusedly. "He'd better be quick. As soon as Jimmy gives the all clear, we'll have to make tracks."

"Well, Laura, I know the truth about you now," said Jack. "My aunt knew too, didn't she?"

"Yes, she did. Eventually."

"I don't suppose you or Clemis have any pictures of home on those communicators?"

"No need. Clemis?"

Clemis showed him Alda Mexa.

Jack became very quiet and sat staring into his glass.

"Now, Roegin," said Laura, "isn't there something you want to tell Darren?"

For what he hoped was the last time, Roegin related the story of the unfortunate Chris Edgewood.

"He's telling the truth," Clemis added in careful English. "Roegin, please picture the area of the tunnel."

He did so, and Clemis relayed it to Darren. His face lit in wonderment but he kept his mind on the matter in hand.

"I know the place. I'll ensure he's found."

"I wish all our loose ends could be dealt with that easily," said Laura. "Tarlion's spacecraft, for instance. I don't like leaving it here to be analysed."

"Not a problem," Roegin declared. "I saw inside and the Drive was totalled."

"All the same," began Laura doubtfully.

"The Earthers already have aldacite. What else could they learn from a burnt-out wreck?"

"The hull must have been intact. Theridolyte doesn't burn."

"True, but it can't be synthesised without therite. And there's no therite on Earth, believe me. A survey was commissioned and if they'd found just one deposit of it, the Eldorian mining corporations would have been here before Covert Ops got a look in."

Laura acquiesced with a tired smile.

"We did find it on Io," Roegin added, "but conditions weren't conducive to exploitation."

"Io," Laura repeated with a broader smile. "I don't think we need worry about that just yet!" She took up the communicator so recently returned by Tarlion, and made a few adjustments to it. "Darren, you've shown your true colours today. If you're in agreement I'm going to leave this with you. I won't be returning to Cheveney as it's no longer safe for me here: so, I want you to send me news. Tidy up those loose ends I talked about."

"How does it work?"

"Press any two edges, and keep pressing until the theridolyte responds and opens. Then touch the screen to start. I've set the device to locate the akron, where I live. The system will authenticate the signal and record your message."

Suddenly the back door was kicked open and the missing kidnapper almost fell through it. He was young, agitated, and held an old-fashioned firearm in one trembling hand.

"I'm here for Laura Gilcoyne. Hand her over."

Jack surveyed him critically. "Where did Tallifer find *you*? Work experience?"

"Hand her over *now*," the boy repeated. "This project mustn't fail. Don't you realise what it means to us – all of us?"

"Oh yes, we realise," Laura said. "That's why it isn't going to happen."

Clemis, her stun-pistol out of charge, looked helpless. With Tarlion absent, what could any of them do?

Laura stood up and moved coolly toward the boy. "Give me the gun."

"Laura, don't!" cried Jack.

"It's all right." She took another step. "You took that Luger from a display case in Sir John's study, didn't you? It doesn't work. How do I know? Because Sir John bought my Uncle Nathaniel's gun collection to help him out financially. That one looks the part, but it doesn't have a firing pin. War souvenir." She reached out and took the weapon. Instantly Roegin seized the boy in an arm lock.

194

A squeal of brakes signalled the arrival of Baz's van, and a moment later Jimmy was at the door. "Sorry, folks. That little toe-rag got away from us. I see you've got everything in hand, Laura."

She realised she was pointing the gun at him, and lowered it hastily. Baz and Miggy hauled the boy outside. "Put him with the others!" Jimmy called after them. Then, to Laura: "It's all secure back there, at least for the moment. We tied everyone up and locked them in a cellar. We – ah – didn't touch the crime scene. Time for you to ring the cops, I think."

"Are you off, then?"

"The lads are. I'm going to look in on Ma. I know this is none of my business, Laura, but will you be doing your usual disappearing act?"

"Yes. We'll soon be on our way."

"Then – what exactly are you going to *tell* the police? You can't report your own kidnap and then vanish. If you go swanning off, *we* might be accused of murder!"

"No, Tallifer will," said Roegin with a degree of satisfaction. "Opportunity, motive, relationship to the deceased ..."

"Oh?"

"Ann was his wife. His estranged, unfaithful wife."

Laura stared. "No wonder he hated you!"

"All the same," said Jimmy, "the rest of the gang's going to walk if you're not around."

"Forget about them." Tarlion was back, escorting Phaedra. "They aren't important. This is.

195

Jack, my friend: I've just explained to Kelly and your wife that I've been working undercover to break up a money-laundering ring. Here - " He produced a crumpled sheet of paper from his pocket – "is all you'll need to nail the men in charge. Offshore accounts, shell companies, and so on. One phone call to HMRC should start the ball rolling."

"Tip of the iceberg," muttered Roegin.

"It's a start."

"I take it *you* won't be making this call, Leon?" asked Jack.

"Sorry. I have to move on."

"I'll call them," Darren volunteered. "My last act as Jonathan Stone."

"Be my guest," said Jack, handing him the paper.

"Isn't it exciting, everyone?" said Phaedra, eyes shining. "Big business corruption in our midst! We could be on the news. Oh, that reminds me, Jack – have you tried our TV tonight? There's some kind of interference. The punters were going mad because they couldn't see the football."

Jack turned on the set. Bursts of silent static cut across the picture on all channels.

"Is that - ?" began Clemis.

"We have to leave," announced Laura. "*Now*."

***

"Idenion, we've got trouble," said Trevone.

"I know. The ground stations are still tracking the second asteroid. What's gone wrong? Why haven't you destroyed it?"

"I can't line up an accurate shot. Every time I close in, those EM pulses interfere with my systems and obscure the target."

"Oh, chaos, it's true then. I thought he was delusional."

"Pardon?"

"Sarune and Lydion turned up with Rinyi, the last surviving reducee. He can read them both. And he claims the EM emissions aren't the by-product of an intelligent life form. He says they *are* the life form. And after what you've just told me I'm inclined to believe him."

"Bizarre, but possible," Trevone agreed. "I'll pass your findings to Space Tech. I spoke with them earlier – I was hoping some of their spheres still carried Lydion's shield or the Tekla Skein."

"But they don't."

Trevone sighed. "No. As Zanna reminded me, each device requires eight modified spheres, and the ones used in battle were decommissioned long ago. We still have the specs, but no working models and no time to build them."

"I'll order the reconstruction anyway. As First Scientist, you should never have allowed the technology to lapse."

Trevone accepted the rebuke stoically. "I admit I was at fault. But – "

"But you thought we'd be fighting Eldorians."

"Exactly. And since we gifted them our sphere-shield, it wouldn't have made much sense to deploy it against them."

"So we're helpless."

"Not quite. Space Tech does have a good supply of space mines. I don't imagine they'll be effective against the EM cluster but I'm aiming to cause a diversion. Zanna will arm a sphere and join me, and I'll give you more news as we have it."

"Understood. Sarune and Lydion have offered to study these motes at close quarters and maybe find ways to neutralise them, but that will take time. Keep targeting that asteroid, Trevone, while the disperser's still an option."

"Should I make another public announcement to contradict the first one?"

Idenion hesitated. "It wouldn't do much for our credibility, would it? We'll wait as long as we can."

"Agreed. Trevone out."

Idenion powered down the transposer and turned to Nefyrra, who was waiting at a discreet distance. "All right, you can come out now."

She complied. "Sorry. I just didn't want him to see me. Trevone's in the middle of a dangerous task, and the last thing he needs is his worried mother staring at him."

"*Are* you worried?"

"He'd assume so. But the answer's no, not for him personally. He's been in danger before and he can handle it."

"You don't change!" Idenion sounded almost grateful. "Nerves of steel. Anyway, how may I help you? I never had a chance to thank you for giving Rinyi lodgings. I hope he isn't being a nuisance."

"Rinyi's no trouble. This visit isn't about him – well, only indirectly. It's about Tonora."

"Oh, chaos. I hope she isn't upset at having Lydion appropriated."

"Not in the least. She accepts that from now on Lydion will speak to her because he wants to, not because he *has* to. She's a mature, sensible child. Which is why I decided to ask her about the EM cluster – how she perceived it, what she thought of it. Tonor gave me permission but warned me not to scare her."

"And?"

"Fortunately she studies complete patterns, not just sentience, so she didn't share Rinyi's alarmist vision. Instead she saw a bunch of small, irritating beings who could only say yes, no, yes, no. It turns out that each EM spark has a neutral companion in tow, alternately masking then revealing its host. On and off, yes and no. It's binary. That's how the particles share information."

Idenion thought this through. "So what we have is an organic computer or a programmable hive mind, carrying out one task at a time. Mapping us, then directing an attack. But it isn't the enemy. It's in the service of the enemy. Or as the Eldorians might say, these entities are only the foot soldiers. We need to find the commander. I'll update Zanna and Trevone; you tell the incorporeals if they haven't left yet."

"It's already done."

"Of course it is." Idenion smiled. "Good to be working with you, Nefyrra."

"Glad to be of service. What's next?"

199

"Well, I think we should bring our codebreakers out of retirement – or assemble new groups. Could you deal with the preliminaries? Contact Ruvrin; she'll help."

"What will they be analysing?"

"Every recording of the interference. We'll have to isolate it from what we were *trying* to record, of course, I'll alert all the receiving stations and tell them not to delete anything. And with your permission I'll put Jarras in charge of a tech team." Idenion straightened his shoulders. "We should reward that little girl. She's given us our first real breakthrough. I've been sleepwalking through the past octal, but now we're defining what we're up against I feel revitalised. And not before time. I wouldn't want Laura to think I've been slacking in her absence!"

Nefyrra returned his smile and started to leave, then paused. "Oh, one more thing. Sheyell."

"What about her?"

"She came to a recital yesterday, caught sight of Rinyi and took off. I don't know what her problem is but could you please sound her out? The scolia made Rinyi welcome so I don't expect administrators to shun him. Fortunately he didn't notice. Next time, he might."

"I'll speak to her and assure her he's harmless," Idenion promised.

"That's just it – she wasn't scared. She simply didn't want to be seen. It may seem a trivial matter but it needs sorting. Rinyi has an important job to do and we can't let personal issues intrude."

+Zanna, Zanna, beautiful Zanna! My penultimate lover. Look at her, Sarune! The strength, the sensuality of that pattern. I remember when we were stranded in a snowboarding lodge on Ninka Heights …+

+Lydion+

+What?+

+Shut up+

+Since you ask me so nicely I suppose I must. I was only trying to make light of things. It isn't easy when someone you've been close to looks right through you – literally+

+Focus on your mission+ advised Sarune after a pause. +We'll soon be as close as we dare get to Trevone and his dispersal engine, so get ready to bail+

+Ejected like toxic waste. I'm really looking forward to that+

+A case of having to. We can't permeate theridolyte. We tried+

+Which probably means those – things – can't either+ Lydion conceded grudgingly. +All to the good, I suppose. But, I'm taking the scenic route home when we're finished here+

+Always assuming you have a home to go to+ Sarune retorted.

Zanna was donning a bioshell. Prior to closing the helmet she paused and addressed the apparently empty cabin. "I'll partially vent the atmosphere as arranged. Leave via the filtration chambers. You have thirty isk to get clear." She paused. "Good fortune, Lydion."

+She *does* still care+ he exulted, before he and Sarune were catapulted into space.

+Are you intact?+ asked Sarune.

+Apart from my dignity.+

+I'll take that as a yes. Now, according to Trevone, there are little pockets of energy at a distance from the main mass around the asteroid. Observers, maybe. These offer the best opportunity for study. We could even capture one or two+

+Now hold on. We don't want the entire gang after us+

+We'll wait until Zanna begins her attack – they'll have plenty to occupy them then. Anyway, they probably wouldn't even notice a missing few. I imagine the attrition rate is quite high+

Lydion didn't reply for a moment, detecting in Sarune's uncustomary eagerness a trace of the former Synectic. Ensnare, possess and control. +I'll let you take the lead on this one+ he responded at last.

Trevone's data was meticulously correct: the tumbling asteroid, the besieged sphere, and several diminutive EM signatures. Sarune chose a small group of particles furthest from the confrontation and began making her approach.

+Zanna's not ready+ cautioned Lydion.

+As I was saying, these things seem fragile+ Sarune went on airily. +So how do they exist in space? How do they cope with natural hazards? This is a trial run. Watch closely+

202

She launched herself at the centre of the group and made a pounce. She missed. The entities had flown apart so instantaneously that Lydion had scarcely perceived the reaction. They had then recombined just as swiftly. Sarune tried again, with the same result.

Lydion framed an oath, catching the significance at once. How could his people take down these beings when the discharge from any weapon would simply go straight through them?

+First things first+ said Sarune, coldly practical. +I have their avoidance pattern. When Zanna makes her move, you lunge at those little beasts and make them scatter. I'll do the rest+

I'm sure you will, Lydion thought. But he kept the remark to himself.

"Right, Trevone," said Zanna, "line up on the rock as if you're going to fire the disperser. When the swarm comes after you I'll intercept and scatter some mines. After that, we improvise."

"Commencing approach," responded Trevone, none too hopefully. "Coming into range, and – no, it's useless, Zanna. Can't get a target lock. Those things are all over me."

"Deploying mines," said Zanna crisply. "The swarm's changing course, encircling them. Can you make another run? Do you have a window?"

"Negative. I'm still surrounded."

"They've caught up with me too. Where are they all coming from?"

"I presume that's rhetorical? Communications are jammed except the transposer. No external readings available."

"I can't locate the mines." Zanna was suddenly tense. "Their signature just vanished. Scanners becoming ineffective. Density of swarm increasing."

"This isn't like the other times, Zanna. We've stirred them up. Let's call this off."

"I can't navigate out, Trev, not without risking a collision with you or the asteroid. It's like being in a magnetic storm. I'll open a transposer link to Space Tech and use it as a homing beacon. I suggest you do the same with Alda Six. And then, since you'll make landfall ahead of me, you can have the pleasure of telling Idenion we screwed up."

Trevone sighed. "Perfect. Ending transmission. I'll give you two astallen to get clear."

"Copy that. Zanna out."

Left alone, Trevone gazed gloomily at the dancing static on the viewscreen. He checked the logic system to verify everything had been recorded, then sat down to wait. But before even one astal had passed, an incoming transposer visual chased away the interference.

"You seem to be in a spot of bother, Trevone," said a voice he knew. "Need a hand?"

Trevone stared. "Ymer!"

"The same."

"Did you break through the Cadence? How many of you are there? No, wait, scrub that. Do you have pulse-cannon?"

"I never go anywhere without them."

"Then would you please destroy that asteroid?"

"We'll be glad to. Hold your position; we don't want you getting in the way. I take it you don't mind what happens to those space insects you seem to have attracted?"

"Not in the least."

"Good. That makes our job easier."

Ymer kept the transposer link active, so Trevone once again witnessed the fire and fury of the Eldorian lasers. There seemed to be only four spheres, which was somewhat reassuring. When the asteroid had been reduced to fragments, Ymer said:

"One space rock, pulverised. I'd like to say we'd got rid of those infestations as well, but I think most of them dodged. They're gone, anyway. And now, you need to make that expanding debris field disappear before it peppers your planet. I take it you've the means to do that?"

"Yes," Trevone said reluctantly.

"Off you go, then. And once that's done, maybe you could let Idenion know we're here? We need to talk."

Trevone, finding himself on escort duty, spoke briefly with Alda Six and alerted Alda Mexa spaceport. Only then did he notify Idenion.

Daphos, at Communications, was still trying to calm the other staff when his viewscreen relit. "Hey, stranger, it's Clemis! When my father condescends to get off the transposer, do tell him I'm on my way back with Laura, Tarlion and a surprise guest. What's been going on? Did I miss anything exciting?"

***

+Well, that was educational+ remarked Lydion. +Did you enjoy the floor show, Sarune?+

+Not particularly. I don't appreciate dodging laser fire+

+Relax, Timidity. We were nowhere near it. Just close enough to warm the extremities+

+We don't have extremities+

+Figure of speech+

+Nor do we actually speak+

+Sarune+ said Lydion patiently, +I know you like to be precise, but could you please cut me some slack on this occasion? I've just seen a bunch of Eldorians demolish a threat to my world!+

+Only because they want something+

+Cynic. All right, celebration over. Let's pool our information+

+About time. You first+

+Well ...+ Lydion wasn't quite up to speed, as concern for Zanna had coloured his observations. +The little beings can transpose, or more likely *be* transposed, at short notice. *How* they do it we've yet to discover. They can't possibly use t-space – they'd be pulverised instantly. At a guess, they'll have a designated dimensional portal to convey them and to channel gravity through when shifting asteroids. Whoever's controlling them knows his stuff+

+Why did the space mines throw them into a panic?+

+No idea. I thought they'd only confuse and distract. But, they're resonance based. And it was a resonance event that kicked this whole thing off+

+And you couldn't tell where the enemy took them?+

+There was rather a lot going on just then+ Lydion reminded her. +Right, let's have *your* info. How are your captives?+

+Sulking+ Sarune answered disdainfully. +I imagine it's the first time they've ever been trapped. They went crazy to begin with – not a comfortable sensation – but now they've gone introvert. Waiting for instructions, I suppose+

+Don't relax your hold. They may be trying to fool you+

+I held onto you for seven years. I'm quite capable of restraining these little pests for a few days. But I *would* like to hand them over to Nohal before I'm tempted to swat them+

+Well, let's drop in on him. Hopefully he'll have prepared a suitable cage. I can move faster than you, so, ready to be towed?+

+As ready as I'll ever be+

Lydion surveyed his surroundings. +Piece of cake, as Laura would say. I'll follow the spheres' auxiliary trail. Stand by for a snowboard ride!+

+Er – Lydion+

+What?+

+You might want to delay our departure. Something's happening+

The entities were reappearing at a discreet distance from the marker Trevone had just left. But instead of the usual inchoate mass they began to assemble geometrically, carefully fringing the boundary of their tiny portal. The shape grew in density till it resembled a shallow bowl.

+Maybe we should have run+ Sarune murmured.

+It isn't a weapon. It's almost like a data conduit. I think they're trying to communicate!+

+I can't decode transposed data. Can you?+

+No need. They're seeking our perception, Sarune, like thousands of little relayists. The bowl's an amplifier. Can't you detect the random chatter it's generating? They'll soon have our range+

+I don't feel inclined to chat with them. They could overwhelm us+

+Can't your prisoners enlighten you?+

+No chance. They've no idea that anything's going on+

Lydion's mind was made up. +Well, threat or not threat, I have to allow the contact+

+Why take the risk?+

+Because they're dying, Sarune. See that irradiated clump at the centre of the bowl? That's the focal point. They're channelling a thought-stream from chaos knows where, and their fellow beings are feeding them the power to do so. The outer layers are sacrificing themselves to keep the link open. Which means one of two things: either the message is of paramount importance, or there's an inexhaustible supply of those creatures. If the latter, we'll never defeat them. If there's any negotiating to be done, I have to do it now+

Sarune cogitated a moment. +All right, I'm in+

They concentrated.

The mind which addressed them, courtesy of its suicide troops, was infinitely old, infinitely weary. +I am Vuli. I command the Clustrals+

+Then call them off+ Lydion suggested. Vuli ignored him.

+I was not aware that your species had created artificial intelligences like myself+

+Lydion bristled with indignation. +Who're you calling artificial?+

+We are evolved beings+ Sarune pointed out loftily.

+You are the guardians of your race?+

+We are+ declared Lydion. +And we demand to know why we were attacked without provocation+

+You have threatened the Protected Realm. I am its defender+

+We don't know what you mean+ Sarune ventured. Vuli, in mid-speech, again took no notice.

+Now you have presented yourselves I am programmed to re-categorise your species. You are entitled to sue for clemency. Your representation should include inhabitants from all planets under your supervision. Hostilities will cease pending the outcome of your appeal. Report to these coordinates in one octal+

+No+ Lydion pronounced coolly.

+What -?+ began Sarune. He hushed her.

+Vuli, we cannot present our appeal under these conditions. We wish to be detailed and thorough, and we can be neither when communication is so laboured. I have a suggestion+

+Proceed+

+Let us come to you. I have your location. We wish to see this Protected Realm and learn how to respect it. We shall require life support for our subjects and a generous measure of your time+

+There is no precedent+

+Then create one, and be quick about it. Your portal's collapsing+

+You are young and impatient+ came the eventual response. +Very well. You may conduct negotiations on my homeworld. But bear in mind this concession does not guarantee a favourable outcome+

+Accepted. We may need a few octals to prepare+

+I shall be waiting. I will detail my Clustrals to escort you once you have transposed. Bring the one who programmed you. I should like to meet with him+

The portal folded upon itself and was gone.

+Would you mind telling me what you're playing at, Lydion?+ asked Sarune coldly.

+Tactics, dear girl. Tactics. A perfect opportunity to know one's enemy+

+A perfect trap to blunder into. And don't call me dear girl+

+Criticise all you like, o mentor mine, but I'm not in error. Laura would call it seizing the day. Come on – let's get back to base, find Rinyi and share our news+

Chapter Eight

The journey back to Celestra was half complete, and all four travellers were anxious for it to be over. Laura and Clemis simply wanted to be home; Tarlion and Roegin were impatient to see the world they'd heard so much about.

As soon as the spacecraft had quit transposal, Clemis was on the communicator – first to Daphos, then Idenion, then to Escir at his clinic. She used a dainty headset to minimise disturbance to her passengers. At least, that was the reason she gave. Roegin, euphoric and exhausted, dozed on a bunk. Tarlion pretended to watch the viewscreen and waited for Laura to speak. Finally, she did.

"Before we land, Tarlion, there are things you should know about your father. There was no chance to tell you earlier but ..."

"You don't have to spare my feelings," he interrupted gently. "I know he's dead. You've been wondering how to tell me ever since we met. And I know *how* he died. Roegin heard about the court-martial, and he saw some of that musical tribute you broadcast."

"Then you know that Lydion was much loved," Laura said quietly. "There are many people in Alda Mexa who knew him well. They'll be happy to share their memories with you."

"There's just one thing I don't understand," Tarlion went on. "You told me, back at the manor, that I had my father's eyes. But at the same time your thoughts, so piercingly sad, were saying how devastated Lydion would be when he couldn't see me. I thought I'd got the syntax wrong. But I didn't, did I? What exactly did you mean?"

Carefully, Laura explained.

"I understand," Tarlion said neutrally after a long pause. "And you've spoken with him via this child?"

"Not personally, not yet. I won't find it easy."

"And Sarune? How does *she* communicate?"

"Only via Lydion so far."

"That doesn't surprise me," Tarlion remarked. "She wouldn't win many popularity contests. Don't worry, I won't make waves. I know she's useful to you. For the record, I've always believed that if the elite of Old Narvella had treated their women better, there'd have been no Synectic net. And something else – something even Sarune might not know – a report was sent to Myrig by the team who combed the ruins of Ipsa base. There was evidence that the overseer, a man named Clovath, had laced the Synectics' nutrient feed with performance-enhancing drugs. It made them act crazy."

"How long was this going on?"

Tarlion shrugged. "Who knows? It might not have started with Clovath. So, I can forgive Sarune. She wasn't in control of her own project."

"Laura!" called Clemis. "Escir wants a word."

"Put him on the speaker."

"It's confidential. Medical matter."

"Oh, chaos, he probably wants me in for a health check. Sorry, Tarlion."

"We'll talk later," he promised.

"We will. And if there's a way for Lydion to see you, we'll find it."

212

"Laura." Escir sounded coolly professional. "Clemis says you're on good terms with Roegin. If he doesn't already know, could you explain about the bio-protections and how ill some of the soldiers were? I still have a few shots of the vaccine we used at Etys Plain, and I want Roegin to have one. Bring him straight to me – but after you've explained. I don't want him thinking he's swapped one institution for another."

"Will the vaccine still work?"

"It worked on Habbon. He's the only reason I kept it. But he says his off-world days are over, so Roegin has priority. I don't know how in chaos he survived that pathogen but he's certainly a unique case."

"What was that you were saying about institutions?"

Escir chuckled. "Relax. I only want a chat about Earther medicine. Once he's acclimatised he's free to go – with your permission of course. Until then, he's quarantined along with the other new arrivals."

"Isn't that a bit draconian? There's no risk to us."

"But there *is*, Laura. You're tired after your ordeal, or you'd never have missed this."

She *was* tired. "A clue would be nice," she suggested.

"Gloriana," Escir replied. "Enlightened? I thought so. Now you'll understand why Idenion wants all our visitors under one roof. I just wish he hadn't chosen mine! They won't have forgotten my crimes against the Empire."

"This all sounds very … temporary."

"It is. It's a breathing space for you and Idenion to decide what to tell them, what to keep from them and how to enforce it. If they learn about the time travellers there'll be no sending them back through the Cadence. They'll have to stay here whether they like it or not! Ah, they've just arrived. Wish me luck, Laura! They've been screened for weapons so I won't get a knife in the ribs, but I'm sure there'll be plenty of insults flying. Fists too, maybe."

"The Empire's a long way off, Escir. They're in no position to start a fight."

"A fight?" Tarlion called across the cabin. "Am I invited?"

Escir overheard. "That's Tarlion, I presume. Yes, bring him along. He might divert some attention from *me*!"

"Landfall in one astal," Clemis announced.

Laura approached Roegin. "Wake up, sleepyhead. Oh, you *are* awake!"

"Awake, and shamelessly listening to your conversation."

"Did you understand any of it?"

"Very little. But Eldor is Eldor in any language. At a guess, I'd say your Cadence escapees have arrived."

"Yes, they have. All eight of them."

Roegin laughed. "That shouldn't be a problem for you, then!"

Tarlion scowled at him across the cabin.

Roegin waited until the hatch was open and the ramp deployed before attempting to rise. Then he sat up, stretched somewhat painfully, and prepared to disembark. Laura offered an arm; he refused with what he hoped was graciousness. He had no idea who was out there and first impressions counted.

As it happened, he needn't have worried. A small crowd surged forward but no-one paid him the slightest attention. Idenion, whom he recognised, proceeded to make a great fuss of Laura. Clemis' partner greeted her with uninhibited passion. And several young women, plus one or two older ones, waylaid Tarlion with hugs and questions. "Can you sing?" they asked, over and over. "Can you sing?"

Roegin permitted himself a rueful smile. "Welcome to Celestra," he murmured.

"They're not groupies." Laura had returned to his side. "They're scolia players. Tarlion's initial message reached me during a committee meeting, so I wasn't able to keep his arrival secret. But no-one knew about *you*."

"Where are the other Eldorians?" Roegin asked.

"With Escir. We diverted them to the hospital landing pad. You'll meet with them soon. I need to debrief you so I'll do that on the way."

"*You're* escorting me?"

"Yes, and Idenion will bring Tarlion once the scolia's finished with him."

"About that," Roegin began.

"Don't feel neglected. You'll get your audition."

"That's what worries me. There's something I didn't tell you about my parentage – and the secret will be out as soon as those eager young things read

215

my mind. My mother, Tressa Halb-Maven, is – or was – an opera diva."

"Chaos, why didn't you say? The scolia are going to *love* you. Have you a voice?"

"Once, maybe. I haven't had much to sing about recently."

A flitter landed nearby.

"Here's our transport," Laura said. "Would you still prefer to walk unaided?"

"Actually, no," Roegin confessed. "May I lean on you just a little? Tallifer stamped on my knee."

Laura sighed. "You don't need to play the stoic any more, Roegin. Come on, let's get you to the clinic. And while you're laid up you can start learning Celestrian!"

During the short trip Roegin stared wordlessly through the canopy at the streets of Alda Mexa. Laura had previously related how Escir – the disgraced Escir with a Three Worlds price on his head – had cured the Celestrians' infertility and singlehandedly turned their civilisation around. He hadn't quite believed her. But now he'd seen the amount of building work going on, he conceded it was the truth. He managed to conceal from Laura – if not from the pilot – how much the little city, with its terraces and delightful jumble of architecture, appealed to him. But he wouldn't allow himself to grow fond of the place. He had unfinished business on Eldor Prime: Celestra could never be his home.

At the hospital Laura left him in the care of Drusa and a younger healer, promising to send Tarlion later to help with translation. Then she went in search of the Eldorian contingent, having agreed to deliver a cautious welcome. Escir caught up with her as she neared the visitors' suite.

"You're still in one piece, then," she remarked.

"If Clemis had told me Ymer was in charge I'd have been much less uneasy," Escir replied, slightly defensive.

"I'm not sure she *knows* Ymer."

"In that case I forgive her." Escir mustered a grin. "Is that an Earther dress? I like it. I'm not sure the boots match it, though."

"I didn't have time to change. I thought you wanted me to meet and greet."

"Maybe ..." Escir hesitated. "Maybe it would be better if you waited for Idenion. They're telling a wild story and we need to verify it." Escir outlined Keska's theory about the perpetual civil war. "It makes sense in a way – keeping everyone busy so they don't look too closely at the Senate. The war with Earth, if it had gone ahead, would have been a more solid diversion."

"Why would the two leading investigators risk their lives breaking through the Cadence?"

"They did it to bring their evidence to Veylis. They'd never have got near him else."

"As you say," Laura decided after the briefest pause, "we need Idenion. Who's with them now?"

"Habbon. They asked to see him. Two of Ymer's men are his former students."

"Habbon taught soldiers?"

"Not soldiers, military scientists. Don't worry, Laura, Habbon knows what he mustn't mention. From what I overheard, all the talk was family related. Starting with news of his ex-wives."

217

"Riveting."

"Quite. Shall we retreat to my office while we wait? I've liman on tap, or resnay if you'd prefer."

"I'd better stay off the resnay. I had two large whiskies just before I left Earth."

"Alcohol?"

"Alcohol. But I'd love some liman. It was late evening in England, and suddenly it's noon again. I need to stay alert just a little longer."

"Liman it is, then. Come on. Idenion will find us."

Once they were alone, Laura allowed her composure to slip a little. "How in chaos am I going to explain away the Gloriana?" she lamented. "We kept it so secret till after the battle – why didn't we go on doing that instead of holding that party?"

"I might be able to help with your cover story," Escir said. "I was on board just as long as you, remember, and I've been thinking around the problem ever since I knew the Cadence had been breached. Supposing we said the Gloriana was an artefact left over from the time Celestra rediscovered space travel?"

"That was thousands of years ago."

"So? It could have been a resurrected museum piece. Everyone who set foot in it will recall how shabby it was, with vast uninhabited areas."

"Exactly. It was vast. Where are we supposed to have kept it?"

"That needn't concern us. The Expeditionary Force was only here a year, and they didn't explore the Alda system."

"Well … no," said Laura, only half convinced.

"Clemis told me the Gloriana used to be a pleasure cruiser," Escir went on. "She said that the generator area used to be a swimming pool where the passengers went skinny dipping under the stars. It *sounds* Celestrian. Use it if the need arises."

"And how do the Earthers fit in?"

"That's easy. You had spheres at the ready, you had the superweapon, but you didn't have enough pilots with the temperament to fight. You recruited Earthers, trained them, then mindwiped them when the conflict was over."

"It's a bold explanation," Laura said slowly.

"And it'll work. Eldor was well aware of your visits to Earth, correct?"

"It's how they found us."

"Then you've nothing more to worry about. There's enough truth in the tale to make it plausible."

"Zanna will need to contact the class of 4024," Laura mused aloud. "Ibri can round up his engineers, and Nefyrra her scolia workers."

"Simple, isn't it? And tell me this: how many of those youngsters set eyes on the torus, or the predictive sampler, or Xorian's weird computer? None, I bet. In my opinion, they're already halfway to believing that the time travel aspect was a myth, or propaganda. I expect it'll be Idenion who instructs them, so make sure he builds on their scepticism. They'll lie more convincingly."

"You've really thought this through, haven't you?"

"Can you blame me? I've as much to lose as any of you. The plan needs fine-tuning, you understand. Don't follow it to the letter."

"Oh, I won't. I'll deliver a personal warning to Trevone and Ibri, for a start. They're the ones most likely to meet up with our visitors."

"Why those two?"

"Weapons tech. They'll be all over the Eldorian spheres, with or without the owners. Either way, they'll have my backing. We need pulse cannon that work! And Escir – before you give our Eldorian friends a clean bill of health, confer with Idenion or me. They'll still have to be supervised."

"Does that apply to Roegin as well?"

"No," Laura said instantly. "I won't confine him. He can go wherever he likes."

Still at the spaceport, Tarlion had a similar intention. "Look, Idenion, I don't know whose idea it was to hospitalise me, but it really isn't necessary. Myrig told me that most Narvellans only had a mild reaction to the bio-protections, and I'm sure my Celestrian half's no different. It makes far more sense for me to stay here, have a meal and get to know the scolia girls better."

"Oh?"

"Don't worry, I'm not planning any conquests. They're taking me to the Lyricon, to see where Lydion worked and to meet his niece Nefyrra. I didn't realise I had cousins. And apparently, Lydion's house is still empty."

"That's right," Idenion confirmed. "It's reserved for the weathershield operator, but it's too small for Tonor and his family."

"I'm not trying to lay claim to it," Tarlion went on hurriedly, "but it might do until I can find somewhere else. If Nefyrra doesn't mind."

"There's no harm in asking," Idenion conceded. "Tarlion – would all this improvisation have anything to do with *not* meeting Veylis?"

"It would. I know, I know – I'm being unreasonable. He's not responsible for what his father did."

"He never *met* his father," Idenion supplemented.

Tarlion sighed. "I know that too. I just need to settle in, unwind. Then I'll rehearse what to say to Veylis – and to whatever survives of my father, if he isn't hovering round us at this very moment."

"Lydion and Sarune are in Tafret with Relayist Nohal. They have vital information about the swarm which attacked us recently."

"Can this Nohal perceive incorporeals? Are they still dependent on that child?"

"No; there's another sensitive. His name's Rinyi, and if your plans work out you'll meet him soon enough. He's staying with Nefyrra."

***

2.7.1.4031

Nohal had been very thorough . He'd studied the quiescent Clustrals under Celestra's most

221

advanced microscope – borrowed from Scapirion – and had bombarded the specimens with simulated brainwave emissions and retraces of actual brainwaves. He's also exposed them to the prill. Selecting an EM waveband typically used by the Clustrals, he'd broadcast static, music and speech at them. There was a singular lack of response, presumably because Nohal was not Vuli. The creatures would, naturally enough, have some means of tuning out the plethora of electromagnetic signals in the cosmos.

+I don't like being trapped+ Sarune grumbled ominously. Nohal had turned the entire research block into an EMF cage.

+Neither do I, but he's almost finished+ Lydion responded, hoping to placate her. +He needed some way to contain those things, otherwise they'd have just flown off. There are way too few of them to trigger a portal but they could still have disappeared into the landscape+

Nohal was unused to Escir's newly devised table of brain activity. Much of the terminology was Eldorian, of course, with extra cycles added to denote routine perception, relayist-strength perception, and the lattice. At the top of the scale were the entrained children, with an amazing 70 cycles. Significantly, the children's frequency had prompted the Clustrals' only reaction. When exposed to it, their random output ceased and they appeared somnolent. To confirm this Nohal had run the test over and over, prompting Sarune's displeasure.

Finally he assembled his data and approached the patiently waiting Rinyi. "I'm ready to draft my report now. Lydion? Sarune? Are you there?"

Rinyi's direct yet slightly vacant stare met his. "Yes, First Relayist Nohal. They're both here."

Nohal cleared his throat. "Then tell them, feel free to embellish or amend my findings. What we have here is a bio-synthetic single-celled construct, carbon-based, resembling the exoelectrogen bacteria found on our world. Much larger, of course: my assistant can see them with the naked eye."

"Self-powering?" inquired Lydion via Rinyi. "I can do that!"

"I'll bear it in mind," Nohal said imperturbably.

Rinyi's expression shifted. "Sarune says: are you sure they're constructs?"

Surprisingly, Nohal grinned. "Really, Sarune, have you forgotten all your biology lessons? You captured a dozen entities, and sequestered them for how many days? Two? Three?"

"Three."

"Then, if they were normal bacteria, you'd be looking at a colony of thousands. These creatures are sterile. At the moment they have two objectives: maintain energy levels, carry out task. If that were to change to maintain energy, divide, carry out task, I doubt if they'd be half as focused on what they do. So far, we've seen they're individually capable of self-determination. As a swarm they can transpose across vast distances and command gravity."

"Don't sound so impressed," Lydion advised. "*I'm* not. Their science isn't that far ahead of ours –

223

they just go about it in a different way. I'm more concerned with their disposability. Vuli doesn't seem to mind squandering them, so, we need to know their numerical strength."

"As you've been invited to their homeworld, that will be for you to find out," Nohal stated.

"I'll put it on my to do list."

"I have every confidence in you, Lydion – despite your levity."

Rinyi assumed a frown. "Sarune says, can we get on with the analysis, boys?"

"I was about to." Nohal was careful not to frown back as Rinyi often took such things personally. "Tonora discovered that each bacterium has a negatively charged companion. She thinks this 'dark twin' is some kind of binary signaller. Do you concur, Lydion?"

"I'm sure she's right, but I'm fairly certain it has other functions. I'd say it's a short-term memory store."

Nohal scribbled. Lydion and Rinyi waited for him to catch up. Sarune fidgeted.

"Most importantly," Lydion then continued, "when the Cluster retreated from the second asteroid, a small percentage of the swarm was destroyed by laser fire. They *can* be eradicated, if only they'd keep still long enough."

"I'm working on that. Moving forward, I believe you have a precise fix on their homeworld?"

"Oh yes. Idenion has the co-ordinates. As soon as he and Laura have selected a crew, I can lead the way."

"This AI. If we delay our departure by much, is it likely to lose patience and return to the attack?"

"I don't think we need worry. Vuli has patience in abundance. It probably sits around for millennia between assaults on unsuspecting planets."

+Lydion+ Sarune interrupted, +I can't tolerate this EMF screen much longer. My energy levels are depleted+

+Mine aren't. What have you been doing?+

+Catching those little vermin and keeping them alive. And thirdly, I've just conducted a small experiment of my own+ She indicated the Clustrals, huddled at the centre of the null-field where she'd deposited them. Lydion focused painstakingly on their tiny patterns. There were now only eleven pairs.

+They haven't escaped+ Sarune informed him. +I, er, crushed a positive and a negative from different couples+

+You'll be pulling the wings off flies next+

+I wanted to see if the remaining ones would form a fresh pair+ Sarune went on. +They did, and immediately started a dialogue+

+So? It's an economy. It reduces losses+

+Clones?+

+Maybe. Or endless duplicates. And that means there must be an original or a template somewhere. Something easier to destroy. Now get us out of here+

Lydion hastily reconnected with the bewildered Rinyi and apologised for the hiatus. "We have to leave the facility now. Send us the full report as soon as you can. And be assured, I'll be recommending that we go prepared for conflict. Appeasement is not an option, except as a delaying tactic. Vuli has to be stopped."

***

Alda Mexa 7.7.1.4031

One octal later, the Eldorians were over the worst of their species-specific fever. Keska had nicknamed it the Celestra love-bite, and the term had immediately been adopted by the rest of the party. After cogitation Escir had administered two of the three remaining doses of anti-virals to Veylis – in view of his father's near fatal reaction – and to Ymer, as the effects were always worse for returning visitors.

Roegin had received the final dose, but even with its help had been laid low. Escir had left him in Drusa's capable hands and stopped by whenever he could. He knew something of the pathogen inflicted on the Covert Ops division, and it wasn't his favourite memory. The virologists had been so pleased with their work, from the initial dormant state of the toxin-producing virus to the way a single missing gene ensured the vulnerable nuclei perished on the death of the host.

"Is that to keep the Earthers from harm?" Escir had asked innocently.

"It won't affect them," came the supremely confident reply. "We just don't want them getting their hands on something that kills *us*."

226

Yet in defiance of their expectations, Roegin had survived. He'd fought off the Celestrian fever too. Six days after being floored by it he was sitting up in bed and yelling at Drusa.

"At last! *You* deal with him," she said when Escir appeared.

"Sorry," Roegin muttered when she'd left. "She wouldn't get rid of this IV line. I thought I was done with all that."

Escir had noticed the needle marks on his arms. "What in Ebbondrear were those Earthers doing to you, Roegin?"

"Preventing a relapse, they said."

"Preventing? With what? Once the virus is active the effects are irreversible – supposedly. I'm very curious to know how they saved you."

"I only know what they told me. They were days away from perfecting a cure, but I didn't have days. I was dying, they had nothing to lose, so they tried an experiment. Lowering my body temperature to ten degrees above freezing, and keeping it there, gave them the time they needed."

"And how long were you in this state?"

"I don't know. Three or four days I suppose."

"With your core temperature that low I'm surprised they managed to revive you," Escir remarked. "A daring procedure. I'm impressed."

"They said it was costly."

"I can believe that. Well, that answers my question. As far as the virus was concerned, you were dead. It self-destructed as it was designed to do."

"They saved me by accident?"

"On the contrary, I think they knew exactly what they were doing. I assume they'd taken blood samples?"

"Many times."

"And, having isolated the virus, they exposed it to extremes of heat and cold. It's the first thing *I'd* have done."

Roegin stared. "Then if I was clear of it, what was all that stuff they kept injecting me with?"

"A ruse to ensure your dependence," Escir surmised. "Something harmless, obviously. Vitamins, iron –"

"That lying bitch!"

Escir raised an eyebrow.

"Ann. The woman who was murdered. I thought she – oh, never mind. She lied."

Escir let him spiral down from that. "Have any of the Cadence escapees been to see you?"

"The girl, Keska. She reckons she has a good case against the warmongers in the Senate and wants me to testify."

"You'd never get a chance to speak," Escir declared. "Don't get drawn in. Not when Laura's given you leave to stay."

"I haven't said I'm staying."

"You'd be mad not to." Escir was unequivocal. "Anyway, you'll have time to think it over. The First Citizens won't be in a hurry to repatriate Ymer and his pals while whoever diverted those asteroids is still out there."

Roegin managed a sour smile. "I heard the pulse-cannon came in useful."

"And will again, no doubt. So before it all kicks off I suggest you acquaint yourself with the good people of this city and start enjoying life. I'm discharging you tomorrow."

***

+Lydion, talk to me+

Sarune was trying to be conciliatory. It didn't quite work, so she gave up the attempt.

+Lydion, chaos take you, stop this brooding!! *You* called this conference, *you* suggested the Alda Mexa observatory as a venue, and everyone's arriving. You've a pivotal role in this. You have to focus!+

At last he replied, but appeared to ignore her plea. +Ever since Sijek told me about Tarlion, I dreamt that he'd turn up one day. And when he did, no-one thought to *tell* me! I didn't know he was on Symerid Three, nor that Laura had gone looking for him. Idenion didn't say a word!+

+Because he had weightier things on his mind+ Sarune declared. +And because we needed to be on top form to handle the Clustrals+

+Fine. We did that. And then we get back from Nohal's and Nefyrra says she has a surprise for me. All so casual. Didn't anyone realise how I'd react? My son can't see me, hear me nor touch me. I can't read him and he can't read me. That leaves Rinyi, who's behaving like the relayist he once was. A conduit for information. Little Tonora's a bit better but she can't show me visuals. It isn't enough, Sarune!+

+Lydion -+

+It's different for Tarlion. He can read Nefyrra's memory, and Tonor's. He can see what I looked like. He can play my retraces if he wants. I don't have any of those options. I can never see him, unless -+

+So *that's* why you were shutting me out! Lydion, you can't do this. You can't push Rinyi's consciousness aside and risk harming him when he's so vital to the expedition. You have to talk with Vuli, and Rinyi has to interpret. No-one else can do that except Tonora, and I somehow don't think Tonor would allow her on this mission+

+You took up residence in someone else's head. It can be done. Did any harm come to Passik's brother?+

+I didn't wait to find out. In any case, he was just a shell. Rinyi's much more than that. And have you forgotten about Dena? I nearly killed her+

+She nearly died of a miscarriage. And you inhabited her mind for how long? A day? Two? I'm talking about moments+

+Moments, is it? Supposing you get stuck? *I* nearly did!+

+Please don't quarrel+ Rinyi's thoughts broke in.

+Chaos, I forgot he could hear us+ Lydion unsuccessfully tried to be surreptitious.

+I want to help+ Rinyi went on. +Sarune, let me do this. Consider it repayment for my new life. Lydion's so kind+

+Is he indeed?+ Sarune remarked.

230

Lydion felt even more wretched.

+But it isn't just that+ Rinyi added earnestly. +Lydion and I have a parallel history. We both had affairs with elite-wives who gave birth to our sons. We both had our partners taken from us. The difference is that Lydion's son survived and mine didn't. If he had, if he suddenly turned up ...+ Rinyi faltered at this point. It had been a long speech for him, but he'd said enough.

+I assumed Rinyi would obey under duress+ said Sarune. +His willingness changes things. I believe, Lydion, that you'll handle Vuli better if you resolve the Tarlion situation first. So, I'll guide you. And if all three of us get into trouble with the First Citizens, so be it+

+Before we start,+ ventured Rinyi, +there's something I need to ask, Sarune+

+Then ask+

+It was because of me that Quetri was recruited, and later sent to attack the Synectics. I just want your assurance that there's no ill feeling+

+At the time, I blamed Quetri for the failure of the project+ Sarune answered candidly. +But he wasn't the cause. Neither was Tralvar. The fault lay with the Synectics' inability to work together. They'd never have been strong enough to take that evolutionary step. And I've gradually come to realise what a lucky escape I had. I could have been tied to those bigoted patriarchs forever. I'm free now. And I'm glad. Now let's go and find Tarlion+

+I know where he is+ said Rinyi.

At that moment Tarlion, newest tenant of Lydion's former home, was in earnest conversation with Nefyrra.

"I know it seems ridiculous to go chasing across the galaxy when I've only just arrived here, but as my father's involved I want to be part of this confrontation – if that's the right word."

"Knowing Lydion, I'd say it's exactly the right word." Nefyrra smiled ruefully.

"You're not going?"

"I'm going to the meeting, mostly to keep an eye on Rinyi. He doesn't like large groups of people. But I won't be going offworld."

"How many delegates are we talking about?"

"Not as many as I'd expected. Thirty or so. As we're at the observatory the other city states can take part via transposer link conferencing."

"I thought transposal was strictly one link at a time?"

"It is. But all our observatories and communications centres now have several transposers each. We did an upgrade after the war with Eldor, to assist with defence. And, since you're about to ask, I've never been offworld. Unless you count orbital flights to Tafret. You take after Lykalion, your grandfather. *He* was the wanderer. Lydion didn't travel much."

"But he did go to Myrma, didn't he? Please tell me it wasn't a myth!"

"Oh yes, he went. So did a lot of young men, at that time. A rite of passage, I suppose, in a more frivolous era. Hardly anyone goes there now."

"I might. Later."

"Then be sure to take plenty of gifts. That's the main reason we stopped: the Myrmians were becoming too mercenary. We felt our presence was disrupting their social evolution."

+Well, there they are, Lydion!+ Rinyi paused at the doorway. +Are you ready?+

+As ready as I'll ever be+

+Can you see through my eyes?+

+Yes. Well, not quite. I'm reading the images as you process them. But I've no audio feed yet+

+He's not a logic system, Lydion+ Sarune remonstrated. +I've told him to close off his perception, so you'll be able to concentrate on sight and sound+

Lydion's discomfort increased. Rinyi hadn't been looking after himself. Impressions of back pain, aching feet and calloused hands drifted in and out of his precariously focused senses.

+Don't forget what we agreed+ Sarune continued warningly. +You're to remain passive. You'll be able to see Tarlion, and hopefully hear him, but don't try and speak. You might not like the result. And let Rinyi do the walking or you could end up flat on your face. *His* face+

But at his first glimpse of Tarlion, Lydion promptly forgot these admonitions. He stumbled forward, arms outstretched to embrace his startled son. He tried to speak, only managed a croak, tried again. "It's …me! Lydion! You look so like your mother …." Then Tarlion's image dissolved in a wash of tears. Sarune maintained an exasperated silence. And somewhere close by, Rinyi was asking if he was all right. Nefyrra echoed the question.

"Yes. Yes, I'm more than all right. So's Rinyi. We did it. I'm delighted. I'm giving back control to Rinyi now …"

Nefyrra scrutinised Rinyi minutely. "He shouldn't have done that. How do you feel?"

Rinyi straightened his shoulders. "Alert. Energised."

"The sharing strengthened you?" asked Tarlion, only marginally surprised. Narvellan medicine worked along similar lines.

"Yes. I'm stronger. It probably won't last, but for now …" Rinyi smiled. "I think it's time we left for the observatory. Shall I send for a flitter?"

"If you –" began Tarlion, then hesitated, not wishing to put a dent in the reducee's newly acquired confidence.

"Yes, I can do it," Rinyi assured him. "I was a leading relayist once. Second only to Kyrin, some said. I think I can manage one simple message."

"Tarlion," said Nefyrra, "if you're resolved on joining the expedition, you *must* set up a recording session before you go. My scolia will be very disappointed if you don't."

"They'll be disappointed if I *do*," he answered lightly. "My voice is mediocre and Narvellan songs are rubbish. Get Roegin to record something. Music's in his family."

"So I've heard. I'll need to choose my moment."

"He could sing a duet with Escir," Tarlion continued.

Nefyrra and Rinyi both chuckled.

"I don't know why we're laughing," Nefyrra added. "Someone's just declared war on us."

"We're laughing because our chief negotiator – our *only* negotiator – is happy, and eager to commence his task," said Tarlion.

"And," added Rinyi, "he knows he can share my consciousness without causing me harm. That could be very useful."

"Where *is* Lydion now?" Nefyrra asked him.

"I'm not sure. He took off in glee, and Sarune followed him."

"He'll catch us up. Come on, you two. Let's head for the pick-up point."

Lydion, euphoric, had spread his energies in a wide ribbon, encircling one of the Lyricon's columns and reaching for the next in line.

+What are you doing?+ Sarune demanded.

+Stretching+

+Well, don't. You do too much of that. Haven't I warned you against thinning out?+

+You have. Oh, you have. Over and over+

+Then calm down. You're proposing to address a hostile AI on behalf of your people, so today's assembly needs to know they can trust you. You have to be the model of sobriety+

+*That* won't work. They know me of old, remember+

+Then at least be polite+

+To the Administrators? I can't see that working either. I think I'll just be me+

Sarune gave the equivalent of a sigh. +Business as usual, then. At least promise you'll treat Rinyi respectfully+

+Agreed. And so must you. *You're* the one he's scared of+

+I think he's over that now+

+Let's hope so. Actually I'm a little daunted myself. Administrators, Prefects, scientists -+

+And Zanna+

+What?+

+She's bound to be there, to explain about the space mines+

+Sometimes, Sarune, you say exactly the right thing. Consider yourself hugged+

+Don't push it.   Now make yourself presentable and let's go+

Chapter Nine

Before the discussion could begin in earnest, Idenion had to ensure that the delegates – including those not actually present – had received all available data on the Clustrals. He and Daphos had previously circulated the earliest scans from Alda Six, Trevone's shipboard logs of the encounters with both asteroids, and Nohal's analysis of the captured organisms. While the distribution was in progress Tarlion and Rinyi arrived late, Rinyi laughing at a remark Lydion had just made. On seeing them, Sheyell suppressed a sob and hurried from the lecture hall. Idenion went after her, leaving Daphos in charge. She hadn't gone far: he found her in the nearest corridor, still fighting back tears and resolutely shielding her thoughts.

"Sheyell," he said gently. "Nefyrra told me that Rinyi distresses you. I assumed you were averse to his mental state, but I see it's more profound than that. As he's necessary to these proceedings, you need to tell me what's going on."

She gazed past him into the middle distance. "He's my son," she said at last. "A product of Alendis' eugenics programme."

Idenion successfully hid his surprise. "Tell me the rest, Sheyell. You must."

She sighed. "I was a trainee relayist, newly pubescent. Alendis selected me and two other girls to be inseminated by leading relayists of the day. He was so plausible, so persuasive – he said it would be like sciesha only more civilised, that we'd get to know our partners first. I was assigned to Hieros of Alcine."

"*Hieros?* But he must have been - "

"Old." She managed a weak smile. "Younger than I am now, but he seemed ancient to me. He wasn't enthusiastic. I was a plain little thing. But, we got it over with. And I conceived. Neither of the others did. I gave Rinyi up, of course, as one would a sciesha child, but I couldn't go back to my training. I didn't have the right detachment any more. City admin was dull and safe. I followed Rinyi's progress of course. He was an excellent relayist. And then he started work for that selfish creature Isylla. The rest you know. It agonises me to look at the poor damaged simpleton he became, all due to Alendis and that obscene programme of his."

"But the programme worked, Sheyell. Rinyi was exceptional."

"And if he hadn't been, if he'd had a different father, Isylla wouldn't have employed him. He'd have had a normal life. Now do you see why I wanted Alendis' records destroyed?"

"I do see, but we can't undo what's been done. If there are other talented people out there, they could be helping us now. Do you know of any others?"

"I had a friend in the scolia. Tiphane. She gave birth to a thoroughly ordinary daughter and Alendis dropped her from the programme. But that daughter became the mother of Patra, Tonor's wife."

"And *she* gave birth to Tonora," Idenion breathed. "Sheyell – you do realise I'll need to follow this up? You needn't be involved but I have to trace the other descendants."

"I won't object," Sheyell said wearily. "I'm sorry I kept this to myself. I thought I'd never have to see Rinyi again."

"Idenion?" Laura had appeared in the corridor. "We're waiting for you. Is there a problem?"

"No, not any more. Ready, Sheyell?"

"Ready."

They ran each datastream twice, as many present had never seen a Cluster at work. There was no sound, as the bursts of static had been rendered into graphs. Laura gazed long and intently at the ever-shifting Clustral formations as they veered this way and that, surging and wheeling.

"They remind me of something," she mused. "Murmuration."

"After all this time, an English word I don't know!" Idenion said, surprised.

"It means, a huge flock of starlings. Birds. I used to see them over the fields beyond Cheveney, flying in similar patterns to the Clustrals."

"Were they attacking something?"

"No. I'm not sure why they do it. Affirming their community, perhaps."

Idenion stared gloomily at the screen. Lydion's right, he thought privately. Beam weapons alone won't protect us. And I now have to go on air and say the opposite.

Nefyrra leant across from her station. "Idenion, Rinyi's ready to speak. Will you announce him?"

"Just as soon as Daphos assures me that all monitoring teams are scouring the spectrum for Clustral activity. Vuli may have stopped the attacks but I don't trust him not to snoop."

"All regions report no change," said Daphos after a pause. "Still clear."

"Very well." Idenion rose to his feet and faced the array of transposer screens, each linked to a different city state. Serious faces looked back at him. "People of Celestra: for the next part of our briefing I present Rinyi, last survivor of the Narvellan punishment squads. Despite the injury he suffered – or maybe because of it – he's able to channel the two beings most vital to our defence. Lydion, resonance expert and creator of the Cadence: and Sarune, the Synectic coordinator whose benign intervention gave Lydion life in his present form ..."

+Benign?+ repeated Lydion, amused.

+Well, what did you expect him to say?+ Sarune retorted. +Totally selfish intervention?+

+We-e-ll ...+

+It's irrelevant anyway. This is your show, Lydion. They don't want to hear from me+

Rinyi wasted no time on further introductions. "Citizens, I speak as Lydion. After the second asteroid was successfully removed, the commander of the Clustrals – an artificial intelligence calling itself Vuli – made itself known to Sarune and myself. It believed that we too were constructs. It seems that, as a civilisation presumed capable of producing AI's, Celestra has been reassessed: now, instead of being summarily annihilated, we get to

240

speak in our own defence. I negotiated a stand-off while we prepared a response. Apparently we're a threat to the Protected Realm, whatever that is. It will be down to our expedition to convince Vuli that we aren't, and that the Bad Resonance, the cause of this unwelcome attention, was an accident. All very civilised. Unfortunately, it won't happen like that. Let's not forget that Vuli is the aggressor, and that it made the mistake of thinking we'd attained the same technological level as our ancestors. If we hadn't surpassed it, we wouldn't be having this conference.

"In a moment, star charts will be displayed, showing the location of Vuli's world as seen from Celestra, the Eldor system, and Earth. Once you've seen this you'll doubtless realise why our explorers never found it. I should also remind you that Vuli has stipulated that we bring delegates from each species involved in the bad resonance event."

"Are *you* going?" someone asked obscurely.

"Yes, and yes," Rinyi answered with a smile. "I, Rinyi, will vocalise Lydion; and I, Lydion, will do my best to handle Vuli's lofty pronouncements. Now, take a look at these charts."

Trevone took over. "The first picture on your screens is of the Cowl, as we call it. A dark nebula bordering a starless region of our galaxy. And here it as it is seen from the Eldor system."

"That's Ebbon's Glove," said Ymer. "I didn't recognise it at first."

"That's because we only see its edge from Celestra. Earth has a better view." He switched pictures again. "Laura's people call it the Northern

Coalsack. And if anyone's interested, Earth, Celestra and the Cowl are equidistant."

"And that's where Vuli's world is?" asked the Prefect of Alcine. "In that cloud?"

"Correct. It orbits a red dwarf star, previously uncharted."

"If it's no further away than Earth, why has no-one been there?"

Moron, thought Trevone irritably. The Prefect had opted for remote conferencing, so couldn't read him, but those present could. Trevone wasn't particularly worried.

"It's to do with transposal and the way it operates," he replied evenly. "One needs to programme a destination – and in the case of a dark nebula full of unknown, unseen hazards, that simply wasn't possible. It *is* possible to transpose without a programme, and I've done so myself a couple of times – thanks to my dear wife when she was too young to know any better. I lived to tell the tale, but I don't recommend the experience. Our early explorers sensibly sought more congenial destinations. Ones they could see."

"Then is the journey still dangerous?"

"No, because we have an exact location and can transpose straight to it. Any more questions?"

"Yes, for the First Citizens," said the Prefect. "Why have you brought Eldorians to this conference?"

Several of the delegates frowned. Idenion and Laura doubtless had their reasons and no-one wanted to object.

242

"They asked to attend," Idenion replied blandly. "Captain Ymer will explain."

Ymer rose to his feet. "Citizens and dignitaries, I speak for my scientist colleague Keska, whose Celestrian is insufficient for this occasion. As we left the region of the Transfix – our name for the Cadence – the schism we had created melded together, shutting us out. Keska set her instruments to record any changes in the structure, and saw something she didn't understand at the time. She had in fact witnessed hundreds if not thousands of Clustrals dashing themselves to destruction against the newly sealed barrier. So, we have a dilemma. We came here in the hope of persuading you to take down the Cadence. But if it were removed, we'd immediately find ourselves under attack by the Clustrals. We want them stopped as much as you do."

Nefyrra spoke next. "Our decryption experts have been looking for patterns in the static generated by the Clustrals. As specific attention was paid to each city-state in turn, we're hoping to find characteristics associated with each location. If we come under attack on a more localised basis, as seems probable after the failure of the asteroids, we hope to determine which area or areas to defend. Our task has been made simpler by the Communications team at Kest, who recorded the interference in its entirety. My thanks to you, Warden." She nodded toward the Kest transposer link.

The Warden, unused to praise, blushed. "You're – you're welcome," he stammered. It had been an accident, of course. Someone had left a channel open and unattended for days. But this time, negligence had paid off.

"Are we presupposing that our negotiations will fail?" asked Sheyell.

"We have to," returned Idenion. "The alternative is to sit around and wait to be decimated a second time."

The next speak was Jarras, co-opted out of retirement to resume his position at Treva Academy. "Our main tactical advantage is that any Cluster, in order to function, has to announce its presence. Students at the Academy and at various other centres across the globe are assembling rudimentary radio receivers. No-one foresaw that we, as telepaths, would depend on radio for our safety; so we can't hope to equip every citizen within the given timeframe. But we can certainly supply every relayist in every city-state. If and when the Clustrals are detected, each relayist can alert his or her neighbourhood."

"And then what happens?" asked the Atrisian delegate.

"The regional administrators, under Dessin's direction, will have circulated instructions to be followed in an emergency," replied Idenion somewhat evasively. An inevitable barrage of questions followed, but he refused to elaborate. The plans were incomplete, and potentially controversial. "What I *can* tell you," he concluded, "is that half the Eldorian contingent, plus two of their spheres, will remain here for the duration of the mission. Our combined armaments will ensure

244

a strong defence, should it be required. Also, while on stand-by, the Eldorian team will work with our engineers in Treva to install pulse-cannon technology in as many of our spheres as possible."

The final item on the agenda was, of course, who would confront Vuli and when. Again, Idenion was unforthcoming. "A date will be set as soon as the mission spacecraft have been serviced and tested. A full list of crew members will be released nearer that time. Thank you for your patience, citizens. This meeting is now concluded." He signalled Daphos, who cut the transposer feeds.

"Spoken like an English politician," Laura said amusedly. "But I suppose you have your reasons."

Idenion did. When people learnt that both he and Laura would be on the crew list, there'd be an outcry – one he was anxious to avoid until Laura herself knew what he was planning. Laura *had* to go: she had to be present following the Clustrals' study of Cheveney. And Idenion had no intention of being separated from her again. It was as simple and incontrovertible as that.

Meanwhile Lydion had cajoled a bashful Rinyi into speaking with Zanna, to determine if she'd volunteered for the trip. The answer, disappointingly, was no. "I thought about it," she said, "but Idenion says my piloting skills will be more useful here. Someone has to fly our upgraded spheres, and our current generation lacks combat experience."

Lydion thanked her and was about to add an endearment, but refrained. There was nothing of

the passionate lover in today's Zanna, just a coolly professional spacewoman.

"Lydion," she continued carefully, "you'll be everyone's spokesman when you meet this AI. Correct?"

"Vuli may be able to read all of us. No-one knows yet."

"But you're the one it considers superior. You said it was lofty, and I take that to mean patronising, high-handed?"

"That would be about right."

"Then take care not to antagonise it. You know what you're like!"

"I shall be diplomacy personified."

"Will you? I know you of old, remember. Just keep it sweet. And stay out of trouble."

"Oh, I will!" Lydion declared with absolute confidence.

"I'm glad you're so sure." Zanna moved away, but before Rinyi could rejoin the Alda Mexa delegation, Ruvrin bounded up.

"Rinyi, are you channelling Lydion at the moment? Oh, good. I wanted to ask him – well, I suppose I should say ask *you* – more about the tiny universes and other dimensions you spoke of at Scapirion."

"What did you want to know?"

"Anything you can tell me. I didn't have a chance to quiz you earlier, as the Cadence took precedence, but I'm still fascinated. Will you have time for a teensy bit of mentoring before you leave?"

Lydion prompted Rinyi to smile. "Since I can't help with building radios and renovating spheres, the answer would appear to be yes. But, I don't do teensy. Expect a full-on brainstorming session. Would tomorrow suit you?"

"Perfect. Tomorrow it is, then. At Nefyrra's."

***

1.8.1 4031

"Hello there, big boy!"

Roegin sat up, puzzled. A small, improbably slim woman with an impish smile was wheeling a rack of clothes into his room.

"Esc says you can leave today so I've brought you some things to try on. Can't have you wandering around town in that dreadful Earther suit!"

"You speak Eldorian."

"Why shouldn't I? I'm married to one!"

He smiled then, tiredly. "You must be Ailsi. Did Escir send you to throw me out?"

"He thought you might need showing round a bit, on your first day of freedom in chaos knows how many years. I've neglected my dance practice to do this, so if you aren't nice to me I'll run off and leave you. Yes, you presume right – you'll be walking out of here emptyhanded. You don't need possessions to make your way in this city."

"So I've heard."

"Then you know how it works. Provide a service to Alda Mexa, and Alda Mexa will look after you."

"Fine. Do you know anyone who needs spying on?"

She grinned again. "I don't think that would work here. But you Eldorian men have good singing voices. Deliver a few songs at the Lyricon and the city will be yours!"

"Don't *you* start!"

"Tarlion's with the scolia as we speak. Care to join him?"

"He's blended right in, hasn't he? I knew he would."

"You could too!"

"I'm not so sure." He inspected the garments: tunics, jerkins and trousers in plain bright colours, indicative of a simplistic way of life. "What about footwear?"

"Sorted. We took those beat-up old shoes you arrived in and used them as templates. You now have a lovely pair of bespoke boots made by one of our best craftsmen. Esc's always complaining of cold feet so I knew you wouldn't want sandals."

"I might want socks."

Ailsi laughed. "Just as I thought. Another fashion disaster, like Esc. I'll get you some of his favourite knee-length firi stockings. Here's your underwear." She took a bag from the rail and tipped out an assortment of thongs and pouches. "Bit too draughty for you? Tell you what – I'll raid Escir's secret stash of Army undershorts, and bring you a few pairs."

248

"Please do."

Ailsi took a step toward the door, then turned back. "Look if you really can't decide how to spend the day, maybe we should concentrate on finding you somewhere to live."

"Will that be difficult?"

"Of course not. I've a few ideas, but we're going to need a flitter and someone to fly it. I never could get the hang of it."

"Where are the other Eldorians staying?"

"The scientists all went to Treva to work on pulse-cannon. The others will be at the akron, I assume, planning strategy with Laura."

"*She's* not going on this weird mission, surely?"

"Earth created part of the Bad Resonance. She's no choice."

"Ebbon's blood!" Roegin paced the room. "I didn't realise. I offered to go, but Escir said I wouldn't survive a second bout of protection fever."

"Laura's a veteran of conflict. She'll be fine." Ailsi put a dainty hand on his arm. "Roegin – whatever your long term plans are, today's all about *you*. You have to start living for yourself now."

"I suppose."

"Try it, just for a while. Now, where to?"

He squared his shoulders. "Is there a gym?"

She read him for a moment. "Not as you understand it."

"A swimming pool, then. There was an outdoor pool at the manor but they wouldn't let me use it. Couldn't spare anyone to stand guard."

Ailsi's eyes lit up. "You're a good swimmer?"

"I was."

"Then I know just the place for a day out. And I know just the person to get you back in trim. She might help with your living quarters too."

"She …?"

"Won't be long!"

The door slammed and Roegin was temporarily alone. He was, he knew, being a sour and ungrateful guest. It wouldn't hurt him to sing once or twice. Except that it would put him in mind of his mother and the life he could have had. He'd inherited her vocal talent, but after the death of General Drice a career in entertainment was no longer an option. He needed a guaranteed salary such as Covert Ops provided, so he could continue his father's task of shoring up Tressa's profligate lifestyle. Silly, flighty, foolish Tressa. Destitute or dead now, he supposed. The Transfix team might know, but he didn't feel like asking.

Presently Ailsi returned. "Here. Shorts, socks, boots. Not chosen an outfit yet?" She yanked a pale green leisure suit from the rail and threw it onto the bed. "This'll do. It compliments your eye colour. Now get dressed."

"Under your supervision?"

She ignored that. "Be outside in one astal. A flitter's waiting to take us to the monorail terminal. Someone's meeting us there."

After a brisk flight across the lower laterals, Ailsi ushered Roegin into the small station with its single platform. There he was greeted by another woman, slightly taller than Ailsi and with the sinewy slimness of late middle age. It was impossible to tell how old she was, as her face was as unlined as a girl's.

"I'm delighted to meet you," she said, in passable Eldorian. "I'm Dena, Idenion's sister."

Ailsi smiled mischievously. "Don't worry, Roegin, you needn't be on your best behaviour. She's used to Eldorians. She gave a home to Geffin, that reporter of yours. Did you know him?"

"I knew *of* him," Roegin said. "There was a rumour going round the service that he was trading our secrets."

"He was," admitted Dena. "And it can do no harm to tell you now."

"Is he still here?"

Dena hesitated. "No. He – disappeared."

"So they got to him, did they? Shame."

"Right," said Ailsi, "you two seem to have hit it off so I'll leave you to it. There's a revue at the Lyricon in a couple of days, so I really should put in some rehearsal time."

Roegin frowned. "A concert? *Now*?"

"Well, yes. We don't know when we'll next get the chance. Tonor says that if the Clustrals show up we'll have to cut the electricity to stop them feeding on it. No electricity means no weathershield. No weathershield means we'll get rained on. So, I'll be at the Lyricon if you need me. Have fun!"

She returned to the flitter and was gone.

Roegin, slightly bemused, followed Dena onto the train. The carriage was half full, mostly young people in groups. He wondered why no-one was staring at him, then remembered that if they wanted to study him they didn't need to stare. "Where are we going?"

"Lake Holpen. I swim there whenever I can. It's a lovely spot."

"As long as the water isn't too cold."

"We're in early summer, so it doesn't get much warmer. You'll be fine. Geffin was always cold but you don't seem to be."

"Geffin didn't spend a decade in England."

"I was there once, the day we found Laura," Dena reminisced. "Warm and showery – not that I was taking much notice. I was terrified. So was Idenion, though he's never admitted it. We'd no idea what we were getting into. But Laura was amazing. She just took charge."

"I can imagine," said Roegin. "She's good at that."

***

"Are you sure that's all of them?"

"Yes. All he wrote down, anyway." Idenion closed one of Alendis' files and laid it aside, taking care not to overturn any others. "I'd made some inroads before Sheyell's revelations."

"Right," said Laura briskly. "Let's put Ansela in charge of this. She's level-headed and trustworthy. We'll tell her to choose her best assistant archivists, go to the registry and check every single one of those names. We want lists of all partners past and present, all offspring and all *their* offspring, youngest generation in particular. We need to know their ages, locations, and if

252

they're currently in a relayist programme or similar."

"And then?"

"Then we let Nohal take over, to find more children who can sustain a seventy cycle lattice in the event of a Cluster attack."

Idenion looked troubled.

"I know it sounds dangerous, but we have to trust Nohal. We don't have a choice."

"There'll be protests."

"I think we've built up enough goodwill to offset that, don't you?"

"The children might not want to do it."

"If you truly believe that, Idenion, then you don't know our kids. And they won't be working in isolation. Nohal says some of our relayists – Kyrin for instance – can reach sixty- five cycles in short bursts. The Guild wants you to authorise the use of starfire in an emergency."

Idenion sighed. "I suppose I'll have to allow it. Do you know what's ironic? The Narvellans could have dealt with this. The Five, the Ten – they were way in excess of that frequency. Maybe we should try Tarlion out."

"You can't make him stay behind now you've agreed he can come with us," argued Laura. "One individual won't make much difference here. Anyway, I've seen him in action and his abilities aren't great. Ask Clemis."

Idenion held up his hands in mock surrender. "All right, bad idea. Maybe it's time to stop talking."

"Maybe it is. Let's find Ansela and get her started on the research."

***

Roegin liked Lake Holpen – a vast sunny expanse of crystal clear water, fringed by trees and a shingle beach. Near the monorail was a drinks bar and a store supplying rugs, towels, beachwear and sun umbrellas. Further away lay a boathouse. Overnight stays were obviously not catered for, which seemed a pity. He wouldn't have minded a few days to recoup and thoroughly unwind, as the current occupants of the beach were doing.

Dena had offered him lodgings, and he'd accepted, but it was beginning to seem as though all roads led to the Lyricon. He still wasn't sure what Dena's job title was, but it involved children, costumes and choreography. Just as long as no-one asked him to sing.

Dena was waving and beckoning to him from a wooden pontoon anchored far from the shore. He hoped she realised he wasn't going to make the attempt. After a few experimental lengths in the shallows he'd realised how out of condition he was. It would be too embarrassing if he got into difficulties and had to be rescued by her.

Eventually she came back and they sauntered across to the bar. He wondered why liman tasted so much better in these surroundings.

"Care for a massage?" she asked.

He blinked.

"Oh, *I* shan't be doing it! There's a spa. See?" She indicated a modest one storey building in the distance, half hidden by a stand of trees. Roegin had assumed it was another storehouse.

"We've always had a spa at Corayn, but this one's fairly new," Dena went on. "You can have a full body massage with pilif flower oil, an exfoliating scrub with Virdan sea minerals, or just soak in a Scapirian hot tub. And afterward, a complimentary glass of fruit and resnay cordial."

"The drink sounds promising, at least. Do you intend sampling these delights?"

"Possibly. First of all, I want to catch up with a friend who works here. She gave palliative care to my late partner. Her medicines may not have prolonged his life but they certainly improved the quality of his last days."

Roegin fell into step beside her. He was quietly enjoying having his day organised, but still hadn't shaken off the wariness and watchfulness that had been so much a part of his life. Here in this laidback place there was no need to keep looking over his shoulder. He needed to relax while he could.

"We can help you with that," said Dena.

To his own surprise he didn't bridle at having his mind read. "I'm all yours," he answered.

Ciela was younger than he expected, around the same age as Clemis, with long brown hair and a warm smile. "Dena! If you'd told me you were bringing someone I wouldn't have been so ill prepared. We're just setting up for the season.

We're short of floral essences and the hot tub hasn't been delivered."

"Then give Roegin one of your deep cleanse specials. Something manly to get rid of all that tension!"

Roegin wasn't attempting to follow the conversation. His gaze remained fixed on Ciela. "I've seen you before."

"Laura warned me about your appalling chat-up lines," Dena said reprovingly. "Apologise to Ciela."

"It wasn't an approach," Roegin protested. "I *have* seen her before. Years ago."

"In your dreams?" Dena inquired sceptically.

"Wait," Roegin said, frowning.

Then he remembered. His colleague Buuth had dragged him along to watch a pirated Celestrian video – the many loves of Pervain's victim Lydion. The women had formed a procession at the end, with Geffin's camera team singling out the youngest and prettiest for close-ups. Ciela had been one such choice.

"You have a good memory for faces," she said, in slow careful Eldorian.

"It goes with the training. But it helps if the face has charm."

Dena gave him an exasperated glare, but Ciela merely smiled. "Let's see if my work impresses you too. This way."

She took his arm. He didn't shrug her off.

Once she had applied the cleansing pack, she left him to snooze and hurried back to Dena. "I'm so pleased you brought him! He interests me."

256

Dena wasn't entirely surprised. "Care to tell me why?"

"Suppressed melancholy. And he's so difficult to read. You must have noticed! How did you become his minder, anyway? I thought all the Cadence escapees were in Treva."

"He didn't escape the Cadence. He's been a prisoner on Earth since the battle."

"Chaos!" Ciela looked even more intrigued. "What else do you know?"

Dena smiled indulgently. "I only met him today. But I guarantee he'll be at the lake again, without me in tow. I'm sure you'll get your answers."

***

3.8.1.4031

Gradually the plan took shape. It was decided that Ymer, reasonably sympathetic to the Celestrian cause, would remain at Treva with his Patieron crewmen Nirik, Thaed and Hyberl. Having their commanding officer present would ensure they followed orders to the letter, rather than in any way that suited them. Also, Ymer's skill with the pulse-cannon had already been demonstrated. All four Transfix spheres had been serviced and tested, and two new pulse-cannon had left the assembly line.

The expedition's fighting contingent would be Trevone, in charge of the one dispersal engine to be assigned; Tarlion, with his useful knack of coping with the unexpected; Veylis, Fley and Keska, who had unanimously refused to be left behind; and science chief Brome, whose political neutrality had been endorsed by Habbon.

That left the non-combatants: Idenion, Laura, Rinyi and the two incorporeals.

"This is poor strategy," Fley was heard to declare. "We shouldn't waste time on conciliation. Now we'll be obliged to watch their backs when we should be finishing the job quickly."

"Gently, father," advised Keska. "The Celestrians may have different methods but they do have a habit of winning. And as we need that to happen, we have to co-operate fully. Agreed?"

It was the morning of the much anticipated concert, and a capacity audience was expected once the announcement was made.

"Where's Rinyi?" Laura asked Idenion.

"Still closeted with Ruvrin, and Lydion of course. And before you ask, I've no idea what they're doing. It'll be Cadence related, no doubt."

"Have you heard from Ansela today?"

"Yes; her people have traced three more eugenic descendants. Scolia hopefuls, every one."

"Good. That makes them easier to train."

Idenion scrutinised her closely. "You've had a disagreement. With Veylis."

"Yes, we had words. I just don't think it's very sensible to take him along when protection fever's such an issue."

"He's young and strong. And we mightn't be away long enough for it to matter."

"I wanted him to take the long view. The Senate will be unassailable without him, *or* without

Fley. But neither one of them will back down. Too scared of losing face, I suppose. And Keska won't be separated from her father. So if we lose one, we quite possibly lose them all." Laura paused to calm herself. "Keska's given Roegin the names of her contacts. In a worst case scenario, he's promised to continue her work. But will he?"

"He does have his own agenda," Idenion remarked.

"Indeed he does, and it includes not singing. I couldn't persuade him, and neither could Dena and Nefyrra. But he *has* agreed to attend. He wasn't going to at first."

"Well, we've plenty of other singers," Idenion said consolingly. "We can do without him this once."

Nefyrra joined them in the First Singer's suite. "I've called the scolia. Unnecessary really, as they were already here, but we have to maintain tradition. Kyrin's trainee will prime the relayist chain."

The chain became active as she spoke.

"So that's Bridd," Idenion remarked. "Nohal made a good choice. I thought only Kyrin could reach Lateral One from the akron."

"Bridd does have a similar autograph," said Nefyrra.

"I'd better change," announced Laura, and vanished into her dressing room.

Presently Dena came in with a slightly reluctant Roegin and several other guests, all having been invited by Laura to view the show from her private balcony. Zanna was there, and Ymer, and –

surprisingly – Veylis. Trevone and Clemis had opted to join the audience below.

"Not lending your voice to the proceedings, Veylis?" Roegin inquired.

"I have to preserve my image," Veylis replied loftily but not too seriously. "Today's masterwork will be recorded, and Transfix or no Transfix, these things have a habit of turning up where they're not wanted. Besides, I don't have a musical education."

"That was remiss of you."

"Lord Ephren didn't consider it necessary. I am, however, well versed in social dancing, small talk and knowing which fork to pick up."

"I'm sure that will come in useful when the battle lines are drawn," Roegin remarked.

"So, what's *your* excuse for dodging the spotlight? And don't give me any more garbage about your mother."

"I abandoned her - "

"That was hardly your fault."

"- and I'm damned if I'll insult her memory by singing."

"You don't even know she's dead," argued Veylis. "When we get home I'll use every resource at my disposal to find her. I swear on my honour and that of my House. Does that make you happier about singing?"

The oath meant something. Roegin offered a concession. "I'd need to prepare. I promise to sing at the next concert, whenever that happens to be. Now shall we watch your Patierade pals make idiots of themselves?"

Fley, with characteristic ebullience, was first on stage. In an impressive bass-baritone, he performed the War Song of the Patierades. The Celestrians remembered to applaud. Science Chief Brome delivered a drinking song, evoking a more generous response.

Then Keska appeared, self-conscious in a borrowed pink gown. In carefully memorised Celestrian, she announced her choice: a folk ballad called The Tree of Wendlissin. Laura, applying her stage make-up, listened curiously. "Fair Wendlissin, lost princess, we guard the tree that bears your name."

"What was all that about?" she asked her guests when the song was over.

"No idea," said Veylis. "Ephren saw to that."

"Patierade tree-worship?" hazarded Ymer.

"It's a myth," Roegin said quietly. "Princess Wendlissin of Patiera was young, beautiful and dying. Venturing into her garden for the last time, she planted a sapling beneath her window and vowed – uselessly, as it turned out – that she'd regain her strength as the tree grew taller. And to ensure it came to no harm, she ordered sentries to guard it day and night. When she died, the order was never rescinded. A sentry still guards the tree."

"Is that required reading for Covert Ops?" inquired Veylis.

"Yes, if you're going into Patierade territory. Not knowing their mythology could get you killed."

"I must write this down." Idenion found a stylus and paper, and began to scribble.

"Will you walk me to the stage, Roegin?" Laura asked pleasantly.

"As long as you don't expect me to walk *on* it."

"That privilege belongs to Tarlion. I'm singing a duet with him."

They took the elevator to the back of the auditorium, and started the descent.

"Shouldn't Idenion be escorting you?" Roegin asked. "Not that I mind."

"I asked you for a reason," announced Laura. "And no, not because I thought I'd look good on your arm. After the expedition leaves you'll be the only Eldorian in Alda Mexa apart from Escir. I want to show everyone that you have the freedom of the city, and my friendship."

Roegin searched for a facile response, found none, and settled for a simple "Thank you."

Later, squeezed onto the front terrace, he watched her support Tarlion through a limp performance of the Gypsy Rover. He hoped no-one saw him wince. Tarlion was *not* musical.

Fortunately, Tarlion knew his own limits. He waved aside requests for an encore and instead seated himself at the edge of the stage. Laura then addressed a wry ballad to him, pretending she could grant him the night vision he'd always wanted.

Further along the front row, little Tonora gazed adoringly at Tarlion's face. "He's my life-bonded," she announced to Clemis as the song ended.

"Don't let your father hear you say that," Clemis advised. "Tarlion's three times your age!"

"Yes, but I'll catch up," Tonora said optimistically. "Our patterns converge. I can see it."

Trevone, overhearing, leant towards her. "What do you mean exactly? What can you see?"

But Tonora merely laughed, leapt to her feet and sped off to join her junior dance troupe, who were to perform next.

Finally Laura returned to the stage, alone. Roegin had been waiting for this, and she didn't disappoint. The bright blue of the weathershield faded to soft azure. One single footlight accentuated the silver gems on her dress. She began to sing, and immediately and effortlessly had her audience in thrall. She sang of summer, seduction, and an affair which would only last a season. Roegin knew the song, though not the Celestrian lyrics. It was from Earth, of course. Ann had liked it.

The rest of Laura's performance consisted of the vocal pyrotechnics her public had come to expect. Roegin would have preferred more ballads, and intended to inform her after the show. But before he could elbow his way through her admirers he was waylaid by Tarlion, who invited him for a drink. One drink turned into several. Roegin, unaccustomed to resnay and its effects, surfaced at noon the following day to find the expedition had set off with both Laura and Idenion on board. An act of folly if ever there was one.

"You knew Idenion had this planned," he accused Dena.

"He's my twin," she said miserably. "How could I not know?"

Roegin saw a tear in her eye and suppressed the rant he was about to deliver. "You need a distraction. Why not come to Holpen with me? Today might be the day I make it to the pontoon!"

"You and Ciela don't want me along," Dena said, though she looked grateful. "You go. Keep using that temporary gym you've set up."

Roegin intended to. If he could get most of his old strength back he might actually be some use in a conflict. And there would be one – he was certain of that. He just didn't know what form it would take. According to Fley, the Celestrians were secretly training child soldiers. Which, of course, was nonsense.

Chapter Ten

4.8.1.4031

At a prearranged location near the outer fringes of the Cowl, the trio of spheres emerged from transposal and waited. Everyone was on edge, and not only because of the nature of the mission. Shortly before take-off they'd bickered over the allocation of crew members. Laura had wanted each sphere to carry one scientist, an arrangement based on common sense. Tarlion, however, refused to be subordinate to any Eldorian. Laura and Idenion wanted to stay together. Trevone wouldn't grant the Eldorians unsupervised access to the dispersal engine. And Rinyi believed that he and Tarlion should travel separately to avoid distracting Lydion. So, eventually, they settled on the less than perfect arrangement of Veylis, Keska and Fley aboard one craft, with Trevone, Rinyi and Brome manning the fully armed sphere. Tarlion, by default, found himself responsible for the First Citizens' safety. Laura had complete confidence in him, Idenion less so.

"Can't you at least *try* to work with the Eldorians?" he asked Tarlion without much optimism.

"I *am* trying. And to give Veylis his due, he's been ultra-polite. But he's a soldier. They all are. They're used to giving orders, not making requests. And, well, I was never any good at following orders."

"You really do take after your father," Laura said ruefully. "Just humour them. Please?"

"Are *you* going to?"

"Yes, because I have to. It won't be for long."

Idenion conferred with Trevone. "Remind me again why we've stopped here?"

"A precaution. Lydion insists the coordinates he was given are genuine, but how old are they? You of all people should know these things need continual updating. Lydion's trying to make contact with the AI as we speak. When he does, we'll complete the rest of the journey very cautiously. I'd appreciate it if you remained here until I've ensured it's safe."

"Very well," said Idenion. He was almost drowned out by a burst of static from the modified EM tuner. "Did you hear that, Trevone? I believe Vuli's little troops are here."

"All over us," Trevone confirmed.

"Then tell Lydion to hurry up."

"Copy that. Stand by."

While they waited, Tarlion spoke again of his lone voyage. "I very nearly *wasn't* alone," he revealed. "I wanted to give some of my students the chance of an adventure. I'm sure they'd have been up for it. But Myrig said they'd be scared, and forbade me to tell them I was leaving. I still think he was wrong."

Idenion wondered why he was closed off.

Finally, Trevone called in. "It's all right – the coordinates are valid. You can resume the programme. Our scanners are only effective at short range within the Cowl, but don't let that worry you. Hold your course and you'll be fine."

"And what's the destination?" asked Tarlion. "A solar system?"

"After a fashion. It's a red dwarf star with one planet. Sending data."

"And Vuli's on this planet?"

"So Lydion says. When we're all assembled we'll be given landing instructions."

"And where's this protected realm we're supposed to have threatened?"

"No idea. I don't see anything that looks like one. Just get yourselves here and then we might find out!"

Several astallen later, the three spheres regrouped near the designated planet.

"Well, what have we got?" asked Laura impatiently.

"Nothing too exciting," Trevone replied. "Uninhabited world, trapped rotation, as close to its sun as Alda Two is to ours. Brome's just confirmed that the atmosphere's rotating even though the planet isn't. That should help equalise the temperature across the globe."

"What type of atmosphere?"

"Not breathable. Look at the data feed."

"Sorry, Trevone, I can't decipher it. I've never had to."

"Here, let me." Tarlion gently moved her aside. "Hmm, that's easy enough to explain. No oxygen, only carbon dioxide. And for your benefit, Idenion, I've just said there's no thuvium. Discord's dreams, I can't believe you still call it

Fire Air. Antique or what? You're still First Poet, aren't you, so why don't you change its name to something more scientific?"

"I'm only permitted to change the name of my homeworld, and then only once."

"Brilliant. Well, there's nothing to stop you naming *this* boring little planet, is there? I've seen hundreds like it. Signs of ancient volcanic activity but absolutely no life."

"Vuli's alive, in a manner of speaking."

"That remains to be seen. Oh, there's one plus point: the air pressure's not much different to Celestra's, so we'll probably get away with wearing masks instead of bioshells." The logic system beeped. "*Now* what?"

Trevone, still manning the transposer, answered him. "Keska's spotted some kind of artefact in orbit round the sun, and has gone to have a look."

"So much for teamwork," muttered Tarlion.

"It might be important," said Trevone, ever the peacemaker.

"Is this what she saw?" Tarlion consulted the image Trevone had sent. "Could be anything."

"It could. So, she needs to get closer."

"Is it Vuli?" asked Laura.

"I might have thought so, but Lydion insists Vuli's landlocked. There's a connection, though. Whatever that thing is, the Clustrals are involved – seriously involved. I'll have to log out now, to keep the mode clear for Keska. You can track her progress on the scanner. As soon as she files a report, I'll share it. Don't go away."

They waited. Soon, Trevone forwarded another screen image. Then another.

"It looks like a rocket," said Laura. "Or a ramscoop."

"A what?" asked Idenion.

"Earther tech. Very slow interstellar travel. Theoretical."

"Hey, look!" As suggested, Tarlion had been tracking Keska's sphere. "She's on the move. She's running!"

"Are the Clustrals after her?"

"No more than before. Something's given her a fright and we need to know what. I'm calling Trevone."

"He told you not to."

"Did he? I must have missed that!" Tarlion grinned and repositioned his chair, but Trevone unwittingly pre-empted him.

"Ready, everyone? I have the landing coordinates."

"About time!"

"Transferring data now. Follow me down."

"Certainly. After you've told me why Keska panicked."

Trevone gave a dry chuckle. "Keska had a solar eruption licking at her heels. Our red dwarf's a flare star. She didn't get much warning."

"But what about that object? Is it derelict or functional?"

"Later. As soon as we've made landfall I'm calling a conference."

"How? The radio frequencies will be swamped and the Eldorians wouldn't understand us anyway."

"We'll manage. We'll all cram into one sphere if necessary. Now stop gabbing and land. Decorously please, as we're being evaluated."

"Can that AI *read* us?"

"I don't believe so, or it wouldn't route all its communications through Lydion. Rinyi can sense the Clustrals but not Vuli itself. All the same, we should be wary."

"Understood," said Tarlion, compliant for once.

They landed on a dusty plain dotted with small rocks. A range of extinct volcanoes was visible to the north; on the other three sides, more desert, bordered by foothills. The region was in sombre twilight, the sun low on the horizon.

But the stillness was illusory. The Clustrals were everywhere. Trevone issued instructions for the life support masks to be broken out, and ensured everyone knew how to use them. "We'll convene in the Eldorians' sphere as Keska has additional information. Remember your drill: don't remove your masks until onboard conditions have normalised."

"Sarune and Lydion wish to remain outside," announced Rinyi.

"Not yet. Soon. First they should be aware of Keska's findings."

Everyone crowded into the cabin space. The moment their masks were off, Brome and Veylis complained of the infiltrating cold.

"Man up," Fley advised them.

"Turn on more heat, " Veylis demanded.

"We'd lose it again when we let everyone out. I'm not depleting our resources so soon."

"We're not all used to Patierade ice worlds!"

"Veylis, enough!" ordered Trevone. "This isn't ideal but it won't take long. Keska, let's have your presentation. Then we can all get back to a temperature that suits us."

"All right, everyone, gather round," Keska said. "Tallest at the back. Brome, that means you. Here we go." She started the image sequence. "I'm in no doubt that this orbiting device is the Clustrals' hive. It collects the raw material for their manufacture. My early analysis shows it's part organic, similar to theridolyte, and possibly self-maintaining as well. The scoop wasn't fully deployed when I took these shots; the demand for new Clustrals must have been scaled back. But whatever the incubation process is, it's still active enough to produce a steady stream of Clustrals from the far end of the craft. I've added artificial colour to highlight the radio emissions."

"Have you enhanced the colour of the craft!" asked Tarlion.

"No, that's how it appears – grey with a hint of bronze. The Clustrals might look like that too, if enough banded together."

"Have you seen any evidence of a propulsion system?"

"No. It holds its position as a satellite would."

"And the flares provide the raw materials?"

"They're obviously the primary source but I imagine it could harvest small asteroids or infalling comets. It isn't likely to run out of fuel in a hurry!" She stood up suddenly and put an arm round Veylis. "It was our Freelord who got us to safety. But I'm sure you conversants know that."

"You and your father were studying the data and Veylis was on watch," Trevone surmised without reading her.

Veylis smiled modestly. "Fortunately my reaction time is second to none." And he kissed Keska on the nose.

Tarlion aimed an exasperated glance at the ceiling.

"We didn't see any flares," said Laura.

"Our spheres were in the planet's shadow prior to landing," Trevone explained. "If the flare was short-lived we'd have had no readings."

"Short but vicious," Keska confirmed. "Less than an astal. Just long enough to chase us away."

"I'll rig some monitoring equipment outside," said Brome. "If this is the start of an active phase we need to know what a safe distance is!"

Rinyi spoke up self-consciously. "May I have your attention, everyone? Vuli is addressing us via Lydion. Message follows. You young species are always in such a hurry. You should have told me you wished to leave your spacecraft. My drones have created a localised biosphere for you, based on my studies of your worlds. You will no longer require masks."

An assortment of sceptical looks greeted this announcement.

"Readings, Keska!" ordered Trevone.

"According to this," she replied, studying the display, "it's breathable. Quite a breeze too."

"Right," said Trevone decisively. "Masks on, people. I'll unseal the hatch and *one* of us will test what's out there."

"I'll do it," said Tarlion.

"Why you?"

"I'm the only one who hasn't been summoned to the presence. So, I'm the least important."

No-one disagreed.

"That's a yes, then. Stand by to revive me with strong liquor if Vuli's got it wrong."

"We don't have any liquor," said Laura.

"Yes we do. Or rather, Fley does. He's acquired quite a taste for resnay, haven't you, Commander?"

Fley shuffled his feet.

"And if this works you'll be able to smoke some of the weed you brought from Eldor Two," Tarlion continued merrily. "Should make a nice change from just sniffing it. Well, as the Earthers say, here goes nothing."

The hatch rippled open. Tarlion drew a shallow breath, then another deeper one. The air outside was fresh and clean, and smelt of loam and dampness. A warm breeze ruffled his hair. He strolled down the ramp and paused, looking down at multiple eddies of grit and tiny stones.

"Gangway, Tarlion," said Laura, behind him. "We're spreading out!" She strode past him, followed by Idenion and Veylis.

"Everyone, keep your masks with you at all times!" Trevone shouted as the group dispersed. "Don't assume this is permanent!"

"You don't trust Vuli," observed Tarlion.

"No. Don't you realise how the Clustrals are doing this?"

"Not exactly."

273

"You might have, if you'd seen how they channelled gravity to drive those asteroids. Channelling air must be effortless for them." He studied the gyrating pebbles. "Imagine this as a full-scale tornado. If the Clustrals can help themselves to another planet's atmosphere, they can manipulate weather systems. That might be Vuli's next attack strategy, if we fail this mysterious test."

"Whose air are we breathing, then?" Tarlion asked suspiciously.

"It isn't Celestra's. Keska's checking the Empire database for a match."

"I wonder if there's a barrier?" Tarlion threw an experimental stone.

"No vacuum so no need for one. It'll just thin out, I expect. Why?"

"Because I'm going exploring."

"Is that wise?"

"Maybe not, but I'm going. I don't need your permission."

"Now look, Tarlion - " Trevone began, but was interrupted by Keska.

"Clash of temperaments? Argue away, don't mind me. I just thought you'd like to know that this pop-up eco-system matches the rain world we spent time on after escaping the Transfix. The Clustrals must have tracked us there."

Rinyi had followed her. He looked more nervous than usual.

Tarlion tried a bright smile. "What's up, Master Interpreter? Where are the incorporeals?"

"Sarune's regaining her equilibrium. She doesn't like confined spaces."

"And Lydion?"

"He's talking with the AI, trying to find out where it's located. He says Vuli has very little self-concept, or sense of surroundings. And it keeps saying we, as if it were a collective."

"Maybe it's just self-importance," Tarlion suggested.

"Or maybe there *is* more than one of them," said Trevone.

"Lydion needs to know," Rinyi stated. "Since you want to look around, Tarlion, he has a task for you. There's a constant stream of Clustrals apparently disappearing into the ground over there." He pointed in the direction of the ever-setting sun. "He wants you to check it out. Take Sarune with you. She'll read the geology and describe what she sees."

"You'll have to come with us, then," said Tarlion a little too casually.

"No, I won't," Rinyi said, gently reproachful. "Lydion knows you and Sarune can communicate. He's accepted it. It was only to be expected, he said. You're more Narvellan than you care to admit, and she's seized on that."

"I've been ignoring her," Tarlion confessed. "I don't exactly trust her. But if Lydion wants me to take her along - "

"He does."

"Then I'd better do it." Tarlion glanced across at the sphere he'd piloted. Brome and Veylis had improvised a griddle near the open hatch, and Laura was toasting grain cakes. Close by, Fley was smoking a roll-up of the noxious weed he enjoyed.

"Home from home," Trevone remarked. "I hope they don't get too comfortable."

"I'll soon put them to shame!" Tarlion bounded past the barbecue, disappeared briefly into the sphere and emerged with a holdall containing his breathing gear, a water ration, an eye-shield, and two pouches for rock samples.

"Souvenir hunting?" inquired Trevone. "Keep your mind on the mission. This isn't New Narvella."

"I'll try to remember that," Tarlion said lightly. "Ah, Sarune's here. Time to go."

"Stay where we can see you."

"Stop fussing." Tarlion shouldered his meagre provisions and set off. As he passed the picnic he helped himself to a slab of cake newly spread with pilif jam.

+You'll get fat+ Sarune reprimanded.

+Let's be clear about one thing, Sarune – I'm not going to flirt with you the way Lydion does+

+Shame+

+And no Synectic antics, if you please+

+As it happens,+ Sarune informed him, +I promised Lydion I wouldn't lose my temper with you, no matter how annoying you were. I hope I won't regret making that promise. Now step on it. I can move a lot faster than you, and I do hate dawdling+

Tarlion obligingly quickened his step, but something about his surroundings – the gravity, the irritating breeze or maybe the gloomy ambience – wasn't conducive to healthy exercise. After half an ild he stopped trying to needle Sarune and made an

276

effort to pace himself, but grew more and more breathless and was obliged to slow up. The air was thinning out, just as Trevone had said it would. He glanced back: the three spheres were mere specks, but the hills ahead of him looked distant as ever.

Something scrunched beneath his boot. He paused, scooped up a handful of rubble and carefully segregated five tiny transparent stones.

+Hey, Sarune+

+What?+ She seemed abstracted.

+I think these are diamonds. Can you look them over?+

+If you think you've found diamonds then you probably haven't+

+Just scan them, will you?+ Tarlion held out his palm.

+Done. And yes, they're diamonds+ Sarune announced disinterestedly. +Too small for industrial use. Throw them away+

+They might make a nice necklace+ Tarlion persisted.

+The Celestrians don't place any value on diamonds+

+Laura might+ Tarlion dropped the stones into a pouch and pocketed it. +Are there any more deposits round here? Sarune?+

No reply.

Tarlion shrugged, studied the scatter pattern of the detritus at his feet, and tried to shift the surface layers with his mind. Powdered sand described a feeble parabola, then fell back upon itself, revealing nothing. He waited for Sarune's derision. None came. Further on, he found some commonplace hexagonal crystals, each with a sheared-off edge. There were broken flints, too, and a row of tumbled boulders.

The sunlight had grown brighter. Another flare. Looking back at his ever more distinct shadow, he realised he was descending a gentle slope. He could no longer see the spheres. The air quality was now so poor that he had to decide whether to call it a day or put on his mask and continue. Where in chaos was Sarune? Had she found the Clustrals' landfall site and not told him? Stubbornness made him keep walking, though the mask obscured his downward view and made it near-impossible to see diamonds or anything else. So, he'd just climb the far side of the hollow, take a final look around, then head back.

There was a sharp crack beneath his feet. The ground gave way. His psychokinetic reflex kicked in, weak to the point of uselessness, but slowing his fall just long enough for him to grasp a spur of rock that had suddenly appeared next to his ear. Sand showered onto his head. Then something struck him hard in the ribs and tossed him sideways onto solid ground, where he lay winded.

+Idiot!+ hissed Sarune. +I leave you alone for one astal and this is what happens. Now crawl!+

+What?+

+Crawl to your right. Now!+

He obeyed.

+All right, that's far enough for safety. Check your air supply+

+It's functioning. I seem to have lost my pack, though+

278

+And you've sliced your hand on that shale. Thanks a bunch, Tarlion! I'll now have to face Lydion's wrath for putting you in danger+

He sat up shakily and looked around. +What happened exactly?+

+There's an underground chasm. I can't read its depth. There's just a thin rocky shelf left on the surface and you were merrily strolling on it. You saw the damage above ground – didn't you realise there'd been a cave-in?+

+I … wasn't concentrating. Thanks for doing whatever it was you did+

+Just a shove. All I was capable of. Pathetic, isn't it, when I could once do so much more+

Tarlion didn't answer.

+And you're heavier than you look+ Sarune added ungraciously. +Now, isn't it high time we went back to the spheres?+

+Not before I mark this danger zone somehow. We may need to come this way again+ Tarlion got to his feet and tried to lift the smallest of the scattered boulders. +Some help here, please?+

The weight lessened.

+Thanks. So, a thin shelf, you said. Maybe if this lands near the hole I nearly fell into - +

+Just throw it, Tarlion, before I drop it+

He threw it. The already weakened shale cracked apart, then plummeted downwards. Sand poured after it in an ever-broadening circle. Tarlion hastily retreated up the slope. +There, that should - + he began.

+Wait+ cautioned Sarune. +The show isn't over+

With an oddly muted rumble the far side of the basin fell away, leaving a black jagged expanse of igneous rock. Embedded in it were layers of iridescent crystals – blue, mauve, yellow, all gleaming in the weak sunlight.

+Congratulations+ Sarune was at her most sardonic. +You've just unearthed Vuli's predecessor. Don't worry, you didn't kill it. It's been dead a long time+

Tarlion stared. Vuli was part of the planet – this crumbling wasteland of a planet. +Call the others! Get them to check the landing site for instabilities+

+Already done, and it's safe. Now walk. And once you're back in range, assure everyone you're well+

He walked. +What precisely was I looking at back there?+

+A data store. Vuli's makers knew how to encode every crystal, every clathrate, every molecular lattice, without removing them from the rock they evolved in. Ingenious. Efficient. Exploitative+

+What? Why?+

+Vuli is robust, secure, shielded from EM emissions – and locked in. For chaos knows how long, its only sensory input has been from the Clustrals. You think me cruel, don't you, Tarlion? *This* is cruelty. To create a steadfast, loyal being and immure it in rock. Fortunately, Vuli has no free will and doesn't long to escape. Neither is it devious. Lydion's been extracting information about its programming, its directive+

+But what keeps it going? What powers it?+

+Isn't it obvious? The Clustral stream we were sent to study. Their trail disappears into solid rock apparently, but I'm sure there's a Clustral-sized conduit leading straight back to Vuli. I'd just begun a closer search when you had your little adventure+

+Vuli's killing them?+

+They're on a one-way trip, so, yes. They'll provide a small electro-chemical charge, similar to the one which powers the likes of *you*+

+But why are they still trying to feed the extinct Vuli?+

+Maybe no-one's told them to stop+ Sarune answered laconically. +Now get a move on. I'm tired of babysitting you+

Back in the sphere they shared, Laura sat Tarlion down with a cool drink and proceeded to fuss over his injury. "You look exhausted," she scolded. "You must have walked twenty silmi or more."

"Have I really? It's difficult to judge distance in this place. No sense of time, either, with that endless twilight. Oh, here, I've a present for you." He handed her the pouch. "Diamonds. Sarune's authenticated them. I was looking for more when the going got tricky."

Laura examined the uncut stones. "You certainly know how to flatter a girl, risking life and limb to bring me these. Thank you seems rather inadequate."

"I'll settle for a foot massage."

Laura laughed. "No chance. Ask Keska."

"Oho, Veylis wouldn't like that. I'd be challenged to pulse-lances at dawn."

"No dawn hereabouts."

"Just as well." Tarlion suppressed a yawn. "Now, I gather Lydion wants to address us all, but could someone ask him to be quick about it? I'm falling asleep here!"

"So are the Eldorians. We've all been up longer than a Celestrian day, and their homeworlds have shorter rotations. As soon as Lydion's said his piece I'm drawing up a sleep roster. Ah, your request's been granted. Here's Rinyi. Up you get, Tarlion — on this occasion we're assembling outside."

"While we still can," Tarlion muttered.

As always when speaking for Lydion, Rinyi's voice was warm and assured. "First of all," he began, "I've the answer to a question that's been puzzling us all. The Protected Realm is a bubble universe."

"I thought they were hypothetical," said Brome.

"Have you seen it?" asked Trevone.

"Yes, and no. It's a self-contained space-time continuum, projected onto *our* space-time. It isn't really here. But I can read the projection."

"Might it be a construct?"

"I did wonder. I've seen other universes, tiny ones, and they're here and gone. Or maybe only their projections are transient, restricted by local conditions. This bubble's different. It appears sizeable. And, of course, its projection's been stable for a very long time."

"It *is* a construct, then."

282

"Maybe. Aren't we more concerned with what it's for, rather than what it is?"

"Where's its point of contact?" asked Veylis uneasily.

"Where we're standing, in a manner of speaking."

"Then why didn't you notice it earlier?"

"Because space-time bubbles aren't easy to discern when I have to stay focused on you lot. Relax, Veylis. It's only a holographic image. Nothing's coming to get you."

Tarlion smothered a grin.

"As I was saying," Rinyi went on more seriously, "Vuli's makers seeded this little universe as an experiment. They wanted to know if civilisations must inevitably fall, or if, given the right start, they could evolve into something eternal. And before you ask, Vuli has no idea who his makers are or were. Nor has he any idea what's inside the Protected Realm. His duty is to guard it.

"I took him to task over the destruction of intelligent species in *this* universe, people like our ancestors who didn't know how or why they'd transgressed. I wanted to know how many worlds had been attacked. I received only unclear answers, and at first I thought Vuli was being evasive. But I now believe there are numerous gaps in his memory – data lost over the years, either by deterioration of the memory medium or corrupted by the subsidence which destroyed the master AI. Which, incidentally, Vuli believes still exists."

"Does this mean Vuli's senile?" inquired Laura.

"Absolutely. Eight times he's asked who created me. Eight times I've explained that I'm not an AI. Over and over, he forgets."

"Can he remember his previous attack on Celestra, and why he did it?" asked Idenion.

"Yes: apparently, the Realm is conjoined with realities other than ours. It has a connection to one of the ten other dimensions in our space-time – the same one our ancestors adopted as an alternative to t-space. A safer means of transposal for them. But the Realm suffered bruising as a result."

Keska handed Rinyi a cup of water, which he drank gratefully.

"Vuli wishes to emphasise that his remit does not include the eradication of any species. His preferred term, which he's used many times, is reset. To remove the harmful technology, not the life-form which created it. Vuli is also not empowered to destroy planetary ecosystems, only to temporarily disrupt them in accordance with the will of the makers."

"He almost wiped us out," said Trevone angrily. "Isn't he even sorry?"

"He can't override his programming."

"Well, where *are* these makers? Can he answer that?"

"Afraid not. He implicitly believes they'll return, but to me that seems highly unlikely. The slow decay of the site and its minder suggests the experiment has continued way too long. The makers have either lost interest or met with a disaster of their own."

"They're dead," Veylis declared.

"And you say this because …?"

"They were trying to create a perfect society, which means *they* didn't have one."

"That makes sense," Tarlion said grudgingly. "What else have you to tell us, Lydion?"

"Nothing good. I was wrong about the augmentation of the Bad Resonance. The three receptors weren't Eldor, Celestra and Earth. They were Celestra, Earth and this world. An almost perfect triangle. Eldor, or rather the piercing of the Cadence, was the trigger."

"So it's *my* fault," said Keska.

"No, you were one element in a cosmic accident. You could say I was to blame for creating the Cadence, Ruvrin for setting it up wrongly, Trevone for bringing Alda Six online when he did, and the Earthers for experimenting with alien tech."

"The Resonance was exclusive to aldacite. I didn't detect any here."

"Sarune did, inside those dead volcanoes. Never harvested, never utilised."

"So Vuli's right," Trevone said despondently. "We *did* threaten his Realm."

"We can't pretend otherwise. It now remains for us to convince him it was unintentional. All right, everyone. We're done here." Lydion ceased channelling, uncharacteristically abrupt. Rinyi, back in charge of himself, looked bashful.

Laura hastily took over. "Keska, Fley, Veylis, Brome and Tarlion. Get some sleep. Tarlion, you and Brome take Trevone's sphere. We'll need the other one for conferencing. We'll wake you in six ilden."

285

"We won't need that long," said Keska.

"*I* will," Tarlion countered amiably.

They dispersed. Rinyi and Idenion struck up a conversation. Laura began to dismantle the barbecue. Trevone contacted Alda Mexa and spoke with Dessin. Lydion, his pattern coiled defensively, maintained a gloomy silence.

+Hey+ Sarune said at last.

+What?+

+If you're having one of your moments, you've picked a bad time. What's the problem?+

+Vuli is. Communicating with him is exhausting. He's failing, Sarune. I can hardly keep him on topic. Is this how *I'll* end up?+

+Maybe, if you regress+ Sarune answered coldly.

+You don't do empathy. Sorry, I forgot that minor detail+

+Sooner or later,+ Sarune persisted, +you'll have to stop holding onto what you were, and look to what you *could* be+

+And that's what *you're* doing, is it? Obliterating your physical life?+

+My past isn't relevant. And returning to your previous question, Vuli isn't like you. He's just a logic system reliant on worn out circuitry. In the end, even rocks wear out+

Again, Lydion was silent.

+You have to stop identifying with him+ Sarune was relentless. +Stop personalising him. You've already got everyone saying 'he' instead of 'it'+

+That was Rinyi's doing+

+Then don't let it go any further. It's dangerous sentiment+ She paused. +What's Vuli plotting now, anyway? Why's he shutting us out?+

+He's reviewing the circumstances which led to the resonance event. I don't think we're in for a long wait, since we're not denying culpability. He'll want to hear our excuses+

+Or not+

+He's programmed to. If he calls us to account while the Eldorians are still asleep, Laura's offered to go first+

+Sarune, Lydion+ This was Rinyi. +The Clustrals are all around Laura. Should we do something?+

There was no time to answer him. Vuli's thoughts boomed across their joint consciousness. +Is *this* the woman who would sue for clemency? She deals in war. She is the node, the sole non-conversant, the one the Gloriana sought through time+

+How do you know all that?+ demanded Lydion, astonished.

+I derived information from the guardian of the time bridge, machine-mind qubitech of Xorian+

Lydion didn't hesitate. +Rinyi, alert the First Citizens this instant. Vuli's been chatting with the Gloriana's quantum computer!+

***

The Akron, Alda Mexa 6.8.1.4031

"Sea-scum."

287

"Mud-brain."

"Mollusc."

"Worm."

"Your mother was a crustacean."

"Your father was a river snake."

The voices grew louder and louder. Ansela, in search of Dessin, found him outside the audience room. "What's going on? Who's in there?"

"That," said Dessin wearily, "is Ribor of Kest. Skipper of the Eprys Blossom, scourge of the Lisir."

The insults grew more inventive.

Ansela frowned. "Shouldn't *you* be dealing with this?"

"Bridd said he could handle it. In fact, he insisted."

"Any idea what Ribor wants?"

"He hasn't got around to that yet. Name-calling comes first. River folk tradition. Didn't you know?"

""I've not seen it in any book," said Ansela, wrinkling her nose. "Well, we'd better start without Bridd. Sheyell and Kyrin are waiting, and Kalyx is standing by in Scapirion."

They assembled at the transposer point.

"I asked you here for two reasons," Dessin began. "Firstly, so Ansela can inform us how our child trainees are progressing. I've been concentrating on other defence matters, so have little idea how the entrainment programme's shaping up. Secondly, we're here because I heard from Trevone this morning." He briefly explained about the bubble universe, the orbiting Clustral lab and the sheer age of the project. "We didn't expect

288

anything quite so bizarre," he concluded. "But, fortuitously, our emergency preparations will still serve. Trevone believes that after the failure of the meteor strikes, the Clustrals will try manipulating the weather. Should this be the case, we'll be ready for them. We've analysed the coded references to our cities. The distribution of radio receivers is almost complete, and the secure storage of food supplies *is* complete. Ymer, Ibri and their team have equipped fifteen spheres with pulse-cannon, and will doubtless add to that figure. And, in case of power failure – or in case we have to turn it off – I've had generating equipment delivered to every prill facility. If the children are to be our last line of defence we must guarantee power to the plant habitats. Sheyell, a word."

She looked up.

"The notes you're making are only to be distributed at administrator level. No public access, not yet."

"Is it sensible to keep everyone in ignorance?" asked Kyrin. "It's been appropriate in the past, but this time they'll be in the firing line."

"I know, and we *will* make them aware, but if we wait a little longer the threat may diminish. Trevone says that in the event of renewed hostility, he and the others will try their utmost to deal with it at source."

"Easily said," Sheyell remarked. "A device which uses raw energy from a flare star? How do you stop something like that?"

"That's our Sheyell, always positive!" said Kalyx, though privately he agreed with her.

289

Dessin appeared to ignore him. "So, Ansela, how goes it with the children?"

"Well enough," she replied. "Thanks to our excellent genealogical records our researchers have found all the eugenics descendants, and of those identified, eighty per cent proved reliable subjects. Most were already in the scolia or relayist training, and their local tutors have run the usual tests, explained to them what's needed and introduced them to the prill farms. Nohal was going to study the borderline talents and give them a yes or no, but he eventually decided we'd need everyone. We're still slightly below our expected targets."

"In that case, Scapirion will forego its allocation," Kalyx said decisively. "I'm sure of this, Dessin. We're better able to defend ourselves than any other city state."

"I believe that to be true," Dessin said. "All the same - "

"It *is* true, trust me. We have different strengths. Permission to sign out? I have to run this past my ministers. Oh, don't worry. They'll comply."

"With you in charge, who'd doubt it? Good luck, Kalyx. Stay in touch."

"Kyrin," began Sheyell, "can you provide - "

She got no further. The door flew open and Bridd tumbled in, followed by a sinewy, weather-beaten man.

"Bridd," Kyrin said reprovingly, "this is quite unorthodox."

"I know, and I apologise. But Ribor did seek an audience with Dessin, and he did have to make do with me. I thought you should hear what he has to say. Straight to the point, please, Ribor."

His request went unheeded.

"Well, if it isn't Dessin the Respectable. Rebel turned penpusher. I preferred it when you were breaking and entering."

"Make your petition if you're going to," Dessin advised.

"Politely, Ribor!" added Bridd.

Ribor glared at them both. "I came here today because something's brewing and I want to know what it is."

"Specify," Dessin suggested.

"Well," Ribor continued warily, "the First Citizens are off-world again. Both of them. The last time that happened we were planning to go to war. And I also know First Scientist Trevone had to destroy *two* rogue asteroids."

Dessin gave him an inquiring look. "You're shielded. Why?"

"I'm not saying how I came by the information. A friend of a friend works at the spaceport, and that's all you're getting."

"As you please," Dessin said curtly. "Yes, two asteroids posed a threat. They've been dealt with. Now, if there's nothing further - "

"I've hardly started. Why are Eldorians working alongside our men in the weapon shops of Treva? We've been transporting materials to them. If my people are helping them re-arm I want to know why. And why are we stockpiling food? We've hauled enough in the past few octals to feed Alda Mexa for a year!"

291

Dessin reached a swift decision. "You're an astute man, Ribor. And you're quite right – we *are* on a war footing, and thus we may have to requisition your fleet. If that happens, I'd like you to be in charge of its deployment. In return you'll be kept fully apprised of the developing situation – starting today."

Ribor tried not to look astonished.

"You seem to have established a rapport with Bridd," Dessin continued. "He can be your liaison as of now."

Ribor grinned and aimed a fake punch at the young relayist. "This boy's a breath of fresh air. I didn't think anyone could better my insults, but he managed it. And he isn't even river stock."

"I come from a long line of Virdan fishermen," Bridd said with a show of pride. "We have our own oral traditions. Ribor, my friend – I've missed most of this briefing thanks to you, so why don't you wait for me in the refectory while Dessin brings me up to date? Then I can tell you exactly what's what."

Ribor departed with an even broader grin.

"Dessin, I hope you know what you're doing," Sheyell said sourly.

"I think he does," Kyrin said, and laughed – much to everyone's surprise.

"And to think I once believed you and Bridd were alike," smiled Ansela. "You couldn't be more different."

"That's easily explained. Bridd's family didn't report his talent straight away. He had a few years of normal life, going to sea and helping with the catch."

"Once this difficult time's over I may go back," Bridd supplemented. "Virda needs relayists too. Then there's my girl, Kythania. I'd have asked her to come with me but she's better off there if things get dangerous."

"Can you and Kyrin provide continuous cover for the city, if the need arises?" asked Sheyell, returning to her unfinished question.

"Yes; we've been rehearsing. Kyrin will head the chain on the eastern side along with his co-worker Alcis, and I'll take the west. I'll have to put a squib under Tylo, no doubt, but it's all part of the job."

"You enjoy startling him," Kyrin accused lightly.

"He shouldn't always be asleep."

"Treat him kindly. He's getting old."

"Just like you, then."

"Enough, you two," Dessin ordered.

"Yes, Bridd, behave yourself!" admonished Kyrin. "Or I'll tell everyone about your poetry."

"What poetry's this?" asked Ansela, intrigued.

"Oh, nothing." Bridd was suddenly evasive. "Just some lines I wrote for Kythania to say I miss her. I ... we ... have a life bond."

"Relayists don't make life bonds," said Sheyell.

"This one does."

Suddenly concerned, Dessin watched as Bridd skimmed through Sheyell's notes and ran off to find Ribor.

"Problem?" asked Sheyell.

"You *know* there is. Relayists and life bonds don't mix. What's that phrase of theirs?"

"Everyone and no-one," Kyrin supplied.

"Exactly. Well, I hope Bridd remembers it. If the Clustrals attack, he might find love's a distraction he doesn't need."

***

"I missed you," said Ciela.

Roegin tried to look contrite, and almost succeeded. "Sorry. I've been in Treva with the Eldorian engineers. I thought I might see my way forward more clearly if I knew what was going on back home. Just more of the same, as it turned out."

"Still hoping for news of your mother?"

"They don't know anything – they're too young. Habbon might have been more helpful if he hadn't quit Eldor Prime when he did. But, news from the expedition arrived just a few ilden ago." Briefly Roegin outlined Trevone's bulletin. "So that's the gist. That crazy old machine thinks we side-swiped its pet universe. You couldn't make it up! Trevone says your cities are most at risk so promise me you won't go to Alda Mexa. Tivenne might be safer but I'd rather you stayed here."

"Will you stay as well?"

"I'll stay as long as you want," he promised.

"Is that possible?" she countered.

They were sitting on the veranda of Ciela's health spa, gazing down toward the beach and the lake beyond. It was twilight. Apart from a couple of litter-pickers and someone dismantling the beachwear stall, they were alone. Roegin's command of Celestrian was still poor, but Ciela's use of conscious telepathy had taught her enough Eldorian to get by. Sometimes she inadvertently mixed Eldorian with Earth-English, which Roegin had fondly encouraged. It was like having their own secret language. But now, he wondered if her muddled speech merely reflected his own state of mind.

He forced an apology. "I really am sorry. I'm not being fair to you."

"Nor to yourself," she said softly.

"I had everything worked out," he continued. "I thought it all through when I first arrived, and decided Escir was right. If I confronted the Senate I'd very soon be dead and the Three Worlds would be none the wiser. I'd almost decided to stay put, make a home here. And then along came Keska with her plans for a coup. With Veylis on her side she might just pull it off. And even if she doesn't, the Patierades have a network of broadcast facilities. They could give me a platform."

"I see."

"I never thought I'd meet someone I could care about," he hurried on. "You've complicated things - "

"Good."

"- and I'm back where I started."

"With one important difference," Ciela said. "Keska and her father may not return from this mission. And you'd be on your own again."

"It could happen, I suppose."

"And until you know the outcome, you can't decide your future. Why don't we take advantage of that, starting tonight?"

"*I'm* supposed to do the persuading," Roegin objected.

"There's no need." Ciela sounded mildly surprised. "I've already made my choice."

"Oh, I get it. Female superiority."

"Not superior. Just equal."

He kissed her while he marshalled a reply. "Tonight, I'll go along with that. Tomorrow I shall race you to the pontoon, and I shall win."

"Take a coracle. You'll get there quicker."

"Just for that, you'll cook breakfast."

She laughed. "Maybe. If you sing me to sleep."

"Absolutely not!" he declared. But he smiled as he said it.

Chapter Eleven

"Everything?   Vuli knows *everything*?" repeated Laura in disbelief.   "Discord's dreams, we've been so *careful* ..."

"How is this possible?" asked Idenion. "Xorian's computer wasn't an AI."

"Vuli hacked it," said Trevone grimly. "Calmly does it, Laura. You were wondering how to present your case. Now you don't have to dissemble. It's just as well this came out now."

"Are the Eldorians asleep?" Laura asked nervously.

Idenion scanned the neighbouring spheres. "Yes, all of them. Tarlion as well."

"Then let's get this done before they wake up. Keep watch, would you?"

"Of course I will. But you're being too alarmist. They can't sense Vuli."

"No, but they can hear my replies. Can't we close the hatch?"

"If we did that, Vuli might think we were trying to screen you against the Clustrals. Theridolyte blocks them, or had you forgotten?"

"It's all about honesty and transparency," Trevone added.

Laura sighed. "All right. Just be ready to cause a distraction if necessary. Rinyi, will you be speaking as Lydion or yourself?"

"Lydion won't have time to chat. He has to channel Vuli for my benefit, and relay your answers back to him. So it's just me, I'm afraid."

"And where's Sarune?"

"Absent by choice. Her feelings toward Vuli are ambivalent. She thinks he's been exploited – he reminds her of when she was similarly trapped underground. And that in turn makes her feel guilty at what she did to free herself."

Laura didn't care to be reminded of that either. Before confronting Vuli, she turned briefly to Idenion and Trevone. "I'm glad you're keeping me company, but please don't interrupt, even if I make a mess of it. I'll be speaking for Earth, remember. Celestra gets its turn later."

"We'll keep quiet," Idenion promised.

"Vuli is ready," Rinyi announced. "Proceed, Laura."

"You know about – " she began, then paused and looked away. "I feel silly."

"Remember that Vuli can't hear you," said Rinyi earnestly. "His only information comes from the Clustrals. To him you're a biochemical profile, nothing more."

"So when I speak, it's just to you and Lydion?"

"That's right. And we'll filter out any mistakes."

Laura gave a tentative smile and tried again. "You know about the timeship, and my role in preventing the Earth-Eldor wars. You will therefore know that in so doing I denied my world interstellar travel, in its own interests. However, we couldn't prevent a number of Eldorians reaching Earth, and although that matter has been rectified, a communication device fell into Earther hands. The Bad Resonance was caused in part by an attempt to

298

duplicate this technology. I personally went to Earth and dealt with those responsible."

"Vuli says: all this is known to me," said Rinyi. "My Clustrals tracked you there."

"Then you will also know that the source of the resonance has been neutralised. There is no naturally-occurring aldacite on Earth. I therefore seek your clemency regarding this world, which no longer constitutes a threat to you or the Realm."

Rinyi's face went curiously blank as he conferred with Lydion. Laura suddenly remembered Darren's communicator and prayed he wouldn't use it just yet.

Finally the answer came. "From the data in my possession I am satisfied that the closed world Earth poses no risk. Reset is deferred."

"I'm sincerely grateful," said Laura. "May I now ask a question?"

Rinyi looked surprised, but channelled the request.

"Proceed," came the reply.

"The Earth-Eldor wars would have torn the galaxy apart. When you read the contents of Xorian's computer, why did you not interfere?"

"I am not programmed for pre-emptive strikes. Without a real and immediate threat to the Protected Realm, I cannot act."

"You saw it all? The battle? The setting up of the Cadence?"

"Are you trying to impress me?" Rinyi's voice had acquired an edge. "Surveillance is a duty. I carried it out. How you resolve your differences is of no consequence provided it does not impact on the Realm."

"But surely - "

"Laura, it's Lydion," Rinyi interjected at this point. "No more questions – he's gone all tetchy. We still haven't discussed Celestra so we need to keep him sweet."

"Sorry. I'll shut up."

"He really doesn't care who's right and who's wrong," Lydion added gently. "You won't help Celestra that way."

"I know that now," Laura said despondently. "All he cares about is that stupid Realm. I wish there was a way to see inside it. I bet it isn't so special. Lydion?"

"Still here. Cogitating. I think the Eldorians should speak next. Vary the perspective, keep Vuli focused. Veylis will probably want to do the honours so I must make sure he's suitably abject."

"Does he know the meaning of the word?"

"I'll remind him. The Clustrals will detect any hostility via his vital signs, so he has to rein it in. I'd prefer Keska as negotiator but I think she'll be outvoted."

"She has *my* vote."

"I'll let her know. Don't worry, Laura, I've got this. The kids won't disappoint us."

Laura thanked him and wandered outside. Beyond the encampment, the landscape was subtly changed: brighter sands, deeper shadows. Another flare. It was, she estimated, about four ilden since the last one.

Idenion came to stand beside her. "You're still angry."

"At Vuli. Idenion, this isn't going to work. I'm sure of it."

"It will if we can buy ourselves enough time," Idenion said, trying to sound reassuring. He didn't quite succeed.

"First Citizens," Rinyi ventured, "I need to rest before assisting the Eldorians. I'm ... suddenly tired. I've told Lydion and he says it doesn't matter, that Vuli's used to waiting."

"Then we'll *let* him wait," Trevone declared. "Get your heads down, all three of you. I'll keep watch till the Eldorians surface."

Laura felt too dispirited to argue. Idenion took her arm and they returned to the sphere, Rinyi trailing after them. Trevone paused by Brome's monitoring equipment and began studying the data it had collected.

+Lydion+

+Oh, hello, Sarune. Back, are we?+

+What in chaos are you up to? Rinyi wasn't tired. And he can't act, either+

Lydion was briefly amused. +No, he can't. If Laura hadn't been so tired herself she'd have spotted that+

+So why did you put him up to it? Why cause a delay?+

+Because I want to see what Vuli's protecting. It was Laura who gave me the idea+

+*What* idea?+

+Of seeing into the Realm. Ever hear of the holographic principle?+

+No+

+Tyvian spoke of it. I'd forgotten. It belongs to the time of string theory, before we moved on to resonance theory. But I'm sure it's still viable+

+Oh, good!+ Sarune exuded sarcasm. +Now skip the history lesson, tell me how it works and stop wasting the time you've bought yourself+

Lydion remained affable. +Fine. I'll keep it simple. You've seen holograms, I presume?+

+I won't dignify that question with a response+

+Just checking. According to the holographic principle, whatever's inside a three-dimensional space is displayed on the surface enclosing it+

+Intriguing. But haven't you already studied the Realm?+

+One small area, just to confirm its existence. If I'm to make sense of what's inside, I'll need to encircle it+

Sarune finally saw where this was leading. +No, Lydion. It's too dangerous+

+It's an image, Sarune. It can't harm me+

+In itself, no. But how far does this image extend?+

+Far enough to be awkward+

+And what if Vuli sends his Clustrals to sort you out while you're stretched wafer thin? That's going to sting a bit+

+He didn't order me not to look+ Lydion retorted, suddenly obstinate.

+He doesn't know you're capable of it+ Sarune shot back.

+Must we squabble? This isn't just about my curiosity, despite what you're thinking. This experiment should have ended long ago – we all know that. What if there are living beings trapped in that universe? Whole civilisations, maybe, with no resources left+

+And what are *we* supposed to do if there are?+

+Sarune, merciless one, listen. I predict we'll end up destroying everything here. But we can't destroy the Realm, even if we wanted to. Before we leave it to its fate we should at least examine it fully+

Sarune capitulated with bad grace. +Do what you must. But don't look to me for help if you land yourself in trouble+

Undeterred, Lydion departed breezily. Sarune immediately regretted being so dismissive. Pique was to blame, she supposed. She couldn't perceive the Realm. Typically, Lydion didn't mind that he hadn't *her* skills, such as reading geological data. Not that there was much to read at the moment – just Vuli's sullen brooding, far below. Idly she observed Trevone completing his analysis of the flares. Industrious, thorough, meticulous. She could admire that.

The constantly shifting air, with its trace of drizzle, fluttered gently at her pattern's edge. It was soothing in a way, deceptively so. The reduced interaction with corporeals was even more refreshing than the rain. She wished it would happen more often.

Then, abruptly, she was startled back to full awareness. Something was amiss. An incomplete contact, a sense of entreaty. Lydion? No, he was engrossed in his work. Tarlion was sleeping contentedly. It had to be Rinyi, then, having an anxiety attack. Not entirely unexpected. Just as long as he didn't impinge on Lydion's concentration.

Seven years, Lydion, Sarune thought with a trace of incredulity. I nurtured you for seven long Celestrian years. So why does a couple of ilden seem so endless? Anyone would think I was worried about you.

Suddenly, he was beside her. +Miss me?+

+Chaos, don't *do* that! Well, what did you detect?+

+Something I wasn't expecting+

+What? Don't drag it out, Lydion – I'm not in the mood+

+Straight to the point, then. The Realm is dead. There's nothing left in it – no stars, nothing. We never asked ourselves, did we, how long it was designed to last from creation to heat-death. Well, at least we don't have to fret about the inhabitants. If there ever were any, they're long gone+

+Be very sure of your facts, Lydion+

+I *am* sure. There are a few wisps of plasma left, and that's all. Entropy's won. It's terrifying. Care to share?+

Sarune demurred. +That won't be necessary. Consider me convinced. When do we tell Vuli?+

+Just what I was wondering. We'd be negating his entire purpose, and I'm not sure how he'll take it+

+He'll call off hostilities, surely? None of us can harm something that's already dead+

304

+We can't rush into this, Sarune. You've had so little contact with Vuli – you don't know how unstable he is. Something as momentous as this could tip him into insanity. For now, we wait+

+I wish you wouldn't cosset him+ Sarune grumbled. +I suppose you know best. Are we updating the rest of the team?+

+How can we not? I'll tell Rinyi as soon as he wakes up+

+Tell me what, Lydion?+ Rinyi always sensed when he was being discussed.

+Discord's dreams, why aren't you asleep?+

+I wasn't tired, remember? Did you spy on the Realm? What was it like?+

Lydion hesitated. +Well – it …+

+Oh, sorry, both of you – I'll have to catch up later. Veylis is awake and demanding some action. The Clustrals are hovering round him and he knows they're there – he says they make him itch+

+His aristocratic sensibilities, no doubt+ Lydion quipped sourly. +Sounds as if Vuli wants to resume negotiations. I'll check on him, you get Keska ready. Laura wants her to take part in the appeal+

Presently the two young people took their places before Rinyi, trying to look prepared.

"I'm never going to convince Vuli I mean no harm," Veylis muttered. "He's like a warmongering old general – and I've met a few of those. Why are we even talking to him? He should be shut down. We should've taken out that orbiting Clustral factory as soon as we saw it!"

"I don't think our pulse-cannon would have had much effect," Keska said reasonably.

"We could have tried."

"When you're ready, Veylis," Rinyi said uncertainly.

Keska suddenly turned and kissed Veylis on the mouth. "There," she said at length, "that should give the Clustrals a treat. Vital signs suffused with … good things."

Veylis grinned, put a casual arm round her and began the speech he'd rehearsed, expressing his regret at the disruption caused by the Transfix breakout. "On our return home we will work together to promote regime change and a peaceful future," he concluded earnestly.

"Lies, all lies," said Tarlion cheerfully as he passed by. "Come and have breakfast, kids. He'll be an age processing that piece of fiction."

But Vuli had already launched a response.

+Lydion, this is bad+ Rinyi quavered. +What do I tell them?+

+Say nothing+ Lydion ordered. +Let's see where he's going with this+

+The Eldorian Empire is synonymous with destruction+ Vuli was continuing. +It has strip-mined worlds, annihilated numerous life-forms, given the star-drive to feral creatures. The war with the Earthers continues interminably - +

+What in chaos?+ Rinyi was stunned.

Lydion cut off the flow of information, leaving the deranged AI talking to itself. +Harmony save us, he's really lost it. That's the alternate timeline from the Gloriana computer. He thinks it's really happening!+

Sarune swooped in. +Lydion! Conference! Now!+

+Not a word of this to the Eldorians+ Lydion reminded Rinyi. +Well, Sarune?+

+Over there+ She moved to indicate the landslip area, and the fissure where the stream of Clustrals fed energy to Vuli. +Notice anything?+

The stream had all but vanished.

+Wake up, Lydion! Has that rock-bound dotard addled your wits so soon? He's run out of Clustrals. We've seen how he squanders them and now there aren't enough to sustain him. He's hallucinating. And he'll continue to do so until the collector's processed the yield from the last flare+

The damp air eddied round them. Briefly in accord for once, they knew the imported biosphere was safe for the moment. Vuli, oblivious to his own failings, had ignored the vital supply of Clustrals on the rainworld.

+The scoop doesn't work very fast, does it?+ Lydion mused. +Do me a favour, Sarune, and keep watch for that Clustral stream. I think we should note the exact time the processing takes+

+What are *you* going to do?+

+Deal with this deputation+ Veylis, Keska and her father were homing in on Rinyi. +Fley's no fool. He knows something's up+

+What will you tell them?+

+Nothing about Vuli's little rant. As you'll observe, he's just gone into sleep mode. When he wakes, he might not remember any of it. No harm in telling them about the missing Clustrals, though. And as we agreed, the dead Realm+

+Dead?+ repeated Rinyi, startled.

+Totally. Channel me, if you will+

The trio of Eldorians came to a halt.

"Gather round, people," said Rinyi with an engaging smile. "I've some interesting news."

Lydion kept his speech short for once, sticking to the facts and omitting his usual adroit phrasing. Of the three, only Veylis could understand such nuances – and he wasn't minded to impress Veylis. He finished the bulletin and paused while the group conversed.

"Oh, that's so sad!" Keska exclaimed. "It's like the Tree of Wendlissin all over again."

"Vuli being the sentry, I suppose," said Veylis. "But where's the similarity between a living tree and a dead universe?"

"The song doesn't tell all the story. Neither did Roegin. The tree died, but as the order was still in force, a sentry stood guard over the dead tree. Later, he guarded the stump. And later still, when even the stump was gone, he guarded nothing. To this day, a soldier keeps vigil – even though we're not sure we have the right place."

"It's an honour to be chosen as sentinel," Fley added. "There's a waiting list."

"So, do we tell Vuli to stand down?" Veylis asked Rinyi.

"Lydion says, wait till the petitions have been dealt with," Rinyi said hesitantly.

Veylis scowled. "We've waited long enough!"

"Hey, you three!" Tarlion had reappeared. "Breakfast! Cereal with hot pilif syrup. There's enough for you too, Rinyi. Hurry before Trevone eats it all!"

"He should be sleeping," Rinyi said. "He must be exhausted."

"Not him! He's been on the transposer for the past half-ild. Says he's used to the very long days on Alda Six. Come on, join us. Vuli's downtime won't end just yet, will it?"

"I don't think so."

"Then let's go."

Rinyi followed them obediently.

+Where are *you* going, Lydion?+ inquired Sarune. +Leave Rinyi alone. He needs a break. So do you+

+I know, but they need watching. Veylis is spoiling for a fight and he could pick on Rinyi+

+So? There are four able-bodied men to keep them apart. Take a metaphorical step back, relax, rebuild your strength+

For once, Lydion heeded her advice – which only proved to Sarune how right she'd been. Elsewhere, the predicted quarrel began to take shape.

"I can't believe you're willing to sit on your collective backsides and do nothing!" stormed Veylis. "The Clustrals are out of action, Vuli's offline – what better chance can there be? We should get airborne *now*, and finish this!"

"We wait," Trevone said evenly.

"And who put *you* in charge?"

309

"Veylis, no-one doubts your skill with the pulse-cannon. But it can't take out Vuli. If you don't believe me, give Ymer a call. Or, you might try asking your girlfriend."

"It's true, Veylis," Keska said hesitantly. "Pulse-cannon are no use against subterranean targets. Particularly not this one. You'd have run out of charge long before you vapourised all that rock."

"Then how did Ymer smash that asteroid?"

"It was exposed on all sides. Your battle computers would have scanned it for weaknesses."

"Sarune can do that," said Tarlion with his mouth full.

Trevone scowled. "Tarlion, you're not helping."

Veylis promptly turned to Rinyi, who had been doing his best to look inconspicuous. "Is that right, sensitive? Can she read the terrain?"

"I ... suppose so."

"Then summon her!"

"I don't think that's a good idea," Rinyi said, greatly daring.

"Do it, wimp!"

"That's enough, Veylis." Brome stood up. "What you're proposing is risky and foolish. We can't rush into something that might fail. All our worlds could be forfeit."

"I never knew you were such a doom merchant," Veylis said witheringly. "You prefer appeasement, do you? Go ahead, see where it gets you."

"Veylis, back off!" ordered Tarlion. "Stop being such a hothead. You're not the only one with a plan."

"Do you have a better one?"

"No, but *he* does." Tarlion jerked his head toward Trevone.

"Yes. Right," Veylis said dismissively. "It's called wait and see."

"Perhaps I should explain," Trevone said coolly.

"Perhaps you should."

"I'd have told you sooner if you'd been minded to listen. Pulse-cannon aren't equal to the job, but therite is."

"Therite?"

"Unprocessed theridolyte, used in quarrying. I've sent for some."

"Now you're talking!" exclaimed Fley.

"Therite is volatile and difficult to work with," Trevone added.

"And I'm the best explosives expert in the Three Worlds. When will the shipment arrive?"

"I don't know yet. Because of our planet-wide building programme, supplies are scarce. Ibri's trying to source some. By that, I mean he's having to convince the quarrymen that our need is greater than theirs. To stall for time, we're trying to make the sham conciliation last longer that we first intended."

The Eldorians were silent.

"You didn't seriously think we'd settle for that? We needed to embed ourselves here, to study the terrain and the way Vuli functioned, before moving against him. How could we ever trust any promise he might make when he's likely to forget he's made it?"

"And how do we destroy the collector?" asked Brome.

"I'm hoping we won't have to. Once it's no longer receiving commands, it might shut down. Then we could take as long as necessary to remove it."

"And if it doesn't shut down?"

"I'm not sure, to be honest. That thing's built to withstand extreme pressures. The dispersal engine might make a dent or two, but it wouldn't destroy it."

"Could we send it into a decaying orbit?" asked Keska.

"That's a possibility. But we'd need more firepower."

"Your attention, everyone," said Rinyi suddenly. "Vuli's Clustral stream has just reappeared. He'll soon be awake."

"Right, people, it's the moment of truth," said Trevone. "I'd better wake the First Citizens."

+Ready?+ Sarune asked Lydion.

+I suppose I'll have to be+

+Do you want me along?+

+Actually yes, I do. You can help fend off whatever madness he slings at me this time+

+I'm sorry I've been leaving you to his tender mercies+ Sarune seemed in a conciliatory mood.

+You can make it up to me now+ Lydion responded, more positively than of late.

+Is Rinyi not joining us?+

+He's on standby. We daren't let him speak yet+

+So, just the two of us then. United front?+

+Something like that+

They concentrated. As the alternate timeline wasn't mentioned, they assumed Vuli was back in control. It mattered little. His new pronouncement was equally damning.

+The Eldorian Empire is covetous and acquisitive, and if they knew about the Realm they would undoubtedly lay claim to it. Those two well-intentioned children are unlikely to bring about change. Therefore I shall do precisely nothing with Eldor. The Cadence will stay, and when the travellers do not return they will be presumed dead. This should discourage further escape bids+

+Doesn't that contravene your pre-emptive strike ban?+ asked Lydion.

+No, it does not. I intend to do nothing, as I've just stated+

+But the Celestrians will take the Cadence down. What will you do then?+

+Again, nothing. The Celestrians will not remove the Cadence as they will be in no position to do so+

+First Citizen Laura has not yet offered her petition+ Sarune objected.

+Nor will she. By their own admission, the Celestrians are guilty. They allowed their technology to fall into undeserving hands, resulting in misuse and experimentation. This, combined with the errors in establishing the Cadence, created adverse resonances which threatened the Realm.

They also launched resonance devices against my Clustrals. That strategy failed, but clearly the Celestrians are willing to make indiscriminate use of resonance as a weapon. This cannot be allowed to continue+

Lydion had expected something of the kind, but it was still a blow. +We need time to vacate your world+ he ventured.

+For the sake of those who are not Celestrian, atmospheric adjustments will continue for the present+ Vuli replied magnanimously. +But you, of course, will not be leaving+

+What in chaos does he mean, Lydion?+ asked Sarune.

+Never mind that now. Monitor him for a bit, would you? I need to stick close to Rinyi while he delivers the bad news+

+So I'm the babysitter again, am I? So much for the united front. Maybe I'll quiz him about that last remark+

+You don't want to know. Please, Sarune, just leave it+

+*Please?*+ echoed Sarune. +Now I *am* worried+

Laura, Idenion and Trevone had just joined the others. Everyone listened in near-silence while Rinyi spoke. Then there was uproar.

"Didn't Lydion tell him the Realm was dead?" demanded several voices. "Well, why not?"

"Lydion must have his reasons," Rinyi said evasively.

Veylis leapt forward, seized the hapless sensitive by the shoulders and shook him furiously.

314

"Are you with him, Lydion? Do as we tell you or by Ebbon you'll feel his pain!"

"Veylis, don't!" Keska pleaded.

Tarlion launched himself across the cabin and grappled with Veylis. Fley separated them with difficulty.

"First Citizens!" wailed Rinyi. "Advise us!"

"Will Lydion abide by our instructions?" asked Laura.

Rinyi's demeanour changed. "I will, but be warned that the truth carries risks."

Laura bridled. "Oh, for discord's sake, Lydion, just speak to Vuli before there's a riot in here!"

"Do it," Idenion added less vehemently. "Find yourself a place with no distractions. Take Rinyi. We'll need a first-hand report."

Shortly thereafter, with both Rinyi and Sarune in attendance, Lydion addressed Vuli. Earnestly regretful, he depicted conditions within the Realm. He pointed out that its external properties were unchanged, and explained how he was able to read beyond them. He expressed his belief that the Makers would not return, and gently asserted that Vuli's task was over.

And Vuli reacted with fury.

"Masks!" yelled Trevone. "The atmosphere's dissipating. Rinyi's down – I'll bring him in." But Tarlion was already out of the hatch and sprinting toward the prone figure.

Rinyi was physically unhurt. As Tarlion approached he tried to sit up. "Perception overload," he mumbled. "Vuli … lashed out. I got in the way."

"Focus on me," Tarlion ordered. "We need to move."

"How – did you - ?"

"React so quickly? Sarune, of course. She values you."

Trevone arrived with the masks that Tarlion hadn't waited to pick up, and together they hurried Rinyi back to the sphere. The hatch rippled shut and the environmental systems set to work replenishing the air.

"You've left Sarune and Lydion outside," Rinyi said anxiously as soon as his mask was removed. He tried to get off the bunk where he'd been placed, but Tarlion shoved him back.

"Sarune doesn't like being confined. Just relax, will you?"

Rinyi remained agitated. "We should let them in. I can't sense them."

"Do you need to? You should close off. You took quite a hit."

"I've had worse." Rinyi shivered, suddenly glad he was lying down. "The Narvellan Five, for instance. No offence, Tarlion."

"None taken. I assume Vuli attacked Lydion?"

"It wasn't simply an attack, more a rejection or repudiation. Sarune deflected most of it."

"And why deprive us of an atmosphere after he said he wouldn't?" asked Laura. "That was gratuitous."

"He panicked. He's just realised how few Clustrals he has."

"Well, Lydion was right. Vuli won't accept the Realm's finished."

"Something else angered him," Rinyi said.

"What?"

"I don't know. But I think Lydion does."

Keska had activated the long-range scanner.

"Careful of the power reserve," Brome advised. "We'll need it for life support."

"I know, and I'll be quick. With the atmospheric turbulence gone, I can study the collector in detail. Just a hunch, but I think we need to check on its status."

"By Ebbon's bloody beard," muttered Fley as the image built. "You were right, girl. Look at this, Trevone."

Trevone looked. The scoop had opened more fully than he'd thought possible, its gaping maw ready to ingest the next flare – which, he realised, was imminent.

"It's like some carnivorous plant," Laura said, eyeing the object resentfully.

"We could take a sphere into it," mused Trevone. "It's broad enough if it stays like that. We might be able to inflict some damage after all."

"You mean, fire the dispersal engine *inside* that thing?"

"That's exactly what I mean."

"A suicide mission," commented Veylis.

"Not necessarily. I experimented with remote triggers after …" Trevone paused in midsentence.

"After what?" Veylis asked.

"There was an accident with our prototype. A bad one. And I've just had an idea." He keyed the transposer. "Daphos? I need to speak with Clemis urgently. Alert the chain. Find her!"

317

***

+You had to do it, didn't you?+ raged Sarune. +Lydion of Atris, teller of tall tales. You *lied* to Vuli. Though how that was possible in a telepathic dialogue -+

+He's a machine, as you're so fond of telling me. Non-intuitive+

+Well, I hope you're pleased with yourself. No wonder you put off telling him about the Realm!+

+Discord's dreams, Sarune, he was the only source of intel on his creators, this world, everything! I had to gain his confidence quickly. You were all depending on me. He'd already decided I was an AI, so I just took it a stage further+

+And I can just imagine how it went. You're so old and wise, Vuli. You've shown me what it's like to have dedication and purpose. Let me share your burden, whatever it is+

+That's more or less right+ Lydion conceded.

+You tricked him into believing you'd stay here and help monitor the Realm. And what about me? Did you nominate me Celestra's sole guardian?+

+How well you know me! But I swear, if I'd known the Realm was dead - +

+Too late now. He thinks you want to usurp him. Well, you've put paid to the stand-off Trevone was hoping for. The next batch of Clustrals will be headed straight for Celestra+

318

+Trevone's delaying tactics ended when Vuli ruled against us. Stop adding to my misdemeanours+

+So you *are* feeling guilty!+

+Rinyi nearly suffered burn-out, Vuli won't speak to us and the collector's gone into overdrive. So yes, I feel bad. I caused this. When the others know the full story my name will be mud+

+Maybe not+ Sarune ceased her diatribe. +Time for some damage limitation+

+Explain+

+I was about to. Thanks to Vuli's incandescent little tantrum, I now know his precise location, composition and vulnerabilities. Under my direction, one set of therite charges will finish him+

+That should save a lot of time+ Lydion answered cautiously.

+Not just time. If we'd failed to take him out with our first attempt, he'd have set the Clustrals on us. He wouldn't have held back, and you know it. That's one less threat we have to deal with. In addition, the removal of the breathable atmosphere means we no longer have freely circulating fire air, thuvium, oxygen or whatever you like to call it. Due to your inspired action, Fley can rig his charges in the knowledge that they won't blow up in his face+

+You make me sound almost virtuous+ Lydion remarked.

+Good. As soon as that hatch opens I'll convey my findings to your son, who shares your gift of eloquence. He in turn can tell the others. Maybe, just maybe, your name won't be mud after all!+

"Clemis. Thank harmony they found you quickly."

"I was with the neonates. I'm now in Escir's office – alone. What's going on?"

"Daphos will explain. I want to ask you something important. Do we still have the data crystals from Theo's accident?"

"I think so. Why?"

"Yes or no, Clemis. They were in my study along with some other … souvenirs. Please tell me you didn't have one of your manic clear-outs while I was on Alda Six!"

"No, I didn't," Clemis replied testily. "Not that I didn't think about it. You never throw anything away. So, what should I do with the crystals?"

"Take them to Daphos. I'll tell him to expect you. And not a word to anyone else unless you happen to see Ibri."

"Trouble on the way?"

"Yes, but with your help we'll contain it. I'll ensure Dessin's up to speed with - " Another argument had broken out behind him and he turned, irritated, to see what had prompted it. Clemis waited curiously.

"Trevone, we need to open the hatch," said Laura once she had his attention. "Rinyi can't stop shivering – some kind of delayed reaction to the psychic attack. And all our thermal blankets are in the sphere we slept in."

320

Trevone frowned. "Don't we have any spare cloaks?"

"We only have what we stand up in. And in case you hadn't noticed, the cabin temperature's way down. Energy conservation."

"We can't keep venting air," reiterated Brome. "We lose the lot even before the ramp's deployed!"

"Trevone, you must have made contingency plans," Laura persisted. "Tell him!"

"He does have a point," Trevone said reluctantly. "We carry a four-octal supply for a crew of three, as do the other spheres. But numerous containment losses weren't factored in. At this rate we could be on recycled air tomorrow!"

"Which won't be very nice," Tarlion commented. "I should know. Fatigue, brain fog - "

"Exactly!" Brome interrupted. "Which only goes to show - "

"Therefore," Tarlion continued imperturbably, "we crank the hatch manually. Difficult, but it works. We'll open it just enough for the smallest of us to get out. That would be you, Keska."

"Trevone?" inquired Laura.

"Yes, all right, do it. If we're quick about it, the thuvium loss should be minimal. Get ready to make a dash, Keska."

Keska adjusted her mask. "Ready and waiting. Stand by to secure the sphere once I'm out. And mind my fingers!"

The hatch unsealed grudgingly. Keska squeezed through and dropped the short distance to the ground. The ever-watchful Sarune slid into the cabin.

At last Trevone turned back to his waiting wife. "Sorry about that, best girl."

Clemis smiled forgivingly. "Oh, don't apologise. It was very enlightening. Well, you'll need to watch for Keska so I'd better vacate your screen."

"Wait!" Tarlion elbowed Trevone aside. "Sarune knows where Vuli's hidden. She says his anger lit him up."

Clemis stared. "You can talk to Sarune?"

"He can," Trevone said. "And her point is?"

"We overestimated the amount of therite needed. Ibri's bound to have enough by now."

"I'll tell him," Clemis promised. "And I'll deliver those crystals. Trust me!"

The screen blanked briefly, then relit to show the monochrome contours of Vuli's world. Keska, carrying several blankets, was hastening back to the sphere. Brome and Fley made ready to crank the hatch a second time.

"Does Sarune have a Clustral update for us?" asked Trevone.

Tarlion paused fractionally. "She says there aren't any, except for Vuli's providers. She thinks they're amassing offworld, awaiting transposal when there are enough of them."

"I'll scan for their EM signature. And what about Vuli? Is he still furious?"

"He won't communicate. Sarune thinks the outburst damaged him. He's started talking to his predecessor again."

"That's good, isn't it? For us?"

"Not exactly. He's still planning to reset us and his former self agrees it should happen."

"We'll see about that." Trevone paused to ensure Keska was aboard, then called Daphos. "Clemis is on her way to Communications with some data crystals. I want them duplicated and safely stored. Give the copies to Ibri for immediate delivery to us, along with the therite he currently has. If Clemis sees him first, she'll advise him."

"What if there isn't enough therite?"

"There will be. Change of circumstance. Lastly, I need more space mines."

"But you said they were a failure!"

"I have a different use in mind for them. Are they at the spaceport?"

"Not here. Treva. I'll have some sent over." Daphos hesitated. "Trevone, I've been on duty for twelve ilden. I'm not sure how much longer I can keep going."

"Can't anyone stand in for you?"

"Not immediately. Dessin ordered maintenance checks on all our flitters. And my assistant's delivering Clustral detectors."

"Essential preparations," Trevone conceded. "Well, once you've seen Ibri on his way, Treva can take the watch and you can go home. It'll be a day or two before anything else happens."

"I'll make the most of it, then." Daphos smiled wearily. "I do have one staffing suggestion, subject to approval. Jarras has been asking if there's anything he can do to help. Communications could certainly use him at the moment."

"Up to you," Trevone said disinterestedly.

323

"Idenion? Laura? Are you happy with that?"

"Of course," Idenion said.

Laura was less certain. "Won't he be nervous in the tower, after what happened the last time he was alone there?"

"Nobody's going to be shooting at him, are they?" Daphos pointed out.

"True. All right, go ahead and reinstate him."

"Gladly." Daphos signed off, looking more cheerful.

"People," said Tarlion, "may I now have a word in your assembled ears? Lydion wants me to speak on his behalf. Sarune's given me the details."

He immediately had everyone's attention. Even Rinyi, nestling under his blankets, opened an eye.

"Is Lydion here with us?" asked Laura.

"No, he stayed outside. He feels he's let you all down. I hope to convince you otherwise."

"Well, get on with it," Veylis said irritably.

Tarlion thought momentarily of his students back on New Narvella. He had embellished the truth in his many stories, and now he'd do so again. With easy confidence, he spoke of Lydion's growing desperation after several failed attempts to win Vuli's trust. In deference to Fley and Keska he kept his language simple, but in no time at all had his audience exactly where he wanted them. Laura dabbed a tear. Even Veylis looked sympathetic.

"And so," Tarlion went on, "what could he do but lie? He promised the ancient, intransigent AI the only thing which would have any effect: unending loyalty. And at last, Vuli confided his secrets. Who amongst us could have imagined that the Realm was dead? But we can, perhaps, imagine Lydion's dismay when he found out. Vuli had believed a lie; now he rejected the truth, seeing it as a plot against him. We all know what followed." He glanced at Rinyi. "Yet, by a twist of fortune, Vuli's rage has saved us time and resources. And time, as none of you need reminding, is in short supply. So let us glean something positive from Lydion's mistake, and forgive him."

A silence followed. Then, unexpectedly, Veylis spoke. "Mistake? Not in *my* book. It's exactly what I'd have said."

Tarlion looked him in the eye and smiled. It was time to build bridges.

Laura nudged Trevone. "Did you hear *any* of that?"

"Er – what?"

"You're exhausted. Daphos looked worn out but you look ten times worse. And don't give me any more waffle about Alda Six and the length of its days. You need sleep and you need it now. Rinyi, give me one of your blankets. You don't need three."

"There's only one bunk, and he's on it," Trevone argued feebly.

"I'll recline the pilot's chair. There we are. All set."

"I really don't think I should - "

"Do as you're told, Trevone," Veylis said amusedly. "Mother-in-law knows best."

"Just until Ibri gets here," Laura supplemented.

"You'll wake me?"

"Of course." Laura tucked the blanket round him.

"You need to … monitor the flares. Record how many …"

Laura waited.

"He's asleep," said Veylis. "Just like that. Amazing!"

Laura politely steered him away. "We must all do our best to be quiet. Trevone will need all the sleep he can get. His real work hasn't even begun!"

Chapter Twelve

"Hello, sleepyhead!"

Trevone opened bleary eyes to find Clemis smiling down at him. For a moment he thought he was home in Alda Mexa, and smiled lazily back. Then, suddenly, reality dawned and his smile faded. "What in chaos are *you* doing here?"

"Salvaging your mission. Here, have some hot liman."

He sat up, stretched his cramped limbs, and took the beaker she offered. As he sipped, he became aware of an odd change in his surroundings. The cabin was empty apart from Clemis, a soundly sleeping Rinyi, and himself. The hatch was open. Beyond it, everything seemed misty.

Addressing a more immediate problem, he looked across at the hygiene unit and was reassured to see it too was vacant.

"Been queueing, have you?" Clemis inquired. "How disorganised. Maybe you should let women plan these expeditions!"

"Hold that thought," Trevone grinned, heading for the cubicle. "We can argue about it later!"

Clemis smiled indulgently. When he emerged, she handed him a large bowl of cereal and pilif fruits.

"Can we spare this?" he asked.

"We can now. I brought supplies."

"Of course you did." Trevone ate appreciatively. "Where's Ibri?"

"With Fley, deciding where to lay the charges. Tarlion's with them, channelling Sarune. The others are resting while they can. We'll have to relocate before the blasting, and after that we're going to be busy."

Trevone decided not to berate her for turning up. He'd almost forgotten how resourceful Clemis could be when she chose. "How did you talk Ibri into bringing you?"

"I might have given him the impression you'd sent for me," she said carelessly.

"And you've got the crystals?"

"The crystals, the mines, everything you requisitioned and more."

Trevone put down his bowl and approached the hatchway. A translucent tunnel of lightweight polymer snaked across the landing zone, branching off at intervals to connect with the other three spheres. Nearby, an airlock of more rigid construction led to the planet's surface. "What *is* this?"

"Habbon calls it his air corridor. It was made for temporary use on the Alda Four dig. It wouldn't work in a vacuum, of course – it would just balloon outwards and split – but as long as there's air pressure on the outside, it'll hold."

Trevone tugged at a section of the material, which was apparently adhered to the theridolyte hatch frame. It detached itself briefly, then slithered off his hand and snapped back into place.

"It's theridolyte friendly," Clemis added.

"Yes, but how's it done? Polymers are chemically inert. Who made it and why didn't I know about it?"

"Habbon said it was made at Ninka. At their refinery."

"And you know this because …"

"Habbon's always visiting Escir. More specifically, Esc had a bale of this wonder-fabric brought to the neonates unit. He thought it might suit the incubators, but he never got around to trying it."

Someone had entered the airlock. It swished open to reveal Ibri, grimy and sweaty, thankfully peeling off his breathing gear and making for the spacecraft he and Clemis had arrived in. He reappeared almost at once with a shatter-proof glass case of therite.

"I wish there was a better way of transporting that stuff," Trevone muttered.

"Relax," said Clemis lightly. "We got it through t-space, didn't we? Every fragment's cocooned in mythol gel. I helped with the packing." She focused. +Ibri! How's it going?+

He changed direction and approached them. "We're getting there. This is the final batch of charges. I wanted to keep some in reserve, but Sarune says we have to use them all. It won't take long to place them but we still have to set theridolyte reflectors."

"Sarune's instructions?"

"Who else? She wants to duplicate the cave-in that killed off Vuli One, and she doesn't want us wasting firepower on empty air. We're going deep down."

Trevone looked slightly sceptical. "You'll need thuvium for the detonation. How do you plan to deliver it?"

"Already there, according to Sarune. Embedded. If you want detail you'd better ask Tarlion what she meant."

"I will," said Trevone, puzzled.

"I'll send him over if you like. I work better when I'm not being watched." He stepped into the airlock, repositioning his mask. Presently Tarlion appeared and let himself in.

"Greetings, lovebirds. I gather you want a chemistry lesson."

"Keep it brief, please."

Tarlion grinned. "Difficult, since I'll be wrestling with many technologies. Firstly, Sarune detected some stray oxygen – er, thuvium – molecules in Vuli's Clustral feed. She assumed they were randomly acquired in space. There were mercury molecules too."

"Sorry, I don't know that word."

"Laura calls it mercury. Idenion calls it hydragyros."

Trevone banished a scowl. "It's about time he and the other aesthetes stopped using Earther-Greek. He means brightflight. Zyltris."

"Two names for the same element? The sooner you rewrite your periodic table, the better. So, this process of feeding Vuli's been going on for – well, we don't know. But long enough for that trickle of odd molecules to accumulate, combine and oxidise. That's Laura's term. Got a different one?"

"Never mind. Go on."

"To separate the elements and free the oxygen, all we have to do is make the area nice and hot. We'll direct low-powered laser fire from a safe height, and wait for the flash-point. If our assessment's correct, the blast should split open a fault line very close to Vuli."

"You've worked very fast."

"Fley's used to that. And Sarune's been amazing."

"So I gather. But where's Lydion? Is he still keeping out of our way?"

"Yes and no. There wasn't a lot he could do – he can't read the ground like Sarune does. So he's with Rinyi, keeping watch and promoting recuperative sleep."

"That's Lydion for you," said Clemis fondly. "Little kindnesses when you least expect them. Maybe he sent a few soothing thoughts in *your* direction, Trevone, since you slept for a whole day. A Celestrian day, that is."

"Chaos! Has anyone been monitoring the flares?"

"The equipment can handle it," said Tarlion, unconcerned.

"How many have I missed? Approximately?"

"Eight or nine. We're not being negligent, Trevone, so less of the disapproval. We're prioritising. First things first."

"That's just idleness. Surely one of you could have found the time to - "

"Trev my sweet," interrupted Clemis, "why don't we run through the data on those crystals, to refresh our memories before we have to relocate?"

Trevone subsided. "Yes. Yes, we should do that."

"Good. And while we're reviewing it, we can decide on the best place to work on the programming. Here, or in space."

"Wait, Clemis, just … wait. You can help with the preliminaries but I'll have to do the rest by myself. You know why. I'll be invoking a t-space portal."

"No, *we* will. You and me. Someone will have to build new circuits. I did it before, at your side, and I can do it again. Like it or not, you need my help."

* * *

Removed to a safe distance on the featureless plain, the scientists, engineers and soldiers waited and watched. A few stood outside, but more opted for a viewscreen link between all four spheres. Veylis, pleased to have an active role at last, fired continuous pulse-cannon bursts at the target specified by Sarune.

"Does he have the right place?" asked Laura.

"Believe me, he does," said Tarlion. "Sarune says there are useful voids near the surface, underneath all the rubble that's being churned up."

"Does she know how long this will take?"

"It's only been half an ild, if that. Just keep watching. We don't need to melt the rock, just toast the oxidised stuff that's down there."

Another quarter-ild passed. Some of the watchers grew inattentive. Then Ibri spotted a flicker of green flame amid the dust. "Veylis, stop firing and increase your height. Brome, start the recorder."

He'd scarcely finished speaking when the therite ignited with a flash and roar, bathing the landscape in eerie green. Moments later, the secondary charges erupted as their dampeners burnt off.

"Status, Ibri?" asked Trevone, icily calm.

"It worked. Look."

The camera on Veylis' craft, focused closely on the blast area, showed a slowly widening crevice.

"Watch the nearside," Ibri added. "We concentrated our efforts there. Vuli's main systems are arranged vertically, just beyond the fracture. I'm hoping for visual proof of his destruction."

The crack turned at a right angle, then again. And halted. Silt and rubble showered steadily into its depths, but the infrastructure held. Veylis, impatient, lined up a further shot.

"Wait!" cautioned Ibri.

A further subsidence left the rock exposed on four sides. The central mass stubbornly held its position, defying gravity. Then, almost gracefully, it collapsed. For one brief moment the jewels and crystals of Vuli's circuitry shone in the light of day. One moment only. The rock face sundered, sweeping everything before it. Finally, all was silent.

Keska was the first to speak. "Rest, soldier, your long vigil over. Wendlissin has fallen, a new era begins."

+He didn't suffer+ Lydion added.

Sarune was incensed. +You *read* him? Are you insane?+

+I had to know+ Lydion answered calmly.

+You had to take yet another risk+ Sarune retorted. Then, curiously: +Was he scared?+

+No. Same old Vuli – proud, obstinate. But at the last, when the light hit, he registered amazement. Sheer wonder. Not a bad way to go+

Keska again had the collector on visual. No-one seriously believed that Vuli's demise would bring Clustral production to a halt, but until there was proof that it hadn't, one slim hope remained. It was soon dashed. Almost lost amid solar static, the Clustrals' EM signature sounded faintly as a fresh cloud was ejected. Their chatter grew louder, then suddenly ceased as they transposed in search of their fellows. Slowly, almost lazily, the scoop gaped wide in anticipation of the next flare.

"Keep watch with everything we've got," ordered Trevone. "The interval between the readying of the scoop and the start of the flare is all the time we'll have for the delivery of our weapon. While we're preparing it I want every one of those sequences studied and measured, including all past readings. Highlight all discrepancies. It need hardly be said that for our safety, we have to match operations to the shortest interval – and then shave more time off that.

"Clemis and I will handle the programming. We've done it before and there's no time to teach anyone else. Ibri will customise a sphere to remotely control the device sphere. Brome, you'll be responsible for the solar data. Keska can assist Brome and Ibri."

"What about me?" asked Veylis.

"You can help Fley with the site maintenance and catering."

"Seriously?"

"Someone has to do it," said Fley genially, "and everyone else will be too busy. I enjoy cooking, anyway."

"It's just for now, Veylis," Trevone added. "Later you'll be Keska's pilot when she deploys the space mines. Rinyi, you and the incorporeals will patrol the site and scan for Clustrals. We can't assume they'll all transpose, not once we start our activities. I suspect the collector's just a machine with no reasoning capability, but we simply don't know. Likewise, we know the Clustrals have self-determination, but how binding was Vuli's last command? We don't know that either. So, we proceed with caution. Now if there are no further questions - "

"I didn't hear Tarlion's name on the roster," Veylis remarked.

"Nor the First Citizens," Keska put in.

"That's because we're going home," said Laura. "I came here at Vuli's behest, and said my piece for what it was worth, but that part of the mission's well and truly over."

"Did Dessin send for you?" asked Clemis.

"Not in so many words, but he'll be relieved to see us. He says the Clustrals have been mapping everything again – planning their strategy. The longer we stay away, the worse it looks. We need to be there for our people."

"I'll navigate, as before," Tarlion said. "Unless you'd care to do the honours, Veylis?"

"No thanks. The space mines sound much more fun."

Keska eyed him coquettishly. "I haven't explained what we'll be doing with them yet."

"Then tell me now, sweetness. What do we blow up?"

"Nothing. They're resonance enabled, so we track them. We launch them into the collector when it opens its ugly mouth, then observe their signal until it stops."

"We just let them be pulverised?"

"Yes, to gauge the maximum depth Trevone's sphere can reach."

"And then what? He fires the disperser?"

"Not exactly." Trevone answered for her. "I'm attempting to recreate the accident that killed my friend. If I succeed, and I'm confident I will, a t-space node will briefly touch the sphere. It will be annihilated along with its surroundings."

"Ouch," said Veylis. "And if you screw up?"

"Then I'll have wasted a valuable piece of equipment. Any more questions?"

"Yes. This is pure speculation, you understand, but have you considered removing the Cadence and getting the entire Three Worlds space fleet out here to blast that thing?"

"With pulse-cannon? With laser fire?"

"Well .. yes."

"No, I haven't. Keska will tell you why."

Veylis looked at her inquiringly.

Keska sighed. "Because you'd be *feeding* it, silly. Listen to Trevone. He knows what he's doing."

Silence.

"Right, team," Trevone said briskly, "you know your duties. Let's get to work. Oh, one last thing – I need a strong-willed volunteer to enforce the sleep rota."

"Me!" Veylis said instantly. "My one chance to order you around, First Scientist."

"You're on."

"Trev," ventured Laura, "it's time we weren't here."

He refocused. "Apologies. Getting ahead of myself. I'll help Tarlion disconnect your sphere from the air corridor, and then you're free to leave. Could you do me a favour? Once you're under way, ask Communications not to chase us for updates. If they don't hear from us, they're to assume everything's on track. Tarlion, you're with me."

"Laura," said Clemis, "safe journey."

"And you take care. Stay well away from that artefact."

"Trevone will look after me," Clemis said somewhat ambiguously.

"And I'll look after *her*," promised Idenion, giving Laura a swift hug. "Hurry home, Clemis. We'll be thinking of you."

***

+*Ibri*!+

Clemis and Rinyi flinched. Trevone didn't usually vent his anger in that way.

+What?+ Ibri's reply was aggrieved.

+My sphere. Now+

Moments later Ibri, still indignant, stepped through the open hatch. "What in chaos is wrong with you, Trevone?"

"Perhaps you can explain this." Trevone gestured at the monitor.

"What am I looking at exactly?"

"Someone from Treva – possibly someone you work with – wrote a subroutine for the disperser and installed it with no reference to me. Without wishing to sound proprietorial, this is *my* weapon and I should have been informed."

"Strictly speaking, it's Tralvar's weapon," Ibri said with a trace of the belligerence he'd once been renowned for. "What's this miscreant done to it?"

"We think some well-meaning person installed a safety feature," said Clemis, attempting to smooth things over. "If an unstable node begins to form, the firing's aborted."

"Unfortunately," Trevone went on, "Theo's accident began and ended with an unstable node. Until I've rewritten this programme I can't even run a simulation."

"But why yell at *me*?"

"You've been at Treva working on spheres. There was a chance you knew about this."

"I've been at Treva working on pulse-cannon," Ibri corrected him. "Before that, I was at the Ninka refineries."

"Sorry."

"And *I'm* sorry that I don't know enough about programming to help unravel this. Can I go now?"

"This is going to cause a big delay," said Trevone, half to himself. "Yes, Ibri. Go."

"I can't test the remote handling until you're done here. Shall I talk Keska through the space mine op?"

"Good idea. At least we'll be making *some* progress."

"I'm on it." Ibri disappeared into the air corridor. He was back in less than two astallen.

"Well?" asked Trevone ominously.

"Problem. Something we both should have remembered. You too, Clemis."

"And what might that be?" Clemis inquired, waiting for the yelling to recommence.

Ibri forbore. "What were the space mines originally designed to do? You know this – you were there."

"They emit a counter-resonance to interfere with the ... oh."

"Exactly. Oh. If Keska launches the mines in their present configuration they'll simply turn around and target her sphere. Which, of course, is Eldorian."

"We needed its pulse-cannon!" Trevone said defensively.

"I'm not criticising." Ibri sounded weary. "We've had to improvise at every turn. Let's just concentrate on putting this right."

"Can you adapt Keska's sphere to remotely access this one?"

"Maybe, but I wouldn't like to try. Eldorian logic systems aren't much like ours. No, the only solution is to deactivate or modify the resonant component in each mine. Keska says she can do it. And Rinyi can help – he can sense changes in the resonance."

Trevone stared morosely at the floor.

"We don't have to convert many," Ibri added. "A dozen or so should be enough for our purposes."

Trevone didn't look up. "Let's hope so."

"Keska won't let us down," Clemis declared. "She broke out of the Cadence, didn't she? Now let's get on with our share of the work."

The nameless sun undulated along the horizon of its single planet. Trevone, Clemis and the rest of the team deferred to Veylis' temporary authority, eating and sleeping at regular intervals. They worked methodically, forcing themselves not to rush, trying not to think of the new batches of Clustrals being spawned every four ilden.

+We should have gone with Tarlion+ Lydion fretted.

"+What use would we have been?+ Sarune answered testily. +We're needed here+

+Rinyi could have done what we're doing+

+Keska required his talents+

+Then we could have dispensed with the patrol. It's pointless. The Clustrals have abandoned this place. Their target is Celestra+

+They haven't left yet. Brome's been tracking them+

+Then it's a tactical delay. They won't transpose until they've maximised their numbers, and we'll still be stuck here when they do. Celestra's my home, Sarune, and I want to go back. I don't belong out here+

+Oh, go and talk to Rinyi. He's homesick too+

+Isn't he supposed to be busy?+

+He was. Keska's just finished neutralising a bunch of the mines, as you'd know if you hadn't been communing with your inner Atrisian. She's just sent for Trevone. Shall we drop in on them?+

+Might as well. If they've made some progress we'll be that much closer to going home+

Trevone, when they found him, was still conversing with Brome. Loudly. "One and a half astallen? Is that all?"

"You told us to look for the shortest interval. I've searched the readings several times, and so's Ibri. See for yourself. The scoop opens – here – and the flare encounters it, here. I've allowed half an astal for Veylis to get clear after the mines are launched."

"I can do it," said Veylis promptly. "Now would you please inspect Keska's work? She's waiting."

"What we're left with," said Keska when they were all assembled, "is a monotonal resonance with a blip effect as the mine rotates. Here's the graph." She indicated the monitor. "And here's an audio simulation."

"Pleasant," commented Trevone.

+Boring+ remarked Sarune.

"I'll launch a couple just after take-off, to confirm there's no backlash," Keska continued. "Brome, how long before the scoop reopens?"

"A little over half an ild."

"Then I don't propose to hang about. Veylis, can we be in position before that happens?"

"Absolutely."

"Then let's go. Right, everyone – out! Unhitch the tunnel, someone."

"Are you sure you don't want me along?" asked Fley.

"Not this time, father. Trust me. I know what I'm doing."

Veylis, outwardly calm and efficient, took the sphere into orbit. There, as arranged, Keska jettisoned two of the tiny mines. They hovered, then drifted away on some unseen eddy.

"Clever girl," said Veylis.

"That was the easy part. Let's get on with phase two."

At close quarters, the scoop was intimidatingly huge.

"Are you sure we won't be sucked in?" Veylis inquired, trying not to sound worried.

"All our readings suggest that it's inert, that it relies on the flare's velocity," Keska said. "But if I order full reverse thrust, you'll know everybody got it wrong."

"I see."

"The mines will be under propulsion this time," Keska elaborated. "They only have one speed, so if they accelerate, we'll have all the warning we need. But whatever happens, we *have* to monitor their signal until it stops – and that means staying exactly where we are."

"Oh?"

342

"Their output isn't great. Also, there are small but persistent interference sources nearby. Resonance sumps, probably, left by Clustral portal activity."

They waited, the adamantine bulk of the collector filling the viewscreen. Keska, ever curious, increased magnification to inspect the alien surface. "Just as I thought, Veylis. Heat damage. Extensive. This thing's showing its age!"

"It doesn't maintain itself, then?"

"Well if it does, it can't keep up." She switched to the original setting. "Any time now, we should see movement."

The scoop began to open, evidenced at first by a change in the vessel's outline. Then, as it widened, sunlight glinted sullenly along its upper edge.

"Recording," said Keska. "Not that there's anything to see yet. It's black as Ebbondrear in there."

Veylis fidgeted. "Shouldn't we be launching the mines?"

"In a moment, when it's opened a bit further. Relax, I know what I'm – hey, did you see that?"

"What?"

"The upper half jolted. Hesitated. I think our scoop's as worn out as Vuli!"

"Maybe, but it's just woken up. Look!"

A red glow wavered in the distant depths.

"Readings nonspecific," Keska said after checking her panel. "We're only seeing a reflection."

"Well, what is it? A furnace?"

"At a guess I'd say it's a fusion device, an ancient one. It must have been bright as a star once." Suddenly she was all efficiency. "Releasing mines. Timer running. Acquiring signals." A medley of blips sounded over the commlink. "We have half an astal before we need to leave. Start the countdown."

"Starting countdown at one-eight-seven isk."

The mines, now invisible to the sphere's cameras, sailed ever deeper into the collector's featureless maw. The distant glow did not increase. The chirping signals continued at full strength.

"Sixty isk," Veylis announced. "Solar radiation's starting to build. We should make a move."

"Not while I still have contact."

"Forty-five isk. Forty. You're cutting it fine, Keska. Twenty-eight."

The chirping ceased in a squeal of static.

"Signal loss timed at fifty-seven isk. Recording archived. Go, Veylis!"

He needed no second bidding. Keska, in a state of high anticipation, forwarded the data to Trevone while still in transit. Both she and Veylis assumed the final stage of the operation would go ahead at once. Such was their faith in Trevone's work that they were looking forward to an early return to Celestra and the start of peace negotiations. After they'd touched down, however, their hopes were summarily put on hold.

"I need another day – perhaps longer," said Trevone.

"Why?" demanded Veylis.

"Do the maths. The length of the conduit, the signature speed of the mines, the time before contact was lost. They were only a third of the way along before they were consumed. I was hoping they'd reach the halfway point. I've finished reprogramming the dispersal engine but I now need to disable some of the safety protocols in the sphere itself."

"Again, why?"

"To ensure I have complete control of the weapon," Trevone answered curtly. To Clemis he was more forthcoming.

"You saw Theo's sphere. Ruined, ripped apart, but still recognisably a sphere. That was because the instant things went wrong, the logic system shut off the dispersal process. It could intervene this time, unless I prevent it. Now that I know we can't centralise our attack, I have to ensure the disperser stays active as long as possible. It may well be only a fraction of an isk more than if I leave things as they are, but in terms of t-space that fraction could mean the difference between success and failure."

"I see," said Clemis with a tiny sigh. "I can't help you this time, can I? Beyond my expertise?"

"Afraid so. That's why I need a whole day. I have to isolate the disperser from *two* logic systems: this one, and whichever one we'll be operating remotely. You *could* stand by to shoo Veylis away if he decides I need sleep."

"You do."

"I'll rest when the work's done. I'm not needed for the final system checks. We're nearly there, Clemis. And if this succeeds it means Theo won't have died in vain."

Despite his estimate of the workload, Trevone completed the task in half a day – then slept like a baby until Clemis woke him. It had been agreed that once the weaponised sphere was in the target area, Ibri would take over the guidance while Trevone concentrated on the disperser. And the entire operation would be conducted from the ground – almost an anti-climax, thought Veylis.

"Come on," said Keska. "They want us to clear out. Once that sphere goes belly-up we'll only have our scanners to show us the result, so, let's find another viewscreen and bag a ringside seat!"

Also banished from the control sphere, Clemis and Fley went to prepare supper in the one remaining craft. Brome went with them, to ready the long-distance monitoring. Latterly, Rinyi arrived, presumably with Lydion and Sarune, although they communicated nothing.

"We're there," said Trevone, scarcely before his audience had settled. "Take over, Ibri."

"Maintaining distance till scoop opens," Ibri responded. "We're a little early. Detecting Clustral chatter. Fading. Gone. They'll be heading to where the others are holed up."

"Hopefully that's the last of them," Trevone said, sounding anything but hopeful.

They waited.

"Scoop opening," Trevone announced at last. "It's all yours, Ibri. Proceed with care – you won't see much once you're in there."

"Setting trajectory," Ibri began. "Entering scoop, adopting space mine progression. Chaos, we're just crawling!"

"Concentrate," warned Trevone.

"External lights on," Ibri resumed. "Chronometer running."

A soft tone began sounding a countdown from fifty-seven isk.

"Readying dispersal engine," said Trevone.

A peremptory chime rang out, startling them both.

"Proximity alert," Ibri said tensely. "Correcting drift. Sorry."

The subdued tones continued.

"Five isk remaining," said Ibri, back in control. "One, zero. In position. Holding steady."

"Commencing firing sequence," Trevone responded. "Powering up. Node acquired. Coalescing. Instability detected - "

Malfunction alarms sounded in the other craft.

"Keep the Drive running!" Trevone shouted. "Node critical. T-space incursion - "

Their screens went dark.

" – inevitable," Trevone concluded in a whisper.

"But did it work?" Ibri asked.

"We'll see. Reinstating scanners."

The viewscreen showed the collector apparently unscathed, and Trevone bowed his head despondently. Then, suddenly, as if punched by a giant hand, a section of the hull caved in. Moments later it crumpled again, untidily, entrails of its secret workings spilling outwards in torn strands. The

347

entire structure had slewed out of its long-held position, the open scoop sagging dismally.

"So … what happens next?" inquired Ibri shakily. "Does everyone head for home?"

"Soon. First, we wait one more flare cycle. If no more Clustrals appear, and I somehow don't think they will, then we're free to go. I presume the collector's past self-repair - "

"Long past, according to Keska."

" – but just to make sure, we'll come back later with enough hardware to send it into a decaying orbit."

The other team members were unusually quiet in Trevone's presence. No-one save Clemis had known what to expect from t-space.

"Should we call Alda Mexa now?" asked Keska.

"Not till we've proof the collector's finished," said Trevone. "It's the first thing they'll ask."

"What about all the Clustrals that got away?"

"Still here, I imagine. For the time being."

"I hope they don't get mad at us for what we've just done."

"You credit them with too much intelligence," said Rinyi, speaking for Lydion. "They'll know the supply's dried up, nothing more. With no new instructions they'll follow Vuli's last command as best they can. We'll be needed at home, so can we please wind this up?"

"Gladly," said Trevone. "To that end, would you and Sarune take part in the final inspection? Certify the wreck Clustral-free?"

"Anything to speed up our departure."

"Fine, let's set it up. Brome, Ibri – help me ready bioshells for the three of us. We'll get Lydion and Sarune as close as they need to go. And as soon as that's done, I'll tell Alda Mexa we're on our way."

***

"They're coming home," said Daphos.

Dessin sighed. "You didn't tell them?"

"It can wait till they get here. But then we'll have some swift decisions to make, before the Clustrals stop mapping and start attacking. Soon everyone's going to know that Laura and Idenion are missing, and we can't be leaderless at a time like this. If *you* don't want to be First Citizen then we must appoint someone who does. Kalyx, for example."

"Not yet," Dessin said emphatically. "They have Tarlion with them, and if there's any way at all of fixing a damaged sphere, he'll find it."

"And if he doesn't?"

Dessin was silent for a moment. "Let's leave it to Clemis," he said at last. "I'll abide by whatever she says."

"Dessin." Sheyell spoke from the doorway.

He turned from Daphos' viewscreen image. "What?"

"If Daphos is meeting Clemis at the spaceport I'd like to be there."

Both men looked surprised.

"Rinyi could have been lost too. And I'd like to make my peace with him – make amends, if I can – before all the trouble starts."

***

Clemis, pale but composed, sat with Daphos in the reception area of Communications. "You were right to keep this news from us," she assured him.

Trevone, beside her, agreed. "It would have distracted us from our work and we'd still be there now, with more and more Clustrals pouring out of that orbiting monstrosity."

Daphos looked marginally less unhappy.

"And Tarlion gave no hint that anything was wrong?" Clemis continued.

"None. He was cheerful. He'd left the Cowl and was in the run-up to transposal. We'll see you in a couple of ilden, he said. And then – nothing. For five days. I'm so very sorry. Clemis ..."

"Go on."

"I hate to press you for decisions, but we urgently need clarity. Do we tell the people now?"

"Yes, we must. I don't want anyone thinking that Laura and Idenion are hiding from danger. It's the one thing they'd never do."

"Then who leads us? Dessin doesn't want to."

"Quite right." Clemis was secretly amazed at how calm she sounded. "He's excellent at his job and he should continue in it, coordinating the plan he helped devise. As for leadership, we should look to history. When Alendis died in a space accident, Tralvar as First Scientist took charge. He wasn't

350

formally elected till later. Therefore, if Trevone's willing, we'll take temporary office until this crisis is over. Afterwards, we can decide who's next in line: Dessin, Kalyx or some other candidate. Well, Trevone, are you up for this? We just have to keep a high profile and act positive."

"Whatever it takes."

Clemis hugged him, allowing her composure to slip a little. "Daphos, can I see Esclevon? I need to see him."

"You can, but ..."

"But what?"

"We can't pull him from his given task. He's essential to the city's defences."

"Of course. He would be," said Clemis expressionlessly. "So why don't you walk us through the set-up? We'll need to know everything."

They took the lift to the top of the tower. Jarras, on communications watch, greeted Trevone awkwardly. He and his son hadn't been on good terms for years.

"I've just had word from Treva. Ibri and the others reported to Ymer and he's granted them leave – subject to immediate recall of course. The girl, Keska, isn't with them. She wanted to see Roegin."

"The akron's now our centre of ops," Daphos explained. "Solid and low-tech. We'd hoped to dispense with the tower completely, but we don't have enough transposers."

Trevone frowned. "Why not?"

351

"Didn't Idenion tell you?" Jarras made an attempt at one-upmanship. "The Prefect of Treva was helping himself to aldacite crystals. Some kind of vanity project. Idenion had to reprimand him."

"We've installed seventeen transposers," Daphos went on. "These will keep us in constant touch with all city states and larger settlements. But we have to keep some extra modes free in case the smaller agrarian communities come under attack."

"Which is why we need the tower," Jarras said. "Someone has to stay on duty and I've volunteered."

Bad idea, thought Trevone. He was shielded, but Jarras guessed his reaction.

"And you?" he asked coldly. "Where will *you* be? Alda Six?"

"No. We can't waste resources defending it, so I've decided to shut it down for the present. I've already recalled the staff."

"Then it's even more important that *one* deep space scanner stays active," Jarras declared. "Keeping watch for incoming spacecraft, for instance."

"Laura and Idenion? That's another indulgence we can't afford. If Tarlion manages to save them he'll find his own way home."

"You think they're dead."

Clemis' hand tightened on Trevone's arm.

"Yes, Jarras, I'm afraid I do. When Tarlion's sphere was caught in the Bad Resonance he kept it going despite catastrophic failures. He sent a distress message and made landfall. Given similar circumstances he could, for instance, create an

352

emergency beacon with just a few working crystals. But nothing's been received. I don't think they'll be coming back."

A cloud passed in front of the sun. At the same time Rinyi's agitated thoughts reached them from the visitors' lounge below.

+They're here! The Clustrals are here!+

Moments later, the Kest monitoring station made contact. "It's one large mass of them. They materialised, hovered, then vanished."

"It's starting," said Daphos. "I should get back to the ops room. Clemis, Trevone – prepare for some hands-on experience instead of a guided tour. Grab Rinyi and his mother, and let's go."

They retrieved Rinyi and Sheyell and bundled them into a flitter. As they lifted off, full daylight was restored. The Clustrals had moved on.

"What are they planning?" Daphos asked Rinyi. "I heard you could read them."

"I know when they're watching us. Not the same thing."

"And they weren't watching us just now?"

"No. Just conversing, babbling, amongst themselves. They seemed troubled."

"Maybe that's a good sign," said Clemis hopefully.

The control hub was situated on the first floor of the akron, in a large room with no outside walls and three exits. Close by, a library annexe now housed several storage batteries and an assortment of rations.

"No generators?" queried Rinyi.

"Not safe. Fuel emissions," Daphos said. "There's one in the kitchen area, where there's ventilation. And there are supply units like this one throughout the city. The hospital's on standby and the river people are ready to assist if the lower laterals flood. We're as prepared as we'll ever be."

"And the other city states? Are they?"

"We've given them autonomy to run things their way. Variety could be a useful defence."

Dessin came to greet them. "We've sent the students home," he reported. "Those who wanted to go, that is. The rest are looking forward to an adventure."

Trevone sighed. "Was I ever that fearless? Well, it's their choice. Who's to tell which areas are safe?"

Dessin led them to a banked array of transposers, each one hastily labelled with the name of a city state. Messages were starting to arrive from all over the planet, detailing a series of Clustral visitations.

"What are they *doing*?" muttered Trevone.

No-one had any suggestions. But as the alerts continued, a pattern emerged. The Clustrals' behaviour never varied; they appeared, did nothing, went away. The intervals between messages grew shorter, but didn't overlap.

"Trevone," Clemis said suddenly, "that's *all* of them – all there is left! There's only one swarm!"

"Chaos! I thought there'd be more."

"That's still one too many," Sheyell declared acidly. "Don't congratulate yourselves."

354

"Do either of you know why they're acting like this?" inquired Dessin.

"I can answer that," said Rinyi unexpectedly. "They're planning to attack one city state at a time."

"It's a possibility," Sheyell conceded.

"It's a fact, mother. Divided, the swarm would be ineffective. They're seeking continuity, perfecting their transference."

"Transference," Trevone repeated almost to himself. "They're not transposing. And if they can't transpose - "

"Or won't."

"- then they can't import extreme weather from other planets. They're restricted to whatever they can summon locally."

"Which can be bad enough," Daphos put in.

"What did you mean by *won't* transpose?" Sheyell inquired of Rinyi.

"Whenever the Clustrals open a portal, some die. So Lydion says. They'd decimate their own number if they attempted it here."

"Is Lydion with you now?" asked Trevone.

"No, he ... took off when he heard about Tarlion."

"Not again!" said Trevone angrily. "We need him here!"

"Be reasonable, dearest," Clemis admonished. "He's bound to be distressed. He'd only just found Tarlion and now he's lost him again."

Trevone relented somewhat. "So where's Sarune? Is *she* here?"

"I sent her after him, "Rinyi said. "I think he went looking for Tonora,"

"That little fantasist!" Daphos said dismissively. "I suppose she'll tell him Tarlion's alive and well and will show up very soon."

"So what, if it keeps him functional?" Dessin was coolly pragmatic. "If they've gone to the Lyricon they've had a wasted trip, so don't expect them back in a hurry. Tonora's in Tivenne."

"I'm sure Lydion will realise that," Rinyi said calmly.

"Of course he will. It's her family home. And now, if everyone would kindly close off, I'm going to instruct Kyrin to announce three deaths before the child starts spreading her own version. Once that's done, the chain will deal with Clustral matters only. Daphos, notify all regions to inform their relayists. We make the announcement worldwide, then we wait."

But Kest was not inclined to wait. After a barely respectful pause, the transposer lit again.

"Hey, Daphos! Listen: when those Clustrals come back we've got a little surprise in store for them."

Daphos glared. "When we gave you a free hand we *didn't* give you leave to be stupid!"

"And we're not. This is a tribute to Laura, in a way: what she'd call a pre-emptive strike."

"You were told to fight defensively. Don't you ever take notice of us?"

"If we'd had that attitude in the past we'd never have beaten the Eldorians."

"Indeed?" queried Daphos. "Remind me of the part you played in that conflict. I can't seem to think of anything!"

Dessin was growing more and more exasperated. Seeing this, Clemis decided to step in.

"Since I'm in charge now, perhaps I can cast a deciding vote. If you have a strategy, spokesman for Kest, then you've permission to employ it. But be reminded that autonomy means just that. If you find yourselves in trouble, no-one will come to your rescue."

"Understood, First Citizen. Thank you." The operator signed off.

"Well done," said Dessin laconically.

Clemis didn't relish her new title. "Can I see Esclevon now?" she asked plaintively.

"As you wish. I'll take you to him."

"Chaos, Dessin, I'm quite capable of handling a flitter. Just tell me where he is. Got it. No, Trevone, you stay here. Vonnie's used to me checking up on him but if you turn up as well he might lose confidence." She glanced at the screens. The Clustral activity showed no sign of escalating. "I won't be long. And anyway – if there *is* such a thing as a safe place, it'll be where Vonnie is."

Esclevon was billeted with two other boys in a disused machine shop. "I'm told this used to be Tralvar's recording studio," he said, brushing aside Clemis' attempt at a hug. "What did you want, mother? Make it quick. We've just received the call to man our stations!"

One of Nohal's co-workers, Lakal, was in charge of the trio. She was equally tense, but more forthcoming. "The children are ranged around this lateral at eight locations. Because they're mostly

357

scolia trainees we've tended to use music venues for our lattice sites."

Clemis' gaze was drawn to the prill habitats, small self-contained domes containing the unlovely plants on which so much depended.

"One of the boys' tasks is to monitor these environments," Lakal continued. "We have to ensure a continuous power source. We're still on the grid at the moment but that could change very soon."

"Daphos inferred that Esclevon's role was vital. Why is that?"

Esclevon answered for himself. "As I'm the strongest sender, I'm the link to Kyrin. He can provide short-term back-up if we need it."

"It all sounds a bit … improvised," Clemis ventured.

"Not at all. When the Clustrals are somnolent they emit a distinctive radio pattern, easily identified. Once we control them they should be easy to destroy. Don't worry, mother. We've practised. And now hadn't you better get back to the akron before the fun starts? It's where people will expect you to be."

Clemis hadn't, till that moment, acknowledged that she'd have to switch residences. Much as it saddened her to do so, she gathered some clothes and other essentials from her home and transferred them to her parents' apartment. It felt like stepping back in time to her younger days, before Space Tech and the Gloriana.

Trevone, of course, couldn't be with her. He was based at the spaceport maintenance block with the city's meagre defence team. At least Dessin hadn't sent him to Treva with Ibri and the Eldorians. It made sense to locate most of the armed spheres at Treva, whose heavy industry offered a prime target, but Clemis couldn't help thinking that Alda Mexa had been left underprotected.

When she returned to the akron hub, Daphos was about to take an extended break.

"Dessin freed up the guest suites to house defence workers," he explained. "I can be on call, in the building, whenever I'm not on duty."

"It was the only way to make him rest," Dessin said when he'd gone.

"You look in need of sleep yourself," Clemis chided.

"And I intend to have it, as soon as I'm sure Trytin over there will take the work seriously."

"Of course I shall. It beats delivering radios," said the duty tech, suppressing a grin.

"What's so amusing?" Clemis asked.

"Kest broadcast the Clustrals' EM emissions back at them. It confused them just long enough for the pulse-cannon boys to take some of them out."

"That's good news, but I still don't see the joke."

"Alcine tried it too. It didn't work, and the Clustrals launched a torrent at them."

Alcine was a desert city, once the twin of vanished Ilonna.

"Do you get it now? Sand plus torrential rain equals mud. A whole lot of mud."

Dessin sighed. "It was amusing to begin with. Their spacefield's now waterlogged and they can't deploy their spheres."

"Then they need reprimanding," Clemis declared. "They shouldn't have copied Kest. Don't they know a strategy only works once? Do the rest of the city-states know that?"

"Maybe not," Dessin admitted.

"Then deputise me."

"Pardon?"

"Put me on your team. You need someone with first-hand experience of battle tactics. I mean it, Dessin! If I'm in my parents' home for long I'll just sit and brood about them. I'd rather be here."

"Report just coming in from Tafret," Trytin announced. "Blizzard again. No serious damage."

"Maybe you shouldn't have given Kest permission to act," Dessin said, still addressing Clemis. "The Clustrals are agitated, inchoate."

"Naturally," Clemis said calmly. "They were pushed into action before they were ready, and that's no bad thing. Now's the time to destroy more of them before they can refine their technique."

Dessin looked undecided.

"Consult Trevone on that particular issue, if you want," Clemis added.

"I believe you."

"Then act as if you do! We may be wasting opportunities."

Dessin smiled wearily. "All right, you're deputised."

"About time," Trytin remarked. "A pleasure to be working with you, Clemis."

"I'll leave you to it, then," Dessin said, heading for the door.

"Just before you go," Clemis said, in a tone which inferred she'd require more than a moment. Dessin sighed and turned back.

"I realise," she continued carefully, "why you chose this sequestered place as the hub. But in my opinion we're *too* cut off from the outside. We need to see out. Eyes and ears, as Laura would say. We're monitoring everyone else's Clustral incursions, but who's monitoring ours?"

"Clemis, sweetness - " began Trytin.

Dessin frowned.

"I mean, First Citizenness," Trytin amended. "Please don't foist this on Daphos and me. When the Clustrals are up to speed, these screens will demand our full attention. We don't need white noise in our ears. Anyway, I can't translate Clustral-speak and I'm sure Daphos can't either."

"Then who can?"

"The relayists in each city have been taught their local cipher," said Dessin. "But we can't station a relayist here. We're overstretched as it is."

"Then Rinyi will have to substitute. Get him back."

"Sheyell won't approve."

"Then she'll have to disapprove. He's a resource and we have to use him, even though he can't interpret. Trytin!"

"Er – hello?"

"Call Jarras for me, please. He's going to be our eyes."

Trytin obeyed without comment.

"What is it you want, Clemis?" Jarras asked suspiciously.

"You've an impressive view of the city from Communications, haven't you? I'd like to utilise it."

"Oh, it's already being utilised. It diverts visitors and stops them asking me stupid questions."

"You sound more like Tralvar every day," Clemis remarked.

"I'll take that as a compliment. Now, let's see: you've just realised you need to be on weather-watch, all your transposers are spoken for, and you need a logic system tie-in to the tower – or rather what lies beyond it. Correct?"

"Can you arrange that?"

"Easily. I can rig a static camera and share the data via a redundant satellite band. Your team will help you set it up."

"What if the Clustrals target our satellites?"

"The Clustrals have shown no interest in them, presumably because the array's damaged. Or, they've decided that if they take out the ground stations the satellites are no use anyway."

Clemis hesitated.

"It'll work, Clemis. I guarantee it. The Clustrals don't even have a binary phrase for satellite."

"Do you have some knowledge of their codes?" asked Clemis with a spark of hope.

"Of course. My physics students decrypted them."

+Well, well+ remarked Trytin. +Maybe he has his uses after all+

Clemis resisted the urge to deliver a telepathic slap. Many of Trytin's generation – *her* generation – had forgotten that Jarras had singlehandedly jammed Eldorian transmissions during the all-important battle, and been seriously wounded for his trouble. Trytin only remembered the dreamdust–addicted traitor of earlier days. Clemis hoped that was about to change.

"When the Clustrals reappear," she said, addressing Jarras, "could you listen to their chatter? It's just possible that they'll name their next destination as they prepare to transfer. Any advance warning, even if it's an astal or less, could be of significant help."

"I'll attend to it."

"Could any of your students assist? We'll need to think it through, but is there any way they could liaise with the regional relayists …?"

"No need for anything so elaborate. The Clustrals have the EM spectrum all to themselves – if Kest stays off the air, that is. I'll use the comsats to track them."

"What about the gaps in the array?" asked Dessin, still loitering by the door.

"You're there too, are you? Well, thanks to your closure of Treva Academy, my students from Alcine and Kassi are well placed to keep a listening watch. They'll do it. They all want to help."

"I'm glad I made the right decision," Dessin said coolly. "Well, you and Clemis seem to have everything in hand, so I'll finally take what's left of the day off. No-one's to wake me unless there's an emergency."

363

Chapter Thirteen

Clustral Offensive, Day One, 1.6.2.4031

The Clustrals returned at dusk. Dessin, overlooked, slumbered on, as everyone was busy trying to remember a drill that had suddenly become too convoluted.

"Chaos, Trytin!" yelled Jarras. "You wanted the camera so why weren't you looking at it? We've got snow, hail, chunks of ice floe in a tight column – and it's heading straight for you! Why isn't the power off?"

Trytin was attempting to instruct Lakal. Bridd and Kyrin were circulating warnings and monopolising the chain. The prill-enhanced lattice belatedly came online, but covered too narrow an area. The Clustrals whirled away from its influence, sparing the akron but unleashing the ice storm on the student quarter. Several roofs were torn off and footbridges pulverised before the children asserted proper control. The Clustrals were held in stasis, low over the city.

Trevone, airborne, was unable to attack. "I can't use the pulse-cannon so close to street level. I'd cause more damage than the Clustrals. I'll have to let them go this time."

The lattice shut down, the Clustrals transferred, and recriminations began. Lakal berated the children for indiscipline, and Sheyell raged at Daphos for keeping the student quarter open. No-one was sure if there were victims beneath the rubble, as no-one was sure who had gone home and who had stayed.

"Daphos," said Clemis, "Sheyell's right. That was a total shambles. We did far better than this against the Eldorians."

"We knew and understood them," he answered morosely. "It's easier fighting dictatorships than weather-wielding swarms. And why pick on Alda Mexa anyway? We're hardly high-tech."

"If anyone's interested," called Jarras, "Treva's next!"

Lydion, contrary to everyone's belief, had paid only the briefest of visits to Tonora. Hitherto, he'd been perfectly willing to trust her abilities, but had no faith in her assertion that Tarlion was alive. He had gone back to his old home beneath the Lyricon colonnade – where Tarlion had all too fleetingly dwelt – and tried to discern some vestige of his son's presence.

+This is so pointless+ declared Sarune. +There's more of *your* ambience here than his. Why are you giving way to this?+

+It isn't just about Tarlion. Or about the Lyricon, though I still feel grounded here. There's something else, something vital, and I can't pin it down+

+You're grieving. Come away. We should be with Rinyi at the akron+

+As you wish+ answered Lydion absently. Then, as an afterthought: +Only half the Clustral swarm carried out that attack. The ones transferring the ice became depleted and they had to take sustenance from the others. It's the first time they've shown altruism+

+And you didn't think to mention it till now? Wake *up*, Lydion! They're following their programming but they're also trying to survive. That will make them harder to defeat. Now get yourself together and let's share this revelation+

The Treva technicians had set up a lure. When Jarras' alert reached them just after nadir, four square silmi around the theridolyte processing plant went dark. Only an occasional solar cone lit the watery landscape of channels where semi-processed theridolyte trickled toward the vats. And in its midst, an incongruity – a cube of loops and coils pulsing with electricity, immediately seized on by the energy-starved Clustrals.

"They're all over it!" cried Ibri jubilantly. "Get ready, kids!"

Eight intent young adepts at the heart of a prill array created and sustained their trance-inducing lattice. Ibri's pulse-cannon lit the night with crimson fire. The cube, and the Clustrals which battened on it, were destroyed. The rest of the swarm withdrew to consider its losses.

"How many did we get?" asked Veylis.

"Not sure. But we hurt them," Ibri said confidently. "Put the word out – but mind what Clemis said. No imitators."

***

Clustral Offensive, Day Two, 2.6.2.4031

The next target was Ninka, but when no news of any kind was forthcoming, Dessin ordered Rinyi and Sarune to the student quarter. The hospital's best readers had already scanned for living casualties; now Sarune read the ruins in search of bodies. She found none. Dessin then assembled a team of workers, who until recently had been furthering Idenion's plans for the capital. "Make this wreckage safe, but don't bother making it pretty. There'll be more to contend with later."

Finally, Ninka reported in. "Sorry we kept you waiting, Control, but we had to be sure of our facts. Put simply, the Clustrals didn't harm us. There wasn't a lot they could do except melt the snow and cause a deluge. But we always get spring floods, and the refineries are protected by underground run-offs."

"Don't get complacent," Daphos advised. "They might try something different next time."

"We know, and we're ready. Where are they now?"

"Good question." Daphos' screens were idle. He called Jarras, who lengthily consulted the satellite array and found nothing.

"Chaos, Jarras, they must be somewhere. Get your students onto it!"

"Wait. Wait. Let me widen the search – there's something I haven't tried. Now that's … odd."

"Specify," Daphos said impatiently.

"I've found them, but they're in mid-ocean. I don't know why – the signal's barely detectable. Should I get Kest to enhance it?"

"Knowing Kest, they'll be on it as we speak. What's the nearest habitation?"

"Virda, I suppose. But it isn't exactly close."

Daphos pondered. "I don't like this. Clemis would say we needed eyes. I think we should send Trevone to overfly the region."

To his surprise, Jarras agreed.

At first Trevone could detect nothing out of the ordinary, but as he maintained his patrol of the undulating seascape, realisation dawned. "They're trying to create a swell, but it isn't quite working. There aren't enough of them."

"You mean they're *underwater*?"

"Well, yes. Hence the messed-up signal. Surprised, Jarras? They can live in space. They can transpose. What's a little sea water to them?"

Jarras was silent, resenting any form of criticism from his son. "You know them better than I do," he said at last. "What's happening now?"

"Their dialogue's stalled, so I assume they've given up. They've still managed to whip up some turbulence though. We'd better warn Virda."

"Why in the name of discord would they attack a fishing community?"

"I don't know *everything* about them." Trevone kept his response gentle. "Maybe they just got it wrong. What's their next target? Did you retrieve a code?"

"Still cleaning up the signal. Come on home. You've been away long enough."

"Sorry, Jarras, I have to look in on Virda. You know what they're like – if I call them it won't get any further than the transposal station."

"Autonomy, Trevone. Remember?"

No answer. Above the communications tower, broiling clouds gathered.

"Jarras!" Daphos' irate tones cut through his preoccupation. "Are you asleep over there? You were supposed to warn us!"

"He screwed up as usual," Trytin remarked in the background.

"The Clustrals went for a swim without consulting me. How is that my fault?" Jarras retaliated. "We couldn't read the last batch of data. If you think you can do better, be my guest."

The purple rain clouds descended on Lateral One, and nowhere else. Jarras watched, perplexed. Targeting the Lyricon made even less sense than attempting to swamp Virda.

"They're still experimenting," he said aloud.

After less than two astallen the storm abruptly moved on. The renewed clarity of the Clustrals' chatter preceded it. Their next destination was Scapirion.

"Oh, chaos," Jarras whispered. Scapirion, which had opted to forego the defender programme in the belief that, as in the past, it could wait out a siege. The dome was doubtless impervious to Clustral attack: the undersea foundations were not.

With shaking fingers Jarras keyed the transposer. "Get Kalyx. Well, wake him up. Ruvrin too. On second thoughts, just get Ruvrin. You're going to need her expertise."

***

"How do I look?" Ailsi, in waterproofs and waders, pirouetted in front of Escir.

"Different."

"Needs must. I borrowed these from one of the river women. I've assembled a few pals to conduct a rescue mission."

"What mission?" asked Escir suspiciously.

"The Lyricon basement's all mud and puddles, the lower reaches particularly, and we want to round up as much of the contents as we can before everything's ruined."

"Who are these pals exactly?"

"Some of the instrument-makers, a few of the scolia, and some dancers."

"But no salvage workers. This isn't a good idea, Ailsi. Call it off."

"But Esc, there's all kinds of valuable stuff down there. We can't just abandon it!"

"Yes, you can. Haven't you been taking notice of the bulletins? I have, and I've only been getting them second-hand. The Clustrals have the Lyricon in their sights."

"I know. Why do you think I'm doing this?"

Escir sighed. "Ailsi, I've never once played the heavy-handed Eldorian husband - "

"I should think not!"

" - so I'm merely asking you now, most earnestly: give up this pursuit. Leave town. Take your friends and go."

"Why? *You're* not leaving."

"I can't. We have to keep the hospital open as long as possible."

370

"Then you've no business asking *me* to go."
Ailsi turned and flounced out.

***

Jarras notified the akron of the danger to
Scapirion, and collectively they waited for Ruvrin's
response. After an anxious delay it was Kalyx who
made contact, insisting on speaking to Clemis.

"It's happening just the way Jarras expected,"
he said tonelessly. "We thought they'd try and
breach the dome, and as you'll remember, I was
confident they wouldn't succeed. But they never
went near it. They went straight for the geo-thermal
pumps. Ruvrin's at the wellhead, trying to figure
out counter-measures. From the temperature
fluctuations we assume they're planning to freeze a
section of pipe. If they do this and thaw it suddenly,
it'll crack. And if they go on doing that, they could
shut us down. We can't track their signals, not
underwater. If we're to mount a half-decent
defence, we have to know exactly where they are. I
know I said we could handle them, and I know your
rule about self-sufficiency - "

"Trevone's just broken that," said Clemis.

"Good. Because we need your help, Clemis.
Specifically, we need Sarune, Lydion and Rinyi. If
that doesn't leave you too exposed."

"The Clustrals haven't exactly been covert in
their dealings with Alda Mexa. Quite the opposite:
open, obvious and full-on. We can manage without
the incorporeals for now."

"Is that all right with you, Rinyi?" asked Kalyx, peering past Clemis.

"I'm just the vessel," Rinyi reminded him. "Sarune says it would be polite of Clemis to ask before hiring us out. Lydion says he'll do it but doesn't want to be away too long."

Trevone, newly returned from Virda, was less positive. "We can't let Rinyi trek all the way from that landing post," he objected.

"You're a little out of date," Jarras remarked. "Scapirion has a docking port now. That isolated cabin still exists as a love-nest, as in the time of Lykalion and Mehedra. And the younger generation hold sled races along the track."

"I had no idea," Trevone confessed. "I suppose your students told you that?"

"Yes, and more. Scapirion's re-joined the world. Speaking of that, how did you get on with those insular Virdans?"

"As expected. They recalled their fleet but still thought I was overreacting. They said they were used to storms." He hesitated. "I met Kythania, Bridd's girl, at the transposer point. She's worried about him. I said I'd give him a message."

"And you haven't."

"I've had no chance. But even if I had, I wouldn't have spoken. He can't have any distractions when we're so dependent on his work."

Jarras concurred. "He's a relayist. She should understand."

Rinyi's flitter arrived at the spaceport. Trytin, piloting, was disinclined to stop and chat, leaving Rinyi alone on the field near the maintenance block.

But, Trevone reminded himself as he hurried toward the small solitary figure, he *wasn't* alone. In fact, he was smiling.

"Good to be back in action," he said breezily. "Let's get started."

***

Ruvrin was still at the wellhead along with several worried engineers.

"I'll have to leave if sent for," Trevone told her without preamble. "But for now, all four of us are at your disposal."

"We need to know exactly where the Clustrals are, and how many there are," Ruvrin answered, also forgoing preliminaries. "We assume they're responsible for these two cold spots - " she indicated the diagnostic screen – "and that their efforts are presently concentrated here. We've purged the system twice, which normalised it temporarily, but if we keep wasting energy we won't be able to sustain output to the city."

Lydion spoke through Rinyi. "First we'll get you a detailed map of the offensive from a Clustral viewpoint. Once we have that, we'll have a clearer idea what to do."

+You hope+ Sarune remarked. +Have you ever risked your pattern underwater?+

+Risk? Is there one? Since I never even learnt to swim, I'm looking forward to the experience+

Sarune urged caution.

+Yes, yes, I know. Stay compact, nice tidy edges, watch out for particles that could pierce straggly bits -+

+Those are instructions for a void, you idiot!+ Sarune shrilled.

But Lydion had already closed off as he drifted beneath Scapirion, down amidst a tangle of pipes and conduits. A swirl of Clustrals passed by, replete with energy, ready to recharge their companions who were transferring frost and ice from the surface. A surge of static from their midst shivered through him, deflecting him from his course. Currents whirled him off a subterranean shelf into deep water, murky and featureless. On the sea bed were layers of dead Clustrals, their inorganic component still registering with him. He tried to turn back, and only then perceived the pressure around him. Too late, he struggled to adopt a softer, more buoyant shape. He was being compressed into something small and heavy that would ultimately sink without trace.

He almost panicked. Dangerous situations seldom worried him, but being stuck and helpless – possibly for a long, long time – did. He attempted to signal his distress, and was unsurprised when there was no contact. He'd yet to define his location, and without that, his efforts at communication would be wildly imprecise. Stoically he willed himself to scan, study and evaluate. Then he again reached out to the world above, cursing the water he'd hitherto had the good sense not to swim in.

Sarune had finished scanning for stresses within the pipework, and had found three areas at risk of fracture. The engineers had just begun to re-route the intake when Rinyi suddenly announced that Lydion was stranded.

Sarune was surprised.   +I didn't sense anything+

+You were scrying+

+I wasn't inferring you were wrong. What's he done this time?+

"He's gone too deep. A crevasse." Rinyi spoke aloud for everyone's benefit. "The pressure won't let him rise."

"He could have ridden a thermal," said Trevone.

"He says they were too far away."

+They wouldn't have been, if he'd had his mind on his work+ Sarune remarked.   +He's constantly distracted since we lost Tarlion. I fear for him+

Rinyi vocalised this, much to her wrath.

"I suppose we'll have to mount a rescue attempt," said one of the engineers.

"We could send an aquasphere to pick him up," Ruvrin suggested.

"We can't crack the hatch at that depth. We'd need a deep sea craft from Ninka."

"But couldn't he attach himself to the outside somehow?" asked Ruvrin uncertainly.

"He says he thinks so," Rinyi said after a pause.

"All right, we'll try it. I'll send Rohunar – he's our best submariner."

Trevone recognised the name. He remembered where he'd heard it when the tall, taciturn sailor arrived and began staring suspiciously at Rinyi. Rohunar had been in charge of the lake expedition which had led to the discovery of the Pre-Impact time capsule – and the subsequent death of Sijek, the Narvellan synaesthete. And in fact there were superficial similarities between Sijek and Rinyi: both frail, both misfits with unusual psi abilities.

"Do I have to take *him* on this dive?" Rohunar inquired brusquely.

"Yes, if you want to accomplish the rescue," said Rinyi calmly. "You may search me for drugs if that's your concern."

"I'll come with you too," Trevone offered. "You trust *me,* I presume?"

"Yes, First Scientist," Rohunar answered grudgingly. "Report to the launch bay in two astallen. Your craft will be waiting."

"Is he always this friendly?" asked Trevone.

"Always. Don't worry, he's the same with everyone. He doesn't even trust Kalyx on board his vessels."

"With justification, maybe," Trevone said, knowing Kalyx's youthful predilection for starfire. "Coming, Sarune?"

"She's with us," Rinyi confirmed. "And still annoyed at me for revealing her concerns."

Rohunar, grim-lipped, took the aquasphere smoothly past Scapirion's infrastructure and into the deep canyon which had entrapped the unwary Lydion. Rinyi, acutely aware of the submariner's disapproving scowl, scrutinised each detail of the

376

seascape as revealed by the craft's powerful lights. His link with Lydion's rueful mindset was clear and steady, but locating his exact position was – as Lydion himself could have told him – a challenge. Being in a moving vessel didn't help.

Sarune, however, fared better. Before Rinyi could impose some moderation, she had addressed Rohunar as Master Miserable and peremptorily ordered some course corrections. Rohunar complied, then rounded furiously on Rinyi.

"You! Speaker for the bodiless! Restrain the Synectic woman!"

"Are these chasms often found so close to the shore?" asked Trevone hastily.

"Not along this coastline," said Rohunar more calmly. "We think it's part of an impact crater."

"A small meteorite?"

"Who can say? There are rumours that the Draldir caused it – a near miss by one of their war machines."

"Your pardon," Rinyi said carefully. "I have positive news from Lydion. He's reading our approach."

"I'm glad to hear it."

"Please reduce speed and I will guide you in."

Rohunar obeyed with an exaggerated sigh.

"Hey!" The switch to Lydion's persona was unmistakeable. "Is that you, Rohunar, giving my sensitive a hard time? Maybe I should tell Trevone about that party in Ninka when we - "

"Enough of that, Lydion. Just tell us where we should set down."

"No need. I'm all over you, literally. And I shall cling like a limpet until we've docked. Just take it easy on the way up."

"Understood."

"I'll call Ruvrin," Trevone said thankfully.

"Tell her to order a debriefing," Lydion added. "There's something very interesting down here. Interesting – and useful."

Rohunar ejected his passengers at the launch bay, then removed his craft to safer waters. Rinyi hoped it would be the last they saw of him.

Ruvrin was waiting in response to Trevone's message. "No time for a proper debrief – my team's still fully engaged at the wellhead. I'll update them later. What did you find?"

Lydion, via Rinyi, told her about the supercharged Clustral stream which had spun him off course, and the layer of dead Clustrals he'd fallen into. "Once again, we've misjudged their intelligence," he concluded. "They obviously know little about seawater."

"And you do?" Ruvrin couldn't help asking.

"I do now," Lydion said, unabashed. "We're all aware the Clustrals are sustained by a fixed electrical charge, a very small one. I don't know how the absorption's regulated but the increased conductivity of salt water is disrupting that function. And it's killing them."

"But not quickly enough," Trevone remarked.

"You're missing the point. Until now, there have been comparatively few ways to destroy them. We could expose them to a wormhole, if we had one handy; and we can zap them with pulse-cannon, first having persuaded them to keep still. But because they only took what they needed there was never any way of turning their power source against them. Now there is."

+You do realise you're being insufferable?+ Sarune asked him, undetected by anyone save Rinyi.

+And you love me for it, don't you? What's more, I haven't even reached the best bit+

"Don't drag it out, Lydion," Trevone advised as they neared the wellhead, "or you'll find yourself without an audience."

"You always did know how to ruin a good story," Lydion retorted. "As I was about to say: where I … landed, near some *very* sharp rocks, there's a heavy duty cable leading out to sea. Or rather it used to, before it snagged on the rocks and got scissored. Can you enlighten us, Ruvrin? What was it for?"

She looked a little shamefaced. "A goodwill gesture that didn't work. We don't have any heavy industry here, and under normal conditions we can generate more energy than we need. Ninka on the other hand has the refinery to run, so Kalyx and I thought we'd help them out."

"What went wrong?"

"We went for trade talks with the other city-states when we should have been supervising the project. I thought the techs could handle it."

They had reached the wellhead. "Ruvrin, we need to purge the system again," said Zaxu, the team leader.

"Not yet."

"We're at imminent risk of fracture!"

"I said wait. Did any of you work on the undersea cable to Ninka?"

"I hope you don't think *we* were responsible for that screw-up," said Zaxu indignantly. "It was Ninka's cable. They brought it over in an icebreaker. A ship that size couldn't get anywhere near our lagoon, so some of our junior techs went out to meet it in a surface craft. They finished unwinding the cable and just fed it over the side without checking where it would settle."

"At least they kept hold of the end," Trevone quipped.

"So where is it?" Ruvrin demanded of Zaxu. "Disconnected? Discarded?"

"No, just isolated. Pending further attempts."

Ruvrin summoned a grin. "Well, *that* isn't going to happen. Alert your colleagues, would you; say we're on our way and want what remains of the Ninka project readied for use. I'll take responsibility. Rinyi, we'll need Lydion and Sarune standing by. Trevone, we'll doubtless need your commonsense."

+Meaning I don't have any, I suppose?+ Lydion remarked.

+I couldn't possibly comment+ Sarune answered loftily.

Zaxu led them at a run toward the switching room, and beyond it to an alcove which resembled a boat deck.

"Does that winch work?" Ruvrin asked breathlessly. "Can you retract the cable?"

Zaxu tried. Trevone joined him. Grudgingly, the mechanism obeyed. The inspection scanners showed no movement amid Scapirion's underpinnings.

"Keep winding," Ruvrin ordered. "Get it out of that deep trench."

"What's your objective?" Zaxu asked, frowning.

"I'm hoping to create an ion trail. Underwater lightning."

"You'll black out the entire city!" Trevone protested.

"Hopefully not for long."

"Sarune's sensed the cable now," Rinyi announced. "So's Lydion. The severed end's just below us."

"Good," said Ruvrin briskly. "Stop the winch and get ready to turn on the current."

"No, wait," said Rinyi.

"Lydion?"

"Of course it's Lydion. When the energy-depleted Clustrals are being charged, most of the swarm's underwater. At the moment only a fraction of them are."

"We can't delay," Zaxu said ominously. "That pipe's going to rupture."

"You've only got one chance at this," Lydion argued. "Either the generator will blow or the cable will melt. Keep your nerve."

They waited. The temperature at the wellhead fell and fell. A warning chime sounded. Ruvrin turned it off.

"*Now!*" yelled Rinyi-as-Lydion. Zaxu fired up the generator and retreated to a safe distance. A mere isk or two later there was a brief white flash and a plume of acrid smoke from the cable coupling. Lydion withdrew from Rinyi's consciousness to escape the chaos of alarms, emergency lights and the thudding of circuit breakers. Instead he took in the surreal spectacle of dead and dying Clustrals drifting, falling, dwindling into the deep implacable sea.

+Result?+ inquired Sarune.

+A localised one. The Clustrals won't come back here in a hurry. They'll very probably stick with soft targets+

+Alda Mexa?+

+Yes. We should go home, Sarune, and quickly+

Not *my* home, she thought, but didn't communicate it. +Very well, we'll go back to Alda Mexa. Trevone won't argue with that+ She paused a moment. +They're very calm, these Scapirians. Disciplined. No panic in the switching room, everyone focused on their duty+

+They come from a long line of scientists+ Lydion replied. +Now let's love them and leave them+

Trevone had less than edifying news. "That was a brilliant idea of yours, Lydion, but it wasn't as successful as it might have been. Perhaps the swarm was alerted when we raised the cable. Anyway, Ninka's radioed in: just before we turned on the current, there was a routine attack on one of the fuel lines."

"So the swarm had divided?" Rinyi looked as disappointed as Lydion felt.

"Afraid so. And now both halves have vanished. Reunited, no doubt, to renew their attack on the north."

"I thought we were winning."

"So did I. But we've only nibbled the edges. If we're ever to stop them, we'll have to up our game."

Chapter Fourteen

Clustral Offensive Day 3: 3.6.2.4031

"Well!" said Jarras to the image on the tower's transposer. "I'd just about given you up, Aronne. Nice of you to think of us!"

The young man looked apologetic, then worried. "I wanted to call you days ago but we didn't have a working transposer. Treva didn't send our order."

Jarras swore under his breath. Was there no end to the damage done by the Prefect of Treva's "diversion" of scientific equipment? "It's a pity Idenion didn't relieve that man of his post when he had the chance."

"The Prefect likes to follow his own agenda," Aronne said unhappily. "Anyway, I personally went to Alcine and commandeered two of their units."

"You must have been very persuasive."

"I was. I had to be."

Instantly he had Jarras' full attention.

Aronne had been studying atmospheric physics at Treva Academy. He lived at Stela, a tiny city-state in a forested coastal region south of Alcine. Thousands of silmi to the west lay the ruins of Ilonna, and it was long believed that Stela too would have insufficient numbers to sustain itself. A floating population courtesy of Alcine, plus the benefits of Escir's regeneration programme, had saved it.

"I'm at Pell offshore weather station," Aronne was continuing. "We were monitoring the radio spectrum as arranged, and I noticed Clustral activity in the same area as a sudden drop in barometric pressure. So we flew out and dropped a weather buoy to study the event more closely."

"When was this?"

"Two days ago. We've confirmed it's a hurricane. Nothing unusual about that, not around here. But the Clustrals are raising the threat level as we speak."

"They initiated this storm?"

"No, no, it's one of ours. We detected it before they showed up. It's building, but erratically. And the Clustrals come and go, come and go. They're diverting it, Jarras!"

Discord's dreams, Jarras thought wretchedly. Trevone was wrong about the Virda attack. The Clustrals weren't creating a storm at sea, they were transferring it. Another of their practice runs. "What's the worst that can happen?" he asked. "Gales? More structural damage?"

"According to our computer model – and I must emphasise that it was written in haste – the wind speed will slacken. We're looking at a tropical depression. Expect rain – very heavy rain."

"I'll forward that warning. Many thanks, Aronne."

"We'll maintain our watch and report any changes," Aronne promised. "Oh, one more thing. Our contacts at Alcine reported a Clustral presence at Ilonna."

"Ilonna," Jarras echoed, with a shiver.

"Crazy, isn't it? There's nothing left standing since the Eldorians pulverised it. But isn't every bit of information important, even if it doesn't make sense?"

Jarras agreed and signed out. Two astallen later, a freak wave destroyed the weather buoy and hammered the walls of the Pell facility.

"We should leave," said Aronne's co-worker. "That transference is disrupting *our* weather. Look at these readings. They're just ... manic." A sudden gust of wind screamed round the building. "Let's go, while we still have a boat."

Aronne hesitated. "I promised to update Jarras."

"You didn't promise to risk your life. You've warned Alda Mexa; the rest is up to them."

Jarras had already called the akron, with predictable results. "Trytin, I know you think my judgement is suspect but I'm certain about this. Tell Dessin that now would be a good time to implement his evacuation plans. And where's Rinyi? I need to talk to him."

"What for?"

"Because I need to talk to Lydion. He knows more about Ilonna than anyone. I think I know why the Clustrals are attacking non-strategic targets, but I want him to confirm it. And he will. Find Rinyi. Mention Ilonna. *Now*, Trytin!"

"All right, don't yell," Trytin said irritably. "I'll find him. Don't go away!" One astal later, he was back. "Well, it seems you've sparked a security alert. Clemis, no less, is on her way to see you. You're honoured! Rinyi's with Nefyrra at the

386

Lyricon, and – surprise, surprise – Lydion's back too. Clemis will escort you."

"I can't leave the tower."

"Which is why she has Daphos with her. He'll man your post until your impromptu conference is over. Whatever it's about."

Jarras didn't elaborate. Leaving the systems on standby he took the elevator to the lobby, exchanging a few brief words with Daphos when he appeared.

+Hurry, Jarras!+ Clemis called from her flitter. +I don't like the look of that sky+

Daphos, alone in the tower, watched until the flitter had vanished into the gloom. Then, fraught with indecision, he took a data crystal from his pocket and gazed at it. Now, Daphos, do it now, he urged himself. This is an unlooked-for opportunity. There may never be another.

Still he hesitated. He could be about to make a bad situation much much worse. Or, it could be the most inspired thing he'd ever done.

He made his decision, presented the crystal to the transposer array, and waited. There was one active transposer at the given coordinates – exactly as he'd surmised. He selected it. His transposer's viewscreen shimmered, indicating an established contact with no visual. No-one spoke. Eventually Daphos did, his voice querulous.

"Myrig? Myrig, is that you?"

"Who is this?" The voice was gruff, elderly.

"Daphos, communications tech, Alda Mexa. Tarlion told me you spoke Celestrian. I guessed you'd be standing by in case he reported in."

"I told him to destroy his flight log."

"He's not to blame. I'm acting alone. He had a systems meltdown on his way to us and sent an emergency databurst. I reconstructed his journey from some damaged files."

"Your reason being?"

"I had a long conversation with Tarlion when he first arrived. He was convinced that his students would have, given the chance, joined him on his quest to find us. You cautioned him against confiding in them, so out of respect for you, he didn't. Which of you was right, Myrig?"

"*He* was," Myrig said promptly. "And I was so very wrong. They would have followed him without hesitation. I suppose he told you that he barely got away, that the Conclave were in pursuit? They weren't. It was the students' vehicles on the horizon that day. Will you tell him that?"

"I - " Daphos faltered. "Yes. When I see him I'll tell him."

"There's more. The Conclave deceived us. One of our Directresses had discovered therite and they suppressed her findings. There's no longer any need to break up our spacecraft, and the Conclave's authority is now at an end."

"A revolution?"

"Nothing so spectacular. A body of concerned citizens, myself included, invited them to step down. They had little choice."

"Then I won't lie to you, Myrig. The reason Tarlion isn't with me is because he's missing. He was on a routine spaceflight home, with Laura and Idenion, and they didn't arrive. I fear they're lost."

"This grieves me. I knew Laura well and had the utmost respect for her."

"So I decided," Daphos hurried on, "that if I could establish a dialogue between our species it would be a fitting tribute to Tarlion and our First Citizens. Will you speak to your young people? Sound them out?"

"I will. But how do I contact you? I'm not reading any coordinates. How is this even possible?"

"Anyone in the Conclave could have answered your transposer," Daphos said evasively. "Please, speak to the students. I'll call you again."

"Very well."

"I have to go now. I'm supposed to be on watch." Daphos broke the contact hastily, noticing how the weather had deteriorated since he'd entered the tower. Then he called Scapirion and asked for Ruvrin.

"I've just tried out your system," he said obscurely, "and it works."

"Not *my* system. Lydion's."

Of course, Daphos thought somewhat sadly. Who else?

Lydion, at that moment, was lamenting his own lack of insight. "I should have known," he repeated several times, although Rinyi only saw the need to say it once. "Sorry to drag you over here, you two, but I couldn't risk Eldorians hearing this. You already know Vuli was senile, but for security's sake I had to suppress some of my findings. He'd managed to hack the Gloriana's quantum computer and get sight of the alternative timeline."

"Trevone told me," said Clemis.

"Not all of it. Vuli then asserted, in my presence, that this version of events was the one he had to deal with."

"Chaos!"

"He rallied, but not for long. He was so very old. He was active thousands of years ago, and witnessed the war between our ancestors and the Draldir. He knew which city-states were important at the time, and saw the defences created by Tekla. Remember what was on the mosaic at Ilonna?"

Jarras did, vividly.

"It's my contention," Lydion went on, "That in the moments before his death, Vuli had another aberration. He believed we were still fighting the Draldir, and modified his plans to take us down. He directed the Clustrals to the relevant targets: Ilonna, Scapirion, Ninka, Alcine."

"But why Alda Mexa?" Clemis objected. "It didn't exist then!"

"No. But the last working example of Ilonna's tech is here now. The Clustrals think the weathershield is a weapon. They won't stop until they've destroyed it and its surroundings. Pull the armed spheres back from Treva, otherwise we'll have no chance. And start evacuating the lower laterals before they're underwater."

"Are you sure about this, Lydion?" asked Nefyrra. "Atris was important in Tekla's day, and it hasn't been attacked."

"Atris was agricultural, as now. Not on Vuli's hit list."

"And where does Virda fit in?" Nefyrra continued.

"I don't know. I wish I did."

"Should we change our strategy, Clemis?" asked Jarras. "Does your autonomy rule still apply when there are other, safer city states which could help us?"

"*Nowhere* is safe," Clemis contradicted. Then, more quietly, "We exchange only information. The one exception will be Treva – they're close enough to be interactive. I'll recall Ibri and Veylis."

"You should return to the akron while you still can," Nefyrra advised. "I'll organise things here, starting with the relayist chain. They'll ensure everyone's updated."

"What about the children?" asked Clemis.

"Without them we have no defence at all. And, knowing them as I do, they'd be bitterly disappointed if we removed them so soon. They'd blame themselves. Be assured, I and their minders will keep them as secure as we can. We'll check all eight lattice points for flood risk and relocate if that becomes essential."

"Have a flitter standing by at each point," Jarras advised. "If Aronne's right about torrential rain but scaled-back winds, then the flitters' repeller fields will cope with a short flight to safety."

Sarune, who'd been absent during the discussion, suddenly reappeared next to Lydion.

+Where have you been?+ he asked peevishly.

+Above+ she replied. +Reading some unusual patterns, while you were beating your metaphorical brow. That cloud layer's nine-tenths artificial and the Clustrals are busy seeding it+

+They're working at that height?+

+For a broader spread across the area, it appears+

Lydion studied the formation. +Finally, something that could help us. Trevone was worried that our pulse-cannon would cause more damage than they prevented, but if the Clustrals stay where they are, it should be possible to target them without incinerating the city. Rinyi, pass that along+

He complied, accosting Clemis as she was closing the flitter canopy. She immediately looked less tense.

"You're staying here, Rinyi?" she inquired, though she knew the answer.

"I must. I'm needed."

"Let's go, Clemis," urged Jarras. "You need to find Dessin and get those river people mobilised. And don't forget we've left Trytin on his own!"

***

"Ciela! Ciela, wait!" Roegin sprinted down the station platform and grabbed Ciela as she was about to board the monorail. "Where in Ebbondrear do you think you're going?"

To either side of him, a straggle of passengers turned irritated glances in his direction.

Oh, great, he thought. Ciela's Eldorian thug yelling at his woman. "Veylis dropped me off at the beach," he continued more quietly. "He's been assigned to Alda Mexa. So's Ibri."

"I heard. I know about the evacuation too."

"Then why are you and these people heading in the wrong direction? Don't you see *that*?" Roegin pointed. To the south, banks of indigo clouds were gathering: symmetrical columns, appearing to slowly rotate like cogs in a vast machine.

"These workers are from the pumping station," Ciela explained. "Those who opted to leave, that is. And they're not going to the city proper, just the marina. The river people will take over from there."

"And that's where *you're* going? Emptyhanded? Not even a rain cape?"

Ciela looked flustered. "I …"

"Don't lie. Believe me, I'll know. I didn't spend years in Covert Ops for nothing."

Two latecomers arrived on the platform. The train powered up briefly.

"Last call," Roegin added. "Talk quickly."

"I was going to find Dena," Ciela confessed. "I'm worried that she won't want to leave Nefyrra and the scolia children. And she has to."

"Fine." Roegin stepped onto the train. "*I'll* go. If she hasn't left the city I'll bring her back to the spa. Just go home, Ciela. Stay where it's safe."

He didn't hear her reply, as the doors slid shut.

Two-thirds of the way to Alda Mexa, a sudden power failure brought the train slithering to a halt. Roegin swore under his breath. The Celestrian monorail system was compact, almost dainty, compared with its Earth counterparts. And it bore no resemblance at all to the Eldorian monoliths that straddled Nova City. But it was still elevated enough to preclude a swift exit, even assuming he could force a door.

By now, he thought, everyone on board will know what's going on and what the options are. Everyone but me, that is.

"*Can* you break us out?" asked one of the utility workers unexpectedly.

"Do you want me to try?" Roegin responded cautiously.

"Please."

Roegin tried. The small servo mechanism offered little resistance. As soon as the door was open, the train lurched and began to move slowly backwards.

"We're on a slight gradient," the spokesman explained. "The operator's rolling us back to the nearest service ladder."

The train halted again. The ladder was close by.

"Well, what's the plan?" asked Roegin impatiently. "You do *have* a plan?"

Everyone spoke at once, contradicting one another, but Roegin got the gist. Half of those present, plus the evacuees in the second carriage, wanted to stay with the train in case the power came back on. The rest had decided to walk to the Lisir, three silmi to the west, and flag down passing river traffic.

Roegin instantly made his choice. He'd spent the past fifteen years sitting around, and he wasn't about to do so again. As he and his companions set out through the woodland, he glanced once more at the swirling mass of cloud above Alda Mexa. Little lightnings flickered in its midst, and a few stray raindrops touched his skin.

"Let's hurry," he said.

***

Trytin did his best not to look relieved when Daphos strode into the hub.

"What have we got? Anything I should know about?"

"Treva called in. Sheeting rain over the theridolyte plant. The sluices had already been cleared so the only damage was to the landscaping. This went on for about an ild, then stopped suddenly."

"Because the sluices were full," Daphos surmised. "It sounds as if the Clustrals were assessing their transfer rate. Another practice run. And we're in line for the real thing, Trytin. A flood, a bad one. Clemis is certain, so's Jarras."

"I don't need convincing," said Trytin. "Virda's taken another hit."

"*Again?*"

"Same as Treva, only more prolonged. It was Kythania, Bridd's girl, who alerted me. Nice little thing. Worried sick about Bridd, of course, and wanting to join him here. But she knows she can't. Trevone made that clear, apparently."

"Never mind Bridd's love life. How are the Virdans coping?"

"Well enough. They've beached their trawlers, or most of them. And the worst of the rain missed the village – Kythania said there were torrents pouring down the cliff face and into the sea."

"Exactly how long were you speaking with her?"

Trytin shrugged. "A while. Does it matter?"

"Yes, because you won't have been paying attention to the relayists. And you really should."

Trytin obliged, then paled. "They're evacuating the lower laterals? Already?"

"If Jarras has the tower camera working, you'll see why," Clemis said, entering the room. "We arrived just ahead of the storm. Take a look."

The screen showed murky twilight, although it was still late afternoon. The cityscape was obscured by a curtain of rain.

"It's localised," Clemis added. "A funnel. The Lyricon's not affected at present. I've asked Nefyrra to contact all the lattice points and hopefully explain what's going on. She'll be thorough. So while we're waiting I want to address the other city-states. It's what Laura would do. I'm not as inspirational, but I'll give it my best."

"What do you want to say? Can we help?"

" I want to strengthen their resolve, but give them a warning too. I'll explain why we're being targeted and say that if Alda Mexa falls, the Clustrals will move on to city after city. We can't second-guess where they'll go. Nowhere's exempt. Oh, chaos, I can't say any of that. I'd scare everyone."

"I've a suggestion," said Trytin. "Jarras, is it right that shutting down our power grids won't

396

starve the Clustrals, since they're getting their energy from the storm?"

"Afraid so."

"Then, Clemis, put it to the people that they can now fight the Clustrals in relative comfort, with plenty of light, and with ample reserves for keeping the prill warm."

"That's very good," Clemis said, impressed. "Any more ideas?"

"Well," mused Trytin, "you could remind everyone that we were knocked back to the stone age once, and it's up to us to prevent it happening again. Say that unlike our ancestors, we know our enemy. The asteroids didn't work; neither will this."

"Maybe I should appoint you my speech-writer," said Clemis, half seriously.

"I'm glad you've found a use for him at last," Jarras remarked, neatly reversing Trytin's earlier jibe.

"I'll set up the broadcast facilities," Daphos said, averting a spat. "We'll have to interrupt the monitoring, so keep it short and to the point. Maybe you should record yourself?"

"Some people still think a recording's insincere," said Clemis. "I'll speak now."

"Good decision," Trytin declared. "Seize the moment before something else does."

"Not funny," said Daphos. "Did you want to include Trevone, Clemis? He *is* co-ruler."

"He is, and he's also servicing pulse-cannon along with Ibri. The weapons have all been fired, some of them recently, and we have to be sure they'll function when needed. And when that's done they'll be moving the spheres to higher ground before the maintenance bay gets swamped. Now, connect me to the transposer network, please."

"You're in charge. Stand by."

"Shouldn't we notify Kyrin?" asked Trytin.

"No," said Clemis emphatically, "we shouldn't. I know it's a break with protocol but I'm not involving the relayist chain. Nefyrra will have given them enough to do. And, I don't want to distract Esclevon from that task."

"Ah," said Trytin.

"My message isn't for Alda Mexa. I told you that."

"You're on," Daphos announced in his usual timely manner.

Clemis spoke a little too rapidly, but with sincerity and conviction. After she'd signed off and Daphos had cut the feed, she allowed herself a small sigh of relief. "Here's hoping there's better news when I have to do that again. And, Trytin – maybe you could refrain from pulling faces at me next time?"

"If you promise to smile more."

"Trytin, you're an idiot," Daphos said irritably, and would have elaborated if a whoop from one of the transposers hadn't interrupted him.

"Hey, Clemis! Clemis? Oh, good, you're still there. This is Augat of Kest City News. May I ask you some questions? We're all keen to know more."

"I - " began Clemis, disconcerted.

"Excellent. Firstly, how do you rate Alda Mexa's chances? What's the mood of the people? What's it like being First Citizen?"

Clemis regained her voice. "What in the name of discord are you playing at? Have you any idea what's going on here? No, you obviously haven't, or you wouldn't be wasting my time with your stupid questions!"

"What *is* going on there?" persisted Augat. "Do tell us!"

Trytin stepped in front of the screen. "You're blocking an emergency channel. Technical information and weather reports only, as of now. Alda Mexa out."

"Thanks," said Clemis, and meant it.

"I detect Geffin's influence," remarked Jarras from the tower.

"Who?" asked Trytin.

"Eldorian reporter. He and his media pals staged Anything to Please You - "

"That I *do* remember. All that amplification!"

"Geffin needed some local help," Jarras continued, "and that meant Kest's recording engineers. They've never been the same since!"

"Sad but true," said Clemis, and went in search of a cold drink. The adjacent ration store had a basic selection of liman, fruit cordial and inferior wine. Dessin had given strict orders that drinks were not to be consumed in the transposer room, so Clemis remained where she was, sipping pilif juice and leaning on a worktop. She could sense the ebb and flow of the relayist chain, the ever-present voice of the city. Kyrin, Alcis and Tylo had been sector leaders well before her birth, and their mental autographs seemed as enduring as the city itself. But today, she wondered how enduring they actually were. Celestra's fate in the alternate timeline had never seemed quite real to her. This did.

+Clemis+ The contact was so gentle it didn't startle her. It was Kyrin, just a few floors above, his amazing range curtailed. +I have Nefyrra's report+

+Thanks. Could you copy it to all the team?+

+Just the three of you. I can't reach Jarras+ Kyrin paused to refocus. +Message begins. The defence can't find a weather transference node. There appear to be several minor ones, which is a first. We can't change the properties of the lattice so we'll have to address one incursion at a time. It won't be as efficient+

+Thanks, Kyrin+ Clemis responded. +Stand by. We'll have a reply for Nefyrra shortly+

"How do we handle this?" asked Trytin.

"We'll improvise," Daphos declared.

"No, we'll devise new surveillance," Clemis said coolly. "What's the point of having all these dedicated screens if the Clustrals have stopped attacking other cities? They've changed tactics – so can we. Who has transposers in Alda Mexa other than us and the spaceport?"

"The hospital," Daphos surmised.

"The hydro-electric plant and the power station," offered Trytin.

"The water treatment works," added Daphos.

"The observatory, except that Dessin sent everyone home," Trytin concluded.

"And still nothing at the Lyricon," fretted Clemis.

"Tradition," Daphos said wisely.

"Outdated," Clemis declared. "What about the river people? Do *they* have transposers?"

"None that they'll admit to."

"All right, we'll work with what we have. Retain the open links to Scapirion, Alcine, Ninka and Treva. Better include Virda as well. Close all others and reassign our freed transposers to the local points we just mentioned."

"The other city-states won't like that," ventured Trytin.

"Then placate them. The system's adaptable – we can change it back if the need arises. Ensure there's one unassigned transposer for emergency use, and also ensure all cities understand what an emergency consists of."

Trytin glanced at Daphos.

"Do it," Daphos advised. "Did you hear all that, Jarras?"

No answer.

"Jarras?"

"We've lost the feed from the tower camera," reported Trytin.

"Since when?"

"I wasn't looking."

"Jarras, report!" Clemis demanded.

"I'm here, I'm here. The camera's offline – it was only a temporary fix, after all."

"He sounds weird," Trytin muttered.

"Jarras," said Clemis frostily, "what's going on?"

He sighed. "There's water coming in the roof hatch. It's never closed properly since the med team kicked it in after I was shot."

"How much water?"

"Enough to short out the camera."

"*How much*?"

"Too much."

"Get out of there," ordered Trytin.

"In this deluge? Talk sense. Wait until the Clustrals switch targets, then send someone over. In the meantime I'll try to minimise the damage. Jarras out."

"He's completely on his own out there," Clemis breathed.

"I don't like it when he's brave," muttered Trytin. "Makes me feel bad."

"He's telling us *we're* on our own," Daphos said. "We've lost our eyes. If we lose another advantage, we'll be in real trouble."

***

Roegin bade a perfunctory farewell to his companions, and stepped off the rescue boat into a rain-soaked Alda Mexa. The marina had been flooded, so the evacuees were assembled on Lateral Six. Minor torrents were still cascading down the paths from the upper laterals, although the sky was temporarily clear.

Roegin spotted Ailsi further up the improvised quay. She was difficult to miss, as she was ineffectually pummelling the bargee who had hold of her. "Let me go, you river zarf. Let *go*!"

"No-one gets off here," he bawled in response.

Roegin elbowed his way toward the pair. "Is there a problem?"

"Roegin!" Ailsi stopped struggling.

"Have you seen - " he began, knowing she'd pre-empt him. He wasn't wrong.

"Dena? She left yesterday with the junior scolia. Nefyrra sent all the resident kids to safety – apart from the defence adepts, that is."

So it's true, Roegin thought. Child warriors. Unbelievable!

The riverman took a firmer hold of Ailsi's arm. "Come on, back on board. You too, Eldorian."

"Not happening. There's somewhere I need to be."

"Holpen?" inquired Ailsi's captor. "You're as bad as *this* one. You won't find anyone to take you upriver."

"Roegin," ventured Ailsi, "since you're going to be here for a bit – could you look for Escir? *Please*? We had a tiff yesterday and I spent the night in Tivenne. It's taken me this long to get back. And now, he's gone missing. I contacted the hospital, they asked around – no-one can find him."

"Can't anyone detect his mind?"

"Trace a nonconversant with all this weird stuff going on? No chance. The fact is, I wanted to salvage some props from the Lyricon and he stopped me. And I think he might have gone there looking for me."

Roegin glanced toward Lateral One. The Lyricon had all but disappeared under a swirl of the now-familiar indigo cloud.

"Please, Roegin!" Ailsi was at her most piteous. "Spran won't let me off the boat."

"How am I supposed to get there? Paddle?"

Spran nudged him. A flitter had just alighted to collect two passengers with minor injuries. "That'll take you as far as the hospital."

"They might not want me along," Roegin objected. But as he spoke, pilot and passengers turned in unison and stared at him. Then the pilot beckoned.

"I asked," Spran said laconically.

Roegin sighed and took the last available place on the flimsy craft. Buffeted by turbulence, it ascended to Lateral Three, and thence to the docking port on the hospital's third floor. The building, on one of the larger intersections, looked solid enough to withstand anything the Clustrals could throw at it. But in anticipation of flooding, the lower floors had been sealed and the remaining patients and staff restricted to the upper levels.

Roegin, familiar with the surroundings, wandered off alone. The transposer station was unoccupied, as was Escir's office. Outside, daylight had turned to sudden twilight. The solar tubes in the corridors attempted to compensate, but hadn't built up sufficient charge during the morning. A woman – small, elderly – was gazing out of a north-facing window, her face rapt and intent. Roegin was about to venture an enquiry when she held up a peremptory hand. Outside, the deluge mysteriously ceased. The sky cleared. Soon after came the spit and flare of a pulse-cannon, far above.

The woman turned to Roegin with a tired smile. "It was the children," she said. "I sensed the lattice, though imperfectly."

"Why risk your children?"

"The frequency which paralyses the Clustrals can only be generated by young minds. They lose the ability when older. We do what we must."

As Celestrians always do, Roegin thought wryly.

"If you want to reach the Lyricon," she continued, "you should start now, before the Clustrals regroup. There's an elevated walkway between this floor and Lateral Two. It was still intact an astal ago." She paused. "Please find him."

Roegin uttered some kind of assurance and set off. The bridge looked strong, not like the fragile traceries that had collapsed on Day One.

He saw no-one at first, and began to think that everyone had obediently left. Then some shrieks of hilarity told him otherwise. A group of young people, clinging to a homemade raft, hurtled by on the rapid-flowing stream that used to be a steep path. Roegin watched them spin into the distance, bouncing off walls and colliding with half-submerged trees.

Laughing in the face of disaster, he thought enviously. That's their strength. I hope it's enough.

Halfway to the second lateral the rain began again, and within moments he was drenched. The Clustrals' focus had shifted further west, and Roegin was now at the edge of the coriolis. Gusts of wind encircled the higher laterals, giant hailstones smacked into the bridge ahead of him.

He sensed, rather than felt, the structure move fractionally. With extreme reluctance he turned back, but as he did so a faint cry reached him from the deepening torrent below. And there, incredibly, was Escir, struggling in vain against the undertow, his left arm trailing uselessly. Unhesitatingly Roegin vaulted the safety rail and hit the water feet first. Escir had been swept past; he swam after him, grabbed him and after a few failed attempts managed to drag him up some submerged steps to a flitter park. Which was, of course, empty. They sprawled on the tiles, momentarily safe.

"Ailsi -" Escir began.

"Esc, she's not at the Lyricon. She sent me to find you."

He subsided thankfully. "Who taught you to swim like that?"

"Dena and Ciela. How'd you break your arm?"

"Hit a tree." He was beginning to shiver. "Where do we go from here?"

Roegin looked about. Floods on two sides. Submerged doors. Walls. Walls. No accessible windows. "We don't," he said at last.

They waited. The hail stopped, but the buffeting wind increased. Then, providentially, a low-flying sphere came into view, hugging the contour of the hill.

"That might be Veylis," Roegin muttered. "Think he's seen us? If he fires his pulse-cannon at this range, we're toast."

The sphere came closer. "I don't see any lenses," Escir said, peering up.

"Then it must be a rescue craft. Wave!"

But there was no need. The sphere, defying the elements, hovered expertly next to the flitter park. The ramp flowed outwards and came securely to rest on the rain-washed slabs.

"Well, get a move on!" someone yelled from within.

Roegin helped Escir to his feet and they trudged gratefully up the ramp – to be confronted by a smiling blonde with an Eldorian-style video camera at her shoulder.

"What was I saying about lenses?" Escir murmured.

Roegin swore. "Ebbon's blood! Who *are* you people?"

A small wiry man stepped forward. "Augat of Kest City News, at your service. You're lucky we were in the area."

"You aren't part of the defence team?"

"Sadly, no."

"I thought Trevone had grounded all non-essential flights?"

"He did, but we believe our work *is* essential. Our viewers have a right to see what's happening here. Vione, find our Eldorian friends some dry clothes. And some resnay."

The pilot, who had said nothing, closed the hatch. The sphere, maintaining its previous low altitude, moved north.

"This isn't the way to the hospital," Escir objected.

"In good time," Augat said coolly. "We haven't any shots of the Lyricon yet and I'm

407

informed there's a window of opportunity coming up."

"And how do you know that?"

A fourth crew member, another woman, swivelled her chair to face them. "I'm relayist Neme, of Kest. According to the local chain, the Clustrals are turning their attention to the power station and the hydro-electric plant."

Roegin suddenly looked uneasy.

"Come," said Vione, "let's find you those clothes – and some pain relief for your arm, Dr Escir. Then you can tell me how you came to be injured and stranded."

"For your viewers?" inquired Roegin.

"Of course."

"Live?"

"Unfortunately not. I can't get a satellite link."

Roegin was pleased about that, and hoped Vione wasn't reading him at that moment. She led him to a clothes repository with such varied content – even children's – that he correctly surmised the team had come in search of people to rescue and subsequently feature on their news channel. To divert her focus, he suggested that she attended to Escir and left him to sort himself out. Then he picked up the least gaudy outfit, grabbed some sandals and headed for what proved to be a surprisingly well-appointed shower room. Were Augat and his crew *living* on this sphere?

The churning column of rain was indeed moving away, joining with a lesser system in the west. But the lashing wind was still in evidence, pummelling the sphere as it hovered over the Lyricon, challenging the pilot to maintain stability.

"I thought Jarras' weather-watch pal said there wouldn't be a hurricane?" Vione inquired of Augat.

"According to my sources, he wasn't sure. Or maybe he got it right and the Clustrals are sampling a different storm. Either way, I don't think we'll hear from him again. Didn't you see what was left of that weather station? Now quiet, everyone – I'm adding voiceover."

"It was *my* turn," muttered Vione. She was ignored.

Keeping a careful eye on the viewscreen, Augat began: "Here, we bring you the depredation wrought by Hurricane Vuli on our beloved Lyricon. The auditorium is strewn with branches, leaves, pots, flowers, awnings, anything not tied down, lifted by this scavenging wind and dumped here. The stage, as you can see, is flooded, but most of the infrastructure is unscathed, thanks to the ingenuity of the Lyricon's forgotten architects." He signalled Vione to zoom in on the mezzanine level. "Not everyone has fled. Custodian Nefyrra has refused to leave, pointing out that the Lyricon is constructed on bedrock and that water does not flow upwards." He paused the recording and turned to Neme.

"Did she elaborate on that?"

"She told me very forcibly to close off and stop disrupting the chain," Neme replied.

"Keep trying. She might come around."

Neme shrugged.

When Roegin emerged, Vione had managed to wrestle Escir into a towelling gown. Drowsed with painkillers and resnay, he was now mumbling some affectionate nonsense about Ailsi. Vione stood over him with the camera, its running light blinking steadily.

The sphere was still prowling round Lateral One.

Roegin strode forward. "Augat, can we possibly get back to the hospital now?"

"Almost done. There was a rainbow! Poetic, eh? That just proves - "

The sphere lurched.

"Zonn, keep it *steady*!"

"Sorry," said the pilot unashamedly. "Wasn't expecting that one."

"Well, I suppose we've enough material. Let's deliver our castaways and head for home."

"Wait!" Roegin was staring at the viewscreen.

"I thought you were in a hurry?"

"The campanile. It moved."

He was right. Augat, calmly efficient, pulled the image back to include not just the stricken monument but a section of the ground beneath. The campanile swayed once more, then tore loose from its base and plummeted end over end to shatter on the stones of the auditorium.

"Thanks for that," Augat said casually. "Neme, maybe Nefyrra will have something to say now."

Neme inquired tentatively, then unexpectedly grinned. "She says, best thing for it."

Augat chortled. "She's a pragmatist, our Custodian. We have our quote. Let's go!"

After being unceremoniously dumped at the hospital by the departing news team, Roegin found the nurse he'd spoken with earlier and left Escir in her care. He then went to borrow some boots and waterproofs from Escir's dwindling stash of Eldorian army wear. On his way back to the ward, he again passed the transposer station. The device was pinging incessantly, and thinking it might be a medical emergency, he answered it. To his surprise, it was Veylis.

"So you *are* there! What in Ebbondrear's going on? I left you at Holpen!"

"Who told you I was here?"

"Kest City News. You're all over it."

"*Already?*" Roegin briefly explained his various errands.

"You need to get back to Ciela," Veylis advised.

"I *know* that."

"I mean, you *really* need to. The Clustrals have switched their activities to the hydro-electric plant, and their mapping pattern's been detected at the pumping station next to Holpen."

"Are you sure they've moved on? It's still so dark here."

"It's dusk, you fool!"

"Ebbon's blood," Roegin muttered angrily. How long had he actually been stuck in the monorail or traipsing through woodland? And, of course, Celestrians didn't care about telling the time. He hadn't seen a single clock anywhere. Ciela was all alone in her beach house. He'd told her she'd be safe.

411

"I can't take you back there." Veylis sounded contrite. "Trevone's off duty, Ibri's weapons system went technical. That leaves me."

"I'll sort it," Roegin declared, though he wasn't sure how. Returning to Lateral Six seemed a sensible way to start.

Escir, his arm in a cast, greeted him with more positivity than he'd shown of late. "I believe you and Nyldra are acquainted. She's declared me unfit for work, so I'm leaving her in charge and going to join Ailsi. That's if she'll speak to me after Augat and his pals broadcast what I was prattling under that narcotic."

"About that." Roegin searched his unfamiliar pockets and located a small data device. "I palmed the clip from Vione's camera as we were leaving. They've got nothing of us except the initial rescue."

"But how did you …?"

"Once a spy, always a spy," Roegin said laconically. "Can I beg a ride as far as the Lisir?"

"That won't get you back to Holpen. The bargees won't take anyone upriver."

"I know. It's the flitter I want."

"Can you fly one?"

"I'll learn."

"You'll crash."

"Thanks for the vote of confidence. Nobody needs a licence to operate one, so how difficult can it be?"

"*I* never mastered it," Escir said loftily.

"Roegin doesn't lack resourcefulness," Nyldra reminded him. "Leave this to me. All he needs is a few pointers from an experienced flyer. Devri."

"Devri? Our orderly?"

"The same. He's been ferrying our expectant mothers to Tivenne all yesterday and most of today. He'll be taking you to the Lisir as his final trip before going to join the evacuees."

"Where is he now?" Roegin asked.

"At a charging point. I've just explained your situation and he wants to ensure the flitter can reach Holpen."

"My sincerest thanks, Nyldra."

"Don't thank me for sending you into danger," she said reprovingly.

Devri arrived almost at once, and, calmly efficient, conveyed the two Eldorians back to the swollen Lisir. Then he helped Escir to board a spacious but crowded riverboat, leaving Roegin to guard the flitter. The daylight was disappearing fast, and it seemed an age before Devri returned – although it was little more than an astal. Then, having found a quieter area for his tutorial, he demonstrated the rudimentary controls two or three times until he was sure Roegin understood the basics.

"If you want the shortest route, forget the monorail. Stay west of the Lisir. There are guide beacons set in the ground and I've set the locator to read the Holpen route only. Keep low, reduce your running lights to conserve power. Got it?"

"I'll manage," Roegin said.

For a time, he did. Heading north-west, he picked up the beacon trail just as the last of the daylight faded. But on his right were storm clouds in their now-familiar columns, shot through with

413

lightning. As he drew parallel the first eddies reached him, threatening to spin the craft around. He increased speed and modified his course slightly, but to no effect. Due east, although he hadn't realised, was the hydro-electric complex.

He forged on. The beacon signals became intermittent, drowned by static. Rain sluiced down the canopy. He engaged the repeller field and the way ahead was promptly obscured by a wall of water. In no time, he was lost. Buffeted by wind and hail, the flitter veered too far west. Cursing, he slammed off the repeller. Then, in desperation and against instructions, he turned the lights full on and decreased height until a proximity alarm sounded.

He was over the lake, only fractionally above the choppy, agitated surface. He hauled on the controls, trying to stay aloft and restore some sense of direction. Then, by a whim of fortune, sheet lightning briefly lit the terrain. Ahead of him were the trees bordering the bay. And to his right, distant but unmistakeable, the steep shingle beach. Yelling Ciela's name he slewed the craft round, aiming for the now invisible shoreline. The engine whined in protest and almost stalled. Bouncing off the water, narrowly missing the pontoon, the flitter lurched to the beach and slammed into the shingle nose first. The shock triggered the canopy.

Roegin, scrambling, stumbling, single-mindedly made his way up the beach. The treeline was ahead of him, black shapes against a slightly less dark sky. And beyond that, Ciela's house, palely lit. He tried calling her name again; uselessly, or so he thought. But she, sensing him, hastened outside in sudden hope. He crushed her to him and for a long moment they clung together, oblivious to the rain.

"I'm so sorry," he began incoherently. "For leaving you here. I couldn't – I didn't - "

She hushed him and led him inside.

The power was out, the faint radiance coming from depleted solar tubes. But the thermally heated stones in the treatment room provided warmth and a place to dry off.

"When did you last eat? she asked, ever practical.

"Er … this morning."

"Thought so. That fool Augat wouldn't think to feed his hero of the day."

"You heard?"

"Kest City News has a long reach. You can tell me what really happened while we have supper. I batch-cooked some soup earlier. We'll have to eat it cold but we can at least toast some grain-cakes."

After the makeshift meal they carried bedding downstairs, not only to stay warm, but because Roegin suspected the roof would soon part company from the rest of the house. They made love while the storm raged above them. And afterwards they spoke of many things, both trivial and profound, but never mentioning their future relationship. When the Clustrals were defeated – if they were – there would have to be decisions. But not tonight. Tonight there would be no promises.

Chapter Fifteen

Clustral Offensive Day 4   4.6.2.4031

"Dessin, you have to get them away from us!" The tired, sweaty face on the transposer screen belonged to Pagnar, chief of operations at the hydro-electric plant. "You must have seen Veylis' report. And those idiots from Kest have been here with spotlights."

Dessin had seen the vidcast. The Clustrals were using the surrounding dense woodland as ammunition – an endless supply of debris to hurl into the river above the dam. The maintenance crew had been out the entire night, using improvised grapples to prevent uprooted foliage from blocking the intakes.

"We can't keep this up. We're exhausted," Pagnar continued. "If any of this stuff reaches the turbines we'll have to take them offline, maybe even remove them, to clear it. And if there's any damage to the rotors we're looking at a major repair which could take octals. Spans, even. The power station says they only have a couple of day's reserve – something I didn't expect to hear when half the city's deserted."

"The solar collectors haven't been much use since the storms. We have to maintain the prill environments, provide power to the spaceport and keep all communications open."

"What about the emergency generators? Have you been using them?"

"Not yet. But they'd only amount to islands of power."

"In terms of days?"

"Two or three."

"As I thought. The Clustrals want Alda Mexa shut down, Dessin, and that's exactly what will happen if we don't act now to stop it. I do have one suggestion, though you probably won't like it."

"Go on."

"Start up the weathershield. The Clustrals think it's a weapon, don't they? They'll be drawn to it instantly."

"If we do that, our reserves will be gone in two ilden rather than two days!"

"Not if we continue to supply you."

"It could work," mused Dessin. "Having them all in one place, I mean. We could concentrate all *our* resources, too. Clemis will be back here soon; I'll discuss it with her and Trevone. We'll need to confer with the scolia-adepts, of course."

"Understood, but do it quickly."

Dessin uttered something bland and ended the transmission.

"Not very convincing," remarked Jarras over the tower audio link.

"Discords, Jarras, why are you still there?" Dessin said accusingly. "I sent Trytin to collect you. I hope he turned up."

"He did, and he's been a great help. He located some flitter canopy sealant in the maintenance bay and fixed the roof hatch with it. Then we mopped up the puddles. Just give me a moment and I'll show you." One of the many transposers lit.

"There, you see? All good, apart from the rooftop camera. The rain totalled that."

"Where's Trytin now?"

"Home, I imagine. He left several ilden ago. I slept in the hospitality suite and I'm now back on duty – if that's all right with you."

"You need to eat."

"Actually, I don't. Trytin brought some fish stew he'd liberated from the river people, along with some really powerful liquor. I slept well after that."

"I'm glad Trytin's been so resourceful," Dessin remarked.

"The sealant was *my* idea," Jarras said. "He just did as he was told for once. We can't abandon the tower, Dessin. Treva can't provide its immediacy. We need access to our satellites." He changed the subject. "I know you don't approve of Kest's vidcasts, but they do have their uses."

"You *watch* that rubbish?"

"Not much else to do at the moment. If you'd just let me explain …?"

"Please do."

"All the debris at the Lyricon was essentially small stuff, anything that wasn't tethered. But now, suddenly, whole trees are being thrown into the Lisir. The Clustrals have a new, more powerful weather source, and I've located it. Or rather, Augat did."

"Discords, Jarras, did you have to involve *him*?"

"What choice did I have? I needed proof, there's no satellite coverage in the hurricane basin

418

and Aronne's probably lost at sea. Augat was happy to chase down the storm. It's a tropical cyclone moving east across the Bay of Espri."

Trytin strolled in, yawning. "Espri? Now *there's* a name from the past!" Then, mistaking the reason for Dessin's frown: "I did pay *some* attention in school. Espri, the biggest aldacite mine in the world, all tapped out and derelict. Back soon!" And he wandered off in search of breakfast.

"Discords," Dessin repeated.

"Annoying, isn't he?" said Jarras.

"It isn't him precisely – not this time. He's just reminded me of a pre-Clustral situation."

"Oh?"

"Our aldacite reserves are almost depleted. We need to source some deposits."

Jarras was unperturbed. "Sarune can help with that, surely.?"

"I suppose. Eventually. Pagnar's suggestion's at the top of today's agenda."

"I heard him. Are you going to do it?"

"Not unless everyone agrees. And I do mean everyone. Clemis, Trevone, Nefyrra, Sheyell, Ansela - "

"And Lydion. He's still the leading expert on the weathershield and the Lyricon in general."

"I hadn't forgotten. I'll ensure Rinyi's notified."

Just then another screen went live. To his surprise, the caller was Nefyrra.

"Can you see me, Dessin? I'm a little new to this."

"Yes, I see you. Where are you?"

"At the Lyricon, on the mezzanine level. I thought my apartment was a little unsafe after last night."

"But where did you get the transposer? No, wait, I think I can guess. Augat."

Nefyrra smiled. "Not precisely. After he'd dropped off Roegin and Escir, I was contacted again by Neme, his relayist. She asked to see me in person. Augat wanted to get his news data back to Kest, so Neme stayed here. We talked late into the night."

"About?"

"Initially she was concerned that I didn't have a transposer. She thought today would be definitive, and that I'd need one." Nefyrra paused. "She probably sensed my mood just after the campanile came down. I stopped being angry with her and Augat, and realised that news communication shouldn't be restricted to a relayist chain. We should work in tandem, telepathic and electronic. Tradition isn't everything. So, here I am. Augat came hurtling back with a transposer, hooked it up and whisked Neme away. She *was* right, wasn't she? About today?"

Dessin explained.

"Then why did you let me talk? We should be helping Pagnar!"

"I agree, but he knows we have to confer. We can start by assembling your team leaders, plus Rinyi and Lydion. And Esclevon too, as he's your only link to Kyrin and Bridd. I'll contact the other administrators."

"What about Clemis and Trevone?"

420

Dessin sighed. "I was hoping they'd wake of their own accord. They're together for the first time this year."

"They'll forgive you. But aren't you forgetting someone?"

"Who?"

"Tonor. We can't run the shield without him."

"Chaos!" muttered Dessin.

"Exactly. He isn't going to like this. He's in comparative safety with his family. So, do we send for him now or wait until we have a decision? Because I think I know what Clemis will say."

"We can afford to wait if we send Trevone for him."

"Very well. But call an admin meeting *now*. And once everyone's alerted we'll need Clemis awake and aware."

Dessin tried to reach Bridd and Kyrin, annoyed when his perception encountered neither. Both asleep? he thought irritably. That's slovenly. One of them should always be on duty. Isn't that why we got Kyrin some help?

Alcis, further off, responded, and set about rousing the administration. But as soon as she'd elicited some replies, Clemis herself joined in.

+Dessin? Alcis? What's going on?+

Dessin framed an explanation, but she cut him short.

+I'm coming down. Wait+

He didn't have to wait long. Clemis swept in, efficient and focused, and coolly took charge. She immediately endorsed Pagnar's idea.

"It's about time we went on the offensive. And, we'll have to give it everything we've got. No half measures. They'd probably fail. Tell the administrators I'm only notifying them as a formality. This is going to happen. Jarras, are you there?"

"Of course."

"Round up Ibri and Veylis, please. They and Trevone will continue as our attack force. The other armed spheres will be on alert. Dessin, get Nefyrra back. I want all the Lyricon participants assembled, if they aren't already. And I need to speak with Esclevon." She headed for the door. "I'm going to wake Trevone and send him to collect Tonor, as per your suggestion."

"One moment," said Dessin.

She paused.

"Do I reprimand Bridd and Kyrin for letting us down?"

She looked faintly surprised. "Not under these circumstances. Their absence means they'll be at optimum strength today. And we're certainly going to need that."

When she returned, she slammed the door.

"Trouble?" inquired Dessin, though he already knew the answer.

"Only from Trevone. He can be so patronising sometimes. He said, and I quote, that I mustn't assume the Clustrals' narrow focus on the hydro dam is all they're capable of now. Why would I assume that? We've killed some, but not that many." She paused to calm herself, then continued: "The Clustrals always surround their target.

422

Therefore they'll form a hemisphere outside the weather-shield canopy. My plan will reflect this. And in case they do decide to vary their approach, Lydion and Sarune will be guarding the projectors and scanning for enemy EM signatures."

"I've asked Jarras to sweep for those too," said Dessin. "He says the other city-states are clear."

Trytin ambled back into the room just as Dessin suppressed a yawn. "You look in need of some down-time, administrator. I'll keep an eye on Clemis till Daphos arrives. Go on, go!"

"One more thing," Clemis said.

"What?" Dessin asked wearily.

"Bridd spoke with me. I mean, he physically came to apologise."

"And?"

"And it was his fault there was no relayist cover. He'd fallen asleep on watch because he'd been writing during his sleep shift."

"Writing what?"

"Poetry to his girlfriend," Trytin offered.

"How would *you* know?"

"She told me."

Dessin sighed. "If he weren't so talented I'd ask Nohal to dismiss him. I still might, later."

Trytin watched him leave. "Dullard. He used to be so much fun. Well, what do we do next?"

"*I*," said Clemis, deliberately emphatic, "am calling a rehearsal. A dummy run, with everyone in their correct role. The children will form a lattice – not the seventy cycle type, just a normal one – to ensure they, and Esclevon in particular, can reach

423

Kyrin and Bridd. And we won't be running the shield yet, of course."

"Will you have a training run for the pilots too?"

"I think they know what to do," Clemis said quietly.

"Any special duties for *me*?" Trytin persisted.

"Keep in touch with Jarras, since you two seem to be getting on so much better. Monitor the other city states alongside Daphos. Oh, and do your best to keep Augat away. We don't want to shoot him down by mistake."

"But what a story," Trytin murmured.

Clemis left him chatting with Jarras, and contacted Nefyrra with details of the planned rehearsal. "As to the main event," she continued," be assured that I'm always mindful of safety, yours and the children's. I'm changing the rescue procedure, should it be needed. Flitters aren't designed to cope with hurricanes so I'm instructing every Eldorian save Veylis to be ready with their spheres. I see Rinyi's with you."

"He's eager to commence – or maybe Lydion is."

"And Vonnie?"

"Edgy, but resolute. He'll deliver."

"Put him on."

Nefyrra hesitated.

"I won't fuss. I just want to see him."

Trytin was engaged in a dispute with Sheyell. As always, his perception had a broad, indiscreet signature. +No, I *don't* think you should be in the library. Get out and take Ansela with you. Haven't

424

you ever *seen* a hurricane? You need to be somewhere with no windows+

"We're ready, mother," Esclevon said over the transposer. "Tell Trytin to shut up."

"You're *receiving* him?"

"Only too well."

Clemis smiled. "That's very reassuring."

"Tonor isn't here yet," said Nefyrra, behind him.

"We don't need him for this. Let's begin."

She elbowed Trytin and he hastily reined in his thoughts. Throughout Lateral One, snug in their heated globes, the prill unfurled their leaves. The children's minds conjoined. On the uppermost floor of the akron, Bridd and Kyrin radiated a dual harmonic. Clemis thought Kyrin had the dominant role, though she couldn't be sure. Esclevon's radiant consciousness reached out and encircled theirs.

"Lovely. Now all we need is some music." Trytin was attempting to be flippant, but didn't quite manage it. "Amazing," he conceded.

Daphos, remarkably calm, walked in. "Dessin's just updated me. When's the main event?"

"Nefyrra will give the signal," Clemis said. "The Lyricon has control now."

***

Tonor, Esclevon, Nefyrra and Rinyi – with Lydion and Sarune in attendance – were assembled in the generator room.

425

"Doesn't anyone else think this is a bad idea?" Tonor asked.

"The alternatives are worse," Nefyrra answered calmly. "If our principal energy source fails, the city will die slowly. This is our best chance of saving both."

"But what if …?" Tonor floundered. "What if Pagnar's got it wrong, and he can't maintain power to the shield? We all know it's a colossal drain on resources. If it fails, the rain could flood the projectors."

"Not going to happen," said Rinyi, speaking as Lydion. "Cast your mind back, Tonor, to your apprenticeship. Floren was custodian, the weathershield was showing its age, and breakdowns were frequent. So were the downpours. But not one drop of rain entered here, due to the genius of the Lyricon's architects. Ever studied those funny little gradients between here and the stage? They protect this room from the elements."

"Did *you* stop the breakdowns, Lydion?" Esclevon asked politely.

"No, the Narvellans did that as part of their reparation programme. A young man called Gryc did most of the work, with help from Tralvar."

Tonor scowled as he remembered being sidelined.

"And where were *you*, Lydion, while this was going on?" Esclevon continued innocently.

"With Tarlatine."

"Oh. Sorry. I - "

Relayist Tylo's slow, patient mindspeech saved him. +Custodian, guests. It's time. The power station and the hydro facility are ready to channel all resources to the shield+

"Sentinels, to your posts," ordered Nefyrra. Rinyi remained where he was; Sarune and Lydion took up positions at opposite sides of the auditorium. In this configuration the trio could pinpoint Clustral activity with added precision.

+Lattice points, report readiness. Esclevon, cue the akron relayists and advise the hub to commence EM frequency monitoring+

"They *and* the incorporeals are detecting Clustrals?" Tonor inquired, puzzled.

"*We* will assist the lattice," Rinyi explained. "The hub will direct the pilots."

Tonor was about to point out the folly of discharging laser cannon near the shield canopy, but a barb from Nefyrra silenced him. Trevone, she reminded him, was the foremost weapons expert on the planet. She and Esclevon then returned to the mezzanine level to maintain transposer contact with the hub, leaving Tonor and Rinyi alone with the lovingly restored ancient tech.

"I still think this is a bad idea," Tonor muttered as he began throwing switches.

Everyone was aware of the turbulence that would follow, but the ferocity of the Clustrals' attack was daunting. Like miniature versions of the hurricane they had brought, they whirled in tiny spirals to maximise their speed before diving at the glowing canopy. The field scattered their formation, leaving them briefly disoriented before reassembling. Lydion, studying this, noted that their approach was more frantic than ferocious. They were even repeating their attack plan.

+Target the spirals+ Lakal advised her team. The children, unused to the density of their targets, struggled to obey. Areas of heavy rain and squalling wind moved randomly across the city as the Clustrals squandered surplus resources, all their efforts being concentrated on the shield.

"It's as Lydion's always said – they're stupid," Clemis remarked. "But how long before they realise the canopy's not the energy source?"

"It's *an* energy source," Daphos said pedantically, "supplied from elsewhere. That's what they don't get."

"For the moment," said Clemis.

In the tower, Jarras was admonishing an Eldorian crew. "Nirik, Thaed, are you joyriding? The whole Treva contingent's here except you!"

"Sorry, Alda Mexa. Thaed here. Nirik thought – "

"No, *he* thought," Nirik interrupted.

"We thought we'd investigate the hurricane itself, to see if there was any way of disrupting its transfer."

"And *is* there?"

"Not at the moment. There's too much static in the air for us to detect Clustral emissions."

"I could have told you that."

"But while we're here," Thaed went on earnestly, "we'd like to explore the eye of the hurricane to check the EM situation from there. Then we'll have done all we can."

"All right," Jarras said grudgingly. "We don't need you at the moment. But stand by to quit your experiment if sent for. And don't go wasting your firepower on insubstantial targets."

"Understood," they chorused.

Jarras sighed. He knew how this would go. Nirik and Thaed would proceed to chase illusions and eventually turn up with weapons depleted.

"A word, Jarras," said Clemis.

"Did you hear all that?"

"Yes, and I don't have a problem with it. But you were wrong about one thing: not all the Eldorians are here. Fley and Keska are still missing."

"Does that matter? Laura did give them freedom to move around."

"And she also gave Roegin permission to stay here permanently – a decision I endorse. I don't want Keska nagging him to change his mind. She's already tried once. So, speak to Treva and see what you can find out. And do it sooner rather than later. We'll be even busier soon."

Jarras obeyed resignedly, thinking this was hardly the time to worry about stray Eldorians. But Treva's disconcerting response not only vindicated Clemis but left him wondering whether to enlighten her. Eventually he decided she didn't need the distraction. The Prefect of Scapirion and his partner had requested a meeting with Keska and her father. To what end? wondered Jarras. Kalyx and Ruvrin seemed in little doubt that they'd be First Citizens in the near future. And where, precisely, did that leave Alda Mexa?

He'd had no status reports from the Lyricon. The driving rain obscured most of the capital, but he could glimpse the blue of the weathershield and see the crimson lightning of the pulse-cannon reflected in the clouds. Everything had begun to seem precarious. The weathershield, which had failed in the past and could well do so again; the children, excitable and easily tired; the lattice, dependent on every individual to sustain it. An early success was imperative, as such a system couldn't remain stable.

At the Lyricon, Tonor was having similar thoughts, though he tried to suppress them for Rinyi's sake. The sensitive's remote, trancelike face showed the pressure he was under. He spoke little, except to murmur that he found Lydion's exuberance taxing. Tonor sighed. So typical of Lydion to find something to enjoy in what was surely the worst of situations.

But Lydion had good reason to be pleased. The latest generation of Eldorian armed spheres had enhanced software for precision flying, and Ymer and his wingman Hyberl were holding a position between the weathershield canopy and the quasi-somnolent Clustrals. Twice, three times the pulse-cannon had raked destruction through their bunched masses.

"We're almost out of charge," Ymer reported breathlessly. "Veylis, Ibri, can you take over? A couple more bursts and we'll be on the way to finishing them."

Veylis signalled his readiness and lined up the shot. And then, in the blink of an eye, everything changed.

Daphos saw the transposer feed from Virda go dark.

A wave of nausea enveloped Bridd. The sudden cessation of many lives had echoed across the improbable distance from Virda, the place he was still grounded in. Beside him, Kyrin gave an anguished wail and began to sob. He too was a son of Virda.

Bridd, thanks to his youth and robust upbringing, held his nerve and thrust away the knowledge that everyone in Virda, including his Kythania, was dead. He could mourn them later. First, he had a job to finish.

"Kyrin!" he yelled, shaking him. "Kyrin, close off!" But the older relayist's grief grew ever louder. Regretfully, Bridd balled his fist and punched him unconscious.

The lattice, a bewildered Esclevon at its head, awaited him. Bridd knew he wouldn't be strong enough alone. Sighing, he took out a capsule of starfire and held it between thumb and forefinger. "To chaos with it," he muttered after the briefest pause. "I never wanted to be a relayist anyway." Then he crushed the tiny capsule and inhaled the vapour.

Several floors below, Clemis and Daphos were well aware of Kyrin's distress and Bridd's decisive action. Clemis promptly called the tower.

"Jarras, you have Augat's ear. Tell him something catastrophic's happened to Virda and we need to know what it is. We need video, fast. Tell him it's an order from the First Citizen."

"On it," said Jarras.

Rinyi's finely honed senses had read every detail of the relayists' plight. Instantly Sarune and Lydion knew it too. And even without Rinyi's input, Lydion knew the presence of starfire.

+We have to help Bridd+ he urged Sarune. +He and Vonnie can't sustain the lattice unaided, and if he takes more starfire it could kill him+

+We can't participate. They can't sense us+

+I know, but we could add our energy to the lattice structure. I've done it before+

+When?+

+When you first brought me back. I used to support lattices here. It made me feel connected to my former life+

+Ingrate+ Sarune remarked.

+It *works*! Help me, Sarune!+

+If you extend yourself all the way to the akron, you won't survive+

+We can do it together!+

+*No*!+ Sarune was at her most chilly. +I won't, Lydion. It would be death. Do this and you're on your own+

+We *have* to!+

+I said no. I *wanted* this life, remember? If you want to kill yourself then go ahead. I quit+

+Sarune!+

+She's gone, Lydion+ Rinyi said. +Not just closed off, gone away. I can't sense her+

+Then I'll manage alone+ Lydion declared. +Don't argue, Rinyi. I can do this+

"Rinyi? What's going on?" asked Tonor anxiously.

"Sarune's bailed on us. And Lydion, harmony help him, is trying to do the impossible."

Outside the canopy, the lattice seemed distant and puny. Lydion found Esclevon, struggling to maintain a diminishing link with the akron. He wished he could tell the boy what he was doing. But not even Rinyi could compete with a sixty five cycle augmentation. Normal perception just bounced off it.

Lydion reached desperately for Bridd's chemically enhanced consciousness, and made contact – but barely. Storm patterns swirled about him, seemingly unchanged despite the losses inflicted on the Clustrals. Lashed and buffeted, his pattern taut as a strelsis-string, he fought to maintain the lattice.

Because he was so intent on his task, he never knew what struck him down.

"Clemis, this is Augat." The hitherto imperturbable newscaster sounded shaken. "I'm sending a video. Stand by."

Clemis, Daphos and Trytin watched in silence. A massive section of the headland above Virda had broken away, burying the little town under layers of rock.

"As you can see," Augat continued, "there's nothing left. We've hovered over the rubble and Neme's scanned for survivors, but so far she hasn't detected any."

"Have you broadcast this?" Clemis asked.

"No, not yet. It needs editing. And anyway, I thought I should ask you first."

433

"Thank you for the consideration," Clemis said formally. "The world needs to see, but maybe now isn't the best time. We still have our own battles to fight."

"Can you go back to your shots of the exposed rock layers?" Daphos asked. "Slow it up. From those striations, I'd say there was a fault line. A bad one."

"The Clustrals couldn't have done that," said Trytin. "There aren't enough of them."

"I agree - it probably existed already. But they *knew* about it, Trytin. They mapped everything before they attacked. And then they sent rainstorm after rainstorm, weakening it."

"Oh, chaos," muttered Trytin. "Kythania. She said the Clustrals' aim was off, that they missed the village and rained on the cliff-top. It wasn't a mistake, was it?"

"What about the fishing fleet?" Clemis asked. "If anything was at sea - "

"All beached," Trytin said morosely. "They thought it was the safest thing to do."

"Then we may never know why Virda was targeted."

"Unless Bridd knows," said Daphos. "And I really don't think this is the time to ask him."

***

"Esclevon, you have to rest," Lakal said anxiously.

"I mustn't," he insisted. "We've lost Kyrin, and Bridd's so drugged up I think he'll soon follow. If I stop now, we'll lose our advantage."

"*What* advantage?" Lakal, agitated, surveyed the murky cityscape. "The weather's worse than ever. How are they still bringing it in? It's as if we haven't destroyed any of them!"

"If I close off from Bridd, I could still add weight to the lattice," Esclevon suggested. "Shall I do that?"

"We're all tired, Vonnie."

"Then let's set up a relay. Half of us resting, half projecting. It won't be our best but at least we can keep going."

"I'll clear it with Nefyrra and the group leaders," Lakal said after a pause. "Close off now. Resume in one astal."

While she spoke with the others, Esclevon mentally surveyed his group. Their output was so ragged and dispirited that he ordered them to share his downtime.

"Nobody said this was going to be easy," he said by way of a pep talk. "We're going to have more rests from now on."

"I want to stop," said Nya, the youngest. "The prill don't like me anymore."

Esclevon, concerned, tilted her sad little face toward him. "Can you show me, Nya? It's important."

"Don't want to."

"It's true," said Arcto. "We grew them. We bonded with them. Now, half of them won't engage. And it's getting worse."

435

Esclevon tried not to show his alarm. "Lakal – can any of us *read* the Clustrals?"

"No, silly. Only Lydion, Rinyi and Sarune can do that. That's why we don't know what effect we're having."

"I knew all that. I just wanted to hear you say it." Esclevon had begun to look much older than his years. "We need Rinyi here. Now."

***

"Jarras!"

"Well, if it isn't my hurricane hunters. What kept you?"

"Visibility," said Nirik laconically. "We can hardly see the ground through all this murk. Could you light the spacefield up a bit?"

"The perimeter flares aren't working. No solar charge. I could light every room in the tower if you want."

"That might help," responded Nirik. "At least we'd see where *not* to land."

A silence. Jarras was staring, puzzled, at a cup of liman as it slid very slowly across his desk.

"Well, *do* it then!" Nirik was growing impatient.

Jarras approached a row of circuit breakers. The cup smashed on the floor. The tower lights shone whitely into the gloom.

"Gods! Jarras, you need to get out of there!" yelled Thaed. "Never mind the comsats. There's a massive sinkhole by the base of the tower, and it's

436

getting bigger. We'll wait near the entrance, but we're not risking a landing. Now hurry up!"

Jarras acted, but too late. The lift jammed a third of the way down. He experienced a moment's claustrophobia, then smiled grimly. This tower's been out to get me for years, he thought. It won't succeed. Then, directing his perception at the unsuspecting Eldorians:

+Nirik! Thaed! Answer please. Slowly+

The usual confused reaction followed.

+I *know* you don't like vocal transference, but it's worse for the sender, believe me. Now listen: something's moved off-centre and the lift's stuck. Not far down; I can't tell exactly. Can you call the hub?+

"Will do," they chorused. "Don't go away."

Trytin took the call and was halfway out of the door before Daphos waylaid him.

"Where do you think you're going?"

"To help free Jarras. Nirik and Thaed have been doing search and rescue in Treva, so they've ropes and harnesses on board. I can't open the tower's roof hatch because of the sealant I used, so the boys will have to lower me to a window. Didn't you hear any of that?"

"I heard them say they couldn't risk a landing."

"Not at the spaceport. It's waterlogged. Which is why I've directed them to the akron roof."

"In a hurricane?" Daphos yelled.

"Visitors' gallery, docking port. Opened last year. Keep up, Daphos!" He sprinted for the stairs. Much as he respected Idenion's concession to tourism, he wished the design had incorporated an escalator or two. It was a long way up.

Nirik and Thaed were there ahead of him, and refrained from remarking on his breathless state. Returning to the spaceport took but moments, although Thaed proceeded cautiously. The tower, all three of them noted, was still intact.

As they crossed Lateral Six they glimpsed three figures waving frantically. They had been trying to escape in a coracle which had wrecked itself on a rapidly diminishing mudbank.

"Why in chaos didn't they leave with everyone else?" Trytin muttered.

"We'll sort it," Nirik promised. "First, let's get you into the tower. Pity you glued up the only sensible way in."

"That was Jarras' idea."

"You don't say. Ever heard the phrase 'single point of failure'?"

"No."

"It means, why in Ebbondrear isn't there a staircase?"

"We couldn't allow casual visitors to mess with delicate equipment. An elevator can be locked. If anyone's stranded, even if there's a power cut, we still have telepathy."

"Don't remind me," Thaed remarked, bringing the sphere to a temporary halt on the roof.

"Can't you shoot the hatch open?" Trytin asked.

"With a pulse-cannon? We'd take the whole roof off and maybe start a fire as well. No, it's the window or nothing."

They buckled Trytin into a harness and attached a coiled rope ladder to the tool belt.

"Sure you can do this?" asked Nirik. "I could take over."

"It's fine. I'm good with heights. So, I kick the window in, then knock out any shards with this handy accessory." He brandished a small hammer, then returned it to its pouch. "Then I climb down to the cage, peel open its trapdoor and return here with Jarras. Just don't take too long rescuing that family."

Thaed keyed the ramp, and together Nirik and Trytin secured the harness to the safety rail. The rain hadn't slackened, and they cursed it by turns. Trytin did his best to abseil down to Communications, but kept rebounding from the featureless walls.

"Are you there yet?" yelled Nirik.

"Bit more. Right, stop – tie it off. This window's cracked. Makes life easier I suppose." Then, after a pause: +I'm inside. Now scat+

They obeyed, despite their concerns. It took longer than expected to carry out the rescue, as they'd not allowed for the trio's lingering mistrust of Eldorian soldiers. At last, with the three reluctant passengers on board, Thaed sent the sphere hurtling back to the spaceport – only to find the tower had fallen. It had broken into three segments, though only two were visible. The midsection had disappeared into the sinkhole. The rest lay darkened and silent on the rainswept field.

Nirik whirled to confront the rescuees, who backed away from him. "Ebbon's blood, don't *do*

439

that! It isn't your fault Trytin sent us away!" Then, more quietly, "I want you to scan for life signs in the tower. Now, please."

They complied.

"Well?"

"Our apologies," said the only woman of the three. "We can read nothing. Nothing at all."

***

"They're here," Rinyi said despairingly. "The Clustrals. All over this room."

"Have they breached the prill containment domes?" asked Lakal.

"No, but why would they need to? They're not attacking the prill. I think they're here unintentionally, tracking heat emissions maybe, or just looking for a way to stop the shield."

"There was a flaw in our plan," Esclevon said. "A big one. We've all been taught about the prill homeworld and the telepathic predators there. If the prill sense a threat, they'll mimic it. And that's what they're doing."

It was a sketchy description, but everyone understood. The prill were ignoring the benign influence of the children and were now augmenting the depleted Clustrals, unwittingly restoring their strength. They could now summon the very worst weather.

Nefyrra, when informed, acted swiftly. +All lattice points, close off. Team leaders, stand by to purge the prill environments+

440

There was an outburst of protest from the children.

+The prill have to be suppressed, and the only way to do it is to kill them+ Nefyrra was inexorable. +Do it. I'll notify the hub+

Clemis listened in dismay, bordering on despair. Following the fall of the tower, there seemed no end to the bad news. She was already aware that Bridd had stopped sending. Sheyell had gone to investigate and found him overdosed on starfire. Then Pagnar advised that a turbine had broken down and the power levels had been halved. If the weathershield continued to run, the city would go dark in less than an ild. Finally, tragically, the hospital called in. A river patrol had found Ansela drowned. She'd left the library without telling anyone. It was thought that she'd been trying to salvage documents from the old archive on the descent to Lateral Two.

"But it was just junk in there!" Clemis wailed, trying to suppress angry tears.

At that moment Trevone strode in, grim and resolute. "That's it – we're leaving," he announced. "I've told the other pilots to cease engagements and pick up survivors instead. Don't argue, Clemis, we can't save the city. We have to retreat and regroup."

"Where?" she asked hopelessly.

"Treva. They're expecting us. Come on, quickly. You too, Daphos."

"I'll shut down the equipment and follow you," he replied. Trevone was already bundling Clemis out of the room.

Daphos, left alone, turned off every transposer save one. Then he keyed in a code he'd used only once before. "Myrig, we're in trouble. If Narvella truly wants to make restitution, now's the time."

"The students have been on standby since your previous message," Myrig answered.

"Then ask them to get here in a hurry. One question: can they emit a combined thought-wave of seventy cycles?"

"Easily. Why?"

"I'll explain once they're on their way – if the power stays on. Sending coordinates now."

**

7.1.3.4031 (3 octals later)

Sarune searched up and down the paths and intersections between Lateral One and the akron. Tonora had told her that Lydion was still alive, but after endless trawls of the area had revealed nothing, she was beginning to think the child was wrong. Then, belatedly inspired, she made her way to the little house in the shadow of the Lyricon. Lydion's former home, empty since Tarlion's disappearance.

And there she found him, lost in some inner darkness, his pattern atrophied and torn. Yet he'd remembered enough of her teaching to coil himself tightly against further harm. She approached, believing he was unaware of her, but he detected her presence and feebly reached out.

+Oh, you idiot. You idiot+ she murmured. +Why did you *do* that? Always hurtling about on some whim+

Then, just as she'd done seven and a half years previously, she encircled what was left of his pattern with her own. She was not optimistic. She remembered how he'd barely survived when newly incorporeal, despite his innate curiosity. Now, after the damage he'd suffered, his chances seemed minimal. Nevertheless, she began lending him her strength. And, as before, she spoke to him, telling him what he'd missed.

+Daphos contacted New Narvella after Alda Mexa was abandoned. Tarlion's students turned up, and soon had the Clustrals immobilised. Did you sense the Narvellan waveforms? I felt like hiding, just like you. I thought the Ten had made a comeback. Rinyi was terrified. But we needn't have worried. The New Narvellans are a friendly bunch; they interacted well with the children and were fascinated by the prill. And, Clemis had to relate every detail of Tarlion's adventures on Earth – how he worked in a tavern under the villains' noses, found time for a romance, and helped rescue Roegin. He'd even had some good things to say about *me*. Incidentally, Tonora's still saying he's not dead+

If Lydion had understood any of this, he gave no sign. Sarune pressed on regardless. +You'll want to know why Virda fell. In one word, aldacite. The investigators found a rich seam of it in what remained of the caves below the headland. The

Clustrals must have thought Virda was a centre of industry.

It looks as though Bridd's the only survivor. He swears he knew nothing about the aldacite and has insisted on being retraced to prove it. But he *did* remember the City Elders declaring several of the caves unsafe and having the entrances walled up. Given the reclusive nature of the Virdans, and of the Elders in particular, Bridd thinks they deliberately concealed the existence of the crystals in order to protect Virda's oral traditions. They didn't want it to become a mining town+

+... Starfire ...?+ Lydion's response was barely discernible, but Sarune marvelled at his resolve. She knew the effort he was making. +Ah, Bridd's heroics. They sent him to Corayn to be dried out, after they'd finished questioning him. His relayist days are over, of course. Total burnout. Kyrin, on the other hand, has resumed his duties+

+Did we ... lose Jarras?+

+We lost the tower. Jarras was trapped in the lift and everyone thought he was dead – even the relayists. But his Eldorian friends didn't quite believe it, and went back to check. He was so lucky! The lift cage is made from industrial quality theridolyte, and wasn't even dented. Jarras was knocked out by the impact but was otherwise unhurt. The Communications tech who'd been trying to rescue him wasn't so fortunate. He was still in the lift shaft when the tower fell, and he didn't stand a chance+ Sarune paused, reading Lydion's compassion for someone he hadn't even known. +Lydion – I understand why you care so much for this city and its people. It's your home. And yes, it's in a mess at the moment. Yes, there were losses. But Alda Mexa *will* recover, and be better than ever. So would you please concentrate on yourself now? Rest as long as you need to. Sleep if you want. I'll be with you+

And for a time, she was. She wasn't needed for Alda Mexa's clean-up operation which saw Narvellans, Eldorians and Celestrians working harmoniously together. But Lydion's sleep was not the recuperative state Sarune had hoped for. His dreams were incoherent fragments; his quieter moments, weary compliance.

She couldn't save him. That had become obvious almost at once. And now, she was being called away.

Rinyi arrived at the designated time. +They're waiting for you+ he said. Then, hesitantly : +There's been no change, then+

+No. And there won't be. Every time I release him, his pattern starts to degrade. With me gone, he won't last a day+

+You need to wake him now+

+I know. I'll do it. Could you stay close, please? I'm not sure how to tell him+

+I don't believe you'll have to+ Rinyi said.

Lydion slowly edged into consciousness. +Has it been seven years?+

+Not even seven octals. But, the city's more like its old self. There's going to be a concert soon: a big one+

Rinyi nudged her.

445

+Lydion, there's no easy way to say this. I can't heal you. And after today I can't even protect you. An expedition to Vuli-world's leaving later today. They're going to send the Collector hulk into the sun, and I have to be there because no-one else can read into the sub-strata. Remember the broken-down AI that Tarlion discovered? Vuli's predecessor? We need to make sure there aren't any others. There are no more Clustrals but a living, vengeful AI could cause damage of a different kind. Do you understand me, Lydion?+

+Of course+ He sounded relieved. +When you first gave me this life, I asked you to let me go. Since then I've had an interesting time, had some adventures and done what I believe to be useful work. So maybe it was worth hanging into me. But now I'll say it again: let me go. You don't have a choice+

+Lydion -+

+I'm content. Truly. It's a rare privilege to die twice, and it doesn't even hurt this time. But seriously – how long before I lose the ability to communicate and become that little frightened thing you found in my house?+

+Three or four ilden+

+That's time enough. Rinyi, could you locate Tonora and bring her to the generator room?+

+I don't have to locate her. She's in the Lyricon with Tonor and some others, tidying up the basement+

+Then bring her. But don't let Tonor see you+

Rinyi hastened off.

446

+What are you planning, Lydion?+ asked Sarune.

+You'll see. One of Tonora's prophecies is about to come true. Escort me to the generator room, please, with all due solemnity as befits the occasion. And then you'd better get your pert little pattern over to Treva, where I believe Trevone and company await your presence+

+Lydion …!+

+Yes, sweetness?+

+You can be so irritating at times+

+Good. Remember that whenever you start to miss me+

Alone with the shield projectors he'd tended in his former life, Lydion soon began to feel the effects of Sarune's absence. Proof, if any were needed, that he was in the right place.

Tonora, when she arrived, took one look at him and remarked: +You're dying, Lydion+

+That's why I'm here. Where you told me I'd be. I'd like you to do two things for me+

+Go on+

+Firstly, talk to Sarune when you can. I wasn't an ideal companion for her, but better than nothing. Now she'll be alone+

+No she won't! She'll meet masses and masses of beings like herself+

As if that's going to happen, Lydion thought privately. But the child's only trying to console me.

+I'll talk to her if she wants+ Tonora supplemented. +What's the second thing?+

+I want you to turn on the weathershield. Now+

+But Lydion, the shield resonance will destroy you!+

+Yes, while I'm still me. The alternative isn't very nice+

Still she hesitated. +Will I get into trouble?+

+No, because Rinyi and Sarune both know what I've been planning. You know exactly what I am, Tonora. An energy pattern. What do your science lessons tell you about energy? That it can't be destroyed, only changed+

She agreed, reluctantly.

+So, even though I won't be in this form, you won't have erased your Lydion. I'll still be here, though I don't know what I'll become. Now please, throw those switches+

She obeyed, calm and dry-eyed. Above the amphitheatre the support matrix sprang into life, and its vortices began to fill with clear blue light.

"Tonora!" An angry Tonor stormed into the generator room. "How many more times do I have to tell you *not* to play around with the shield?"

Tonora quietly explained why she'd disobeyed.

"And you didn't touch the spectrum filters?"

"No, Fa, I just turned it on."

Tonor didn't try to read her. Tonora was already capable of stalling him. And besides, he believed her. "There's something I think you should see," he said, and led her onto the nearby stage. Above, the weathershield was now a solid mass of colour – but not the sky blue Tonora was expecting. Instead she saw a deeper blue, warm and welcoming, casting a benign radiance on the workers who had paused to stare. Then gradually, as they watched, its unique properties grew paler, until nothing remained except the colour it had briefly displaced.

Father and daughter silently left the stage.

"I'll let everyone think I was testing it," Tonor said at last.

"All right."

"And it's just occurred to me that I ought to give it a full systems once-over before the concert. We don't want it breaking down halfway through. Care to help?"

"*Can* I, Fa?"

"Of course. You'll be running it yourself one day. No harm in starting young!"

***

Vuli-world without Vuli was even more desolate than Sarune remembered. While the team pored over their previous flight logs and made calculations, she scoured the landscape for any sign of sentient geodes. The scars of the previous visit were just as before. No Clustrals were trying to revive the tumbled wreckage. She probed further and further from the landing site until Trevone finally told her she could stop.

Now, with only Rinyi for company, she waited in a solitary grounded sphere while the others attached explosives to strategic points on the derelict Collector. Eldorian bioshells were more substantial than their Celestrian counterparts, which meant improved safety but less dexterity. Every charge had to be in place, and the detonation sequence completed, before the next solar flare.

They made it with time to spare. Sarune never doubted their ability. What she didn't realise was that instead of shaking the dust of this miserable world from their assorted shoes, they'd settle down to see the Collector's hulk safely into its decaying orbit.

+More waiting+ she complained to Rinyi.

+They said something about a tipping point+ Rinyi offered. +Observation's the only way to ensure it happens+

+I don't want to *be* here+ Sarune reiterated.

+You're missing him+ Rinyi commented softly.

+Yes, and Tarlion too+

+Yet you complained that Lydion was exasperating+

+He was. But he knew how to *live*. I can never aspire to that+ She paused despondently. +Let me out of here, Rinyi. Crack the hatch, just for a moment. I need some space to think+

Rinyi unhappily complied. +Don't stray too far+

Sarune didn't answer. Without conscious volition she found herself drifting past the area where Tarlion had found the diamonds. A sense of not being alone, which had troubled her several times that day, was suddenly very pervasive. Fool, she told herself. There's no Tarlion, no Vuli, no Clustrals. What else can there be? Nothing!

But she wasn't imagining things. Someone, or some thing, *was* trying to contact her. A composite entity which spoke in unison.

+You perceive us at last. This gladdens us. We celebrate+

+What *are* you?+ Sarune demanded. +Show yourselves!+

+You do not observe us fully. Phasing. Wait. Wait+

Sarune waited. At first she could only perceive white light. Then, many points of light – the life radiance of beings too numerous to count, like stars at a galaxy's heart.

+We are the Concordance of Everness+

Finally, she understood. +You're from the bubble universe. You got out+

+Yes+

+You tried to contact me while Lydion was examining the bubble+

+We did. We also tried to converse with the entity Lydion, but he could not sense us. Where is he? He handled the shell of Everness with much care+

+He is gone. Destroyed while defending his homeworld+

They seemed genuinely regretful. +We must know more about you, Guardian Sarune. What is your species? Where are they? We must learn - we require – we need -+

Sarune, at risk of being swamped, tried to fend off the barrage of questions. She didn't fear these beings, artless as children and just as impatient, but if she were to communicate effectively she had to settle them down.

They solved the problem themselves before she could act – so swiftly that she wondered if they had the same perception of time. +We are the three founding Stays+ announced an authoritative trio-pattern. +We perceive you are also a Stay+

Whatever that is, Sarune thought.

They read her. +Will you permit we three to unite with you, Guardian Sarune? It would greatly improve our future dialogue+

Sarune hesitated warily. This was much too reminiscent of the Synectics. And besides, these Stays might not like what they found.

+Our Concordance was not built without sacrifice+ the trio informed her.

Despite her misgivings, Sarune was intrigued. Steeling herself, she allowed the Stays to read her. They were circumspect, almost deferential – a welcome contrast to the rigorous grasp of the Synectics. In return, they allowed her to view the perfect symmetry of their subjects' existence.

Sarune felt almost bereft when the study concluded. Resignedly she awaited the censure she was convinced would follow. None came.

+Your project could never have succeeded+ the Stays remarked. +The life-energy of organic beings, no matter how numerous, would not have sufficed. When the material resources of Everness began to fail, we had no shortage of volunteers for similar endeavours. Our attempts were fruitless. Only the heat-death of stars had the necessary power. Our first step was to liberate ourselves from our bodies but not seek to leave the confines of Everness. We sacrificed three island galaxies to achieve this. For a time, a very long time, this was enough. But eventually we realised we had to move on, while Everness still had sufficient entropy to make this possible+

Sarune was amazed. +You destroyed your universe to escape it?+

+We did. And now we wish to find the ones who gave us life+

+You knew that Everness was seeded?+

+We guessed. Then we freed ourselves, discovered the sentinel Vuli, and had our theory confirmed. But we're still no nearer to identifying our creators. Will you accompany us on our quest?+

+*Me*?+

+You are an exemplary Stay. You kept those ill-assorted quarrelsome Synectics united for years. We are at the limit of our capabilities. As our numbers increase, we risk losing cohesion+

+How can your numbers increase?+ asked Sarune, although the truth was already dawning on her.

+You compared us with children. And you were right – many of us are. We're still evolving: we grow, we divide. We believe our makers will be impressed. Join with us, Sarune. Fulfil your vocation+

Sarune didn't take much longer to decide. +To paraphrase Lydion, I've found what passes for adventure around here. I accept your invitation. But first, let me say goodbye to Rinyi. The expedition needs to get home now, not waste time searching for me+

Rinyi, in wonderment, promised to tell the others. Afterwards he was never sure, but he fancied he perceived the Concordance as the starry globe gathered its energies and headed for unknown space.

Chapter Sixteen

"We'll soon be home," Tarlion said cheerfully.

"Good," Laura said thankfully. "I didn't mean to be away this long. As soon as we're out of transposal, call ahead."

"Programme ending," Tarlion announced. "Hello, what's this? Stay in your seats, both of you – I'm getting some skittish readings. Engaging safety protocols - "

The sphere lurched violently several times, as if some outside agency had hold of it and was shaking it. The Drive and control systems shut down, the emergency lighting came on.

"Life support functional," Tarlion said calmly. "Don't worry, people, I've dealt with worse than this. We still have our spin. Circuit breakers prevented damage to crystals. Powering up." He studied the panel intently. "Everything seems normal now. I've no idea what that was."

"I think *I* do," said Idenion reluctantly.

"What?" asked Laura, ominously quiet.

"The marker from the second asteroid."

"I thought the Eldorians blew that one to bits," said Tarlion.

"They did, and then Trevone dispatched the bits into t-space."

"And once again you failed to note where that happened," Laura said accusingly.

"Not fair, Laura! I never knew the location. I *was* rather caught up with the Eldorians' return, and your arrival back from Earth - "

"What did you mean, once again?" Tarlion asked curiously.

"On his very first visit to Earth, he nearly ran into a cloud of space rubble. And then didn't tell anyone about it."

"Because I met *you*!" Idenion said, aggrieved.

"Get him to tell you the full story when you have a spare ild or two," Laura advised Tarlion. "Now, shouldn't someone call Alda Mexa?"

Tarlion complied. "That's odd – they're not answering. Something's wrong. I can't even detect a portal."

"Are you sure?" Laura said apprehensively. "Could it be our equipment?"

"See if you can raise Treva," Idenion suggested.

Treva responded immediately, but after Tarlion had announced himself there was a long silence. "Direct your call to Tivenne," the operator said at last. "Here's their portal code. They'll give you landing instructions."

Mystified, Tarlion obeyed. Tivenne was, so he believed, just a village. Why were they handling space traffic? The mystery deepened when the next voice was one he recognised.

"Daphos? It's Tarlion! Yes, we're all here. Laura, Idenion and me. Why? Weren't you expecting us?"

"Yes, we were," Daphos replied. "Eight years ago."

"*What*?"

"Put yourselves on visual, please. I need verification."

456

"You're not the only one," said Tarlion, engaging the main telescreen.

They all stared at one another for several moments before Tarlion began to explain their bumpy emergence from transposal.

"Let's not conjecture," said Daphos, ever practical. ""We'll examine your flight log in detail. Then we'll know more."

Laura had her own opinion, though she didn't voice it. This had to be some remnant of the Gloriana's time bridge, augmented by Trevone's use of the dispersal engine. Eight years, Daphos had said. How long was that in Earth years?

"Twelve," Idenion said laconically.

"You're both very laidback about this," Tarlion remarked, still bemused.

"They've seen it all before." Daphos was similarly unfazed. "May I suggest you overfly the old spaceport location before heading for Tivenne? I'll talk you through it."

"Fine. Bring it on!" Tarlion switched to hover mode.

The change was startling. In place of the tower and maintenance block was an elegant complex of buildings arranged round a central courtyard. A monorail spur and a broad walkway lined with half-mature trees connected the new development with Lateral Six.

"That's Trytin Place, our hospitality centre," said Daphos. "It's only half full at the moment. We're still working on it."

Laura frowned. "It's impressive, but won't it be surplus to requirements?"

457

"Not at all. Alda Mexa gets many more visitors than it used to." Daphos paused, catching Tarlion's eye. "And some of those visitors are Narvellan."

"My students?" Tarlion hardly dared hope.

"I invited them. They've been invaluable."

"I knew it. I *knew* it!"

"They helped us kick-start this project. Telekinesis comes in very handy on a building site!"

"Quite a showpiece," said Idenion. "What was its name again?"

"Trytin Place."

"And what did Trytin do to merit such an accolade?"

"Got himself killed."

"Oh," said Idenion, nonplussed. "How, exactly?"

"Idenion, you and the others have a great deal of catching up to do. We should keep things simple for now, otherwise we'll *all* get confused."

"Too right," agreed Tarlion. "Let's make landfall first and save our questions for later."

"The spaceport's to the south of Tivenne. You can't miss it," Daphos told him. "Now I'd better end this conversation and attempt to head off Kest City News. Chaos knows how they found out you were back."

"The Treva operator, I'll bet," Tarlion muttered.

The spaceport was, as Daphos had inferred, unmistakeable. Instead of a tower was a squat round structure in the shape of a sphere. Much larger of course, with encircling windows, four main entrances and clearly delineated landing sites. The monorail terminus was close by, plus outbuildings and flitter parks. Tarlion brought the spacecraft to a slightly uneven touchdown and attempted to open the hatch. It was then that he realised what Daphos and the other spectators already knew – that the eight-year-long homecoming had almost been a trip to oblivion.

Instead of the smooth rippling transition from hatch to ramp, the process degenerated into ribbons and rivulets. Eventually the damaged theridolyte gave up the struggle and solidified into an inchoate mess. Tarlion, grim-faced, went forward and broke off one of the brittle shards.

"We're on this," Daphos called. "Stay put. We'll bring a wheeled ramp."

Laura accepted Tarlion's help in negotiating the ruined hatchway and the unsecured steps. Once on the ground, she turned to look at the sphere – and for the first time became aware how their very survival had hung by a thread. The entire hull surface was blackened, warped and lacerated. The early afternoon sun, pitiless after the twilit Vuli-world, spared no detail.

Things became confusing after that. Trevone appeared from somewhere, ordering maintenance workers to have the wreck transported to Treva for analysis. Several techs hurried forward to download the flight data for detailed study. Kest City News then put in an appearance, but not the media intrusion that Daphos was expecting. Instead, the welcoming committee consisted of Vione and one cameraman.

"Augat sends his apologies," she began, slightly flustered. "He's setting up the live broadcast of Dancers' Challenge. We're on air this evening. It's the final!"

Laura looked blank.

"The show from your Earth, which Clemis intercepted?" Vione prompted.

"Oh. Yes." Laura was enlightened. "She wanted Ailsi to see it."

"And Ailsi did, but not before it had spent a year on file at the akron hub. We have Daphos to blame for that."

Daphos contrived to look abashed.

"Augat invites you both to attend the show as guests of honour," Vione concluded importantly. "He's put the news of your arrival on hold."

Idenion looked uncomfortable. "I really should look for Dena. I'd rather break the news to her myself."

"Dena's with us. She's chief choreographer."

"And Ailsi's with you too?"

"Dance director. Clemis and Nefyrra are judges and Ninfi's in charge of costumes. And the First Citizens –" She paused guiltily. "Since we have no celebrity culture, Kalyx and Ruvrin decide which profession should compete."

"How long's this been going on?" Laura asked, ineffectually shading her eyes from the sun. Vione produced a parasol from somewhere and handed it to her.

"Five years. So far we've had dancers versus engineers, logic techs, river people – that was a mistake, it ended in a fight – and herbalists. This

460

year it's the turn of the scientists, and they've been amazing. Please say you'll come."

Idenion, ever the diplomat, took charge. "Vione," he said gravely, "this competition is obviously very important to you and your audience, and our sudden presence would only detract from it. Why not have your winner announce our return, at the end?"

"Great idea!" Vione enthused.

"But we will, of course, grant you an interview now. Shall we go inside?"

"If no-one objects," said Tarlion, "I'll make myself scarce. I want to look for my students."

"I'll talk with you later!" Vione called over her shoulder. "You're right, Idenion, this show *has* become important. We'd like to go worldwide with live coverage, but some of the satellites are still defunct. Now that you're back, perhaps you ..."

Tarlion smiled to himself and headed for the nearest flitter park. He wondered how long it would be before Vione was in charge of Kest City News.

It didn't take long for him to trace – via their unmistakeable mindset – a group of his former pupils at one of the many hostelries on Lateral Three. He fully intended to surprise them. But when he found himself across the street from these men and women of his own age, studying their lively faces and listening to their cheerful banter, he knew he wasn't ready to make the mental leap from past to present. Instead, he reboarded the flitter and ascended to Lateral One. He was expecting to find the Lyricon deserted, and he wasn't wrong. Doubtless the scolia had been summoned to Kest.

461

Augat would want only the best live music for his show.

A soft footfall, amplified by the Lyricon's acoustics, startled him. He hadn't realised his perception was closed off. "Hello, Rinyi! Not taking part in this dance-fest?"

"You know how I hate crowds," the sensitive replied. "Sorry I sneaked up on you."

"My fault. I was preoccupied."

"You were. Ever since you turned away from your noisy friends."

"Have you been shadowing me?" Tarlion demanded. "Did you have something to do with my reaction back there?"

"Well, I might have let a trace of my crowd phobia rub off on you."

"Why? Why would you do that?"

"As a favour to a friend. She's waited for you all these years and she didn't care to wait a moment longer."

"Who are we talking about?" Tarlion asked, still ruffled.

"Me!" said a voice from the back of the stage. A slender young woman, with the most beautiful smile Tarlion had ever seen, appeared from the shadows.

"You'll remember Tonora," Rinyi said casually. "She's our weathershield operator now. Well, I'll leave you to get reacquainted."

He tiptoed away, unnoticed. Behind him, Tarlion and Tonora embraced. Then, holding hands, they walked unhurriedly to Lydion's house – the perfect place to affirm their life-bond.

***

"I suppose you want us to step down?" Kalyx inquired.

Laura and Idenion had returned to the akron and to the apartment which had been their official home since Tralvar's day. Clemis had retained it, as Kalyx and Ruvrin preferred to govern from Scapirion. Administrator Dessin was now Prefect of Alda Mexa, and was presently hovering in the background, fearing a dispute. Clemis had sensibly absented herself from the transposer point.

Dessin craned forward to read the on-screen code, and was relieved to see it was Scapirion and not Kest. If Kalyx had still been at the broadcast hub, someone would almost certainly have been recording him.

"Relax, Dessin, this is a secure channel," Kalyx advised. "Well, citizens? Yes or no?"

"Patience, Kalyx," said Idenion. "It isn't as straightforward as that. We won't necessarily want our old lives back."

"We'll need to review everything that's happened in our absence, and then decide," Laura added.

"Get Dessin to make a list," Ruvrin said impishly. "He's good with lists."

"Should we come to Scapirion?"

"Not unless you want to! All the archive material you'll need, and the people who can update you, are in Alda Mexa."

"But not the Eldorians, surely? You'll have sent them back?"

"Of course. They stayed to give a hand with the clean-up, and then they insisted on leaving. I reconfigured the Cadence in accordance with Lydion's instructions, so there'll be no more escapes. Oh, and I … gave them a bit more space. Forty light years instead of ten. They now have access to more habitable worlds."

"It's a good compromise," said Laura. "I'd have done the same."

"As would I," Idenion confirmed. Then, reflectively: "Keska and Fley were so anxious to make their move against the Senate. A pity we'll never know how it went."

"But we *do* know!" Kalyx hadn't lost his sense of the dramatic.

"How, may I ask?"

"Do you remember when – oh, of course, it wouldn't seem very long ago to you."

"What wouldn't?" Idenion asked patiently.

"When Lydion and little Tonora came to Scapirion, as the Cadence needed work. While they were here, Lydion told Ruvrin he could see tiny universes that appeared and disappeared in moments. Tonora could read what he saw and was able to show Ruvrin. It didn't take her long to realise that these little universes offered a way of sending messages into the Cadence. We use an antimatter waveform to - "

"Kalyx, desist!" Ruvrin interrupted forcefully. "Don't forget I'm joint First Citizen. And I have one absolute rule: no bad science will ever come out of Scapirion. It's antiphon, not antimatter. And since you wouldn't know a wave antiphon if it bit you on the backside, please allow me to complete this story."

+I can see who's really in charge here+ Idenion remarked to Laura.

Kalyx, with an exaggerated flourish, complied. "My wife, the scientist. Do continue, my love."

"With pleasure." Ruvrin took a playful swipe at him. "Contrary to what you've just heard, the mini-universes only had curiosity value at first. But later, I did begin to wonder if they could carry a databurst through the Cadence. The Cadence only blocks t-space traffic and the tiny universes seemed independent of t-space. Also, the brief uniqueness of each could potentially serve as an encryption. I had a chance to work on this with Lydion and Rinyi, after the all-cities conference. It was Lydion's final contribution to Cadence theory."

"He kept saying the Cadence was wrongly named." Kalyx was unable to stay silent for long. "But transposal dampener doesn't have the same vibe, does it?"

"Ruvrin," Laura said seriously, "how are the communications with Eldor handled? They'd have to be regulated, surely?"

"Believe it or not, most people don't want to stay in contact," Kalyx said. "Not because they're opposed to the idea but because they aren't interested. Augat did a survey to that effect."

"Augat? Oh well, that's all right then," Laura said with a mirthless laugh.

"And even if the interest was there," Kalyx went on, "only a handful of experts can initialise a call."

"We put through the request at pre-arranged times, send the one-off encryption details and wait," Ruvrin said. "It's usually Keska who answers, but we've also had contact with Veylis and Ymer. There's an audio library of all conversations. Daphos maintains a copy."

"I suppose …" Laura was reluctant to ask the next question. "I suppose you've heard nothing from Roegin. He *did* go with the others?"

"We did our best to dissuade him," Ruvrin said gently. "He felt he had no choice. He's never contacted us, but we do have news of him."

"Let me tell it." Clemis had come back into the room. "What time is it in Scapirion? Then get to bed, you two. Don't forget I've scheduled a transposer meeting tomorrow, between yourselves and Trevone, to finalise the official version of what befell my parents."

"Downplaying the time travel, you mean?" grinned Ruvrin. "Don't worry. Now that everyone's seen the state of that sphere, I think we can say anything we like!"

"And the dispersal engine's habit of messing with space-time's in the public domain now," Kalyx added. "*I* know about it, so it must be!"

"I'm glad you have it all in hand," Laura said.

"We do." Ruvrin was coolly confident. "And as an afterthought, it might interest you to know that my colleagues discovered a particle stream which moves backwards through time. According to

466

resonance theory there must be an opposing stream moving faster than linear time. I'll be looking into this, of course. All right, Clemis, we're going. Goodnight!"

Laura turned to confront her daughter. "Roegin. Why wouldn't he stay?"

"We tried, Laura. We really did. Ruvrin sent for Fley and Keska as soon as she had proofs of the new communication process. She thought Roegin might be persuaded to give his evidence from here."

"But nothing doing?"

"He said that it might be construed as cowardice. In order to make his accusation stick, he had to *be* there." She smiled unexpectedly. "Daphos heard about the confab with Ruvrin and thought there was some kind of plot to oust me! He took a bit of reassuring. And, I do have one piece of *good* news: Roegin was persuaded to sing at a tribute concert to yourselves. You can watch it later." She paused a moment. "For the rest of Roegin's story, you'll have to see Escir and Ailsi."

"What? Why?"

"You need to see them," Clemis repeated. "Tomorrow."

***

The Lyricon, Alda Mexa, 8.2.3.4038

She was, Laura estimated, about six Earth years old.

She was, thought Idenion, about three and a half Celestrian years old.

467

Roegin's daughter, born to his lover Ciela three spans after his departure for Eldor. She had her mother's brown hair and her father's dark eyes, and thus seemed more Eldorian than Celestrian. Her confident gaze was currently fixed on Laura.

"You saved my father from the bad men on Earth," she stated.

"I had some help," Laura said, disconcerted.

"Now he'll save Eldor from more bad men. You made this possible. Thank you."

"Go on, Tressa," Escir prompted.

The child remembered her manners. "And greeting also to you, First Citizen Idenion. I am Tressa of Holpen. Will you be our First Poet again, now that you're back?"

The possibility of losing his position hadn't occurred to Idenion. "Who is First Poet at the moment?" he asked.

Escir was about to reply, but Tressa pre-empted him. "I know this, from school. Bridd of Virda is our First Poet. He writes of the Fall of Virda, and of his lost love Kythania." Then, while Idenion was digesting this: "Will you be giving concerts again, Laura? May I sing with you?"

Ailsi laughed. "If you want to sing with Laura, little one, you'll have to practise. You're late for today's music lesson, so hurry along. I'll let Nefyrra know you're on your way."

Tressa, after hasty goodbyes, disappeared in the direction of the elevator.

"She isn't telepathic," Idenion commented.

"No, and it doesn't seem to worry her. She says that any fool can be a telepath and she'd rather have a voice!"

Laura, naturally enough, wanted to know why Ciela hadn't kept her.

Ailsi looked exasperated. "Chaos, Laura, this *is* still Celestra we're on! You know how this works. Tressa loves to visit Ciela at the spa, but she couldn't have lived there full-time. There's no provision for education, for a start. This way, with Escir and me, she has all the benefits of her dual heritage. Ciela knew how much I'd longed for a child with Escir, so the arrangement suited everybody."

"And did it suit Roegin?"

"She didn't tell him she'd conceived. He was already so conflicted about his future."

"He assumed our species couldn't interbreed," Escir added. "We let him go on thinking that."

Laura knew the truth, of course. She and Ailsi had history. After giving birth to Clemis, Ailsi had launched into a punishing regime of dieting and exercising in order to regain her status as a leading dancer. That regime had become a way of life. In the end, her reproductive system had shut down, and not even Escir's genius could restore it.

"It was selfish and un-Celestrian, and I've paid," Ailsi said. "But maybe some good will come of it now. Tressa will have the best of *all* our worlds."

It seemed an appropriate moment to conclude the meeting, but Escir called Laura back. "When you arrived, which entrance did you take?"

469

"The backstage one, of course. Then up the stairs to the mezzanine level."

"I assumed so. I think you should leave by the main portico. There have ... been some changes."

She thanked him, puzzled.

Idenion said nothing, and continued to say nothing as they walked.

"You know, don't you?" Laura said at last. "You read what Escir meant, and now you're not saying. Please tell me there isn't a huge crowd of people out there. I'm not ready for a comeback just yet."

"Nefyrra and the relayists have ensured everyone knows that," Idenion reassured her. "Just keep walking."

The massive golden door was half open. Beyond it was the colonnade and the memorial to the fallen in the war with Eldor. And further on, at the top of the steps leading to the square, stood a sculpture of a family group. Idenion, book in hand, dreaming, gazing across the city; Laura, poised and assured, smiling at an unseen audience; and the child Clemis, gazing up adoringly at her parents. Master-sculptor Cleve had depicted them in the prime of life, so accurately that Laura felt a mirror was being held up to her past.

"Hell's teeth," she said, inadequately. "I never thought .. I should have realised ..."

"Did you want it taken down?"

"No. No, of course not. Not unless anyone else does."

"They won't," Idenion declared.

470

"Then that's settled." Laura resolutely turned her back on the tableau. "So, what else is on the agenda for today? Any more surprises?"

"No, just the boring stuff. Dessin's anxious to bring me up to date with the post-Clustral admin – how the stored food and grain lasted, and so on. I'd far rather inspect this poem of Bridd's."

"And I'd like to hear the messages from Eldor – and from Earth, if Darren's managed to send any. But I don't feel like going back to Tivenne without you."

"I'll enquire," Idenion said. "I'm sure Daphos will have lodged copies at the akron. And if he has, Sheyell's bound to have them to hand."

***

"How was your day?" asked Idenion.

"You *know* how it was," Laura replied with a gentle smile.

"I do. I'm just being polite. So, how was it?"

"Entertaining and disappointing in equal measures. How was yours?"

"Enlightening and humbling in equal measures."

"Humbling?" inquired Laura.

"Very much so. Dessin let me off lightly – said I could look at city statistics at any time, and referred me to Kest City News for archive recordings of the Clustral Offensive. So I had plenty of time to read Bridd's celebration of Kythania. It's beautiful, Laura. He's kept his love for her as a foundation and built an entire homage to

471

Virda around it. The simplicity of childhood, the lure of the sea and its legends – it's all there. I can't possibly reclaim my First Poet status after this, and I give it up gladly. He's better than I ever was. I'll go on writing poetry, no doubt, but the title stays with him." Idenion paused for emphasis. "Your turn."

"Sheyell did have Darren's recordings, but they hadn't been translated – simply because with us missing, no-one's command of English was good enough. Or in Roegin's case, his Celestrian wasn't up to it. So, I played as much as I could, and made some notes."

"I'll help you with the rest later."

"Thanks. It's going to take a while, but not as long as it might have. Darren reported problems with the communicator and stopped sending shortly afterwards. This was in 4035." She rustled her notes. "Sheyell told me to search for keywords, so I started with Sir John. He confessed to being aware of the money laundering but denied having any part in it. The tabloids weren't very kind to him, saying he'd squandered his fortune on crackpot science – alternative energy sources which didn't deliver, for instance. He received a minimal jail term but had to sell the manor. It's now a culture centre."

"You're sorry for him," Idenion accused.

"Well, yes, I suppose I am. He was basically a decent sort, just obsessed with the idea of making contact with us. I don't think he quite realised what a bunch of thugs he was involved with. And don't forget it was his money and his medical team that saved Roegin."

472

Idenion remained sceptical.

"All right, he had an ulterior motive there," Laura conceded. "But he wasn't obliged to keep his researchers out of trouble. Darren was keen for me to know that. Adam Preece, the astronomer who identified Alda, has returned to his old job at UCL. And the brothers Frank and Edgar Bellingdon are still trying to synthesise aldacite."

"Does that mean we can look forward to being pestered?"

"I don't think so. Not yet, anyway. Investors don't take them seriously."

"Thanks to your pal Sir John. He didn't *protect* them, Laura. He cut them loose and ridiculed their work." Idenion was at his most censorious. "Sorry, dearest, but I'm not about to forgive the man who took you prisoner. Now, what about the crashed sphere? Does Darren know what happened to it?"

"It's a bit of a mystery. Both Tarlion and Roegin saw the wreckage put onto a low-loader for delivery to Frank's laboratory in Basingstoke. Only it never arrived."

"And that means ...?"

"It means years of endless pleasure for whoever's trying to figure it out. Tarlion gave a retrace, didn't he? Everything was trashed. Now stop scowling. I've some better news, which is why I left it till the end."

Idenion's frown didn't budge. "Promise me, Laura, that you'll never go to Earth again."

"You're serious, aren't you?"

"Very."

"I told Roegin I'd never go back, and I meant it. It's as he said – breaking up the Cheveney cell was just the tip of the iceberg. There must be many more collaborators who know about the Eldorians, and Celestra, and me. Earth's not safe for any of us. Now, do you want to hear the rest of my news, and will you pretend you don't already know what it is?"

"Your thoughts are always clearer when you articulate them," Idenion reminded her.

"What, even after all this time?"

"Some things never change. And I don't want them to change." Idenion's gaze had become warm and loving. "Go on. I'm waiting."

"It's about Jack," Laura began. "As he was unable to write the truth about Cheveney, he wrote it as a conspiracy thriller entitled They Wait. The book was a huge success and earned him enough to purchase the Green Man from Kelly. She'd been looking for the right buyer. It's now renamed the Little Green Man and Phaedra's cooking has won several awards. And lastly, Wickens Clump's been designated a Site of Special Scientific Interest. An apparently new species of wild flower has been discovered there. Darren described it, and I think it's Eprys."

"Is that possible?"

"Eprys will grow anywhere: we all know that. Either Clemis or me could have had the seeds on our boots." She paused. "I'd like to think it is. A little bit of Celestra in the English countryside. It makes up for having to stay away."

474

***

"We did it! We did it!" Keska, exuberant, spoke from a recording that was already six years old. "Daphos, Escir, I hope someone can translate this. Veylis will send a message as soon as he can get away, but I couldn't wait to tell you. I presented my dossier, or rather Veylis did, and it, combined with Roegin's evidence, toppled the Senate. Roegin was – amazing. So calm and dignified. We sheltered him until the hearing as we knew there'd be some attempts on his life. Oh, and we found his mother living with a stage-hand in Nova City and brought her here as well, in case the corrupt senators tried to get to Roegin by threatening her. And there's so much more! But, I have to keep it short before this baby universe self-destructs. Imagine that! Anyway, we have representatives in the new Senate. We're really going to shake everything up. Oh, and I married Veylis. It helped politically, but I don't need to tell you how much in love we are. Thank you all!"

Laura, at Tivenne Communications, sat gazing at the audio player after the recording had ended. The system had evolved so radically that she wasn't sure how to close the programme. After a moment Daphos showed her how to eject the data crystal.

"Surprised at the improvements? That's Kest for you. Their tech teams are never satisfied."

"So it would appear," Laura said, smiling. "I'm pleased for them. Kest used to be such a backwater. Now, what else have you chosen for me today? Did the peace initiative last?"

"Just about. Veylis sent this report two years ago."

"I won't pretend it's been easy," Veylis began. "After what Keska likes to call the big reveal, many of the conspirators tried to disappear and we had to send agents to weed them out. It wasn't the best of beginnings. Despite the armistice, we had to accept that after decades of war, the Patierons and the Patierades simply didn't like one another. There were skirmishes. What we really feared was an Army rebellion. We had a huge fighting force with too much time on its hands. Fortunately we were able to channel its energy into a new space initiative – colonisation, mining, reconstruction. We're gradually turning things around and we're now politically stable – just. Roegin's my head of security. Keska wanted him to send a message but he believes a clean break is best."

Laura sighed and leant her elbows on the workstation. "He's probably right."

"Heard enough?"

"For now. I need a rest from playing catch-up. There's still this evening to get through."

She, with Idenion and Tarlion, had been invited by their various friends to a special screening of the memorial concert which had been staged in their honour. It had taken place just prior to the Eldorians' departure. Outside of Kest, Tivenne had the most modern viewing room.

"We thought you'd be pleased," said Daphos in justification. "Everyone joined in. The Narvellans sang some college songs, Bridd recited Idenion's poetry, the scolia excelled themselves."

"That's just my point. All these beautiful tributes make me feel such a fraud. Survivor's guilt. Well, for everyone's sake I'd better show willing. Who are we expecting first?"

"The caterers, I expect. They're bringing a special buffet from the Lyricon kitchens. And Ailsi's bringing you a dress."

"Oh dear."

"One of yours, apparently, from your old apartment."

"As long as it isn't one of her designs. They're a bit too ..."

"Skimpy?" suggested Daphos.

Laura chuckled.

"Hey, I've made you laugh. Now, before the others get here, how about a small – very small - glass of pilif brandy?"

"A drunken First Citizen?" Laura returned lightly. "Just the ammunition Kalyx is waiting for. Daphos?"

He refocused hastily. "Sorry. That was the duty operator. Idenion's calling from the akron and needs to speak with you. There's a problem."

"Oh, what now?" Laura followed Daphos up one floor to the control centre where Idenion's apologetic face was displayed, many times larger than life, on a huge transposer screen. Kest's influence was indeed everywhere.

"I'm so sorry, Laura," Idenion began as soon as he saw her. "We'll have to cancel our gathering."

She tried not to look relieved. "Why?"

"Because there's sciesha, all across laterals two and three. I'm stranded in the akron with Clemis."

477

"Where's Tarlion?"

"He *was* with us, but he's gone missing. Tonora's already in Tivenne, visiting her parents, and Tarlion was going to bring us over later. He went to collect a flitter, and didn't come back."

"And you think the sciesha might have drawn him in?"

"It started soon after he left."

"Was it our students?" asked Daphos.

"Of course. It always is. I hope Tarlion didn't think his Narvellan heritage made him immune. The only protection the Old Narvellans had was their prudish temperament."

"I remember," Laura said with a rueful grin.

"So, as soon as it's over, I'll have to organise the city maintenance crews to straighten everything out and mop up any inebriated revellers. And, chase off Augat's people if they put in an appearance." Idenion paused. "I've spoken with the Lyricon and explained why we're stuck. You might get a call from them."

"I'll be fine," Laura assured him.

The screen blanked.

"Pity about the feast, though," she supplemented. "I'm getting hungry."

"I'll see what I can rustle up," Daphos said.

While she waited, Laura gazed out of the encircling windows at the changed and proliferating Tivenne, its outlines warm and mellow in the early evening sun. A group of maintenance workers strolled past, heading for home. A freight train rattled along the adjoining monorail on its way to Treva. The duty operator spoke quietly to inbound craft, reminding them that Alda Mexa was off limits till morning. Then, unexpectedly, a flitter appeared. It deposited one passenger outside the terminal building: Ailsi, carrying a hamper and wearing a broad smile. She spotted Laura and waved.

Daphos appeared, emptyhanded. "What's Ailsi doing here?"

"No idea," said Laura. "I thought you'd sent for her."

"Nobody sends for *me*," said the newcomer. "I'm the original free spirit. Right, Daphos, you're free to go. I'll look after Laura."

"But - "

"Go. It's girl-talk time. And you can take that hamper to the data room on your way out. It's heavy. Thanks. Bye."

"What's going on, Ailsi?" asked Laura suspiciously, following her downstairs.

"Well, when Idenion cancelled the party I didn't like to think of you stranded here, so, I made an alternative plan. I picked up some goodies from the Lyricon, and once we've eaten, we can have a civilised chat with Nefyrra about your comeback concert. Because there'll have to be one. Also - " She produced a data clip from her tunic pocket. "I've brought the best bits of the tribute concert. We can watch while we're eating."

"I'm not really in the mood - " began Laura.

"Oh, I think you'll want to see this. It's Roegin. Singing."

"Clemis told me he'd relented. Did *you* talk him into it?"

"Didn't have to. He'd made some kind of pact with Veylis and couldn't get out of it. The honour of one's house, and all that. I'm looking forward to seeing it again myself. That man was – rather special. But I don't have to tell *you* that, do I?"

There was an awkward silence.

"I thought sciesha might have been eradicated by now," Laura said, changing the subject.

"Well, it doesn't happen as often. But it'll be a long long time before Nature gives it the stop-signal." Ailsi smiled impishly. "I didn't know if I could still spark it off. But I needn't have worried!"

"Ailsi, you *didn't*!"

"It got you out of a situation, didn't it? Now let's eat this beautiful fish pie and watch the show."

Roegin's first song was "The Summer Knows." Laura had performed it, in Celestrian, just over eight years ago; but Roegin sang it in Earth-English, the version he knew best. The weathershield was set to midnight blue. A soft white illumination bathed the stage. Roegin was alone, the scolia somewhere out of shot, and Vione's adroit camera lingered appreciatively on his face.

"Oh, Ailsi, look at his eyes," Laura whispered. "Distant. Expressionless."

"Avoiding stage fright?" Ailsi murmured back.

"No, that isn't it. I think he was already far away from us."

"We repatriated everyone four days later," Ailsi confirmed.

"Next," Roegin announced with quiet confidence, "I'd like to sing an Earth ballad which Idenion translated long ago. It bears Laura's name,

480

and she'd never perform it as she claimed it would make her sound conceited. So here it is, for the first time on this world. I give you – Laura."

Roegin's warm baritone was pitch-perfect. The audience, uncharacteristically demonstrative, called for an encore.

"And who can blame them?" said Ailsi with her mouth full. "Ooh, that voice. Makes me go all tingly."

Presently Nefyrra appeared on stage, and Roegin stood aside to let her speak. "As you doubtless know," she began, "Roegin is a professionally trained singer, and while Earth love songs are wonderfully evocative, we felt they didn't display his voice to the full. And so, with the able assistance of Commander Fley, we present the Patierade Friendship Anthem."

The two voices, with alternating melody lines, complimented one another in a way Laura didn't expect. She'd heard Fley sing before – his voice was acceptably tuneful and he wasn't afraid to use it – but she suspected he'd had some coaching ahead of this event.

"Ailsi, could you pause it a moment?"

Ailsi complied. "Problem?"

"I'm having some gender issues. They're singing about their god Ebbon, but they keep saying she."

Ailsi assumed a bored expression. "Keska explained all that, sort of. The Eldorian invasion was Patieron-led, so we never got to hear the Patierade version of anything. Patierade women take a more active role in things. They have girl soldiers for a start. So, in *their* mythology, the benign aspect of Ebbon is female."

"Makes sense," Laura conceded.

"Not to me it doesn't. Nice song though. Two estranged friends are reunited." Ailsi moved to restart the playback. "Nefyrra had Augat turn off the amps and station a recordist at the back of the tiers. Just listen."

Roegin's voice soared effortlessly through the auditorium. Laura thought she knew how he, a Patieron general's son, had known that song: the same reason he'd known the tale of the dead tree. He'd been an excellent field agent.

She hoped someone would tell him she was alive.

"Before we speak to Nefyrra, I've a favour to ask," Ailsi said.

"What?"

"The winners of Dancer's Challenge were going to perform for you tonight, and they'll be disappointed. I'd like to tell them they can appear in your comeback concert instead, and I've taken the liberty of bringing their winning performance. May I?"

Laura smiled wearily. "Go on."

The recording began, the music almost drowned by yells of encouragement from the Kest audience. Laura watched, slightly taken aback.

"Brilliant, aren't they?" enthused Ailsi. "The girl's one of my trainees. Her name's Riti. And that gorgeous young man's called Pytor. He's a geologist from Alcine. What a mover!"

482

"But," said Laura lamely, "I thought they'd be doing Earth dances. In costume."

Ailsi gave a shriek of laughter. "What? All those *rules*? No chance!"

"And don't you think they're a bit – underdressed?"

"How are we to award marks if we can't see what they're doing?" countered Ailsi. "Anyway, it's tradition."

Laura was aware of that. It seemed as if her life was turning full circle. She recalled a day when, newly arrived from Earth, a flitter had deposited her outside the Lyricon into a crowd of near-naked young dancers, all eager to catch a glimpse of their new First Singer. "Some things never change," she remarked. "All right, Ailsi, book them in."

"With pleasure. And now we'd better find ourselves a transposer and call Nefyrra. She really does want to speak to you."

Nefyrra, as always, had sensible ideas for Laura's return to the stage. Laura agreed to everything except a revival of the Bell Song. It would, she said regretfully, involve too much rehearsal time. And she wasn't sure she'd manage the high notes any more. "And I'm not singing 'Laura', so don't ask," she concluded.

"Agreed," said Nefyrra. "One last thing. I want to speak to you and Idenion together, so once you're home, call me again. Tonight if possible."

"Both of us? Is this about Kalyx and Ruvrin?"

"No, this isn't a leadership matter. It's – scolia business. We'll speak again soon. Goodbye."

***

"And you've no idea what she wanted?"

"No, Idenion, I don't. She sounded mysterious."

"Well, I can check if the Lyricon portal's still active. But it's very late."

Nefyrra was still awake. "I'm speaking for myself and Nohal," she announced. "We'd like to invite you both to Tafret Academy for a private presentation. For some time now, the best of the lattice enhancement teams, led by Esclevon, have been engaged in a special project. We're now ready to reveal it."

"Is it defence work?" asked Laura.

"Nothing so sinister. Lattices have always been easily disrupted, so Nohal closed the facility to outsiders." She paused for effect. "Believe me, Laura, this is astounding. I'll see you tomorrow, early."

Coda

"You've done *what*?" Laura, amazed, confronted the seemingly ageless Nohal.

"Restored the art of song. More specifically, strengthened and expanded the lattice to carry additional content generated by scolia minds. They're achieved accurate vocal simulations, provisionally called weavesong."

"And is it only scolia-adepts who can do this?"

"Yes, but not always our best instrumentalists nor our strongest telepaths. As on your world, it appears to be a quirk, a wild talent."

"I still don't see where *I* fit in. I can't even sense a lattice."

"But you can! That's precisely why we invited you here. We can use the retracer to share our discovery."

"Oh. That." Laura was suddenly uneasy.

"Don't be nervous! In the past, you've only *given* retraces. Today you'll be absorbing one from a person you trust. That could be me, or Nefyrra, or any scolia-adept you've worked with. And Idenion can keep you company. More than one person can absorb a retrace at a time."

"First, I'd like more background," Laura said cautiously.

"Which is why I'm handing you over to Lattice-Master Esclevon. He's waiting in the rehearsal suite."

Laura, face to face with her adult grandson for the first time, simply stared. "Oh, Idenion, he looks just like Tralvar!"

Idenion had to agree. The sinewy frame, the untidy hair, a torn sleeve – every detail was reminiscent of the iconic First Scientist. Everything except the broad smile, which was pure Esclevon.

"I assume you need a less rarified account of my work?" he inquired. "Here goes. Would you believe this started as a vanity project? I wanted to restore the lattice's reputation, which has been side-lined by recorded music. But to entice people back, I needed something new. We all know what the lattice is – a group of musicians telepathically linked, enjoying their performance and sharing that pleasure with an audience. It's restful and peaceful, gently drawing you in. And it's bland, unchanging. No-one's supposed to interrupt a lattice, even in a contributory way. But why not? Why not add things?" He paused. "Sorry. I get a bit carried away. I'll try an analogy. It took an upstart species like ours to realise that naturally-occurring radio waves could be harnessed to carry information. Similarly, so can a basic lattice. It's just that no-one ever tried it before."

"Has this anything to do with Narvellan higher brain activity?" asked Idenion.

Everyone laughed.

"The Narvellans are hopeless at weavesong," Nefyrra elaborated. "Their forensic, incisive mindset is inimical to the process."

"Sheer overkill," Nohal added.

The scolia-adepts were arriving and tuning their instruments. Two young women and one man seated themselves slightly apart from the ensemble.

"Those are our weavesingers," Nefyrra whispered to Laura. "Remember Bekta, the girl on the left? I tutored her and Esclevon as children."

"What are they performing?" Laura whispered back.

"Esclevon's setting of the Clemoridys finale. The Dream Homecoming."

It *would* have to be about me, Laura reflected.

Esclevon took his place and thereafter remained motionless. The scolia played languid ethereal chords. Idenion kept gazing at Laura throughout the piece, and at one point kissed her on the head. She resolved to tell him off later for not concentrating on whatever the weavesingers were doing. Naturally enough, she could detect only silence from them.

The piece was modest in length, scarcely three astallen, and ended before she felt the need to fidget. When consulted she chose Nefyrra as the retracee, and Esclevon to channel the memory recording.

The retracer looked exactly as she remembered it – a heated cube with several prill inside, and pairs of aldacite crystals at each corner. She shivered momentarily. But Idenion was with her, loving and reassuring, and Esclevon looked positively benevolent as he took his place at the monitor.

The playback began, and the truth about weavesong revealed itself to Laura: unique, beautiful, and very very Celestrian.

***

That evening, back in Alda Mexa, she finally quizzed Idenion about the retrace. She'd refrained until then, not wanting analysis to chase away the lingering wonder.

"The weavesinger Bekta," she began. "The one who portrayed Clemoridys. What did she sound like? *Who* did she sound like?"

"Why, you of course," said Idenion, surprised.

"Of course. To you, she would."

"You heard something different?"

"Yes. She sounded like my mother when I was little. I loved to hear her practising before a show. She didn't have the most beautiful voice in the world, but it seemed so to me. Don't you see, Idenion? Weavesong depends on the recipient as much as the performer. We hear what we cherish most. Tralvar would have heard Tristell. Lydion would have heard Tarlatine. And that boy Arcto, the one who weave-sang the poet: if you had a singing voice you'd sound just like that. To me, anyway." She paused. "What Esclevon's done is phenomenal. I'm only just beginning to realise it."

Clemis put her head round the door. "Sorry to intrude, you two, but I've just had Kalyx on the transposer. Again. He wants to know if you've made a decision."

"We made it long ago," Idenion said. "We were discussing retirement the day we found Alendis' effects in that locked room. Tell Kalyx and Ruvrin that we're no longer the First Citizens. *They* are."

Clemis hadn't expected such a swift answer. "But what will you do now?"

"Do?" echoed Laura. "These years of turbulent history began when Idenion came looking for a singer. Maybe Celestra will have some peace if we lie low for a change. That's a joke, in case you're wondering. We're going to be busier than ever. Idenion still wants to design buildings, and I'd better appoint myself music adviser to Kest City. They're bound to go on harvesting Earth's songs, and they won't know melody from mayhem. But before all that, there's the small matter of my comeback concert. And Nefyrra's going to need help with the first weavesinger tour."

"I'm so proud of Vonnie," Clemis enthused. "Or rather I *would* be, if I knew exactly what he'd done. Do we really have our voices back?"

"In a sense," Idenion replied.

"What kind of an answer is that? You're the wordsmith, Idenion – what *is* weavesong?"

"Well," he smiled, "when the music theorists get hold of it they'll say it's about lattice enhancement, perfect pitch, resonance, the cosmic balance and so on. But in the end, it's all about love."

THE END

GLOSSARY

CAST OF CHARACTERS

Celestrians
Ailsi - dancer, birth-mother of Clemis
Alcis - relayist, eastern sector of Alda Mexa
Ansela - archivist
Arcto - scolia boy
Augat - broadcaster at Kest City News
Bekta - scolia girl
Bridd - relayist
Ciela - proprietor of Lake Holpen spa
Clemis - daughter of Idenion and Laura
Cleve - sculptor
Daphos - engineer and IT expert
Dena -Idenion's sister, costumier
Dessin - Administrator, Alda Mexa
Devri - hospital orderly
Esclevon - son of Trevone and Clemis
Ibri - engineer
Idenion - First Citizen/ First Poet
Jarras - senior communications worker, Nefyrra's partner
Kalyx - Prefect of Scapirion
Kyrin - senior relayist
Lakal - scolia-adepts' group leader
Lann - Guildmaster of music
Nefyrra - Custodian of the Lyricon
Neme - Augat's relayist
Nohal - First Relayist, based at Tafret
Nya - scolia child
Pagnar - chief of ops, hydro-electric plant
Ribor - river captain
Rinyi - a sensitive

Ruvrin - mathematician, wife to Kalyx
Sevet - warden of Kest
Sheyell - recordist at admin meetings
Spran - riverman
Tonor - weathershield operator
Tonora - Tonor's daughter, a sensitive
Trevone - First Scientist, son of Jarras and Nefyrra
Trytin - communications tech
Tylo - elderly relayist
Vione - broadcaster
Ysara - tech, Alda Six
Zanna - Space Academy tutor
Zonn - Augat's pilot

Earthlings:
Ann - Roegin's nurse, Tallifer's estranged wife
Joel Bartlett - Cheveney estate manager, project leader
Edgar Bellingdon - engineer
Frank Bellingdon - engineer, Edgar's brother
Sir John Cheveney - baronet, incumbent of Cheveney Manor
Laura Gilcoyne - singer, now First Citizeness of Celestra
Bryn Harmsworth - private investigator
Bill Jellicoe - Cheveney estate worker
Geoffrey Little - accountant
Jack Moffat - reporter
Phaedra Moffat - Jack's wife
Pavel - hired thug
Adam Preece - astronomer
Jonathan Stone - (formerly Darren Stone) gardener, UFO researcher
Jimmy Stretton - eco-warrior, Laura's "old flame"
Caitlin Stretton - Jimmy's aged mother

Rod Tallifer - head of security, Cheveney Manor
Kelly Thorogood - landlady of the Green Man

Eldorians:
Brome - science chief
Buuth (deceased) - Roegin's partner, Covert Ops
Escir - ex-Army physician, naturalised Celestrian
Fley Dhuvin-Mytyl - sub-commander, Patierade
Free Territories
Habbon Mol-Varna - elderly
professor/archaeologist, naturalised Celestrian
Hyberl - Patieron crewman
Keska Fley-Talt - scientist daughter of Fley
Nirik - Patieron crewman
Roegin Drice-Tressa - former Covert Ops spy,
exiled on Earth
Thaed - Patieron crewman
Tressa - half-Celestrian daughter of Roegin and
Ciela
Veylis Pervain-Opna - Pervain's bastard son, heir to
the Patieron title
Ymer Coll-Preda - soldier, seasoned space traveller

Narvellans:
Myrig - Councillor, New Narvella
Tarlion - half-Celestrian explorer, son of Lydion
and Tarlatine

Place Names:
Akron - administration centre and ruler's home
Alda - Celestra's sun
Alda Mexa - Celestra's capital, City of the Sun
Atris - city to the north

Corayn - centre for herbs and medicines

Dral - dead planet: was once home to the Draldir

Eldor - home planet to the Eldorian Empire, 1200 light years from Celestra

Ilonna - a ghost town

Lake Holpen - beauty spot near Alda Mexa

Lisir - river which runs through Alda Mexa

Lyricon - cherished theatre, situated in Alda Mexa

Miiyat - planetary empire of cat-like creatures

Myrma - humid planet near Celestra

Nevri - the Scapirians' name for Celestra – "mother"

Scapirion - town on the south polar continent with reclusive inhabitants

Symerid - Sol

Symerid Three - Earth

Tafret - town where young relayists are sent for training

Tivenne - village near Alda Mexa

Treva - town to north-east of Alda Mexa, industrial heart of Celestra

Virda - fishing village, home to Kyrin

Earth:

Cheveney - Laura's village

Wickens Clump - wood where UFO's have been sighted

Windbourne - Nathaniel's house

Alien Terms

Aldacite - versatile crystal used in logic systems etc.

Astal/Astallen - unit of time, equivalent to six minutes

Dispersal Engine - superweapon created by Tralvar

Firi - filmy material worn by dancers, etc.

Ild/Ilden unit of time equivalent to just under 50 minutes (eight astallen): there are 30 ilden in one day

Isk - unit of time equivalent to a second. Used only in stellar navigation and music

Kyffu - waterfowl

Liman - milky drink native to Celestra

Octal - a period of eight days

Patierades - rival faction in Eldor's civil war

Patierons - the most powerful ruling family on Eldor

Peisistrata - Celestrian festival

Pilif - small succulent yellow fruit

Relayists - telepaths who circulate news and conduct commerce

Resnay - strong alcoholic drink

Retracer - a device for recording peoples' memories

Scolia - Celestrian orchestra

Sciesha - mating fever

Scieshanar - medallion, Celestrian, denoting one's ancestry

Silmos/Silmi - a measurement of distance, equal to one-third of a mile

Span - Celestrian month

Sphere - Celestrian spacecraft

Starfire - powerful stimulant (proscribed substance)

Strelsis - stringed instrument in various sizes

Theridolyte - a strengthened and stabilised version of therite, used in the construction of spheres

Therite - a mineral, unstable when processed, used for quarrying and weapons

Total Unity - the telepathic element of the sex act

Transposal - the Celestrian hyperdrive

Transposer - hyperspace transmitter/receiver

Ylur - coarse material from which overalls are made

Ytil - material normally used for garments

Zarf - a mythical Celestrian beast with a voracious sexual appetite

Zirid - keyboard instrument

Zytl - Eldorian measurement of time equivalent to one minute

9 781786 957818